Book Two of the Lady Blade Series:

Lady Blade

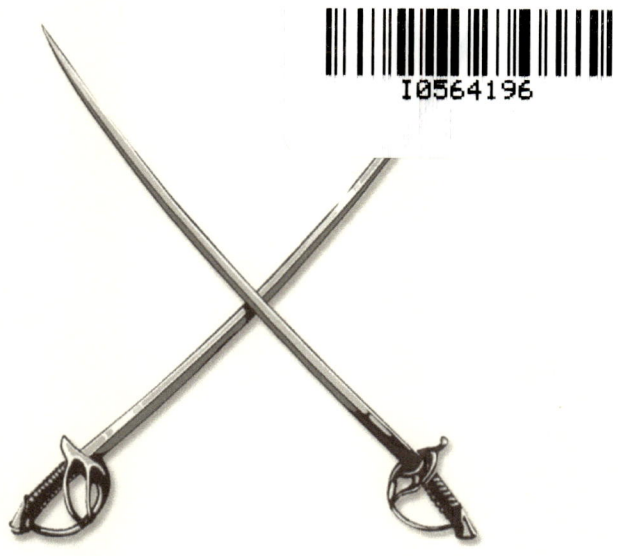

I0564196

by

Catherine Thrush

DEDICATION

For Tom, my captain, my first mate,
and my traveling companion through life.

CONTENTS

*P*art III

A New Path

ACKNOWLEDGEMENTS

Special thanks to all my friends in the Monday Night Writers and the Potluck Publishers who read these chapters as I wrote and rewrote them over and over and told me how bad they were—until they weren't. Thank you for your patience and your sage advice.

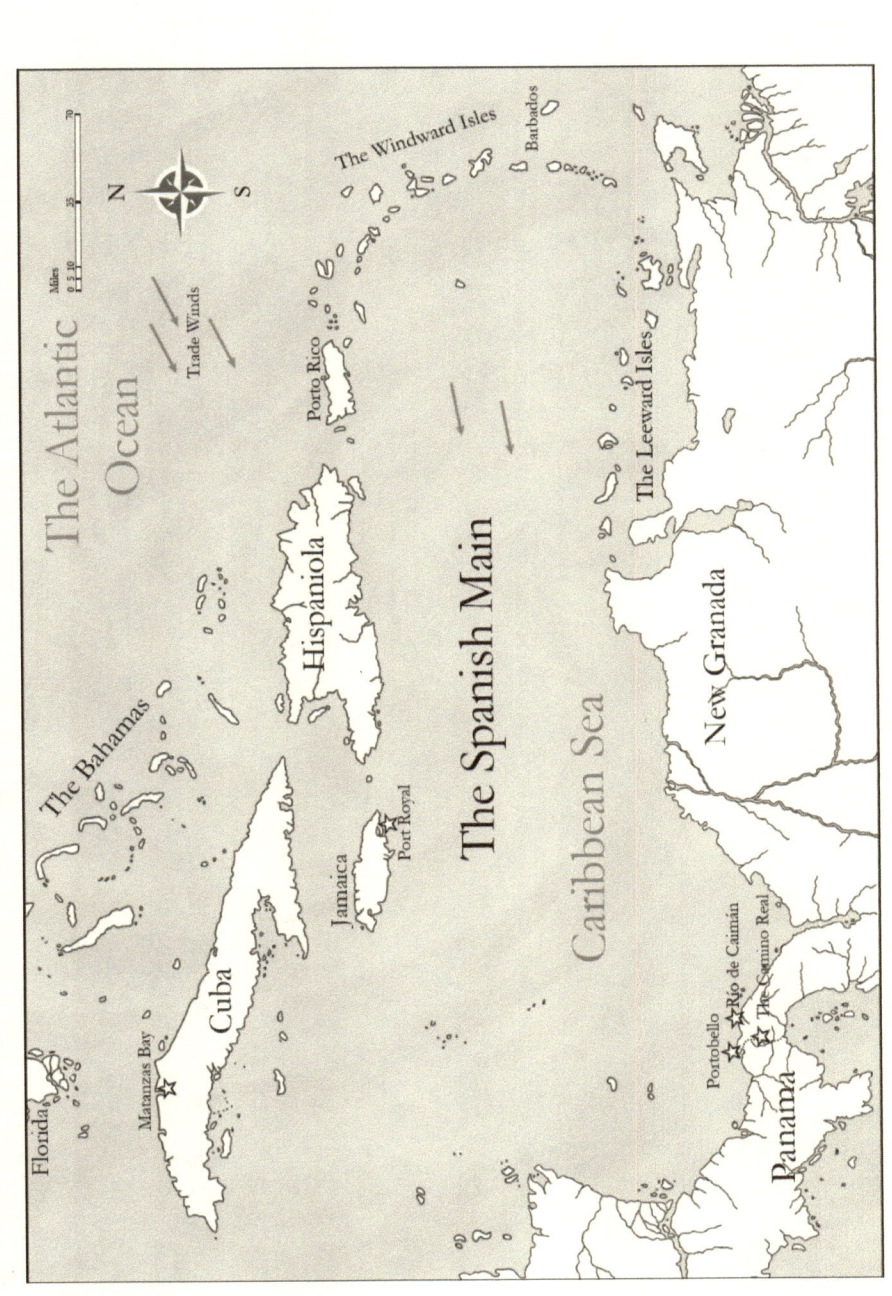

PART I

BEGINNINGS AND ENDINGS

*The world is round
and the place which may seem like the end
may also be only the beginning.*

George Baker

CHAPTER 1
DAWN

Francesca DiCesare knew Papa was the best swordsman in all the states of Italy, perhaps all the world, yet she couldn't shake the foreboding that had settled on her as they journeyed toward the dueling grounds.

The gray dawn wasn't helping. The only things visible through the surrounding mist were her two brothers and Papa on their horses, looking colorless and ghostly, and a dozen paces of dirt road. Only a lightening of the haze indicated where the sun rose.

The damp air seeped through the wool of her red cloak thrusting icy fingers up her sleeves and down her collar.

Francesca sat sidesaddle atop her black horse, Achilles. He rumbled deep in his chest, and she rubbed his neck knowing he was disgruntled at being taken from his warm stable so early, and without his morning oats. He tossed his head and snorted.

A few yards ahead rode her two older brothers, Antonio and Sebastian. Antonio, the eldest, tried to joke with Sebi to lighten the mood, but Sebi's replies were half-hearted, and his shoulders hunched.

It was easy to guess what was on his mind—what was on all their minds. The duel he had fought two years ago. That duel had cost Francesca her closest friend, and Sebi his first love.

She tried to keep her thoughts from going to that heart-rending day. Her breath caught as the image arose of Catalina throwing herself in front of Sebi to take the blade that was meant for him. Guilt flooded her for her involvement in the affair. And the blood … *Stop. Just stop. I can't think about it,* she told herself fiercely, *or I'll fall apart completely.*

She took a deep, steadying breath and turned toward Papa, who rode alongside her. The gray mist made his face pallid and lined, highlighting the scars that slanted across his right cheekbone and ran down his broad forehead.

It's just the light, she told herself. *He's not old.* But lately she'd noticed he tried to hide a limp when the weather changed and the old war injury to his thigh acted up. And he'd asked Signora Bianchi for a salve for the arthritis in his shoulder.

There was no hint of worry on his face, though. His back was straight and his expression serene.

Francesca wanted to lay a hand on his arm and say, "Please, Papa, let's go home," but it was pointless. He had been challenged. Now it was a matter of honor, and his honor meant more to him than anything, even his life.

She looked away. *Everything will be fine. He's fought a hundred duels, maybe a thousand. He marched with armies and faced down kings. He always wins.* But she couldn't stop her traitorous mind from adding, *so far.*

Her reluctance had slowed her pace and she had fallen a few paces behind. He turned to her, crinkling his steel-gray eyes and bunching his goatee at the corners of his mouth. "Come along, Cesca, we mustn't be late."

She hurried Achilles' pace.

"Are you sure they can spare you today?" Papa asked.

"Yes, Papa. Signora Elena will meet the deliveries and everyone else has their duties. They'll be fine without me for the morning."

He nodded. "Have I mentioned lately how proud I am of the way you've been running the salle?"

She smiled at him. "Yes, Papa. But I'm always happy to hear it again."

"I don't think it's ever run so smoothly."

It was nice of him to say so, but she doubted that was true. Problems arose constantly. Although maybe no one else noticed since she and Signora Elena took care of them.

Sebastian glanced back. An errant lock of auburn hair fell over one brow. "Don't tell her that, Papa," he said with a crooked grin. "The power has already gone to her head. Even Leo thinks so. He's heartbroken."

Heat crept into Francesca's cheeks. *Stupid cheeks.* Leo was one of Papa's fencing pupils who fawned over her. She didn't give a fig about any young man but Phillip, her Phillip, but she blushed at Sebi's baiting all the same. Sebi laughed.

Francesca tried to control her cheeks, which only made the blushing worse. Antonio joined in the laughter.

Francesca straightened her shoulders. "Remember who orders our provisions before making fun of me—if you ever want a steak again."

Sebi feigned being pained. "See what I mean, Papa."

"Enough," Papa said.

As Francesca came alongside him, he nodded sympathetically, leaned over, and patted her wrist. He and Signora Elena were the only ones who knew how much she still loved and missed Phillip, and that she'd never see him again. She sagged in the saddle, the loss of Phillip and Catalina carving a hole in her heart.

They rode on, the rhythmic clop of the horses' hooves the only sound. Slowly the mist thinned.

A wraithlike tombstone came into focus to their left.

The Church of the Madonna dell'Acqua's bell tower loomed out of the mist, its usually cheery red-gold color dark and ominous this morning.

"We're here," Papa announced.

Foreboding rushed back over Francesca. She shivered as she and her family dismounted. They let the horses loose to crop grass in the swirling mist among scattered tombstones.

As they headed behind the church, she took Papa's arm. It felt reassuringly solid, and her fingers tightened. She looked up at him. "Papa," she said, hearing the anxiety in her voice.

He patted her hand. "Not to worry, my Cesca. This will be quick. Then we can visit your mother."

She nodded and forced a smile. There was no point in worrying him. *He's right. He always is.*

Francesca's mother was buried in the cemetery where the horses wandered. Although Francesca had never known her mother, she usually felt close to her here, as if something of her spirit remained in the russet stones of the church, the swelling green hills, and the murmur of the Arno River nearby. But not today.

When they rounded the church, Signore Tarrentino, Papa's opponent, stood in the open amid thinning fog. He wore a powdered wig and a sneer curled his lips. He ran a hand down his embroidered blue velvet waistcoat.

4

Finery won't help you here, thought Francesca.

Rumor at the salle had it that he was the youngest son of some disgraced, minor baron. The Signore had grown up poor but had blackmailed his way to a villa and a seat in the senate. He was rich now and made sure everyone knew it. Francesca wasn't one to listen to rumors, but he certainly looked the part with his showy clothes and superior attitude. And yesterday he'd proven himself a thug who lacked honor.

Market day had started so pleasantly. Her family and Signora Bianchi, or Elena, had taken the carriage to Cascina. Elena had chatted merrily. The day before, Elena and Francesca had assisted as the groundskeeper's wife gave birth to a burbling boy, which always made Elena happy.

When they arrived at the market, Antonio and Sebi bounded out of the vehicle to visit friends, setting the carriage rocking. Elena hurried off to Santi Ippolito to talk to the priest about the baby's christening. That left Papa and Francesca to wander the market stalls together.

The air felt like spring. The colorful canvas awnings on the stalls swayed in the breeze. People in their Sunday best filled the square and talked over the clucking of chickens, bleating of sheep, and shouts of the fishmongers. The bright smell of ripe fruits and vegetables mixed with the darker smells of the animals.

Francesca had a long list of supplies needed for the school's pantry, so she and Papa moved from stall to stall and chatted with the vendors, sharing news and jokes, and haggling over prices.

She had never been more content than the last few months. Her afternoons were jam-packed with chores and lessons. There were so much to attend to as Mistress of the Salle that sometimes her head whirled. But after dinner she would have a wild gallop on Achilles across the hillsides to clear her mind before getting back to work. At night she would flop exhausted into bed. But the mornings, mornings were heaven.

She would rush down the stairs to join her brothers and the other students outside in the courtyard for fencing lessons from Papa. Joining the class hadn't been easy. Many of the young men resented having a girl among them. A few even left the school. Others refused to work with her, but some students didn't seem to mind, and several, like Leo, developed crushes on her after she beat them. Win or lose, training with Papa made her happy.

So she was in a light-hearted mood as she and Papa headed to the cheesemaker's stall, munching on crisp apples. They laughed, dodging a dog with a loaf of bread in its mouth that was being chased by a bunch of rowdy children.

Papa had just hailed the cheesemaker when they heard cries and shouts behind them. They turned to look, but a crowd had formed so all Francesca saw was people's backs. A *thwack* and a shriek of pain rang out.

Papa's face clouded and he moved toward the crowd. Francesca followed, her stomach tightening. As more *thwacks* and yelps followed, the crowd murmured. Papa pushed through the people with Francesca behind him.

When they reached the center, she gasped. Tarrentino, red-faced, wielded a dark wood cane with a silver head. At his feet lay a chocolate-skinned boy of about twelve. For a moment Francesca thought the boy was dead, but his chest moved slightly. The boy's forearm bent at an unnatural angle, obviously broken. Raised welts on his face and neck darkened to blue-red.

Tarrentino raised the cane to swing again, but Papa caught it mid-air. Tarrentino tried to yank it away, but Papa held on.

"Let go!" shouted Tarrentino.

"I'll not let you beat this boy further," Papa growled.

Tarrentino sputtered and shook with rage. "That's my property. I'll punish it any way I like."

"This is not punishment," Papa replied. "This is murder." He turned to Francesca. "Get the boy out of here. Take him to the physician."

She nodded and hurried to the boy's side.

"Damn you! I'll have you up for theft!" blustered Tarrentino.

The boy's eyelids fluttered. He groaned as Francesca got an arm under his slight form and raised him to his feet. He collapsed, but a young man in the crowd grabbed the boy's legs and helped Francesca carry him out.

"You can collect him tomorrow at the doctor's office," Papa said. "After you've calmed down and he's been seen to."

As she worked her way through the crowd, Francesca heard Tarrentino shout, "This insult demands satisfaction!"

"So be it," Papa replied.

So here they were, on this cold, gloomy morning.

Francesca wondered what could have possessed Tarrentino to challenge a fencing maestro. Tarrentino was a politician, not a soldier, barely passable with a blade. He had no hope of winning. *But even beginners get lucky sometimes.*

Next to Tarrentino stood his two seconds, almost equally as foppish in satin finery. They too wore wigs and blades that, from their high sheen,

6

looked more decorative than functional. The seconds rubbed their hands and stamped their feet to keep warm. With them stood Signore Russo, a white-haired, solemn man in a tan cloak who would officiate the duel.

The maestro squeezed Francesca's hand and disengaged it from his arm. She went to Antonio, who draped one side of his charcoal cloak over her shoulder, giving her a glimpse of the sword that hung at his hip. She huddled into his side for warmth.

Francesca wished she wore a sword. She craved a pommel to finger, a hilt to grasp, something to relieve her anxious tension, but Papa had forbidden it. Few people outside the school knew about Francesca's fencing, and Papa wanted to keep it that way as long as possible.

"Don't look so worried," Antonio said. "He'll be fine."

Antonio had Papa's grey eyes, black hair, and high cheekbones. He shared Papa's confidence as well.

"I know he will," she replied, trying to believe it. She rubbed her hands for warmth as Sebastian came along side them. Sebastian also wore a sword.

"I wish I had a sword," Francesca murmured.

"You know the law," Sebi said.

"I don't want to use it, I just want to have it," she snapped testily.

While duels were technically against the law, it was seldom enforced. Judges tended to be lenient with a man who killed or injured another in a duel. If Antonio or Sebi, as Papa's seconds, were called upon to step in and fight, they could count on the court's indulgence. Not Francesca. Any woman who killed a man received a death sentence, no matter the circumstances.

"And anyway," she teased Sebi, "I'm better with a sword than you are."

"You can't prove that," Sebi said, with a smirk.

"Only because you'll no longer fence me."

Antonio laughed. "Precisely." He gave her a gentle squeeze. "You know there's never been a woman second."

"I know, I know." Francesca had no desire to hurt anyone, despite how much Tarrentino deserved it. But she'd had years of practice alone in her room before Papa finally agreed to teach her, and she'd spent hundreds of hours training since then. It was strange to think she'd never use her skills.

After speaking with Signore Russo for a moment, Papa approached Tarrentino.

"Apologize," Tarrentino demanded, "so we may all go home."

"I will not apologize for preventing a murder."

Papa removed the black cloak he wore over his brown jacket and breeches. Sebastian took the cloak and Papa pulled on a pair of leather fencing gloves. "Let's get on with it."

As the sun finally broke through the mist, Tarrentino slowly removed his velvet coat and handed it to one of his seconds. Tarrentino ran a thin hand over the ruffles at his throat and glanced around nervously, as if expecting something.

Signore Russo took his position between them. "Come, gentlemen, take your places."

"The weapons must be inspected," Tarrentino said.

"There's no need," Papa replied. As the challenged party the choice of weapons was his. Tarrentino had no right to object.

"But I insist."

Annoyance showed on Papa's face as he handed his rapier to Signore Russo. The Signore took both weapons and gave them a cursory examination comparing their lengths and flexing the steel in his hands. He nodded and handed them back.

Papa fell gracefully into *en garde* position, knees bent, weight centered, blade pointed at Tarrentino's heart.

"The rules must be stated." Tarrentino plucked at his collar.

Francesca's fingers tightened on Antonio's arm. If there was no way to avoid this duel, she wished it would be over quickly. The man seemed to be stalling, but why? Was he too cowardly to draw his blade?

"We all know the rules," Papa said. He looked around the gathering then focused on Tarrentino. "We fight until first blood is drawn. Now get on with it, unless you've come to your senses."

Tarrentino reluctantly took his stance. The men saluted each other by raising the tips of their blades vertically toward the lightening sky, pointing them at each other, then slashing them toward the ground. Tarrentino's eyes flicked right and left as Signore Russo called, "Begin!"

CHAPTER 2
THE DUEL

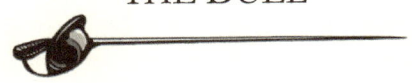

As the duel began, Francesca's fingernails bit into Antonio's linen shirt, her heart pounded, and she felt Antonio's muscles tighten.

But nothing happened. Papa waited, perfectly calm and at ease in his *en gard* position. Tarrentino inched forward, then edged backward again, licking his lips.

The man's stance was all wrong. He leaned too far forward, off balance. If Papa lunged, Tarrentino's retreat would be too slow. He also held his blade in the center of his body giving Papa targets on either side of his blade. His distance was off as well. He was so close Papa could easily hit him with a simple lunge, yet Papa didn't move.

Tarrentino slid closer, then moved back, circling left. Papa merely turned to face him.

For a moment Francesca expected Papa to call a halt and go to Tarrentino and correct his form as he would with any beginning student.

Then Tarrentino attacked lunging clumsily, his blade flailing wide.

Papa merely took a step back and moved his wrist to parry the blade. The clank and hiss of metal on metal sounded crisp and harsh in the morning air.

Tarrentino backed off, panting with the effort, his eyes full of fear. But he seemed committed now. He attacked again and again but Papa slid out of reach. Papa feigned an attack, and then let Tarrentino counterattack, hopelessly overreaching. Papa could have drawn blood and ended the duel a dozen times over.

"What's he waiting for?" Francesca whispered to Antonio.

Antonio nodded toward Tarrentino's seconds. Then Francesca understood. Papa was honor bound to fight this duel, but that didn't mean he thought it wise. Tarrentino was rich and connected. He could cause political trouble for Papa and the salle if he chose to. If Papa ended the duel too quickly, he would humiliate Tarrentino in front of his friends. Papa wouldn't want to make him look worse than absolutely necessary.

Papa let Tarrentino make a few more futile attacks before he went on the offensive. Francesca watched the change come over Papa, like a cat fixing on his prey. Tarrentino saw it too. His eyes widened and he backed away, but he was too late.

Papa lunged, his sword flashing too quickly to see. His blade twisted around Tarrentino's in an *envelopment*, wrenching Tarrentino's weapon from his fingers. The blade spun away. Tarrentino lurched backwards and fell on his rump. Papa stood over him, sword extended, as Tarrentino raised an arm and cowered.

Papa flicked the tip of his blade across Tarrentino's chest and a thin line of red appeared through his clothing.

"First blood," Papa said. "It's done. Honor is served."

Papa extended a hand to Tarrentino to help him up, but Tarrentino looked away.

Papa gave a slight nod. "I'll hear no more of this." He turned toward Francesca and Antonio.

Relief flooded her. It was over. Nothing terrible had happened. Her worry had been a product of the gloomy dawn which was burning away under the bright Tuscan sun.

She and her brothers ran to Papa who handed his sword to Antonio and tugged off his gloves. "Come, we'll visit your mother before we go."

The family walked toward the gravestones where Achilles tossed his head and trotted toward them. Francesca felt so happy she wanted to skip, but she took Papa's arm instead.

She glanced back at Tarrentino looking pathetic, sitting motionless where Papa had left him—legs splayed, a pile of blue velvet and white ruffles against the green of the grass. His face had darkened to purple as he stared at Papa's back. One of his seconds offered him a hand up, but Tarrentino slapped it away. Francesca turned back to Papa.

"I knew you'd make short work of that peacock," Sebastian said with a laugh, hurrying ahead of them.

"Keep a civil tongue, my boy. After all, the man is a senator." The laughter in Papa's eyes took the bite out of his words.

She squeezed his arm. "Let's light a candle in the church for Mother."

Papa patted her hand. "A splendid idea."

She gave him a kiss on the cheek.

Maybe she caught something out of the corner of her eye. Maybe she heard footsteps in the grass or felt the vibrations of pounding feet. Something made her jerk her head around to look behind them in time to see Tarrentino's charge.

His lips were curled back, his face contorted, and his sword extended toward Papa's back.

Her mind froze in shock and fear.

But her body reacted.

Her hand grabbed Papa's blade which dangled from Antonio's fingers. Her body whirled toward Tarrentino who was nearly on top of them. Her legs lunged forward, and her arm drove her sword out.

Tarrentino, intent on Papa, lunged, thrusting his blade past her.

Horrified awe swept over Francesca at what little resistance his body offered her steel. Tarrentino's fury melted into shock as his eyes fixed on hers. His gaze dropped to the sword thrust into his stomach. Her sword. Francesca let go of the hilt as if it burnt her. The blade vibrated there, quivering. Behind her, Papa gasped.

Tarrentino let out a spasming cough and reached for Francesca, grabbing her arm. His eyes went blank, and he fell backward, yanking her off balance before letting go.

She stared at the fallen man, her mind numb and reeling, until the calls behind her penetrated the fog.

"Papa! Papa!" shouted Sebastian.

"Francesca, help us!" called Antonio.

With growing horror, she turned.

Her brothers knelt beside Papa. He lay half on his side, gasping for breath. The tip of Tarrentino's blade protruded from his tan waistcoat. For a second it looked harmless, like a piece of jewelry, just two inches of polished silver. Then deep red blood spread rapidly outward.

"No! No! No!" Francesca cried, flinging herself to her knees beside him. She stared at Papa, mind and body paralyzed as bubbles of blood formed at his lips.

Antonio grabbed her arm and shook her. "You're the healer! Do something!"

Her training from Signora Elena kicked in. *Stop the bleeding. Assess the damage.* She pressed one hand around the blade where the tip exited Papa's ribs on the near side. Reaching her other hand around him she felt for the entry point and closed her hand around that too. "Bandages! For God's sake, we need bandages." She pressed hard on the wounds and Papa groaned.

Hot blood welled, dark and sticky. Then Catalina's blood gushed between her fingers. She struggled for breath. *It can't happen again! Not again!*

Antonio was stripping off his coat and shirt to rip into bandages, but the officiant held out a handful of linen strips. Sebi, on Papa's far side, took the bandages. Then he reached for the sword to pull it out.

"No!" she shouted.

Sebi froze, staring at her.

Tears filled her eyes, and she shook her head. *Assess the damage.* From the angle of the blade and the bubbles of blood at Papa's lips, she knew. His lungs were filling with blood and there was nothing she could do.

"But," Sebi's chest caved in as he understood the implication. "Oh, God!"

Antonio let out a strangled cry.

Papa tried to look over his shoulder. "Tarrentino?" he gasped.

Tarrentino's seconds stood behind them, their faces pale.

"Dead," Signore Russo pronounced.

Francesca shivered. *I killed him.*

Sebi let out an impotent howl. "I wish I could kill him myself!"

Papa, breathing heavily, put a hand to Francesca's face. "Then he's doomed us both."

She didn't understand, but Antonio and Sebastian cursed.

Francesca blinked away her tears. "I'm sorry Papa, I thought … I should have pushed you out of the way."

Papa caressed her cheek. "My Cesca. There isn't much time."

She shook her head, tears blurring her vision. She didn't notice that the others had turned toward the church until Sebi swore. "That rat bastard! He never meant to fight. He meant to have Papa arrested!"

Francesca followed their gaze. A company of foot soldiers and two on horseback rounded the church.

Antonio shook his head. "They're too late."

Tarrentino's seconds ran toward the soldiers shouting and pointing at her.

Papa coughed red flecks. "Cesca, your life is forfeit if they catch you."

They'll hang me, she realized. Now, here, it seemed irrelevant. Her world already lay in ruins. And she couldn't move. She was holding Papa's life in her hands. "I love you, Papa. I won't leave you."

Antonio and Sebastian rose, their faces grim masks.

"Go!" Sebastian said to her.

"We'll slow them down," added Antonio.

They ran toward the soldiers.

Papa struggled to breathe. "You shouldn't die for his dishonor. Go."

"I can't."

"England, Ces… Reverend Falk, Portsmouth," Papa rasped, his voice weakening so that she had to lean close to hear him. "He'll take you to Billy. Billy will…"

"No, Papa." Shuddering uncontrollably, she pressed her hands harder around the sword as his blood and his life drained away.

Papa gulped for air.

Antonio and Sebi reached the soldiers. They argued with Tarrentino's seconds, pushing and shoving. Her brothers drew their swords and faced off against them. Soldiers stepped in and grabbed all four men wrenching the swords from their hands.

Signore Russo yanked Francesca to her feet. "Go! You've no time to lose!"

"No!" Francesca cried, watching Papa's blood well out. She wobbled; her legs seemed unattached to her body.

"Billy England. Promise." whispered Papa.

"I promise, and I swear to live as you taught me, with honor. To show the world—"

Papa went deathly still.

"—that DiCesare is a name of honor."

The mounted soldiers kicked their horses and veered around her brothers. They sped toward Francesca, drawing pistols. "Signora, you are under arrest!"

A shot rang out and a lead ball thudded into the ground nearby. Instinct took over. She ran for Achilles. With one look back, she flung herself into the saddle. Her brothers' faces writhed with anguish and Papa lay still.

"Hold!" barked the soldiers.

Francesca kicked Achilles' side and bolted away.

CHAPTER 3
ESCAPE

Francesca flew on Achilles across the countryside with two blue-coated soldiers galloping after her, pistols drawn.

The morning sun blazed, but the wind ripped the warmth away. Tears blurred her vision. She wiped her eyes with her sleeve and shuddered at her blood-covered hand.

The thundering hoof-beats grew closer. Seated sidesaddle, her right leg bent in front of her, Francesca kicked her left heel into Achilles' side. "Go, boy! Faster!"

He surged forward; his arched neck stretched, his chest pumped, and his black coat shone blue in the sun.

As their speed increased, so did the pull of Francesca's cloak at her throat, choking her with each stride. She glanced back but saw only her dark hair tangling in the wind and her scarlet cloak waving like a matador's cape. She tugged at the pin and the cloak billowed away.

Francesca tried to clear her head, to think. But only one thought came, *Papa's dead. Papa's dead. Papa's dead*, over and over with the beating of hooves.

A sob escaped and she shook her head. *What do I do?* She had headed home on instinct, but what would happen when she got there? Would the soldiers shoot those who tried to protect her?

She imagined Papa's pupils closing ranks around her. Leo would do something "heroic" and foolish to protect her and get himself killed. She imagined soldiers shooting their pistols, lead balls ripping through muscle, and shattering bone, and Signora Elena, lying dead in a pile of gangly limbs.

Steel-cold pain spiked through her. She couldn't go home. Ever. She wiped her tear-blurred eyes, trying to see the way ahead.

Achilles' iron horseshoes clattered across a stone bridge that arched over the sleepy Arno River. The soldiers' horses pounded over seconds behind. *They're gaining!* She urged Achilles on, faster.

She was northwest of Cascina, nearing home. She raced up the dirt road that wound into the foothills. Gnarled grapevines blurred past to her left. Pockets of woodland flew by, dark against pale grass. Soon she would see her home perched on a hill, but before that point there was a hedge …

A pistol fired and something tugged at a loose strand of hair. Her heart skipped a beat. Fear bunched in her stomach. She yanked the reins to the right, steering Achilles into a dirt field.

Twenty yards ahead loomed the hedge. A tight tangle of holly wound around the border of the field; behind it lay a woods. She urged Achilles on.

She and Achilles knew this area well. They'd jumped this hedge last year for fun, but it had grown a foot since then. They streaked forward.

As they approached, Achilles' stride shortened. She bent over her thigh which lay along Achilles' back and tightened her knee around the pommel of her sidesaddle. Grabbing handfuls of mane along with the reins, she braced herself.

The hedge was nearly six feet tall. Achilles gathered and sprang. Francesca's body rose, buoyant. She yanked herself down firmly into the saddle.

They crashed down on the far side. Francesca's chest slammed against her thigh, her face into Achilles' mane. Pain shot through her mouth and she tasted blood. They were in the woods. Leaves and branches slapped her face and caught at her skirts.

Francesca angled sharply right, went a few more yards until she was out of sight of the hedge, then slowed. She listened over Achilles' labored breathing and the crunch of his hooves in the leaf litter.

She heard two strings of angry curses. The soldiers' horses had balked at the jump. They would have to return to the road and go around.

She collapsed forward onto Achilles' neck as relief flooded her. A pistol shot yanked her up straight again, the bullet spattering through the leaves to her left. She urged Achilles on, though his sides heaved.

After half an hour they came to a brook meandering through the trees. She paused to let Achilles drink.

Now that the immediate threat had passed, her body shook, her head spun, and her breath came in gasps. A flood of nausea hit her. She slid from the saddle, leaned against the rough bark of a tree and, as her stomach convulsed, threw up. White lights whirled through her vision and she retched again.

Eventually her stomach calmed and the woods stopped reeling. She stumbled to the brook and knelt. She stared at the dark red covering her hands. Papa's blood.

It's not real. It's just paint. Papa will scold when I get home.

A shiver cascaded down her spine. Papa was dead and she had killed a man. Impossible, but there was the proof, on her hands.

She made fists, holding onto all she had left of Papa as a wave of racking sobs broke over her.

When the surge passed, she lowered her hands into the cold water and opened them. The blood curled away downstream, disappearing, taking with it everything she had known.

She was exhausted. She wanted to lie down next to the brook and burrow into the dirt, become part of the land. She curled into a ball.

Achilles' breath warmed the back of her neck. He nudged her shoulder and rubbed his muzzle against her cheek. Francesca wrapped her arms around his head and dried her tears on his black coat. At least she wasn't alone.

"You're right, we haven't much time before they find us."

She splashed her face, took a drink of water, then forced herself to get up. She trembled so wildly she had trouble climbing into the saddle and gathering the reins.

Francesca turned Achilles away from the road. He shook his head and headed toward home. She knew he was tired and wanted his stable and his oats. She rubbed his neck, her voice quavering, "I'm sorry. Breakfast will have to wait."

She had no idea when or how they would eat again, much less sleep or live. Words rose in her mind. *Fugitive. Criminal. Hunted. Hanged.* She needed to think. *What do I do?*

Papa's words echoed: *To England, Reverend Falk, Portsmouth. He'll take you to Billy.*

Why had she promised Papa? It was ludicrous. How was she supposed to get to England by herself?

She urged Achilles on and bent flat, her cheek against his neck. She felt chilled to the bone and was grateful for his warmth. She let him pick his way through the thicket.

They emerged into a sheep pasture. Her breath caught with a fresh wave of pain. A half mile away, perched on a hill, stood Salle DiCesare, the world-famous fencing school where Papa taught young noblemen the art and science of the sword. *Home.*

The villa's tan stones and terracotta roof glowed in the sun. A stone wall wound around it like a ribbon of gold. She could just glimpse the fuchsia of the bougainvillea covering the south wall of the courtyard.

Achilles neighed and she patted his neck. She ached to gallop across the fields, through the main gate, throw herself on her bed, and wait to wake up from this nightmare. But the salle's iron gates were closed to her.

Besides, she knew the soldiers would expect her to run home. She was only nineteen, and a girl. They would expect her to be frightened and confused. She hoped they would spend hours searching the salle while she slipped away.

She could see that the soldiers had regained the road and were galloping up the cypress-lined lane toward the salle.

Francesca turned Achilles in the opposite direction, away from her family, her home, her world. It was just the two of them now. She and Achilles would have to escape Tuscany. They'd travel south across country until they met the road west to the port of Livorno, and the sea.

CHAPTER 4
LIVORNO

After three hours of hard riding, Francesca and Achilles reached Livorno's gates and lost themselves amid the bustling crowds.

Papa used to say that Livorno displayed the arrogance of the Medicis. They built it to intimidate their enemies. Wide avenues and straight canals, laid out in a fan pattern, led from the harbor. Sunny piazzas held sparkling fountains. Marbled palaces and municipal buildings towered in grandeur.

Those bright open spaces made Francesca jerk around, expecting soldiers rushing toward her, so she kept to the dark back streets and reeking alleyways.

Two and three-story buildings pressed in above the narrow cobblestone streets, leaving only a slit of blue sky. Horses, carriages, carts, and people jostled for space. The smell of roasting chestnuts softened the stench of urine and dung.

Francesca hadn't seen any soldiers behind her on the road, but each moment she felt their eyes on her back. It wouldn't take long for them to guess where she had gone. Livorno was the quickest way out of Tuscany. They'd be after her soon if they weren't already.

While Francesca had little idea where she was, she knew the sea lay to the west. Guided by the direction of the sun on the upper stories of houses, she led Achilles through a maze of backstreets toward the docks.

As she walked, she took stock. She had left home without money or food. Her clothes were a mess. She ran a hand over the ruffles at her throat and came away with a few leaves from the woods. Her tailored gray riding coat was snagged and soiled, the cuffs stained with blood.

She brushed herself off, then ran her fingers through her tangled hair. She couldn't unsnarl the knots, so she twisted it into a bun and secured it with a strand of hair. It would have to do.

She paused in front of a darkened window and stared at her reflection in the wavy glass. *You don't look like a murderer.* At the thought, her stomach heaved, but there was nothing to bring up.

After a few deep breaths she rubbed away a smudge from her cheek and blood from a scratch along her eyebrow. She tried a smile, then a scowl, but neither got rid of the fear in her green eyes. She hurried on.

She would need money for passage to England for her and Achilles. The only thing she had to sell was Achilles' sidesaddle and bridle. It was a fine saddle, but would it be enough?

As Francesca neared the fishy-smelling docks, she found a comfortable looking stable with a yard out front where a half-dozen horses munched piles of hay.

After some negotiating, the sinewy stable manager agreed to trade Francesca's saddle for feed, a dozen liras, and a handful of soldi. The coins chinked woefully in her hand. The manager was getting the better end of the deal, but she had no choice.

Francesca brushed Achilles and left him in the stable yard with plenty of hay while she headed for the harbor to find a ship.

Sunlight painted the forest of masts gold, reflections rippling like quicksilver around the hulls. But a chill, raw breeze flowed out from the nearby hills. Angry purple clouds crept through the valleys. Hurried longboats loaded with men and stores rowed between the ships, preparing for a storm.

To the right of the harbor sat Fortezza Vecchia. Francesca had always thought the fort's massive walls and round towers lent a noble air to the scene. Now it seemed menacing since it served as barracks for the soldiers.

Soldiers.

Francesca tried not to think of them, or the duel. She needed to focus, but as she searched for the harbormaster, the image of Papa overwhelmed her. She clamped her jaws until her muscles ached. Digging her fingernails into her palms, she held the tears at bay and forced her back straight. There was nothing she could do for Papa, but she could keep her promise: England.

The overdressed harbormaster told her there were two ships bound for England. He waved a dismissive hand. "Over there."

The first ship, the *Amsterdam*, flying a Dutch flag, seemed tidy and well maintained. The rail-thin captain stood on the docks directing his men as they loaded barrels. He had a surprisingly booming voice for such a spindly man. He spoke little Italian, and Francesca knew no Dutch, but they both spoke English.

The captain looked Francesca over as she offered him her handful of money. "My dear," he said, "that trifling sum would not be worth the headaches carrying you would cost me."

"I'd be no trouble. I'm skilled with a needle and thread and I can cook."

"No doubt," the captain said. "But an unaccompanied female will distract my men no end. And worse, sailors believe women to be bad luck aboard ship. I'm sorry, you'll have to try elsewhere."

The second captain, a disheveled Englishman with a stained shirt front, told her the same thing but in ruder terms. And when she said she could cook and sew he leaned forward, eyes raking her body. "What else can you do?"

Francesca recoiled and hurried away. She swayed with fatigue, trying to decide what to do next.

If she couldn't afford passage to England, anywhere was better than here. She headed for the nearest ship but spun toward the sound of marching feet. A company of infantrymen trooped down the main road. Her breath hissed out. She steadied herself. *They're probably headed to the fort.* Still, she rushed in the opposite direction. *Do not run. Hurry! But do not run.*

She twisted and turned randomly through the alleys as dark clouds moved in, blocking the sun. *They weren't after me. They can't be. It's too soon.* But she had no way to be sure. Perhaps word had spread more quickly than she imagined. Tarrentino was rich and powerful. The search would be fierce.

Francesca headed back toward the stable clutching her money. Going to sea was no longer an option. *I'll buy back the saddle and we'll head north to Viareggio. Perhaps we can get a ship there.*

But as she rounded the corner to the stable, she stopped in her tracks. Two soldiers were dragging Achilles from the corral. Achilles reared and bucked, but they held on to his harness.

"No!" cried Francesca. She clamped a hand to her mouth and dodged back behind the corner. She put her back against the wall as the world spun. *Achilles!* Her sweet Achilles.

She peered around the corner again. No one seemed to have heard. They were still focused on Achilles who shook his head and tried to pull away.

She looked around helplessly at the passersby who didn't even acknowledge her. Wasn't there anyone who would help?

As she racked her brain for some plan, the soldiers mounted horses and tied Achilles between them. Then they kicked their mounts and headed straight towards her.

She ran.

CHAPTER 5
SOLDIERS AND ROGUES

An alley she followed dumped her out into an open plaza. Francesca stopped. In the center of the cobblestone square, workmen were erecting the rough timber outline of a gallows. Her mouth went dry. Her shoulders crumpled as she backed away. *It's not for me. Please God, let it not be for me.*

Francesca walked on legs that didn't seem quite attached to her body. She looked up at the sky, feeling exposed.

Eventually her body refused to go any farther. She lurched into a recessed doorway and huddled in a corner, sliding to the hard stone floor and wrapping her arms around her knees.

It's all gone. Were her brothers in prison? Even if they were free, she couldn't contact them.

Alone. The word cut like glass. Never in her life had she been on her own. Nurses, governesses, tutors, there had always been people watching over her.

She missed them all with a hollow ache. She missed Papa and her brothers; she missed Leo and Papa's other students. She missed Elena, with her gangly limbs and serious face. She missed Catalina and Nana. And she missed Phillip, her Phillip. The ache in her chest spread in waves.

She sat for a long time in the tomblike doorway, watching strangers pass and disappear like memories. As the cold from the stones crept up her back and legs, she longed to feel safe—the way Papa had always made her feel.

Papa.

But her mind veered from those thoughts. *Phillip then.* She tried to remember a time when she'd been secure in his arms, but those memories would not come. Instead, her last night with Phillip flooded back to her with all its pain and horror.

She had knelt on the dueling grounds, next to the blood-soaked spot where Catalina had died. No, where Francesca's dishonor had killed her. Francesca shivered in the cold and the dark, wishing she was the one lying dead, not her dear friend.

To defend God and country. To keep one's word. To avoid lying, and cheating. To exhibit courage in word and deed. To live for freedom, justice, and all that is good. To die with honor.

How could I have said those words so many times without once understanding them? They weren't rules to limit my freedom, they were guides to save me from this. If I'd acted honorably Catalina would still live.

The shifting leaves in the trees overhead murmured to her. *"Selfffish."*

"Stop!" Francesca had yelled up into the branches.

"Francesca?"

It had been Phillip's voice. Then he was kneeling beside her. She made out little of his face, but she knew the feel and smell of him.

"Francesca, are you alright?"

"No," she gasped as he eased her shoulders up into his arms. "Oh, Phillip, nothing will ever be right again."

"I'm so sorry about Catalina. I came out just in case you needed me."

She clutched him. "I do need you. It's my fault she's dead."

"You didn't stab her."

"I might as well have."

"Don't say that. You loved Catalina. I know you did."

Francesca nodded.

He put a hand to her cheek. "We can still get away from here. We can put this all behind us and start new. I love you, Francesca."

Her heart leapt. She wanted more than anything to run from the pain, but then she heard the leaves overhead.

"Oh, Phillip, I can't go."

"You can," he said, smoothing her hair. "There's nothing to it. We saddle the horses and ride away."

"But Papa would be heartbroken. And Signora Bianchi would be crushed. I know she's hard sometimes, but only because she loves me. I can't do that to them."

"But Francesca…"

"I can't leave Sebi now. He's lost his love. He may hate me, but he'll still need me. And I can't let him and Leandro take all the blame."

She gave a hiccupping cry. "And I can't do it to you. I love you. I want to be with you, but I can't let you give up so much for me."

"I'm not giving up anything important," he said. "Only you matter."

Phillip's fingers touched the bare skin of her arm, "Good Lord, you're freezing. Let's get you up off this damp ground."

He got to his feet and helped her up. Her legs wobbled and she leaned against him. He rubbed her arms to get some warmth into them.

"Maybe you don't care about your future now, but what about five years from now, or twenty? Someday you'll resent all you gave up for me."

"No."

"I tricked you into fencing with me. I nearly got you expelled. I don't deserve your love."

He wrapped his arms around her and rocked her. "Hush. I fenced with you because I chose to. You couldn't have made me if I hadn't wanted to. Besides, what does it matter, as long as we fell in love?"

"I do love you, with all my heart," she said. "That's why I can't go with you. I can't let you dishonor your name, as I have."

"Francesca—"

"Please, Phillip. You must go home and do as your father commands."

He turned away. "If I go home," he said bitterly, "it's to challenge him for killing my mother."

Her heart twisted. She couldn't be responsible for more loss.

She put a hand on his shoulder. "You said yourself he didn't kill her. That she … she made a choice. You can't kill your father over a choice someone else made. That's not justice, it's revenge."

"But he drove her to it."

"Like I drove Sebi to challenge Leandro," she said, her voice thick.

Phillip turned back to her. "It's not the same. Sebi and Leandro chose to pick up those sharps. Catalina chose to leap in front of Sebi."

Francesca took a deep breath. "Your mother chose, too," she said softly.

He looked away. "The man is violent and greedy. Why should I do as he says?"

"Because it's your duty." Her voice shook. "Catalina tried to teach me how important that is, but I wouldn't listen."

"But the man has no honor!"

"It's not about him. It's about you. If you give up your honor, you become him."

He was silent.

She held him tight. She'd lost her best friend, and now she was losing Phillip as well.

"If this is what you really want, I'll leave in the morning," he said, his voice raw.

Francesca gave a sob. "It's the last thing in the world that I want, but it's the way it has to be."

She held him. She listened to his heartbeat and wondered if it was possible to hear a heart break.

Bouts of violent trembling overcame Francesca and so they retreated to the relative warmth of the stable. Piling hay in the corner of Achilles' stall, they lay together in the dark, wrapped in each other's arms, wishing the morning would never come.

It seemed like her last night with Phillip had happened yesterday, but at the same time it seemed like a lifetime ago. Cold then, cold now. The world seemed to have lost all warmth.

She would have to move soon. The chill was sapping what little strength she had left. Besides, whoever this doorway belonged to might find her. She forced herself to rise and inched back to the street. She looked both ways before stepping from the doorway.

As the afternoon waned, the temperature dropped. Channeled into tight gusts, the wind howled up the narrow lanes. She thought of her red cloak lying on the road trampled by horses' hooves and rubbed her upper arms to keep warm. Hunger gnawed, but she didn't dare spend any of her money. She would need it to get out of town.

Francesca found a spot out of the wind and slumped against a stone wall. Yesterday her biggest concern had been whether to ride Achilles in the olive grove or the vineyard. Now she wanted to scream at the injustice, but the scream did not come from her. The scream came from around a corner, shrill and cut off.

A shiver crawled up Francesca's spine. She moved silently down the alley. Ahead was the dark canal with a few tethered boats, and beyond, the towering city wall. She looked to the right down a row of darkened warehouses fronting the canal.

In the gathering dusk she made out two sobbing women huddled in a doorway. A body lay at their feet. Two men examined something in their hands, probably money they had stolen. A third man waved a rapier at the women. He held it like a hammer, not like a sword.

"What about them?" asked one of the men.

"He didn't mention no women," said the man with the sword. "We only got paid for him." He motioned to the man on the ground.

"They'd fetch a good price," the first man said.

"They saw us cut him. They gotta go," the swordsman said.

"That don't mean we can't have a bit of fun first," said the third man.

Anger rushed up, heating Francesca's chilled muscles. She clenched her fingers, wishing for a sword hilt to grasp. She couldn't let those women be raped and murdered, but what could she do? She had no weapons, and it was three against one. From the looks of the women, they would be little help. It would be foolish, suicide.

She gave a harsh laugh as the image of the gallows surfaced in her mind and a wave of recklessness washed over her. She'd likely be dead soon anyway. Better to go out fighting than dangling from a noose. If Papa were here, he would try to save them. So would Catalina. But she'd need something to use as a weapon.

She ran back toward a garbage pile she had passed around the corner. The wind whipped at her skirts and raised goosebumps on her arms. A man wandered down the street and she called to him. "Please, help! Please!"

The man hurried away. Francesca swore under her breath.

The trash heap held mostly broken bits of crates and barrels, smashed pottery, and torn linens, but she found a sturdy wooden cane about the length of a sword. Good enough.

She hurried back. Peeking around the corner, she saw the women huddling over the prone figure. The rogues had moved in closer.

Francesca squared her shoulders. She couldn't fight three men with just a wooden cane, but maybe she could trick them and take them on one by one.

She saluted her opponents, as she had done almost every day at the fencing salle, holding the stick vertical, pointing it at the men, and then whipping the tip toward the ground. "Papa, help me," she whispered.

I'm here, Papa's voice said. She felt his hand on her shoulder, steadying her, and took a deep breath.

Francesca headed toward the group, tapping the cane and staring into space as though blind.

As she drew closer, she realized the women were only girls. One appeared to be around sixteen and the other a few years younger.

The prone man struggled to rise, and the younger girl knelt, helping him. The older girl faced the men, shielding the struggling pair.

The girls' wind-whipped golden hair tangled about their faces. Gusts lashed their traveling cloaks revealing silks underneath. That suggested they were nobles, but what would nobles be doing here?

The older girl put her palm against the chest of the man with the rapier, holding him at arm's length. "Please! Stop!" She spoke in French.

The leader's dark goatee accentuated his sneer as he turned to the other men. "I'll take the feisty one."

The injured man had gotten to one knee. "Leave her be!" he rasped. He clutched his neck and dark blood spilled between his fingers.

"I want her. She's mine," said a lanky man with sharp features. He grabbed the girl's wrist, wrenching her toward him. She cried out.

"Says who?" said the third man. He put a hand around the girl's waist, pulling her against him. He was swarthy and squat — apelike.

Francesca, now twenty feet away, caught their attention. The lanky man let go of the girl's wrist and approached Francesca. His angular features were feline. He stood, back to the canal, drawing a knife. "I'll have this one."

"Who's there?" she said, hearing the quaver in her voice. She had meant to sound frightened, but it was no act.

She tapped her stick up the man's body, staring over his shoulder.

He grinned hungrily.

Francesca brought the cane down on his knife, knocking it from his fingers. As he bent to pick it up, she swung her knee up under his chin with all her strength.

His head snapped back.

She shoved him as hard as she could.

The man stumbled backwards across the narrow street. His heels caught on the lip of the canal and he pin-wheeled his arms, then went over with a splash. Seconds later, a string of profanities echoed off the stone walls.

Francesca grabbed the knife and turned toward the others. The bleeding man had slumped back to the ground and the younger girl bent over him. The ape still held the older girl. She stared, open-mouthed at Francesca.

The leader approached Francesca, sword ready. "You see well enough."

She advanced to meet him. She fell into *en garde* position, knees bent, back straight, cane in her right hand, knife in her left. "Leave them be."

The leader laughed and lunged.

She parried. The rapier shaved a curl of wood off her cane.

The leader lunged again.

Francesca twisted her cane around his blade, binding his sword in an *envelopement*. The blade spun from his fingers, clanged against the stone wall and clattered to the ground.

She lunged, jamming the cane in his stomach. It broke with a *clack*. The man sunk to one knee, gasping.

Francesca grabbed the rapier and moved toward the remaining man. He pulled out a knife and put it to the girl's throat. "Stay back." He moved away, dragging the girl.

Francesca switched her knife to her throwing hand. She hesitated. She couldn't risk hitting the girl, and she could hear the leader behind her coughing as he rose to his feet.

The girl stomped on the man's toes and pulled partway free. He swore as he tried to regain his hold. Francesca threw her knife. The blade skimmed along his cheek and ear, slicing open the skin. With a guttural yell, he released the girl, clapping the hand to his face. She ran for her sister. Blood oozed between his fingers, and he hurried away, swearing.

Francesca spun to face the leader. He was winded, but on his feet. She advanced and put the tip of the rapier to his throat. "What's it to be?"

With a snarl, he backed away, then fled.

Francesca let out a breath. Papa's voice said, *well done, my Cesca.* She raised her eyes to the black clouds for a moment, then hurried to the girls who knelt over the body on the ground.

The man was of considerable girth. Blood covered the hand he held to his neck. Red spattered his cheek from his thick spectacles to his mutton chop beard, coloring the stones beneath him. His eyes fluttered, barely aware. "They'll be back," he said.

"Who are they?" Francesca asked. "Why were they sent to kill you?" But his eyes were closed, and he didn't answer.

"We need to go," Francesca said to the girls. They stared at her, tearstained and uncomprehending. She switched to French. taking the older girl's hand. "We must go."

The girl shook her head. "We must get Father to the doctor."

The sisters were delicately built and shook violently. Francesca thought it unlikely the three of them could transport the man anywhere. "I'll fetch help."

"No!" cried the younger girl. "Don't go!" She clutched at Francesca with icy, shaking fingers.

Francesca hesitated, unsure what to do. A few cold drops of rain landed on her head and spread through her hair. She heard the man in the canal climbing out again somewhere in the darkness. She couldn't leave the girls unprotected.

Their father opened his eyes and laid a hand on the younger girl's arm. His breath sighed out and his body relaxed, his eyes staring and unseeing.

There was a horrible moment of stillness. In that moment the sky opened, and the rain came down in dark, cold sheets.

CHAPTER 6
TO SEA

"We must go!" shouted Francesca over the moan of the wind, the hiss of rain against stone, and the piercing keen of the younger girl.

In the darkness, Francesca could barely make them out. The younger girl knelt beside her father, face upturned. The sound pouring from her seemed too great to be contained within her slender form. Francesca tasted salt tears mixed with the rain on her face. She wanted to keen along; it was her pain too. But wailing would not change things, and they were still in danger.

The older girl slumped over her father convulsing with sobs.

Francesca pulled at her arm. "We must go."

The girl's fingers clamped onto her father's lapels. "No!" she cried, whether to her father, Francesca, or the world, Francesca couldn't tell.

Francesca put a hand on the girl's shoulder. "I'm sorry, but we have to leave him. We must get to safety before they return."

The girl shook her head. "I, I can't."

Francesca's chest heaved. She had said the same words only that morning at Papa's side. She knew the impossibility of abandoning her father.

She wiped her face. "What's your name?"

The girl swallowed her sobs, "C, Claire."

Francesca pushed back the hair slicked to Claire's face. "Claire, I know you love your father, but he's gone." She steadied her voice. "You need to take care of your sister."

Claire looked at the younger girl as if seeing her for the first time. "Belle!"

She grabbed the girl in a fierce embrace. Claire's voice joined Belle's high-pitched howl, reminding Francesca of the banshees, lost spirits who travel the lands keening for the dead.

Francesca stood, shivering, leaning her weight on the sword still in her hand. Her sodden wool skirts and jacket sucked her to the earth. Even the whipping wind barely ruffled them. She looked around. She was lost, but the city wall towered next to them. If they kept it on their right they would find the harbor, and hopefully a warm, dry place where they could get help.

The girls still knelt, wrapped in each other's arms. Francesca took Claire's upper arm and tried to raise her to her feet. "Come," she insisted. She said it three more times before Claire got to her feet, pulling Belle with her. Claire wrapped one arm around Francesca, leaning into her, and the other around her little sister.

Francesca swayed with exhaustion but got the three of them moving through the dark streets. She tried to listen for men following them, but the roar of the storm and the girl's sobs made it impossible. Twice she thought a shadow detached itself from a larger shadow and followed them, but she couldn't be sure. As they reached more populated areas, lighted windows broke the darkness making it easier for Francesca to find her footing on the uneven cobblestone streets.

As they neared the harbor, Francesca stopped under the awning of a tavern. She wiped the rain from her eyes. Amid the golden glow inside, men sang to the scraping of a fiddle. The scent of baking bread and roasting ham wafted out, and her empty stomach twisted. Yet she hesitated.

"Should we go in?" asked Belle in a trembling voice.

Ordinarily, none of them would set foot inside a tavern of this sort.

"I don't know," Francesca said. She had meant to enter, but as she scanned the men inside, their faces and clothing reminded her of the rogues in the alley. If the killers followed them in, whose side would these men be on?

She turned to Claire. "Do you have rooms somewhere? Is there a place we can hide?"

Claire spoke through chattering teeth. "We were returning from mass when we found men searching our rooms. Father said they meant to kill him. He had learned of an intended assassination and had warned the victim. It must be the conspirators after us."

"Who was the victim and who the plotters?" asked Francesca.

Claire shook her head. "He didn't say."

Francesca slumped against the wall. She couldn't very well go to the authorities who wanted to hang her, and had no idea who they could trust.

"Where were you going?" she asked Claire. "Your father must have had a plan."

"He said there was one ship captain he could trust, an old friend, Captain Ramirez. He promised he would help us. He said he would take us away from here."

"Do you know where to find him?"

She shook her head.

Francesca let out a breath. Now that she had stopped, the strength leeched out of her. She couldn't take another step, much less go back out in the dark rain filled with assassins and soldiers.

Claire and Belle stared at her. Their delicate features trembled. Their tight lips were purple with cold and their wide eyes full of unquestioning faith. *I'm all they have.* Then she realized *they're all I have, too.*

Well, this captain must have a ship and she knew where the ships were.

As Francesca wrapped an arm around the girls and lurched them all back out into the rain, a pistol spat in the darkness and a lead ball pinged off the stone wall.

Belle shrieked and Francesca propelled them all forward. "Run!"

By the time they reached the docks the wind and rain had waned, but the cold had grown intense. The lighted windows fronting the harbor lit the docks here and there, plunging other parts into deeper darkness. The dual lanterns on the stern of each ship glowed like pairs of unblinking eyes.

Francesca stared into the darkness at a loss for what to do next. She had only moments before the rogues arrived. She had to do something.

She spotted an orange glow flickering off the face of a man lighting a pipe just up the dock. She ran toward him with the girls following. She grabbed the front of his coat with her free hand, and the man grunted in surprise.

"Captain Ramirez, do you know him? Which is his ship?" she cried.

The man shrugged and shook his head. A puff of pipe smoke enveloped Francesca's face and she coughed it away. She wasn't sure if the man didn't know the answer or if he hadn't understood her. She tried every language she knew and still the man shrugged. Her stomach bunched in desperation. She yanked on his jacket, but then felt Claire's small hand on her arm.

"He can't tell us what he doesn't know," Claire said.

Francesca exhaled, released the man's coat, and backed away. She bent over. She was so tired and lost. Belle hugged her and Claire put an arm across her back saying, "I don't know your—"

"Ahoy," called a voice out of the darkness, "If you're looking for Capt'n Ramirez you're out of luck. That's his ship, the *Santa Ana* making ready to sail."

"Where?" Francesca pitched blindly toward the source of the voice.

She found a young man, a few inches taller than her, who pointed her toward a ship out in the bay. Lanterns lit the ship's deck and men aboard swarmed with activity.

"He must be in a powerful hurry to leave at this time of night, and with the tides against him," the young man mused.

"We must get on that ship," Francesca said.

"Good luck." The young man moved away. Francesca grabbed his arm, hard. "You don't understand, we'll be killed if we don't get aboard."

"It's none of my affair," said the youth, trying to disengage her fingers.

The sound of scuffing feet and low voices came from somewhere in the darkness. The rogues were nearby. She suddenly remembered the sword in her other hand. She pressed the tip against the young man's chest. "It's your problem now." It was a terrible thing to do, but she was desperate.

"Careful with the pig sticker!" the youth said.

Francesca pitched her voice low. "I already killed one man today. Don't make me kill another."

"Fine. Fine. There's a skiff just over there. Take it." He nodded his head to a spot further out on the dock. Francesca made for it, towing the young man. "You're going to take us there." She doubted she had the strength left to row all the way out to the ship.

"I'll not," said the youth.

"You will or you'll be run through," growled Francesca, though she could barely lift the sword.

They piled into the skiff and pushed off from the dock. The choppy waves slapped at the side of the little boat. As the youth took up the oars a shout came from land and booted feet clomped down the dock toward them.

"Hurry!" cried Francesca.

"Oh dear God!" Claire said.

The young man hauled at the oars and the boat shot away. There was a flash and pop from the dock and a lead ball thumped into the skiff's side.

The girls screamed and the youth swore.

"Get down in the bottom of the boat!" Francesca ordered the girls.

As they hunched down the young man mumbled something under his breath, released the oars and jumped over the side. He swam toward the far end of the docks.

"Christ almighty!" exclaimed Francesca as she threw herself into the youth's seat and grabbed the oars. She strained against the handles and the skiff moved forward. Pull. Reach. Pull. Reach. It wouldn't take long for the man to reload his pistol.

Francesca looked over her shoulder at the *Santa Ana* about fifty yards away. A sail spilled loose and then snapped taut. Another shot pounded into the side of the skiff and the girls screamed.

Francesca heard the youth climbing out of the water and then the squeak of another set of oarlocks. The rogues had found a boat and were coming after them.

Francesca pulled for all she was worth, but she was past exhaustion and running on fear. The farther out in the bay, the rougher the water became. The boat wallowed into channels between waves, the oars popping loose at the crests sending Francesca flying backwards. Water splashed over the side.

She glanced back at the ship again. Forty yards, and another sail unfurled.

On the next rise of the waves, Francesca saw the other skiff pulling closer. *Please, God,* she thought as she worked every muscle and gasped for breath.

Thirty yards, three sails, and the *Santa Ana* was beginning to move. She was leaving without them. Francesca gasped to the girls, "Call them. Yell!"

Claire and Belle sat up, screaming to the ship. "Captain Ramirez! Help! Wait! Help!"

Indistinct voices buzzed from the ship, but Francesca didn't look back. She was watching the other skiff drawing closer. They would catch up before she could reach the ship.

A gruff voice shouted from the ship, "Identify yourselves."

"Claire and Belle Henry," shouted Claire.

"Saints bless! Back the sails! Get them aboard quickly," ordered the same voice.

More indistinct voices, then a pale float attached to a rope sailed over Francesca's head, the rope landing across the skiff. With a cry of relief Francesca dropped the oars and grabbed the rope. She and the girls held on as men dragged the skiff as it pitched across the waves.

In moments the craft bumped against the wooden hull and a voice shouted, "Get them aboard quickly now!" Calloused hands helped the girls up the side. Francesca grabbed the rapier before she too was whisked up onto the ship.

She crumpled to the deck, her chest heaving. A sailor wrapped a blanket around her shoulders.

A bull of a man, with a square, handsome face and dark eyes, took Claire's hand as a crewman draped a blanket around her shoulders.

"Where's your father, Lady Henry," the captain said.

Claire teetered but pointed back to the second skiff. "Captain, those men killed him and tried to kill us." Her breath caught and her shoulders shook, but she held in her sob.

"Ah, my condolences, child." The captain laid an oversized, fatherly hand on her shoulder. "He was a good man, doing what was right. I had hoped… well, anyway, you're safe now," the captain said.

He turned to a handful of men who stood at the rail looking out into the dark water toward the other skiff with pistols in hand. With a snarl, he said, "Open fire!"

When the volley of gunfire died away, Francesca's body relaxed. As her consciousness faded one thought exploded through her mind. *Achilles!*

CHAPTER 7
THE SANTA ANA

Francesca awoke confused. She stared up at a rough plank ceiling, swaying gently, and couldn't sort out where she was. Then she heard an inrush of breath and Belle threw herself across Francesca, hugging her neck and exclaiming, "You're awake! Finally!"

At the sight of Belle, the previous day came crashing back; blood spilling from Papa's chest, the feel of the sword as it entered Tarrentino's side, the panicked flight, the fight in the alley, the pull for the ship.

As Belle rushed from the cabin calling for Claire, Francesca's chin quivered, and her body began to shake.

When Claire, Belle, and the captain entered, Francesca was curled in a ball. Sobs strangled her throat and nose and she coughed, gasped, and wept all together. Claire sat on the bed rubbing her back and the captain looked on, his eyebrows drawn together.

"We're fine. We're safe. Everything is…," Claire trailed off, a waver in her voice.

"I know" mumbled Francesca, but it did nothing to stop her bawling. Soon Claire and Belle were crying as well, the three of them piled together on a cot, wrapped in each other's arms, letting waves of grief pass over and through them. At some point, the captain slipped out of the cabin.

When their tears finally quieted Claire said, "What are we to call you? We don't even know your name."

Francesca wiped her eyes and nose. It seemed so odd. Claire and Belle were loved ones, sisters almost, yet she knew next to nothing about them.

"Call me Francesca." As she said it, she realized they were speaking English. Had they been speaking it last night? They'd spoken French at first. "Where are you from? Where are we going? Are they still after us?" A thousand questions piled into Francesca's mind, but Claire put a finger to Francesca's lips.

"We're safe," Claire said. "We're headed north along the coast. We can set you ashore at the next port if you wish."

Francesca thought of Achilles. He was all she had left of home, but going back for him would be suicide. She shook her head.

"Don't you want to go home?" asked Belle.

Francesca tried to bite back the tears, but they came anyway. She told them about Papa's duel, Tarrentino's death, and the soldiers searching for her. They were family now, or as close to it as she was likely to have. They deserved to know. Before she finished, they were crying again as well.

Claire pushed the tangled hair back behind Francesca's ear. "Then you shall come home with us," she said, as if that settled everything. "Our family is your family."

"Where?" asked Francesca.

"To Mother," Belle said.

"Wildewood England," said Claire.

"England!" Francesca whispered. Then her stomach gave a growl, reminding her it had been more than a day since she'd eaten.

"Either you swallowed a tiger, or we'd better find you something to eat," said Belle with a giggle.

The three rose, but Francesca's back muscles seized up and her head spun. She sat down as the room swam around her.

"Perhaps we should bring you some food," Claire said.

Francesca nodded.

"We'll be back in a moment," Claire said, and she and Belle left.

Francesca wore a knee length linen shirt which must have belonged to one of the sailors. The small cabin was simple with whitewashed walls and low overhead beams that would make it just possible for Francesca to stand upright. There were three small cots, and to her left sat a sideboard holding a pitcher and basin; to her right, a dark wood cupboard. There were no windows, but a lantern glowed from a wall sconce between the cots.

The girls returned with a tray of bread and cheese, two oranges, and tea.

As Francesca tucked in, there was a knock at the door. Belle bounced up to answer it. A large man filled the doorway. He had his hands full, and he bobbed his head apologetically.

"Sorry to disturb your ladyships," he said with an awkward bow. "Seein' as I speak English, the men elected me to … We heard what happened, and seein' as you gots nothin'." He bowed again, "We took up a collection." He held out his handful to Belle.

"Oh! Aren't you just the sweetest!" exclaimed Belle as she took the items from him. "A comb and soap, handkerchiefs and ribbons, all sort of things!"

Claire rose and crossed to the man. With his hands now free, he snatched off his wool cap. Claire took his hand, her palm engulfed in his. "Thank everyone for us. This is most generous of you, and we hope we can repay your kindness."

After the man left they admired the handful of items.

Francesca said soberly, "When the captain learns I'm a fugitive he'll be obliged to turn me over to the authorities."

"Then we shan't put him in that position," Claire said. "We'll have to come up with a story."

Francesca's stomach clenched. She had not told a lie since the day that Catalina died. Since the day she had caused Catalina's death with her half-truths and manipulations. Not in three years. And her last words to Papa were about honor.

Belle clapped her hands. "I love making up stories."

"Francesca and I shall make up this one," Claire said sternly. "And you will not mention anything about Francesca's duel."

"I can't let you lie for me," said Francesca.

"Why not?" said Belle, scrunching up her face.

"Because I can't make you complicit in my crime. It's wrong."

Claire gave her a strange look. "So is hanging you. So is forcing the captain to choose between protecting you and turning you over. So is you leaving us."

Francesca looked down at her hands, picturing blood on them.

"We've already told the captain about the fight in the alley," said Belle.

"And that's all he need know," Claire said firmly. She took Francesca's hand. "We'll tell him the truth. Once we're well away from here."

The *Santa Ana* was a tidy, square-sailed vessel, black from the waterline up, with red and gold stripes beneath her twelve gun ports. Taut-bellied, cream-colored sails skipped the three-masted ship across a tumultuous sea barely outrunning the squall behind them. Atop her mizzen-mast crackled a red and gold Spanish flag, contrasting sharply against the grey-blue cloud-filled sky, so low it looked like it might scrape the masts.

She tacked north pushed in a rush by the wind along the coast of France. At this distance from shore, France was no more than a blue smudge on the horizon.

Francesca stood at the starboard rail in her stained riding habit.

They'd been at sea a month and she enjoyed the fresh wind buffeting her skin and tugging at tendrils of her hair.

Francesca had learned, to her surprise, that she loved the ocean.

Papa had traveled the world, first as a soldier, then as a sword master who taught princes and kings. He always came home complaining of the sea journey. He had hated feeling off-balance and had been bored by the monotony.

Not Francesca. She loved the feel of the deck bucking under her feet like a living creature, and how the sea was never the same from minute to minute. One moment it might be deep indigo with soft-edged waves *shushing* along the side of the ship, as if lulling her to sleep, a half hour later it might be steel-blue with feathered whitecaps topping glittering waves. Now it was gray-green, with tall, hard edged waves knocking at the ship's sides from the storm behind them.

Claire and Belle, below in their cabin were seasick, which was part of the reason she was up here.

Francesca watched a bird hover in the wind stream a few feet away. The dusky bird, so small it could nest comfortably in her hand, regarded her in return. She turned to Captain Ramirez who stood nearby. "What is it, Captain?"

He pulled at his mustache and his leathered cheeks stretched into a smile. "She's a storm petrel, Señorita. The men call them 'Stormys.' They like it out here, on the cusp of the storm."

"She's lovely."

"Si. And she's a hardy little chica. She'll spend her whole life out here."

Francesca stared at the fragile spark of life. She tried to imagine a life lived alone in the immensity of the ocean. What would it be like to exist on a thin plane between wind and wave, to live your whole life with no one knowing or caring about your fate? She shuddered.

The bird banked away, falling back behind the ship. "Where's she going?"

The captain shrugged. "She's a mystery."

From the way he said it, and the gleam in his eye, Francesca guessed he wasn't talking about the bird. She looked away.

She knew the captain was curious about her after her sudden appearance with Claire and Belle and the story of her saving them. They had put off his questions with vague answers.

He, however, told them what he knew about that night. Captain Ramirez said that Sir Henry had been the English ambassador to Florence. It was mere happenstance that he overheard a plot against the Grand Duke. He had taken the captain into his confidence, and they had gotten word to the duke. The traitors had been apprehended, but not before they sent the assassins. Captain Ramirez had returned to his ship and made ready to depart as soon as Sir Henry and the girls could join him.

Captain Ramirez hadn't insisted on knowing who Francesca was or where she came from, for which Francesca was grateful. Over the past month she'd come to like the smart and industrious man.

"We'll see Brest soon," the captain pointed in the direction of France. "And we'll reach Le Havre in a few days, if the storm doesn't catch us."

Francesca nodded. France. From there a quick trip across the channel. *England.*

She understood why Papa wanted her to go there. He had spent much of his life in England. There he had married her mother, and he had fostered a boy named Billy. She had never heard why Papa loved Billy so, but it had been clear that he did. His eyes would light up at the mere mention of England, and he was continually posting letters to the boy.

One day, when she was five or six years old, she had found Papa at his massive mahogany desk in his office. He looked down at her and smiled, crinkling his gray eyes. Francesca climbed up on Papa's lap and found him finishing a letter to Billy. She frowned and looked up at him. "Papa, do you love him more than us?"

He set down the quill. "Now why would you ask that?"

"Because you're always writing letters to him."

Papa smiled. "Yes, but when I'm in England I'm always writing letters to you and your brothers."

"But who do you love *the most?*"

Papa chuckled. "I love each of you the most."

Francesca scrunched up her face. "No, Papa. You can't love everyone the most."

"Indeed I can." He put an ink-stained finger to the tip of her nose and her eyebrows released. "You see, it's magic. And one day when you have children of your own, you'll understand precisely how it works."

He rearranged her on his knee and picked up the quill. "Would you like to say hello to Billy?"

Francesca nodded. The maestro dipped the quill in the inkwell and handed it to her. She wrote, *Dear Billy, I hope you like England. Francesca.* She neglected to add that she hoped he liked England so he would stay there and keep away from Papa.

Papa had been pleased. He had blotted the paper gently and sent her on her way.

Sometime later she had gotten a reply in a postscript. It read: *Dear Francesca, I like England very much. Billy.* That was all the contact she had ever had with him.

Francesca and her brothers called him "Billy England." Between them his name was a whispered threat, synonymous with exile. "Stop it, or I'll tell Papa, and he'll send you straight to Billy England." If she ever knew his last name, she had forgotten it long ago.

Papa's dying wish had been that she seek out Billy and that he take care of her.

Well, if the last month had taught her anything, it was that she didn't need someone to take care of her. Besides, Billy would be a man now and might have a family of his own. How would he react to a strange woman appearing on his doorstep claiming some vague kinship? She would go, after she had seen Claire and Belle safely home. She would go to keep her promise to Papa, and out of curiosity, but not to stay. Afterwards, perhaps she would go back to Claire and—

"Sail ho! Abaft the larboard beam," a bass voice bellowed from the crow's nest.

Francesca and the captain looked back at the storm that was following them. Through the webbing of rope Francesca saw pockets of mist and rain roiling the waves, but no ship. The captain excused himself and headed aft.

They'd seen many ships over the last month. Most passed by, smudges on the horizon, or white flecks of sail against the dark sea. A few had been close enough to hail, and one Spanish ship had backed her sails and hove to so the captains could shout news back and forth with bull horns.

Francesca's eyes traveled around deck. There were twenty feet from starboard to larboard rail and eighty feet from bow to stern. In the center, between the foremast and the mainmast, sat the ship's boats, one inside the other on wooden braces. On each side of the deck hunched six cannons on wooden carts, muzzles roped tight against the gun ports. The black gun barrels absorbed the sunlight rather than reflecting it. Their bulk felt both menacing and comforting, a reminder of the threat around them and the means to repel it.

A half-dozen men, on hands and knees, scrubbed the honey-colored deck with sandstone blocks they called "prayer books." Another half-dozen sat beneath the mainsail repairing a sail that had torn in a gust the day before.

Francesca had come to enjoy the easy rhythm of life aboard ship. The men knew their business and did it well. Sailors might be drunken louts ashore, but at sea they were disciplined professionals. They worked hard—harder than she'd ever seen anyone work—but they did so with camaraderie.

Francesca headed aft, curious about the ship the crewman had seen. The deck from the mizzenmast to the stern was called the quarterdeck and was the domain of the captain, his officers, and guests. Crewmen were prohibited, other than the helmsman and the sailors working the mizzenmast.

In front of the wheel and helmsman sat the binnacle, a wooden cabinet housing the ship's compass. Other than that, the quarterdeck held only the captain at the rail, his spyglass trained out to sea.

Francesca saw nothing but waves and mist and circling seabirds.

"She flies the black flag!" yelled a man on the foremast.

Francesca froze. *Pirates!* Then she saw it, emerging from the mist.

Every pair of eyes flashed out to sea and a wave of fear washed the deck.

"Hard to starboard!" shouted the captain. "Señor Covas, raise the jibs and the royals. I want every inch of canvas we've got! And clear the decks. Now!"

"Aye, Sir," said the first mate. He shouted orders and sea men rushed to obey. The helmsman brought the wheel over and the ship tilted, changing course. Men scurried into the rigging to unfurl more sails.

Francesca steadied herself with a few quick breaths as fear and hatred roiled in her stomach like a ball of snakes.

Nana had said that Francesca's mother had died in a pirate attack along the southern coast of the Kingdom of Naples. Francesca, unborn, had been cut from her mother's body. It was their fault she grew up without a mother.

The crew scrambled to set the royal sails with clenched jaws and tense muscles.

"She's seen us, Capitán!" called a man aloft.

"Maldiga!" spat the captain. "Señor Covas, head across the face of the storm, maybe we can lose them in the mists."

He turned to Francesca, but she was already heading below deck.

Francesca paused outside the cabin. She took slow breaths to calm her racing heart. She had known this moment might come. No ocean journey was without the risk, but they were so close to their destination she had thought they were home free. She put on a brave face and opened the door.

The scent of vanilla enveloped Francesca and she inhaled deeply. That the sisters could make the cabin smell good on a ship reeking of tar, creosote, and livestock amazed her.

Claire and Belle, in their shifts, sat together on a cot, sewing. They looked pale and sick, and hadn't kept any food down all day, yet they were working on a dress for Francesca from emerald-green velvet the captain had supplied. It was a thank you for saving their lives, and it helped distract them from their sea sickness.

Claire saw Francesca's face and rose, her work falling from her hands. Her voice wavered. "What is it?"

Francesca threw open the cupboard. "Pirates."

The color drained from Belle's cheeks. "Have they seen us?"

Francesca nodded and pulled Sir Henry's rapier from the cupboard. It gleamed golden in the lamp light.

Claire made the sign of the cross. "You mean to fight them, don't you?"

Francesca forced a smile. "I mean to protect you." She hoped she sounded more confident than she felt.

Her fingers fumbled with the buttons on her riding jacket; she shrugged off the coat and it fell to the floor. Claire's hands trembled as she picked it up and folded it.

Francesca stripped off the ruffled stock from her throat. She breathed deeply but couldn't get enough air. She loosened the laces on her corset, which helped a little. "With luck we'll outrun them, but just in case, put on your dresses and jewelry."

"Our jewelry?" Claire said. She put a hand to her throat as she sank back to the bed. "Shouldn't we hide it?"

They had little, only what they'd been wearing when Francesca found them, but it was of some value.

"If they take the ship, they must believe you are worth a ransom, or…"

Claire's mouth stretched tight, her lips pale lilac. Belle's eyes were wide as she huddled into Claire's arms.

Francesca looked away. Their fear was catching, and she couldn't afford it. She was frightened enough.

Belle whispered, "I wish Father were here."

An ache filled Francesca's chest and she bit her lip hard to dispel it.

She said to the girls. "Once I go, bolt the door and don't let anyone in."

"You're leaving us?" cried Claire.

"No!" wailed Belle. The girls rushed toward Francesca with eyes wide. Belle's arms wrapped around her waist and Claire's around her neck.

"Don't leave me!" cried Belle.

"Stay with us," pleaded Claire.

Francesca gave the girls a hug then tried to disengage their arms. "I can't fight the pirates here; there's no room to move and you might get hurt. I mustn't let them get this far."

"You can't go out there," Claire cried. "You'll be killed!"

Francesca gave up and let them cling to her. She wrapped her arms around them. They felt so fragile. Her desire to keep them safe overwhelmed her, calming her fears and hardening her resolve.

"Claire, you and Belle need to get dressed."

Claire nodded and let go. She helped Francesca unclamp Belle's hands from her waist. Belle whimpered, but Claire put an arm around the girl and ushered her to the cupboard where they pulled out their dresses.

A wooden crash and deafening rumble filled the room. Francesca jumped. The girls fled to the corner, hugging armfuls of silk.

"I think it's the crew running out the cannons," Francesca said, putting a hand to her chest.

Claire and Belle nodded stiffly but didn't move. Francesca crossed to Claire and put a hand on her shoulder. "Lock the door, and don't open it for anyone but me."

Claire nodded numbly. Francesca wrapped the girls in her arms then pulled back. She gave Claire a determined nod and Belle a kiss on the cheek. Her jaw set, she headed for the door.

CHAPTER 8
BATTLE

Francesca stepped onto the main deck, where Capitán Ramirez stared out to sea. Next to him, the First Mate, Mr. Covas awaited orders. Francesca moved within earshot. In a terrible quirk of fate, the rain had stopped, and the clouds were thinning.

"Blast it!" said the captain. "What a time for the storm to let up."

"Should we run for Saint-Malo, Capitán?" Covas said, "It's well-fortified."

"And a pirate haven." The captain shook his head. "They may hail from there." He peered through his spyglass. "He's too quick," he muttered.

"We could dump the cargo, Sir."

"We'd still do little more than seven knots and he's running eight or nine. No, we surrender, or we fight."

Francesca stiffened at the mention of surrender.

"If we surrender, would they be satisfied with our cargo and leave us our skins?" Covas asked.

She wondered if they considered their three women passengers "cargo." Her body tensed.

"Possibly," the captain said. "But we've no way to be sure. No, I'll not take the risk."

Francesca exhaled.

"She'll be manned to the gunwales, Sir," Covas said.

"Aye, but we've got twelve guns to her eight. If we can keep them from boarding…" The captain's face looked grim. "Turn her about. Let's see if he has the stomach for a fight."

"Aye, Capitán."

Francesca's fingers tightened around the hilt of her sword. At least she and the girls wouldn't be handed over like chattel.

Covas turned to the crew, shouting orders. Men scurried up the shrouds into the rigging.

The captain lowered his glass and faced the main deck. When he spotted Francesca, sword in hand, his eyebrows shot up. "What do you think you're doing?"

"The ladies saved my life. I mean to defend them."

The captain gave a sharp laugh. He motioned to two crewmen. "I'll naught have her death on my conscience. Take her below."

Francesca fell into *en garde* position. "I've no quarrel with you, Captain. I'd rather wet my blade on the pirates, but I *will not* go below."

The two crewmen looked to the captain. Nearby crewmen, still at their duties, stared at Francesca.

"Captain, my father was Maestro DiCesare." She saw his eyes flicker in recognition of the name. A murmur ran across deck.

"He taught me well. I've no small part of his knowledge and skill. I can help you fight."

"Ah," the captain said. "That's how you fought off three men with a wooden cane." He looked out toward the pirate ship. "But nothing can prepare you for this."

The ship spun, tacking close to the wind. The sails fell slack, then snapped taut as the ship came round. Men hauled on ropes and salt spray shot in through the larboard gun ports.

The captain shrugged. "In your place, I'd rather die fighting too." As he turned away, he said to a thin, sinewy man, "She can't fight in petticoats. Take her to my cabin. You'll find clothes in my chest that might fit her."

"Aye, Sir."

In the captain's cabin the man threw open a trunk. Among his things they found a pair of buckskin breeches and a leather vest about Francesca's size.

"They're gifts for his son," the crewman said gruffly. "Don't let anyone put holes in them."

Francesca gave a nervous laugh.

"You'll get a better grip on the deck barefoot," he said as he left.

Francesca yanked off her shoes, stockings, skirt, and petticoats. She squeezed into the breeches and could barely fasten them. She felt naked and exposed. Still, better than fighting in heavy skirts. The jerkin she yanked on was of oiled ox hide, with maroon edging. It flared over her hips, held at her waist with brass buttons. She ran her hands down her sides. The hide felt solid enough to turn a blade or two.

A blade or two.

Her legs felt weak and her mouth dry. She looked toward the door. It wasn't too late to go back to her cabin and lock herself in with the girls.

Papa had said, "Courage is not the absence of fear. Any man of reason will be afraid when given cause. Courage is acting honorably in the face of fear." She swallowed hard and gripped her sword until her fingers turned white.

Back on deck, Francesca moved to the rail. They were headed directly toward the pirates now. Waves slapped hard at the ship's side, but the sky was lightening. The approaching vessel was quickly closing the distance, skull and crossbones at the masthead. She thought of her mother and shuddered. Then she imagined Claire and Belle, their dresses torn, and their faces anguished. She shook her head to erase the image. She wouldn't let that happen.

Papa had borne scads of old scars from previous battles. Some of them had ached terribly whenever the weather changed. She'd never considered what those injuries must have been like when they were raw and bleeding. If he, the consummate swordsman had been so injured, what would happen to her? A wave of nausea washed over her.

She was glad Papa had been so merciless in her training. He hadn't wanted her to learn the sword, but living in a school of boys talking of nothing else, she'd been obsessed. Every day she mimicked their actions, watching them practice in the courtyard from her bedroom window. Eventually she convinced Phillip to fence with her. It wasn't until she'd been caught and punished twice that Papa agreed to teach her.

She remembered that the whitewashed walls of the schoolroom had been bare that first evening of serious work.

She'd worn calf length skirts and shivered as the maestro, her father, rested the cold hilt of a practice blade in her palm. She saluted him and took her *en garde* position.

Papa had walked around her correcting the position of her hand and elbow, the distribution of her weight, and the turn of her head, until her position was perfect.

"Remember this," he'd said. "Burn it into your brain and into your muscles and sinews. This position is your best defense and your best offense. It's nothing short of life and death."

She'd closed her eyes, feeling each joint.

"Hold this position until I return."

Then he left.

After ten minutes her arms dipped. After twenty her legs burned. After thirty, fire ran from her fingers, up into her neck. When the maestro returned, sweat poured down her back and her legs and buttocks trembled. The maestro examined her position and nodded.

"Good," he said. "Now lunge."

Pain and relief shot through her as she stretched into a lunge. He examined her position. "Don't lean forward or you'll slow your retreat." He straightened her back and rearranged her sword arm so her thumb was on top and the blade point chest high. He nodded, then left.

When he reappeared, a half hour later, Francesca's body shook. She ground her jaws together, her breath ragged gulps. He released her and let her rest for ten minutes. Then he drilled her on footwork for two hours, back and forth across the floor until she could no longer lift her arms.

Stifling a sob, Francesca had looked up at Papa and seen not even a shadow of pity. She knew he had never driven anyone so hard—not even her brothers. When her legs gave out and she crumpled to the floor she asked, "Why, Papa?"

He shook his head, "Cesca." He sat on a bench and dropped his face in his hands. "You know this is not what I wanted for you, but you've given me no choice, so I must do what I can." He looked at her sharply. "A woman with a sword will always be the target of small-spirited men. She must be the best, better than the best. No half measures will do."

She had grown stronger each day. By the time she was eighteen, her brothers, tired of being beaten, would no longer fence her. She was fast, she was strong, but mostly, she was smart. She loved the mental challenge as much as the physical challenge.

But the game had changed. Now she was the game, and the pirates were the hunters. She focused on the closing pirate ship, painted blood-red up to the black rail. It was smaller than the *Santa Ana* but looked fast and dangerous with raked back masts. It bristled with cannons, fewer than the *Santa Ana* had, but more imposing since they were pointed her way.

The *Santa Ana's* crew had brought chests of weapons up on deck and men handed out muskets, pistols, axes, cutlasses, pikes—whatever might do damage to a human body.

A large man with long sideburns approached Francesca. He bent down and undid a sheath with a knife strapped to his calf. "Little Lady Belle," he said. "She's a bit of sunshine on this dank ship." He handed the sheath and knife to Francesca. "You protect the ladies; let us see to the rest."

"I will."

The man strode to where sailors were using a winch to lower the ship's boats over the side, probably to keep them out of harm's way.

Francesca bent to strap the sheath to her calf, but the strap wouldn't tighten enough. She wrapped it around her thigh instead as she watched the preparations.

There were two companionways leading below. The forward stairway had been battened and secured. The aft, which led to the girls' cabin, also led to the shot locker and the powder magazine. Men carefully carried cloth bags stuffed with gunpowder to the cannons, as if handling infants.

The pirate ship was fifty yards away now. A puff of smoke appeared from one of her forward guns. The report followed, and a shot crossed the *Santa Ana's* bow, a clear warning to yield.

Captain Ramirez ignored the warning, and the two ships passed each other.

Pirates crowded the deck and rigging yelling for blood. Francesca estimated at least a hundred men. The *Santa Ana* had only thirty—odds more than three to one. She rubbed her sweaty palms on her thighs to stop the trembling in her legs.

Mr. Garcia, the captain's steward, appeared at her side. He held a sash and two pistols.

"Complements of the captain," he said, handing them to her. "Primed and loaded." He hurried away.

Francesca looked to the captain on the quarterdeck. He wore a similar sash around his waist, two more pistols stuffed into it. He caught her eye and gave her a brief nod before turning to his men.

Francesca pressed the armful to her chest.

The *Santa Ana's* starboard cannons bellowed. The deafening *thoom* reverberated through her ribcage. At the same time the ship bucked, sending her reeling. Acrid white smoke smothered the deck, burning her nose and throat. She doubled over, coughing, a hand to her ringing ears. When the smoke cleared, she saw that the pirate ship had tacked to follow them.

She quickly tied on the sash and stuffed the pistols into it.

The *Santa Ana*, sails taut, jumped across the waves searching for room to maneuver. But she was sluggish with merchandise, and the nimble pirate ship drew abreast, upwind.

Again the cannons roared. This time Francesca braced herself. Splinters and screams erupted from both ships, and smoke covered the deck. A severed rope tumbled down next to her. The ships were yards apart now.

"Polers to the side!" shouted the captain. "Keep her clear! Don't let them board!"

Crewmen with long pikes ran to the side, into a barrage of musket fire. Bodies slumped to the deck and more crewmen ran to take their places. Francesca leaned heavily against the binnacle. Men dead already and their numbers were so few.

Grappling hooks snaked out from the pirate ship, bit into the rail, and tangled in the rigging. One caught in the ropes nearby. "Cut them free!" shouted Francesca. She sawed at the taut rope with her sword but made little headway. A man with an axe pushed her aside and sliced it away, his axe biting into the wood of the mast behind it. Hatchets and blades slammed into the rail, hacking the *Santa Ana* loose from her tethers.

The pirate ship, pulling ahead, backed her sails, spilling her wind and slowing. Another broadside thundered, most of it missing its target. Then the pirate ship veered directly into the path of the *Santa Ana*.

"Hard to larboard!" shouted the captain, but he was too late.

With a jarring crash the *Santa Ana's* bowsprit hit the rear quarter of the pirate ship. The impact sent Francesca sprawling.

The ship lurched as the bowsprit, two-feet-thick, solid oak, snapped. The bow of the *Santa Ana* staved in the side of the pirate ship. Instantly the ships' riggings were entangled.

"To arms!" yelled the captain, bounding down from the quarterdeck to the main deck. "Follow me!" He charged forward as a wave of pirates swept over the bow and swung into the rigging.

Fire flooding through her body, Francesca bolted for the companionway.

No one would go down it while she lived. She faced a wave of cutthroats coming toward her, breath catching in her throat.

The *Santa Ana* crew formed a wall in front of her and fired into the onslaught. Muskets and pistols thundered. Francesca drew a pistol and fired at a pirate climbing through the rigging. He dropped into the mass of bodies below. The pistol held only one shot. She stuffed it into her sash and readied her sword.

A bald pirate broke past the *Santa Ana* crew and scrambled toward Francesca swinging his blade. She dropped beneath his cutlass, impaling him on her blade. He fell to his knees in front of her. She froze, staring into his gray, dying eyes. Bile rose in her throat, and her limbs refused to move. She might have died there, but Papa's voice urged, *Get up! Protect them!* Then the face of Papa's killer, Tarrentino, arose in place of the pirate's. Fire boiled up until Francesca was aflame. She rose, pressed a foot to the pirate's stomach and with a harsh yell, pushed him off her blade.

The wall of fighting bodies moved aft, forcing the *Santa Ana* crew back. Francesca caught sight of the pirate captain. Tall and well-muscled, he stood atop the bow railing directing the attack. With a raw and visceral electricity, he might have been handsome, except for his twisted expression of rage and hatred. He wore the red coat of a Spanish officer stripped of sleeves and insignia over a white, blood-spattered shirt.

Francesca aimed her second pistol at him, but another pirate broke through the *Santa Ana* crew and rushed her, axe raised. She twisted, aimed, and fired. The pistol spat and the pirate spun and fell.

Then the wall of chaos reached her. The battle became a blur. Bodies heaved and writhed across deck, pressing in. Swords, axes, weapons of all kinds flashed and spun around her. Screams and oaths filled her ears. The smell of gunpowder, sweat, and blood clawed her throat. Her senses vibrated. Her attackers seemed to move in slow motion as she parried, slashed, and stabbed. Bodies fell. Her sword carved a circle of space from the chaos, dropping anyone who entered. There was no time to think or strategize. Her body moved on its own, faster than she thought possible, obeying years of training.

As another pirate slumped to the deck, her eyes caught those of the pirate captain across deck. A mob of fighting bodies separated them, but he stared with such intensity the air between them seemed to vibrate. Then the battle swirled, and she lost sight of him.

Hopelessly outnumbered, the crew of the *Santa Ana* fought savagely.

Three pirates surrounded Francesca. She twisted away leaving her knife in the stomach of the first. She parried the second with her sword. A kick to the groin dropped the third to a knee, gasping.

The second pirate's blade nipped in and sliced open her shoulder. She barely noticed. She spun and buried her sword in his stomach.

As she pulled it free, she heard pistols cock close behind her.

"Hold!" commanded the pirate captain.

CHAPTER 9
PIRATES

The battle had ended, and for all its chaos and destruction it had lasted less than a quarter hour. Blood slicked the deck. Everywhere Francesca looked, bodies littered the ground and rigging. Some moaned or grasped at wounds, but most had the eerie stillness of death.

The storm had calmed to a whisper that merely spread the smell of gunpowder and gore, refusing to carry it away.

The *Santa Ana's* deck was torn ragged by cannon balls, and her rigging and sails hung in tatters. Her bowsprit emerged askew from the pirate ship's gaping side. The ships looked like two terrible birds of prey, killed in a battle to the death.

Of those left standing, none had escaped injury. The ten remaining of the *Santa Ana's* crew had surrendered. Herded together, they stood with hunched shoulders, and bowed heads.

Francesca, her sides still heaving, had her back to the companionway. Wiping sweat from her eyes, she smeared blood across her face. She pushed away wisps of hair clinging to her throat and cheeks. Blood from the gash on her shoulder striped her left sleeve crimson.

Francesca itched to fight, to run, to scream, to do anything but stand still. Body tensed, she held her sword at the ready, but she knew it was in vain. A dozen pirates encircled her.

The pirate captain studied her with an insolent smile, his powerful body lounging against the larboard rail. He was tall and wide-shouldered with lean, muscular arms, as if he'd worked in a smithy. He wiped blood from his blade as he looked her over.

The captain's expression of seething hatred had evaporated. Against her will, Francesca noticed how handsome he was, though not in the way Phillip was. Phillip had perfect, refined features she longed to see carved from marble or cast in bronze. This man was striking the way a wild stallion was. An animal vitality coursed under his skin. *Dangerous and unpredictable.*

He looked young for a captain, under thirty, she guessed. There was something cat-like in the strong lines of his cheekbones and jaw and in the way he moved. He examined her so intently that she felt naked, and her cheeks flamed. Her eyes narrowed and her fingers tightened around the hilt of her sword.

"Mr. Baldric!" bellowed the captain, making Francesca jump.

A short, grim man appeared at the captain's elbow. A ragged white scar ran from temple to chin, puckering his right eye.

"Search those men and see them secured," the captain commanded, nodding toward the *Santa Ana* crew.

So, he's English, thought Francesca.

"Aye, Sir." Mr. Baldric motioned to the pirates watching the *Santa Ana* crew, and they prodded them down the forward companionway.

A few pirates wandered among the fallen, checking for life and carrying those still alive below deck. They rifled the pockets of the *Santa Ana* dead and tossed the bodies overboard.

The captain turned his attention back to Francesca. "I saw you kill eight of my men."

Francesca twisted one side of her mouth remembering what Papa had always said about pirates. *They are craven animals not fit to be called men.* She shook her head. "I killed no men."

The captain scowled. "And those poor bastards lying at your feet?"

"Pirates."

An angry murmur surrounded Francesca. She raised her chin and stared hard at the captain. "I'd like to try for one more."

The pirates bristled, but the captain laughed and shook his head. He moved toward her, stepping over a dead pirate, and stopped in front of her. He looked around at his men. "She's got a tongue on 'er." Then he motioned toward her bloody sword, which she held between them. "But I'll pull that tooth, lest anyone else be bitten."

Francesca hesitated, her eyes on the base of the captain's tan throat. One quick thrust and he'd be dead. Of course, she would die a second later.

It would be an honorable death, a satisfying one, but it would leave Claire and Belle alone with the pirates.

She loosened her fingers on the hilt of Sir Henry's blade and the point dropped toward the deck. She shoved the hilt flat against the captain's chest, pushing him away.

The captain's face grew hard as he took the blade. "Watch yourself, girl." His eyes ranged from Francesca to the stairway behind her and back again. He motioned to her with the tip of her sword, and she reluctantly stepped aside over a fallen body.

The captain nodded to two pirates. "See what's down there."

Sneering at Francesca, they descended.

Francesca squeezed her eyes shut, willing this to be a dream. How could she have failed again? First Papa, now Claire and Belle. The fire drained from her veins.

She listened to the men searching the cabins below. There was pounding and yelling and then splintering wood. A shriek echoed and she stiffened. A rough voice drifted out, "Bloody hell, girl!"

Seconds later Claire and Belle were shoved roughly up the companionway. In their pastel silk dresses, they looked ludicrously out of place, like butterflies in a butcher shop. Belle peered from behind Claire, whose hands trembled as she smoothed her skirts and straightened her shoulders with dignity.

Francesca caught Claire's eyes. Francesca expected recrimination, but she saw Claire's shoulders ease and a slight smile cross her face.

Baldric leered at the girls as he approached, eyeing their jewelry. "Cap'n, the crew is secured, and Pitt says we're ready to part the ships."

"Well done," the captain said. "First, bring over the stores and have a look at the bow. Once we're clear, set the Spaniards on the other ship."

"She'll likely sink, Sir."

"Aye."

Francesca seethed at the casual way he condemned the sailors to death. "That's inhuman."

He snarled. "It's a chance. That's more than Spaniards deserve."

The captain turned to a dark tower of a man with a pock-marked face. The man stared at Claire and Belle with combined lust and disdain. "Mr.

Agar, I want swivel guns fitted fore and aft once the bowsprit is repaired. See to transferring the guns."

Mr. Agar's deep voice rumbled. "Aye, Sir."

He and Baldric left, taking most of the men.

The captain approached the girls. "So, the tigress was protecting cubs. Who are you?"

Claire wore a pale blue brocade dress edged in seed pearls at the neckline. Her golden hair was piled high, and a crucifix glittered at her throat. She looked far beyond her sixteen years. She lifted her head. "Courtesy would require your name first, Sir."

The captain laughed and shook his head. "We've taken a brace of tongues." He made an extravagant show of bowing and kissing Claire's hand. "My apologies, m' lady, your humble servant, Captain Will Massey." The remaining pirates snickered, and Claire jerked her hand back.

Claire straightened to her full height. "I'm Claire Henry, daughter of Lord and Lady Henry. This is my sister, Belle." A hint of a smirk crossed her face as she added, "And I believe you've met Miss Francesca DiCesare."

A murmur ran though the pirates. The captain's eyes flicked to Francesca and held. He slowly brought his attention back to Claire. "And what are two English ladies doing on a Spanish ship?"

"Trying to go home, Captain," Claire said. "Though I see no reason I should explain myself to you."

The self-assurance in her voice made Francesca proud. The captain moved closer. He raised a blood-spattered hand and fingered the necklace at Claire's throat. Claire shuddered. A frown crossed the captain's face, and he dropped his hand.

Claire cleared her throat as she steadied herself. "I must ask, what are your intentions?"

The captain chuckled. "I see no reason I should explain myself to you."

He headed toward the bow, pausing next to an enormous man. "Lock them in their cabin and guard the door."

Francesca paced the cabin in her blood-stained clothes. Five steps to the ornate Jacobean cupboard. Five steps back to the sideboard that held the porcelain pitcher and a washbasin full of bloody water. Up and back, up and back. She'd been pacing for hours, ever since Claire and Belle had bandaged her shoulder. Her mind and her blood kept racing, and she couldn't hold still.

In the back of her mind, the image of blank-eyed bodies lying at her feet gnawed at her. Remorse hovered at the edge of awareness, but she refused to acknowledge it. It would sap the strength she might need at any moment. She held onto the anger boiling through her, and to Papa's words: "Such blackguards are without shame and without honor."

Francesca paused to test the door for the hundredth time. The frame had broken when the pirates kicked in the door. The lock was useless, but the door wouldn't budge. She resumed pacing.

Not long after they had been locked in, the anchor rattled out and splashed when it hit the water. Later the cabin trembled and bucked, and the ship's timbers groaned. Francesca guessed the pirates were parting the two ships. The *thunk* of hammers against wood and *clang* of metal against metal amid shouted orders followed, hour after hour. And the girls waited, tired, hungry, and seemingly forgotten.

A dozen plans of escape had occurred to Francesca, none with the slightest chance of success. They were trapped. Despite all that had happened, she'd never felt so completely helpless.

Francesca knew her pacing was driving Claire mad, but she couldn't help it. Claire sat against the headboard with Belle lying half asleep in her arms, exhausted by fear. Claire had suggested that Francesca rest, arguing she might need her strength later, but it did no good. She was a caged animal.

Francesca's eyes ran round the cabin again. "If only I had a weapon."

With a yawn, Belle raised her right palm showing Francesca a jagged scar across it. Francesca had noticed the scar before but she'd never asked about it. "I did this when I broke a porcelain pitcher."

Francesca's eyes shot to the pitcher and washbasin.

"Actually," Claire said, "when you tried to hide the evidence."

Belle settled back into Claire's arms. "Why must you always tattle?"

Francesca crossed to the pitcher and basin. There were a few inches of water left in the pitcher. She took a drink then had Claire and Belle drink the rest. She poured the bloody water from the basin into the pitcher, wrapped the basin in a sheet, and set it on the floor upside down. She jumped and came down with her heel on the basin. With a *crunch* it gave way.

Francesca parted the fabric. The basin had broken into wedge-shaped pieces. She chose the longest and held it up. The edges were razor sharp. She carried her skirt with the rest of the shards to the corner and resumed pacing. She felt better at least nominally armed.

Francesca's pacing went on for another hour. It almost came as a relief when they heard voices and something heavy being moved away from the door.

Belle clutched at Claire.

Francesca pressed against the wall next to the door. She tensed as the door opened.

A pirate moved in past Francesca, eyeing the girls on the bed. He was Francesca's height and wore a buckskin vest. Gray hair, tinged with yellow, straggled out from beneath a black wool cap.

Francesca surged forward. She wrapped her left arm around his chest putting the shard to his throat with her right hand. She pulled him, stumbling backwards, until her back came up against the wall. The smell of spicy pipe tobacco filled her lungs. The man carried a set of manacles.

A second pirate entered. His rodent eyes, pinched face, and sinewy body reminded Francesca of a ferret. He held a pair of pistols.

"Put down the pistols, or I cut him," Francesca hissed.

"Go a'ead," he said in nasal voice, calling her bluff. "'E's nigh useless anyhow."

"Watch yer gob," said the pirate in her grip.

"Or what?" the weaselly one retorted. He cocked his pistols and pointed one at Francesca. When she didn't move, he raised the other pistol and pointed it at Claire and Belle. He laughed as Francesca sagged and dropped her makeshift knife.

"Clap on the irons an' be done," he said.

The older man snapped the manacles around Francesca's wrists, *snick*, *snick*. Francesca's eyes met Claire's. She struggled to keep her terror from showing, but judging by Claire's expression, she failed.

Claire and Belle rose. Panic crept into Claire's voice. "What are you going to do?"

The men dragged Francesca toward the door.

"Where are you taking her?" cried Belle.

Francesca fought, but they pulled her from the cabin with Claire and Belle grasping after her, until the pirates shut and blocked the door.

They shoved Francesca into the *Santa Ana's* great cabin, the captain's domain. Others were allowed only by invitation or permission. It served as the ship's conference room, navigation room, a reception room for important guests, and the captain's private dining room.

It had survived the battle unscathed. The walls were white and spotless. Burgundy oriental rugs covered the honey-oak floor. A dark-stained oak table with turned legs and six chairs took up the center of the room.

Francesca knew the cabin well. She, Claire, and Belle had dined there often with Captain Ramirez and his officers. She'd often admired the beautiful arc of aft windows and the delicate scrollwork carved into the low overhead beams.

Captain Massey, washed, shaven, and wearing a gray silk vest over a crisp muslin shirt, lounged with his feet up on the table, sipping from a golden goblet. His dark, wavy hair was pulled neatly back at the nape of his neck. A blushing pink and lavender sunset lit the windows, softening the lines of his face. His eyes twinkled with amusement.

Francesca gripped her chains as she took in his attire. His good looks and finery did not fool her. No amount of silk and ruffles could disguise what he was. But there were more pressing matters. "If you touch them, I swear—"

The captain raised his hand. "The ladies are in no danger."

"They have means. Surely you must see they have more value to you un…"

The captain set down the goblet and rose. He moved to the stern windows, staring into the sunset. "Unspoiled?"

Francesca frowned.

The captain faced her. "And you? There must be a doting father anxious to ransom back his loving daughter." There was an edge of ridicule in his voice.

"My father is dead." Francesca turned away so he wouldn't see her anguish. She wouldn't give him the satisfaction. She heard him sit heavily on the window seat. When she looked back, sunset silhouetted his head.

"No brothers?" he asked. His voice sounded strained.

She strode angrily toward him around the table, her chains held taut in her hands. "I'm sorry to disappoint you. You'll squeeze more gold from a fish. All I have are my clothes and the weapons you've already taken."

"How can that be?" The captain leaned against the window frame and looked up at her with surprise on his face. "A woman with your … abilities."

Francesca flared. "I am not a dancing bear, prancing for lira. And I assume you didn't bring me here to tell my tale of woe."

The captain's face darkened. "No. I brought you here to tell you who I am. I—"

"I know who you are," she said. "You're a murderer, a thief, a pirate." She spat the words like curses.

"Francesca, I—"

"You are the worst sort of scum. You prey on the weak and the helpless, you have no honor, you're not fit to be called a man."

The captain leaned forward, his face reddened, his hands clenched, his jaw muscles worked, but he said nothing.

She smiled smugly as he fought for control.

"Perhaps," he hissed through gritted teeth, leaning back against the window frame.

Francesca silently celebrated her victory.

The captain's face smoothed to a haughty sneer. "But I saw your face during the battle. I know that expression."

Francesca frowned in confusion.

"I know a pirate when I see one," the captain said.

She lunged at the captain using her chains to pin him to the window frame by the throat.

The captain gave a coarse laugh. He pulled at the chain with one hand. "You prove my point," he rasped.

Francesca's face was inches from the captain's.

When he spoke, his breath stirred her hair. "I can offer you freedom, adventure, wealth; the finest of everything from every realm on earth."

"I'd rather be fed piecemeal to the sharks."

Anger darkened his eyes and a pistol cocked. "I can offer that too."

She looked down to see the captain's pistol pointed at her side.

"I should have killed you when I had the chance," she said.

The captain quirked his mouth to one side. "But you didn't. Why, I wonder?"

Francesca glared at him but backed off.

The captain rubbed his throat and rose from his seat. The sunset behind him was fading. Gloom enveloped the room. He released the hammer on his pistol and shoved it into a sash under his vest. He lit a lantern that hung from a bracket next to the windows, and a warm glow spread around them. Recovering his goblet, he perched on the edge of the table looking at her, considering.

61

She wanted to tear that self-satisfied look from his face. She twisted her chains until they cut into her wrists.

The captain took a drink. "If treasure won't sway you, perhaps duty will. I propose a wager, a duel: rapier and dagger, you and me."

At the word "duel" her pulse raced. She clenched her hands imagining them covered in blood; Papa's blood, Catalina's blood, seeping between her fingers while she could do nothing to stop it. She wobbled and had to lean against the table.

She squeezed her eyes shut, forcing the image out of her mind. She couldn't let *him* see her like this.

She opened her eyes and stepped toward the captain cautiously. "What is the wager?"

"The stakes are these. If you win, you and the ladies will be delivered unharmed to the nearest English port, minus a few baubles to satisfy my men." He leaned forward, watching her face intently. "If I win, the ladies are delivered unharmed, but you swear loyalty to me and my crew."

She shook her head. "So, if I agree, either way, Claire and Belle go free?"

He shrugged. "I want them off my ship. They're distracting my men. The *English* port is to sweeten the deal."

"And you want me to…"

He grinned. "Become a pirate."

"Why?"

"Do pirates need a reason?" When she didn't respond he shrugged. "You have some useful skills. I want you on my crew. Oh, I could force you. We press men all the time, but I don't fancy giving you another go at my throat."

He tilted his head to one side, sizing her up. "But you strike me as someone who'll stick to a bargain once you've clapped hands to it."

Her eyes narrowed. "And if I kill you?"

"If you kill me, how can I be certain my men will honor our agreement?"

"What assurance do I have *you* will honor it?"

Captain Massey shrugged. "None." He spread his hands wide. "What choice do you have?"

Francesca's teeth clenched. "And if I don't agree?"

"I withdraw my protection and I doubt any of you will survive the night, or care to."

A spike of ice ran down Francesca's spine. She had no option, but at least she had hope. She held out her manacled hands to shake. "Very well."

CHAPTER 10
DUEL AT DAWN

After the pirates shoved Francesca back into her cabin, she told Claire and Belle about the duel.

Claire went pale. "I forbid it!"

Francesca looked at her in confusion. "You do?"

"We almost lost you once."

"Don't you see?" Francesca said. "This is good news. It's a chance for us to get off this ship alive."

"But what if you lose?" Belle shuddered.

"I was trained by the best swordsman in Europe. I won't lose."

Claire paced. "There must be a way that doesn't involve risking your life again."

Francesca stopped Claire and took her hand. "This is good. It's more than I could have hoped for. Trust me."

"Maybe he's toying with you," said Belle. "Maybe he plans to kill you."

"If he wanted me dead, I'd be dead."

Francesca noticed a tray of food on the sideboard: bread, cheese, and a bowl of stew. Her stomach growled.

"We saved most of it for you," said Belle.

"Eat," Claire said. "Then you'll need rest."

Francesca tore off a hunk of bread, nodding. "The duel is at dawn."

Despite her exhaustion, Francesca couldn't sleep. The cut on her shoulder ached. Every time she nearly nodded off, cannon fire echoed in her ears, and blood was everywhere. Then she was staring into the eyes of the man who had run onto her blade. She woke with a jerk and tossed and turned.

She should have been relieved. After all, win or lose, the girls would be safe—*if he keeps his word.* That was part of the problem. She was relying on a pirate to keep his word.

But why propose the wager if he doesn't mean to honor it? We're already under his power. He can do as he pleases.

Was this some sort of perverse game, like a cat with a mouse? That seemed more likely. Well, when morning came, she'd be the cat. After all, she was the best. Papa had seen to that.

Yet, she hadn't actually observed the captain fight during the battle. She had no way to judge his skill. Could he be better than her? Could he beat her? And if he did …

She tried not to think about it. She would win tomorrow. She had to.

Eventually, Belle climbed into bed and snuggled into her. Francesca wrapped her arms around the girl, burying her face in Belle's hair, and fell asleep.

She slept fitfully and woke early. Lying on her back, staring at the beams overhead, she rotated her shoulder; it was sore and stiff from the gash. She listened to Belle's even breathing. There was so much riding on this fight. What if she failed again? She couldn't bear it.

Papa's duel rushed back, as if she were living it over again. If only she had saved him. If only she had seen Tarrentino sooner or pushed him out of the way instead of grabbing the sword. If only. *How do I live with "if only?"*

There was a knock on the door and a low voice. "It's time." Claire and Belle stirred. Francesca shivered, wiped her eyes on her blanket, and swung her feet out of bed.

———┝———

It was a cold, hushed daybreak, not unlike the morning of Papa's duel. The ship floated in mist, dreamlike. The pirate crew, seventy men and boys, crowded the deck or hung from the rigging.

Claire and Belle, in their cloaks, huddled with Francesca for warmth.

The chill air magnified the smell of tar and unwashed men. The rope from the winch used to move the cannons dangled above deck with a sturdy metal pulley and hook attached to the end. Crates and barrels, stores brought over from the destroyed pirate ship littered the space.

The ship's doctor, a grizzled Scot, shambled over. His wild white hair stood out in every direction, but it was the twinkle in his eye behind thick glasses that caught her attention. He gave Francesca a wink and leaned close. "I've twenty shillens ridin' on ye, lass," he whispered.

Francesca blinked in surprise. He thought she'd win?

The doctor cleared his throat and held out two swords and two daggers. He assumed an official voice. "Choose yer weapons."

As the challenged party, the choice of weapons was hers. Francesca examined them. They looked expensive. She checked their lengths—an inch of reach could mean the difference between life and death. They matched, so she chose the sword bearing the fox insignia of Solingen, Germany—known for their craftsmanship. She opted for the wider dagger hoping that meant greater strength. She felt their weight and balance. Satisfied, she nodded, and the doctor handed the other weapons to the captain.

Captain Massey raised his voice as he took off a buckskin jacket. "Victory will be declared when one of us is unconscious, dead, or concedes. No weapons are to be thrown. Beyond that, all's fair."

The doctor shooed crewmen out of the way. "Give way, men. Clear the deck."

Francesca disengaged Belle's fingers from her arm. She wore the leather vest and trousers from the battle. The captain had supplied a clean linen shirt.

Francesca and the captain moved into the open and saluted each other. He gave her a penetrating stare, his storm-blue eyes glowing like sunlight through a wave. His expression was calculating and smug, as if he'd added up her chances of winning and found them lacking.

Her pulse raced and fire rushed through her. Suddenly the duel couldn't start soon enough. She couldn't wait to wipe that expression from his face.

They took their *en garde* positions.

The doctor shouted, "Lay to!"

The captain and Francesca circled and feinted, testing each other.

"Are you certain you want to do this, Captain?" she taunted. "These men will never follow you if you lose to a woman."

He made a quick attack. "I don't intend to lose."

Francesca slipped aside. "No one ever does."

Their different styles were immediately apparent. Francesca fenced in the Italian style. She was the essence of finesse, not an ounce of energy wasted. She glided to and fro, her rapier tip always pointed at the captain's heart, waiting to strike. Captain Massey fenced in the English style: fast, hard, and aggressive, swinging his blade more often, counting on his strength to wear her down.

The captain attacked twice in quick succession.

The first, Francesca ducked. The second, she parried, striking in to nip his forearm. A line of blood appeared.

A man shouted from the rigging. "Come on, Cap'n, she's just a slip of a girl!"

"Aye," he shouted back. "But for a girl she's got a mighty long prick!"

The pirates laughed and bellowed encouragement.

Francesca attacked, backing him across deck.

Against the rail, he crossed his weapons, catching her blade. A kick to her stomach sent her reeling.

Francesca dropped to one knee, winded.

The captain rushed her, sword raised. She rolled into his legs, sending him tripping over her.

In a flash they were back on their feet, blades ready. They fought across deck through cannons and supplies.

Captain Massey leapt atop a crate. He vaulted over her, catching her collarbone with his blade. Claire and Belle gasped. The crew tensed and moved closer, vultures waiting for the kill.

The sting and trickle of blood heightened Francesca's concentration. Every detail grew clear. With intensified senses came a feeling of fate, as though she had been preparing for this moment all her life.

The captain tipped over a barrel, kicking it toward her, and followed close behind.

She spun aside, sword outstretched. Her blade caught his back as he passed, slicing open his shirt, drawing blood. Wide, white scars laced his back.

He spun and attacked. She parried, riposted, and retreated.

———————⟊——

As the sun rose, boiling away the mist and drawing steam from the ship's damp timbers, the duel continued.

Francesca tried every move Papa had taught her. Nothing could get past the captain's guard. Blood-stained, sweat-drenched, she could see the captain was in no better condition. They were evenly matched and equally determined.

Wiping sweat from her eyes, Francesca gasped for breath. Her feeling of destiny had long since faded. Only numb resolve remained. She would fight until she could no longer stand. She had no choice, and neither did the captain; if he lost to a woman, he would likely lose his command.

Francesca, backing, bumped her head on the block and tackle that dangled over the deck. The captain's eyes narrowed.

"Concede!" he growled between gasps for air.

"I'll concede that you're better than I thought," she said. "But I still mean to beat you."

The captain attacked, corkscrewing his blade around Francesca's, trying to twist her sword from her fingers.

Francesca held on, countering, matching his moves, but her mind reeled. The *envelopement* was the maestro's signature move, how could he know it? Anger flashed, white hot.

She yelled and attacked fiercely, her sword slicing across the bicep of his blade arm. He cried out and at the same time, swung the block and tackle. The solid metal hook slammed into Francesca's forehead above her right eye. Everything went black

CHAPTER 11
POOLE

She was falling. Francesca couldn't remember how or why, but she had been tumbling down for some time. Although she couldn't see it, she knew the ground was coming to meet her. Hitting it would hurt, almost as much as her head, which was splitting in two. She tensed for impact and opened her eyes.

"Thank God," Claire said as Francesca came to, groaning.

The doctor was removing a bloody bandage from her forehead.

"Ohhh," she moaned, putting her hands to her head. Her brains throbbed against the inside of her skull as if to burst.

The doctor moved her hands away. "Let et be, lass."

She lay in her cot and fingered her right eye. Her eyelid was huge, nearly swollen shut. The doctor covered her good eye with one hand and held his other hand in front of her, thumb and pinkie down. "Hou many fingers am I holdin' up?"

Francesca squinted, then winced. "Three."

"Splendid," the doctor said.

"How long have I been asleep?"

"The duel was yesterday," said Claire sitting beside her and taking her hand.

"Yesterday!" Francesca sat up, instantly regretting it. She fell back, nausea raging through her stomach, her head both exploding and spinning.

"Lie stell!" The doctor glared over his spectacles.

She started to nod and thought better of it. "Where are we?"

"We're nearing Poole Bay," said Belle.

"Poole?"

The ladies nodded. "Home," said Belle.

Claire smiled. "England, anyway. West of Southampton."

"The captain says he'll set us ashore in a few days," said Belle. "After he's sold off his loot and given the men time ashore."

"I suppose he doesn't want us causing trouble for him with the locals," Claire added.

The doctor chuckled. "I doubt ye could. Poole es one o' our regular ports-o'-call."

"Have you been with them long?" Francesca asked the doctor.

"About two years nou, I'd say."

"Can't you get away from them?" asked Belle.

The doctor snorted as he gently examined Francesca's swollen eye. "I'd be daft tae leave."

"How could an educated man stand living among these cutthroats?" Francesca took note of his gray silk vest and white ruffled stock. Despite his wild hair, he looked refined.

The doctor shook his head. "Twenty yairs I've been asea, 'board merchants and navy ships as well as pirates." He peered over the top of his glasses. "I'll take the pirates, thank ye."

"In heaven's name, why?" Claire said.

The doctor faced her. "Fourteen yairs I worked for the Navy and the East India Company stitchin' their wounded and treatin' their sick, and what did I have tae show for et? A bag o' instruments, and the clothes on my back. Nou I'm rich. I've enough saved tae buy a London estate or a plantation en Jamaica when I've a mind to, and the work es easier. Tae be sure, there are more battles, and more men tae stitch after, but the men are better fed and better treated. I have all I need tae do my job. Nae like the merchant ships where every draught I gave, every foot o' cat gut I used was counted and begrudged." The doctor shrugged. "Nae, if et's all the same. I'll stay."

He finished bandaging her head and stood. "Nou, lass, ye've a nasty lump on yer noggin, but there's no swelling o' the brain so far as I can tell. You're lucky tae have such a theck skull." He chuckled, then turned to Claire. "Keep her stell. Sit on her ef need be. I'll be back at next watch."

Claire promised to send word if problems arose. The doctor left, giving them a glimpse of the guard outside their door, no doubt keeping the pirates out, rather than them in.

Claire sighed and her shoulders relaxed. "I'm so glad you're awake. We were afraid…"

Francesca squeezed her hand. "I'm sorry that I failed you."

"No," Claire said. "We're going home. You saved us."

"The captain's keeping his word?" Francesca asked. A pit opened in her stomach. A part of her had known he would, because by doing so he forced her to do the same. Her bruised face grew grim. "Then I'm bound to keep my bargain."

Claire looked at her sharply. "You'll swear loyalty to these cutthroats?"

Francesca nodded, then groaned.

"Don't be foolish!" Claire had an edge to her voice Francesca hadn't heard before. "You accepted those conditions under duress, upon pain of death, or worse. No one would hold you to it."

"I would," Francesca said, "as would Papa."

Claire shook her head, dumbfounded. "Why?"

"If a pirate can keep his word, how can I do less? Besides, to keep one's word is foremost among the rules of honor."

"But he cheated!" wailed Belle.

"You mean the block and tackle?" Francesca held a hand to her forehead. Belle nodded. "It was a dirty trick."

"The rule was, no weapons were to be thrown. A block and tackle is not a weapon, and he didn't throw it. There are no rules against using your surroundings to your advantage." *And I would have done the same if I'd thought of it,* Francesca added to herself. He was clever; she had to give him that.

"Whether he cheated or not, you're a woman," Claire argued. "The rules of honor don't apply to you."

"They apply to all who bear arms."

"What rules?" asked Belle.

Claire scowled at her. "How can you ask? You're the one who is always reading those books of chivalry."

"To defend God and country," Francesca said. "To keep one's word. To defend the weak and innocent. To never abandon a friend, or a noble cause. To avoid lying and cheating your fellow man. To exhibit courage in word and deed. To live for freedom, justice, and all that is good. To die with honor. That's The Code.

Belle gaped at Francesca. She turned to Claire. "Is she serious? I thought that was only in books."

Francesca scowled and put a hand to her aching head. "My father lived and died by those laws. I've sworn to do the same. Papa said honor is what sets man apart from the beasts. It makes us fit to sit at the knees of God in the hereafter."

She paused and took Belle's hand. "But it's more than that. I've broken those rules before. I've made dishonorable choices and it cost my best friend her life. Catalina was kind and good. She was like my sister, and I caused her death. I can't do that again."

"It's not the same," said Claire.

Francesca nodded. "It's not, no. But we never know what the results of our choices will be. We only know, if we make the honorable choice, then we are not to blame when bad things happen. And…" she trailed off. *And maybe I won't spend my whole life mired in guilt.*

Belle sat down next to her. "I don't care about the rules. Stay with us, please."

Francesca brushed back Belle's hair. "I'd like nothing better. But you'll be home soon with your family. All I have left of my family is my honor."

"Exactly how do you intend to maintain it among these brigands?" demanded Claire.

"I don't know." She closed her eyes. "I'll find a way."

"How can you choose them over us?" wailed Belle.

"Choose?" Francesca thought about the night she had almost run off with Phillip. Not going was the hardest "choice" she had ever made. But then, there never really was a choice.

"Papa used to say choice is an illusion, for women doubly so. Most of our decisions are made for us by fate or necessity. Our only choice is whether to respond honorably or not." She fingered her bandage. "I choose honorably."

On the fourth morning after the duel, the three women appeared on deck, Claire and Belle in their dresses and cloaks. Francesca, her head swathed in bandages and her eye plum-purple, wore the clothes from the duel, cleaned and mended. Sir Henry's rapier, returned by the captain, hung at her hip, though she doubted she had the strength to use it.

Francesca stood at the rail staring shoreward both relieved that Claire and Belle were heading home, and wishing they weren't leaving, though she felt guilty for the latter. They'd given her strength when she needed it badly and she would need it even more now. She shivered, frightened at being alone with the pirates.

Claire and Belle joined her, gazing toward the town of Poole. Morning haze hid the buildings, but they heard the voices of the townspeople, the neighing of horses, and rattling of carriages and carts. Below them, one of the ship's longboats knocked against the side.

The captain approached and Francesca turned toward him. Something flashed in his eyes as he looked at her swollen face. Pity? Remorse? The look fled, replaced by calm certainty.

He wore a black coat, tan waistcoat and breeches, his hair pulled back in a ribbon.

"Is this how you convince the townsfolk to deal with you?" Francesca said. "By making them believe you're a gentleman?"

A few pirates chuckled.

The captain smiled. "You underestimate the power of greed. Our partners have no illusions as to who we are. As long as we don't harass British ships, they are happy to do business."

The captain's eyes swept over the girls and came to rest on Claire's throat where a golden crucifix hung. He nodded at the cross and held out a hand.

Claire covered the necklace with her hand. "It was a gift from my father at my first communion!"

The captain twitched his fingers impatiently. Claire looked around at the pirates who stared hungrily. She glared as she unfastened the necklace and laid it on his palm.

The captain smiled. "I wish you a pleasant journey."

Francesca's temper flared, making her head pound. "And how do you expect them to get home when you've taken all their valuables?"

"On their backs," someone shouted. The rest laughed.

"I'm sure they'll manage," the captain said. He motioned to some of the men. "Get them ashore."

They roughly handed Claire down to the boat. One of the pirates gave Belle's rump a squeeze as he handed her down and she squealed in fright. The crew laughed, but Francesca's rapier hissed as she pulled it from her scabbard.

"Settle down! All of you," snarled the captain. They quieted and Francesca sheathed her sword.

She scowled at the crewmen who tried to help her down the side and they retreated. She started to descend, but Captain Massey grabbed her arm.

He held a piece of paper toward her. She took it and read. It was the ship's articles, her vow to remain faithful to ship and crew. With a glance at the longboat, Francesca shoved the paper out of sight of the girls. Her decision was difficult for Claire and Belle to understand. She had no wish to remind them of it. "Captain, I mean to see them safely on their way. I will return and sign whatever you like. You have my word."

The captain hesitated a moment, then released her arm. "The tide turns at noon—be back by then." She gave a brief nod as she descended to the boat. The oarsmen pushed off, rowing for shore.

Francesca watched Mr. Baldric appear at the captain's side as he leaned on the rail. Baldric said indifferently, "She'll show us her heels, Cap'n."

"No, Baldric," the captain said. "She'll be back."

The rest was lost to the wind and the squeak of the oars, but a smile crossed the captain's face.

As the boat moved away, Claire touched Francesca's arm and pointed toward the ship's stern. Two men, perched on wooden swings had almost finished painting out the name of the *Santa Ana*. Gold letters on a red background read: DESTINY.

When the boat reached the bustling docks, Francesca, Claire, and Belle were set ashore.

"What do we do now?" said Belle.

"How far is it to your home?" asked Francesca.

"Wildcombe is a full day north by carriage," Claire said. "I doubt anyone will take us for free."

Francesca slid her sword from its scabbard. "Not for free."

"Would you force them at sword point?" said Belle.

Francesca laughed, pain rattling through her skull. "No, silly. Your father's sword will protect you one last time. It will pay for your way home."

Concern spread across Claire's face. "We can't leave you with cutthroats unarmed."

"I'm sure there are more than enough swords aboard the *Destiny*," Francesca said. "I wouldn't be of much use to them without one." She said it cheerfully, but she gave the sword a longing look. She hated to lose such a beautifully crafted blade.

"Do you think it's worth enough?" asked Belle.

"It does have some pretty filigree on the handle," Claire said.

"It's called a hilt." Francesca pointed to a small mark on the blade. "That tells me it's a Spanish blade. Spanish blades are always highly prized." She tilted the sword in the sun. "See these light and dark striations? Pure Toledo steel, folded at least fourteen times."

Belle's eyes widened. "I thought it was tarnished."

Francesca showed them the grip. "The tang is solid, running all the way through the hilt." She spun the sword in the air, catching it easily. "The balance is perfect. This sword should more than pay for your way home."

"I had no idea," Claire said.

"You two stay here. I'll see what I can arrange."

A fisherman directed Francesca to the town swordsmith and carriage house. As she headed down the main street a few people looked suspiciously at her mode of dress, but there were far stranger folk about. Twice Francesca saw natives from America in buckskins and feathers. She even saw a man in scarlet robes with the slanted eyes of the Orient.

After selling the sword and visiting the coach house to arrange a carriage, Francesca returned to the docks. She found the girls on a bench in the shade of a shop awning.

"Did it work?" asked Belle nervously.

"The carriage leaves in half an hour."

The girls slid over and made room for Francesca between them. She sat and took out the remaining bills.

"That's what's left?" said Belle in astonishment.

"It was a beautiful rapier."

"Keep the money," Claire said. "You've earned it as our guardian."

Francesca shook her head, cringing at the pain. "You'll need food. And there may be delays on your journey. You should take it."

Claire took half the bills. "Keep the rest. This will be plenty for us." She took Francesca's arm. "I wish there was something more we could do for you."

"I do have a favor to ask," Francesca said.

"Anything," said Belle.

Francesca stared out into the busy street. The morning haze had burned off leaving bright sun. Hurrying merchants, ladies with parasols, sailors, and fishermen wandered past, ducking between horse-drawn carriages and carts.

"In case I…" she cleared her throat. The image of her body swaying in a noose leapt to mind. "I want you to get word to my brothers, and to Phillip." The words caught in her throat. She closed her eyes. "Antonio and Sebastian DiCesare of Cascina, Tuscany, and Lord Phillip Worthington—"

"Phillip Worthington?" said Claire and Belle in unison.

Francesca opened her eyes and saw their astonished expressions. "Do you know him?"

"We know *of* him," Claire said.

"His cousin, Abigail, is a friend," said Belle. She sighed. "Such a sad story."

Francesca's chest tightened. She didn't think she could stand it if something terrible had happened to Phillip. "What sad story?"

"His marriage," Claire said softly.

"Everyone heard about it," said Belle.

"Heard about what?" Francesca's voice quavered.

"His father forced him to marry the countess," said Belle. "She was exceedingly wealthy, but so sickly she had to be carried up the aisle at her own wedding in a litter. She died three months later."

Claire put a hand on Francesca's arm as Belle continued. "There were rumors that Phillip's father was involved in her death." Belle waved a hand and looked toward the sky. "Not that we listen to such things."

Francesca sat stunned. *Not married.* The last letter she had received from him was written right before his wedding. She had assumed he stopped writing because he had fallen in love with his wife.

"According to Abigail," Claire said. "Phillip just had to get away from his father after her death."

Francesca tried to keep her voice steady. "What did he do? Where is he?"

"He took a commission with the navy. When we left for Livorno, he was stationed at Port Royal, Jamaica, but that was months ago," Claire said. "He might be anywhere now."

Francesca tried to control the wild beating of her heart, which echoed through her skull. *Phillip, my Phillip.* Surely now his father would let him choose his own wife. He'd done what duty demanded. *Certainly now.*

"How do you know him?" asked Belle.

"He was a student of my father. We…" She felt her color rising.

"You what?" asked Belle with eyes aglow.

"Belle," reprimanded Claire, "a lady does not pry."

Francesca gave Claire a grateful look. "Could you get word to him? Please tell him, and my brothers, what happened. I want them to know, if I'm … that … that I had no choice. That I tried not to dishonor Papa."

Claire squeezed her arm. "We'll tell them, I promise."

They were silent, Claire and Belle holding her tight. Tears gathered in Claire's eyes, and she shook her head, "You do have a choice, you know."

"Only one that is honorable."

"So you've said." Anger mixed with sorrow in her voice. "But a woman's honor has nothing to do with swords and battle. It comes from loving and tending her family, from worshipping God, and avoiding sin, from keeping her heart and soul pure. How can there be honor in this path?"

"I've given my word. I must keep it. Besides, I can't reach my brothers without putting them at risk. I have no family left to tend."

"You have us." Belle laid her head on Francesca's shoulder.

Francesca kissed Belle's hair as a carriage approached.

Claire squeezed Francesca's arm. "I worry that you've chosen this path, not out of honor, but out of a need for … I don't know what – that you couldn't abide a quiet life in the country with us. I love you, Francesca, but I'm concerned for your soul."

The carriage stopped in front of them, but no one moved.

Francesca stared at the carriage door. All she had to do was step through. *So simple.* She would be free of the pirates. Free to go with Claire and Belle, free to keep her promise to Papa and find Billy, and then to make a new home for herself here, or perhaps to find Phillip. A rising tide of excitement gripped her. Perhaps she and Phillip could still have the life they had dreamed of. She ached for the warmth of his arms. Just step through the carriage door—the *Destiny* would sail with the tide and that would be the end of it.

But she knew it wouldn't be the end, not for her. Every day, when she looked in the mirror, she would know a pirate kept his word and she did not. She had once told Phillip that duty doesn't change with the worth of the recipient. *We act honorably for ourselves, not them, so we may look in the mirror and know ourselves worthy.*

Francesca squeezed her good eye shut. She rose and faced Claire and

Belle, taking their hands. "I love you both. Go home, be well, and pray for me." She turned and headed back toward the ship.

As Francesca climbed aboard the *Destiny* she heard Baldric, the first mate, say to the captain, "The men are grumbling about her already, Sir."

The captain growled. "They'll do as I say."

Francesca pretended she hadn't heard.

The captain approached her. "Safely on their way?"

"Yes, Captain."

He handed her the articles. "Great cabin."

She nodded, winced, and followed him.

Once seated at the great cabin's table he handed her a pen and inkwell. She took her time and looked the paper over, reading carefully hoping to find a loophole.

There were ten articles. The first gave each pirate a vote on matters of import to the ship. Article two determined the amount of loot each crew member was to receive, and three prohibited gambling with dice or cards.

The fourth article read: *"He that shall desert the ship or his quarters in time of battle shall be punished by death or marooning. If any man shall offer to run away, or keep any secret from the Company, he shall be marooned with one bottle of water, one small arm, and one shot."*

She looked nervously at the captain, realizing what her signature would mean. She was glad she was sitting; her legs felt weak. The captain folded his arms across his chest, watching her closely. She continued reading.

The fifth and sixth articles prohibited stealing and fighting among the pirates on pain of death. The seventh prohibited smoking or carrying unprotected candles in the hold. A wise precaution, she thought, in a tar- and gunpowder-laden ship. The eighth charged each man to keep his weapons clean and ready for battle at all times. The ninth allotted money for each limb or eye lost in battle. And the tenth, to Francesca's surprise, read: *"If at any time you meet with a prudent woman, that man that offers to meddle with her without her consent shall suffer death."*

She wanted to ask if this applied to her, but the captain's face was distant and unreadable. She looked for some sign, encouragement, sympathy, understanding perhaps. He only waited patiently.

Francesca took the pen with shaking fingers. Her hand hesitated above the paper. How could she sign her allegiance to *him*? She searched his unflinching eyes. She saw no evil intent, but that only meant he was good at hiding it.

Her gaze traveled down his set jaw, his broad shoulders and muscular chest. Even waiting patiently, he possessed an air of lithe power. If she signed, she would be his to command. Her skin tingled and her heart beat faster. Her eyes flew back to his. If anything, she saw a grudging respect. But he was a cutthroat. She couldn't trust anything about him.

Still the pen tip trembled above the paper. She closed her eyes and heard Papa's words: *Your word is your bond.* Her body went cold as she added her name to the scores of others at the bottom of the sheet.

Without a word the captain blotted the ink, folded the paper, and slid it into his pocket.

Francesca stood unsteadily and the captain noticed the missing blade at her side. "Hold," he said. He left the room and returned a moment later. He carried the Solingen sword Francesca had used in the duel. He handed it to her. "This is the second best blade on the ship." He smiled mischievously. "It should belong to the second best swordsman."

Francesca's scowl shot a dagger of pain through her swollen eye.

"I wasn't completely sure you'd come back," he said, his eyes intent on her face.

"I gave my word. That means something to a woman of honor."

"And what does it mean to a pirate?"

She started to protest, but the captain patted his pocket which held the articles she'd just signed. She bit her lip. Technically, she *was* a pirate.

Instead, she regarded the sword. "I've killed a handful of your men. They'll never accept me."

The captain headed out the door and up the stairs with Francesca following. "Nearly all these men came from prizes we've captured. They've all fought one another at one time." He shook his head. "No, that won't be the problem."

He stepped onto deck and Francesca followed, wondering what the problem would be.

The captain shouted toward the bow, "Mr. Carter!"

A gangly, ten-year-old boy high tailed it across deck and came to attention in front of the captain. "Sir!"

"We have a lubber here, Mr. Carter," the captain said. "Show her the ropes."

Carter's shoulders sagged. "Aww, but Cap'n…"

The captain's glare stitched the boy's lips.

"Aye, Sir," Carter mumbled.

The captain strode to the quarter deck and faced the main deck. "Hoist anchor! Men, say goodbye to England! Helmsmen, set a course for the New World! We head for the Spanish Main!"

Francesca gasped as a "Huzzah!" arose from the men. *The Spanish Main!* If memory served, the Spanish Main was the coast of South America and the Caribbean Sea. That included Jamaica and Jamaica meant *Port Royal and Phillip!*

Crewmen scurried up into the rigging and loosed the sails. Men hauled on ropes, pulling the sails taut. The anchor chain thumped in as more sailors turned the capstan. As the canvas swelled, the ship began to move.

Francesca's emotions whirled while the ship gained momentum. The *Destiny* was taking her toward Phillip. Phillip who was not married. Hope fluttered through her chest. She might still find a home, even if she could never return to Salle DiCesare. Phillip would come up with some way for her to honorably end her vow to the captain. And then… A tremor of anticipation ran down her spine.

The faces of her crewmates caught her eye. Many of the cutthroats stared at her with narrowed eyes. Her fingers gripped the rail. First, she had to stay alive until she could find him.

She looked shoreward. Claire's words surfaced. "I worry that you've chosen this path, not out of honor, but out of a need for … I don't know what."

Francesca shook off the apprehension growing in the back of her mind. Perhaps she did crave adventure. What of it? Perhaps she did love the sea, and the fire that ran through her veins during battle. That didn't make her a pirate. *I promise, Papa, I promise.*

PART II
THE NEW WORLD

My visions were of shipwreck and famine;

of death or captivity among barbarian hordes;

of a lifetime dragged out in sorrow and tears,

upon some gray and desolate rock,

in an ocean unapproachable and unknown.

Edgar Allen Poe

CHAPTER 12
BAD LUCK

Francesca watched the town of Poole dwindling in the distance. She ached to be cocooned in the carriage with Claire and Belle, bumping their way through the green countryside. She missed them already, but she'd made her choice. She hoped someday she would see them again. For now, at least they were safe.

She heard Carter behind her kicking at the deck and grumbling. "Bad 'nough I gotta fetch fer ol' Barnacle."

She turned to face him. There was something elfish about the boy's freckle-splashed face, wide mouth, and up-tilted nose. His bright eyes and mop of sun-bleached hair seemed more puppy than pirate. But he glared at her as though she were an embarrassing younger brother he was forced to let tag along.

"I'll brook no charity," Francesca said. He crossed his arms and scowled. "But as you're ordered to help me, I'll make you a bargain."

"What sort a' bargain?"

"You make a sailor of me, and I'll make a swordsman of you."

Francesca saw interest in his eyes, but he frowned. "Maybe I don't want yer 'elp."

Francesca shrugged. "It's all the same to me. You're under orders to help me anyway. I thought you'd like something for your trouble."

Carter considered, then laughed. "I'll clap fins ta that." He shook her hand heartily, "But a tailor's only as good as the cloth 'e's given. Yer a flash hand with a blade but 'at don't make ya no sailor."

"No, that's your job."

Carter looked her over. "First, cast off the pig sticker," he said pointing at her sword. "It'll git caught in the lines."

Francesca grimaced. "I'm keeping my dagger."

Carter nodded. "Aye."

"Very well." Francesca headed down the aft companionway, Carter following. She'd been assigned a new cabin next to the one she had shared with the girls. She undid the sturdy lock the carpenter had installed. The windowless cabin was just large enough for a cot and her few possessions. She set down her sword, then bumped her head on the low ceiling as she straightened. She grimaced.

As she and Carter headed back up, they ran into the weaselly pirate who had dragged Francesca to the captain's cabin. He leered and moved in close, his eyes running over her body. "If it ain't the Cap'n's pretty little pet."

"Leave off, Hal," Carter said.

Francesca's hand went to where her sword had been. "I'm no one's pet," she snapped.

Hal laughed. "Cap'n says any man what touches ya 'll be swimmin' home." He grinned. "But ya know what I say?"

Francesca's hand dropped to the dagger strapped to her thigh and eased it from the scabbard.

Hal circled his index finger then poked her in the shoulder. "It's hard ta know who bumped inta ya in the dark."

She put the tip of her dagger to Hal's chest. "And I suggest you take care, or it may be a dagger you bump into." She pressed him out of the way with her knife and pushed past him, seething. Carter followed her up the stairs.

Anger pounded through Francesca's head as she stepped on deck. She looked toward the quarterdeck and met the captain's eyes. She headed toward him.

He gave her a friendly smile. "Francesca, how's our newest crewman?"

Francesca, head throbbing, spat, "Don't you mean your newest *pet*?"

The captain's face stiffened. "Where did you hear that?"

"I told you I'm no dancing bear and I have no intention of ever *dancing* with the likes of you!"

The captain's eyes narrowed.

"You forced me to become a member of your crew," she snarled. "And I demand that you treat me like one. I want no special treatment."

His jaw tightened. "So be it, DiCesare. You'll join Old Nob's mess."

"Fine!" Francesca said, though she had no idea what that meant.

"And let me assure you," he said in a tight voice. "I have no designs on any living woman."

He growled at Carter who stood wide-eyed. "See she knows the basics by the end of the week. Now I'll give you two seconds to get her off my quarterdeck before I have you both thrown in the brig."

Carter grabbed the back of Francesca's jerkin and dragged her away from the captain. "Are ya daft! What did ya do that for?"

She stumbled away, her head pounding. "I was just so furious." She put both hands to her exploding skull.

Carter shook his head. "Ya best git that temper under control, or ya'll git yerself killed 'fore I can make a sailor of ya."

Francesca nodded gingerly. "I'll try to stay alive until then."

"Now we'd best git ta work. Ya gots a bucketful ta learn."

"What did he mean, 'You'll mess with Old Nob'?" she asked.

"Yer ta be a topman," Carter said, his voice worried.

Francesca gasped. "You're joking." The topmen worked in the rigging, managing the sails and lines above deck.

"Ol' Nob and his messmates gots the mainmast sails, second watch," Carter said. He shook his head. "It's a flash job, but dangerous. Either the Cap'n's impressed by ya, or he's trying to git ya killed."

Francesca's spirits sank. She thought about requesting a different assignment, but after her tirade, it would be too embarrassing. She looked up at the men on the yard arm. If they could do it so could she. Couldn't she?

"We'd best git to it," said Carter. He grasped a taut black rope that ran from the deck up to the mast. "What's this then?"

"A rope?"

Carter rolled his eyes. "A backstay. Without backstays the mast'd topple o'er."

"A backstay," Francesca repeated.

They worked their way around the ship, Carter touching, naming, and explaining whatever he laid his hand on. They had to step over or around off-duty pirates who lounged on deck. She ignored the leers, stares, and occasional lewd comments.

Within half an hour her head was throbbing. She fingered her bandage as they stopped near one of the cannons. Carter ran through the firing sequence.

She had watched the *Santa Ana* gun crews and understood the principles. Her mind wandered. What did the captain mean when he said, "no designs on any *living* woman."

"Bloody hell!" bellowed a deep voice a few feet behind her.

Francesca turned to a tower of a man with a pockmarked face hidden by a black lion's mane of beard and hair. In one hand he held a pocketknife with a marling spike. Blood ran from a cut across the heel of his other hand. He pointed the knife at Francesca but railed at Carter. "Git that bloody woman away from me. Can't ya see she's bad luck."

Her hand went to her dagger.

"Aye, Sir!" Carter pushed Francesca away, hurrying her around the nearest cannon. "That's Mr. Agar, master gunner," Carter said. "If he tells ya ta jump, ya does it. He's a hard bla'guard if 'ere there was one."

He leaned toward her. "He was watchin' yer aft instead a' the rope he was splicin'. 'At cut was his own fault."

Eventually Carter led her to the shrouds leading up the mainmast.

"Must I?" Francesca squinted up the web of rope ladder to the maintop swaying fifty feet above.

"Well, I've never yet known a topman who could reef or furl from down here. 'Sides, it's rippin' up top. Ya can see nigh forever and yer clear a' the smell a' ol' Bottom's cookin' and Willy Brown's arse." He raised his voice on the last part so Willy could hear.

Willy stood on the deck with a bucket and a brush, slopping tar on a backstay. He flicked a glob at Carter, who ducked it neatly. With a laugh Carter scurried up the shrouds like a monkey.

Fifteen or sixteen, Willy had curly honey-colored hair that drifted into wisps of undeveloped beard at his chin. His gray-green eyes looked at Francesca with curiosity as he slathered the rope with tar. He inspected Francesca's goose-egg eye. "First-rate painted peeper."

She shrugged, sending a bolt through her skull. "Is that to preserve the ropes from the weather?" She peered up the rope towards the top of the mast.

"Lines," Willy said, nodding.

"Do you do all the lines?" She noticed that the shrouds, at least, weren't covered in sticky black tar.

"Naw, we just does the standin' riggin' what stays in place fer months on end. If ya did the haulin' lines, ya'd gum up the works."

Carter hollered from above and Francesca looked up. She had no particular fear of heights, but the swaying rope ladder and pitching mast daunted her, especially with her aching head. With a deep breath she grabbed hold of the shrouds and started to climb.

The ropes cut into the arches of her bare feet. The webbing swung with the ship so one minute she was laying in the ropes and the next hanging out over the water. The higher she got, the more pronounced the swing. Thirty feet above deck her stomach had had enough. She clenched her eyes shut and groaned.

Carter laughed at her. "Watch the 'orizon!" he shouted.

Francesca opened her good eye and kept it glued on the stable horizon line. Eventually her queasiness subsided enough for her to continue climbing.

Carter helped her through the opening and onto the maintop. The wood-grate platform was about ten feet across, with a hole in the center for the mast and entrance. That left about three feet of platform on each side. A railing ran along the back, but the rest was open to the air—and to the fifty-foot drop. Francesca sat, wrapping her arms through the railing, her legs shaking with fear and fatigue. She dropped her head. How was she to be a topman if she could barely climb to the top?

Carter gave her shoulder a playful shove. "First time up, I naught made it 'alf so far, an' I shot the cat after."

"You shot the cat?"

"You know." He made retching noises and mimed throwing up.

"Oh," she said, laughing.

Once her heart stopped pounding, she looked around. If the sea and sky seemed vast from deck, they seemed ten times more immense from fifty feet above. To the north the blazing white cliffs of Dorset grinned like teeth. Fishing boats dotted the sparkling gray sea. For a moment, wonder and awe rose at the beauty and sweep of it, but Carter and his lesson brought her back. "'At's the mainsail below us and the tops'l above, and the top gallant 'bove that," he explained.

Francesca looked up. There were at least thirty more feet of mast above her. A watchman perched on a tiny platform above the next higher sail. "That's the crow's nest, right?"

Carter nodded. "Some calls 'em the topmast trees. And them," he pointed to ropes running along the edges of the main sail, "is the clew lines, fer raising and lowering."

Carter went on, but her attention was drawn to the captain, pacing the deck below. She watched his catlike movements and wondered again what he meant by "any living woman." Surely it implied he had lost someone.

To Francesca's amazement, Willy climbed over the side of the platform and joined them. Carter explained that only lubbers use the hole in the platform specifically made for easy entrance. It was a sign of weakness.

"Willy 'ere is in Ol' Nob's mess," Carter said to Francesca. "She's yer new messmate," he said to Willy.

Willy nodded amiably as he sat down dangling his feet off the platform. All their legs dangled, but only Francesca's fingers were white where she gripped the rail. Willy gave her an overview of topman duties, most of which sounded horribly dangerous.

"Don't worry," Willy said. "Long as ya keep yer feet under ya and yer eyes on yer work, you'll be fine."

"There's ol' Miller blowin' a cloud," said Carter pointing to the man Francesca had threatened with the ceramic shard. He sat on a coil of rope smoking a pipe below them.

"Bet ya a bob I kin gob 'im," Carter said.

"Done," Willy said, shaking Carter's hand.

Carter leaned over, carefully judging the wind and the sway of the ship, and spit. His careful aim was in vain.

"Carter!" she said, "What if you had hit him?"

Carter shrugged. "I'd a' won a bob. 'Sides, Miller wouldn't give it no mind. He and I are ol' pals. It's cuz of 'im I joined up."

"What about your family?" Francesca said.

Carter stared off toward the cliffs. "Pa chipped and ma did fer eight. The lot gripped while I coopered, 'cept my wee brother."

She looked from Carter to Willy blankly.

"He said his pa was a carpenter and his ma looked after their eight children," Willy said. "The grip, influenza took 'em while 'e was away, apprenticed to a cooper makin' barrels, exceptin' his younger brother."

"I'm so sorry." She put a hand on his shoulder.

Carter shrugged her hand off. "My brother was blewed up in the big-house, but I tipped my boom toward the docks."

Francesca looked to Willy again for a translation.

"His brother died in a work-house but Carter ran away ta the docks."

"Didn't I just say 'at?" Carter shook his head.

"Go on," she said.

"Well, I beak-hunted an' cabbaged when I got banded, 'til I ran afoul a pack of bludgers."

"He stole chickens and pilfered when 'e was hungry, 'til 'e ran inta a gang a' cutthroats," Willy translated.

Carter frowned, exasperated. "'At's what I said!" He looked at Francesca. "Don't they teach ya Italians how ta talk?"

She shrugged and winced. "Apparently not."

"Well, they'd a' done me if I hadn't met Miller. Miller run 'em off. After that I signed on with 'im and the cap'n. It's almost a year an' I gots no complaints. I loblolly fer Barnacles, fetchin' and runnin'—"

"Who?" Francesca asked.

"Barnacles—the doc. I fetch fer the doc. Workin' fer 'im is easy; I got a hammock, belly-timber, grog on Sunday, an' only a cuff on occasion. Not a bad bargain."

Francesca nodded. "What about you, Willy?"

"'Willy's a son-of-a-gun," Carter said.

"A what?"

"My pa was a sailor a' some sort, I expect," Willy said. "Me mum worked the docks."

She stared blankly for a moment, then blushed. "Oh."

"She was right good ta me 'til she went toes up. Been on me own since I was six an' at sea since I was somewheres 'round ten. It's a good gig, mostly. Exceptin' the food."

Orphans all. They had that in common. She may have spent her childhood in the salle among young noblemen, but she knew what it was to end up alone. How many such stories ended aboard ships like this?

She breathed in the salt air. Much as she disliked being among pirates, she loved the snap and hum of the sails, the smell of salt spray, the vastness of the sky, and most of all, the curiosity about what lay beyond the horizon.

The bosun's whistle tweeted, calling them to duty. Willy climbed farther up into the rigging, and Francesca followed Carter back down to the deck to clap hands on ropes and haul sail to tack the ship.

That evening, as thin clouds tempered the sun's heat, Francesca gave Carter a fencing lesson. They worked in the waist of the ship, between the stacked longboats and the rail. A few men lounged nearby. Carter held Francesca's sword as she corrected his *en garde* position and showed him how to advance and lunge. Then she had him move back and forth across the deck, lunging.

Carter threw himself too far forward and lost his balance. He swung his arms to right himself and caught his blade in the rigging. He went down in a heap, practically in Miller's lap.

"Mind yer flippers, Carter," growled Miller, "or ya'll put out someone's peeper." He blew pipe smoke in Carter's face.

"Sorry," mumbled Carter.

"Keep your weight balanced," Francesca said as she helped him up. "That way you can move quickly in any direction."

"I know. I'm tryin'. I'm just a bufflehead."

She clapped him on the back. "All you need is practice. Let's try something simpler." She set him lunging at the mast, trying to land the tip of the sword in a knot hole in the wood. "Keep going until you hit the knot twenty times."

"Twenty!" said Carter. "That 'll take days."

She smiled. "Then you best get started."

As she watched Carter drill, her mind wandered. Carter's unruly blonde hair reminded her of Phillip. She thought of the first time she had fenced.

She and Phillip had ridden in secret to an abandoned barn a mile from home. Cotton-puff clouds dotted the sky, and a few lingering wildflowers freckled the field. To their right stood a crumbling stone barn that had long ago lost its roof and doors—the wood probably taken for other uses. Only a pile of rubble wrapped in morning glories remained of one corner of the building, and saplings and brush threatened to swallow it all into the forest.

Francesca pushed back some of the white morning glories and retrieved the practice blades she had hidden there. As she handed him one, Phillip said, "I owe you a bout."

Emotion created a lump in her throat as she nodded. Her first real bout! Until then he'd only let her do drills.

Phillip grinned as they took their positions. "Are you ready?"

"Yes, maestro."

"Fence!"

Delicious fire ripped through her veins and she attacked in quick, controlled movements.

Phillip parried and backed away. His grin spread. "You'll have to do better than that."

She lunged again and again, attacking in high and lowline. She changed the timing up to keep him off guard. Phillip backed away, parrying and riposting. His blade flashed toward Francesca, and she responded.

The world fell away. Only they remained. In a fraction of a second her body reacted to the tiniest movement of his shoulder, the slightest shift of his weight, the tightening of his muscles that indicated an attack. Time and again, her body knew where his blade would be, and blocked it quicker than her mind could react.

It was a beautiful dance, give and take, as they moved first one way across the dirt floor then the other. It was like nothing Francesca had ever experienced. It was instinct, bone deep, but new and thrilling. For the first time in her life, she felt free.

At the same time her mind floated above the bout. Her mind analyzed tactics and, watched for weaknesses, assessing with a sharpness of focus, clarity, and elation she'd never felt before.

When Francesca had landed the tip of her foil on his chest, Phillip called "Halt." They panted for breath.

Phillip shook his head slowly, mouth ajar. He said nothing, but the look of admiration on his face made Francesca's skin tingle. It was the first time someone had looked at her and seen the real her, not the façade she wore daily, not the person they wanted to see. Her. Her passion, her skill. She blinked back tears.

"That was incredible," Phillip said after a moment.

Francesca nodded eagerly. "Oh, yes! It was a hundred times better than I ever dreamed."

"You'd beat more than half the boys here, and that was your first bout!" Francesca glowed.

He shook his head again. "If your father taught you, you'd be the best in the salle by now."

Francesca's breath caught. *If.* She dropped her blade and burst into tears.

"I'm sorry." Phillip let fall his foil and moved toward her. "I meant it as a compliment. I didn't mean to upset you."

She stepped into him, pressed her face against his chest, and he wrapped his arms around her. She felt ridiculous. *Stop it!* She bit off her tears. *He'll think you're an idiot.* She pulled away.

"It's just … that's what I've always wanted," she said. "To be included. To be able to go to class with Papa, and you, and my brothers. To be able to fence openly. But I'll always have to hide. I'll always have to be someone I'm not. I'll never be able to prove what I can do to anyone but you."

"You never have to pretend with me," he said.

She gave a weak smile, turned away, and wiped her face. "I know it sounds silly, but I always dreamed that someday, if I were good enough, Papa would love me enough not to care what was 'proper.' He wouldn't care what anyone said. He'd love me enough to teach me."

She took a shaky breath and glanced at him, afraid he'd laugh at her.

He didn't. His blue eyes shone. He gently turned her to face him. "It doesn't sound silly. I know what it is to want a father's love. And I, for one, know who you are and what you can do, Francesca DiCesare. You're the most amazing woman I've ever met."

Suddenly she wasn't thinking of fencing, or Papa, or who knew what. Her whole world was his blue eyes, his dimples, and the sweet arch of his lips as he smiled. Yearning set her skin on fire. She placed her palm on his chest. His heart thundered under her hand. Her own pulse rushed to match it.

Eyes locked, he moved toward her and wrapped his hands around her waist. she shuddered in anticipation. Her heart beat in her ears as she slid her arms around his neck. As he bent to kiss her, she lifted onto her toes to meet him.

His lips were soft and eager. Wherever his body touched hers ripples of flame spread outward. She pulled him harder against her to fan the flames. The passion overwhelmed and frightened her, which made it all the more thrilling.

Bereft, Francesca coughed and shook away the memory. She looked past the ship's rail at the distant horizon. *Phillip, please be in Port Royal.*

"Twenty!" Carter announced triumphantly.

She was sure he hadn't gotten anywhere near twenty. But he was gleaming with sweat, so she let it go. She'd watch more closely next time.

That night Francesca walked wearily to her cabin. She checked the lock twice before she took off her vest and breeches and fell exhausted onto her cot. Her hands and feet ached from rope burns. Her throbbing head swam with belaying pins, buntlines, gudgeons, hawsers, capstans, and a thousand more items she couldn't quite remember.

But even worse, every time she closed her eyes, she saw the faces of the pirates she had killed during the battle. She rubbed at her good eye to erase them, but they only became clearer. She lay awake, staring into the darkness.

They would have killed me without a second thought; I did what I had to. But still, their deaths felt like a weight, pushing her against her cot, smothering her. Panic plucked at her. Living men she could fight, but how did one fight the dead?

Papa had never spoken of the battles he had fought. How many had died by his hand? If there was such a thing as—

The doorknob rattled.

Her hand slid to the dagger under her pillow. Her eyes flicked to where her sword rested two feet away.

The carpenter had done a good job with the lock. The rattling stopped and Francesca exhaled. So much for worrying about the dead—it was the living who were still a threat.

She released the dagger and tried to relax. She concentrated on Carter's lessons, going over the things he had touched and named until she drifted to sleep.

But her dreams were filled with the faces of dead men.

The next day, Francesca woke tired. Three times during the night someone had rattled her doorknob. Was it the same man each time or different men?

During the day she felt reasonably safe. Except in her cabin, privacy was impossible on such a crowded ship. She was never alone with any of the men. But everywhere she went she felt their eyes on her and saw them look away when she met their gazes. Some would "accidentally" bump into her or hover close when Carter was explaining something. She needed to make it clear that they should leave her be, but had no idea how.

Then disaster struck. Two of Francesca's messmates fell ill. One had a toothache that swelled his face like a grapefruit. The doctor gave him laudanum and chipped out the tooth, but his screams smothered the mood on the ship. The second man was diagnosed with consumption. Beyond bleeding him with leeches, there was nothing the doctor could do.

Francesca had not met either of them, nor had she begun to learn her topman duties, but everyone felt the illnesses were her fault. She had brought bad luck to her watch, even before she joined it.

She knew of the deep-seated superstition that women were bad luck aboard ship. Life as a pirate was precarious. Accidents, battles, diseases, shipwrecks, and the gallows were constant threats. For topmen it was even worse. One bad step or missed handhold meant a long plunge and sudden death. They couldn't afford bad luck. But understanding didn't make the men's resentment any easier to take.

Some men took to spitting at her feet or making the sign of the cross if she passed in front of them. Those who weren't leering either grumbled or fell silent when she came near.

At least Carter and Willy seemed unconcerned about her "bad luck." Carter shrugged when she asked him. "Luck comes, luck goes, good an' bad alike," he said. "Ain't no use worryin'."

Francesca ignored the men as best she could. By the end of the week, she had learned most of what Carter could teach her. She had a basic working knowledge of the vessel and her duties, though she realized it would take a lifetime to become an expert.

She had learned to scrub or sand the decks and equipment, and to untwist old rope and use it with tar to caulk the seams of the ship. She could tie a half-dozen different knots and had the end splice and the cut splice down, though not the eye splice or horseshoe splice. Most of all, she had come to understand that a ship was a fragile creation, always under attack by the salt water it sailed on, and only the crew's constant diligence kept it afloat.

It was time to learn to be a topman if her messmates would teach her.

On Monday morning Francesca groaned and rose from bed when she heard the ship's bell ring four times. It was four o'clock, time to join her new crew. She dressed, braided her hair, and went up on deck.

The sky was brightening to gold when she stepped into the cool morning air. Two lanterns still glowed at the stern of the ship. Old Nob and his crew waited for her, arms crossed, eyes narrowed, and lips pursed. Only Willy gave her a smile. They were all small, wiry men, which made them perfect for scurrying about the maze of ropes above deck.

Old Nob's lined face was chestnut brown from the sun. The elements had preserved him in a state of agelessness. Francesca couldn't tell if he was thirty or seventy. He glared at her with pale grey eyes. "We've orders ta take ye, agin' our wishes. We're puttin' ye in Able's place since ye done him in."

The others murmured agreement. Able was the man who had come down with consumption. Francesca opened her mouth to protest that it was not her fault, but then shut it. There was no way to convince them otherwise.

"Fer now," Old Nob went on, "ye'll follow Willy. Watch what 'e does and do what 'e says. He don't seem ta mind yer company."

"Yes, Sir," Francesca said.

"Don't call me 'Sir'," growled Nob. "I'm no bleedin' officer." Old Nob and his crew turned their backs.

"Come on," Willy said, "I'll show ya yer station."

Francesca followed Willy up the mainmast shrouds. They didn't stop at the top platform, they climbed higher. Her stomach dropped with each foot she climbed. They reached the crow's nest, not much more than a few boards for a person to stand on.

"We'll be workin' the mains'l and tops'l," Willy said. "Able worked starboard so that's where ya'll be. Nob'll take the far end, I'll be next an' ya'll be closest in." Willy slid out along a rope that ran beneath the wooden yardarm. He held on to the top edge of the sail as he glided his bare feet out to the side.

Francesca's breath came in gasps. "You expect me to…"

"It ain't so bad, once ya gits used ta it."

She let out a strained laugh. How could anyone get used to this? The deck was eighty feet below, and the sway and pitch were terrifying.

Willy moved back to her side. "Just try."

He helped her get her bare feet onto the rope he called the "horses." She clamped her hands onto the sail edge. She even managed to move one foot out along the line, but her hands refused to budge.

"Ya don't need ta let go, just slide yer hand," Willy said.

Francesca tried, but the muscles in her hands and forearms were clamped into knots. "I, I can't."

The bosun's whistle tweeted and Francesca's messmates swarmed into the rigging. In a flash they surrounded her.

Old Nob snarled and shoved her against the mast, out of his way so he could get to his station. "Bad luck *and* useless."

He scurried out onto the horses like a squirrel. Willy followed cautiously. Francesca, flushing red, inched along the rope, determined not to be useless. A few feet out she stopped. The deck and the ocean flashed by beneath her with each sway of the ship. There was nothing between her and death but the rope she stood on. Her heart pounded so loudly she thought it would burst. She watched Willy lean over the yardarm. He grabbed a short rope that hung in a line of others from the face of the sail. After pulling up the rope and tying it off, he slid over a foot and a half and did the same again, working his way back toward Francesca.

"That's called reefin' the sail. See, it's not so bad. Ya, just—" Willy missed his footing on the horses. He wrapped his arms around the yardarm, legs dangling free.

"Willy!" shouted Francesca. She slid the few feet to his side. Breathing heavily, she let go of the sail with one hand and guided his searching foot back to the line. Willy got the rope under him and steadied himself.

"Thanks," Willy said.

Nob glared at her. "Ye'll be the death of us all."

Their watch lasted four hours. At eight bells they were off duty and headed for breakfast.

They messed forward in the forecastle on the lower deck. The fo'c'sle was also where most of the pirates slept. It was dark and gloomy with only a couple light vents, and had low overhead beams that made one stoop. It smelled of sweat, tar, and roasted pork.

At night the hammocks hung so closely together it was impossible to walk between them. During the day the hammocks were stowed, and oak tables and benches attached to the beams by canvas straps were lowered. On the starboard side, toward the prow, sat the massive cast-iron stove where Bottom, the cook, and his two mates prepared food.

Francesca's nerves were taut as she descended into that dank hole. As she approached the bench, the men slid together, closing ranks so there was no space for her. She went around the other side. Again, the space disappeared; they filled each spot she headed for. Finally, she stood, wavering.

The cook's mate, a heavy-fisted man in a smudged apron, delivered a platter of food to the center of the table. He gave Francesca an indifferent glance as he walked away.

Francesca's mouth watered, not because the scent was enticing, but because she had worked up a powerful appetite climbing through the rigging for four hours. She stood behind the men, trying to see what smelled like roast ham and biscuits.

Nob turned to her. "We gits ta choose who sits at our table." He spat, nearly hitting her foot. "Yer not wanted here."

Francesca's stomach growled, but she stepped back. The topmen glared at her. Willy gave her a sympathetic shrug. Francesca looked around at the other tables. They all stared at her with narrowed eyes.

Francesca's hand strayed to her dagger. She thought about forcing her messmates to give her food, but that would only antagonize them further—a bad idea if she would be spending her mornings with them eighty feet above deck.

Instead, she moved toward the cast-iron stove. Beside it, along the ship's hull, were stacked barrels, baskets, and bags of foodstuffs and even a few chickens in coops. Bottom stomped around looking for something. He kicked a copper pot aside with his wooden leg causing a clatter.

Bottom was a pear-shaped black man with a face that looked sculpted from mashed potatoes and dipped in beef gravy. He gleamed with sweat from the heat of the cooking fire. He stared at Francesca with emotionless eyes when she asked for food. "Ya eats wit' yer watch," he said with a gravelly voice.

"Yes, I know," Francesca said. "But they won't let me."

"Ya eats wit' yer watch," he repeated.

"But—"

"Or not at all."

"I can pay you," Francesca said, thinking of the money the girls had given her.

Bottom grinned, his eyes drifting down her form. "I don't needs money…"

She took a step backwards.

Bottom's grin widened, harsh white against dark lips. "I'll wait, 'til you is real hungry."

Francesca headed up the companionway nearly plowing into a man descending. As she pushed past, she felt the man's hand on her buttocks. Francesca hurried on with the men laughing behind her.

CHAPTER 13
TAKING A STAND

As Francesca came up on deck, she gasped as though surfacing from underwater. She huddled at the rail, shivering. There was something primal in this threat to starve her to death. While she knew it was not her but her gender they objected to, it didn't make it less frightening. She closed her eyes and imagined Phillip wrapping a comforting arm around her, but it was Carter who appeared at her elbow.

"I 'ear Old Nob won't let ya grease yer gills."

"If you mean he won't let me eat with my mess, you heard right. How did you find out so quickly?"

Carter shrugged. "Secrets last 'bout as long as a lump 'a sugar in a cup 'a tea on this ship."

"Don't talk about tea and sugar." Her stomach ached.

"You can mess with us," Carter said.

Francesca thanked him but shook her head. She'd been eating with Carter and the other boys—Rolly, Finn and Kimball—until today. But the ship's boys, anyone under sixteen, only got half rations to begin with. They had little enough food without sharing with her.

"We oughta tell the Cap'n. He'd make 'em shape up."

"No! I'll solve this on my own. I don't want *his* help." Francesca hated to have anyone fight her battles for her, especially a pirate.

Carter shook his head. "What ya gonna do?"

"Come on."

Francesca and Carter headed down the aft companionway to the landing on the lower deck. Toward the stern was the great cabin. Toward the bow, next to Francesca's new tiny cabin, was her previous cabin she'd shared with the girls, now set up as the doctor's infirmary.

The room had not changed much, except for the addition of the doctor's desk and another cot. A hint of vanilla still clung to the place, reminding Francesca of Claire and Belle. A pang of loneliness shot through her.

Two of the cots were occupied by her would-be messmates. A third cot held a man who gleamed with sweat. All seemed to be either asleep or unconscious. The doctor rose from his desk with a smile as Francesca and Carter entered.

"Ah, lass, I was goin' tae send the lad tae fetch ye. Ef I could find him." He gave Carter a scowl and led Francesca to a seat on an unoccupied cot. "Time to take a peep at yer noggin."

The doctor unwrapped the bandage around her head. The swelling in her eye and forehead had subsided, though the color had deepened to reddish-purple. He examined the wound. "'Tis healin' nicely, but I expect ye'll have a wee bit o' a scar." He replaced the bandage.

Francesca's stomach growled. "It's not my head I came to see you about, Doctor, it's my stomach."

"Bein' a bit puckish es hardly a medical condition."

"Starvation is," Carter said.

The doctor shot Carter a narrow-eyed look.

"It's my messmates," Francesca said. "They won't let me eat with them."

"Botheration!" The doctor sat down next to her. "I was afeard o' that. Bloody superstitious lot."

"Would it be possible for you to get me something to eat?"

The doctor looked thoughtful. "Aye, I can get ye vittles. But that will nae solve the problem, will et?"

"What do you mean?"

The doctor rubbed his face. "I was on a navy cutter off Majorca a few yairs back. The men took a powerful dislike to one o' the hands. I cannae say what he ded to upset them, but they took turns keeping the man awake 'round the clock 'til he was so beat out, he fell from the riggin'. Landed on the stove chimney. What a mess that made, I can tell ye."

"Crikey!" Carter exclaimed.

Cold desperation seeped through Francesca. "What am I to do?"

"I haven't the foggiest," the doctor said. "It's nae as though ye can become a man to please them." He tilted his head. "The captain may have a notion. He's a knowin' lad."

"I'd rather handle this on my own," Francesca said.

"Why, lass?"

"I don't trust him," she said. And the idea of owing him her life made her squirm uncomfortably.

The doctor watched her for a moment, then shrugged. "As ye will." He turned to Carter. "Fetch a plate from Bottom. Tell him et's fer me."

As Carter opened the door, Kelsey, the captain's steward, a mousy man with an eye patch was exiting the great cabin. He stopped when he saw Francesca. "Cap'n wants ta see ya."

The doctor gave her a wry smile and shrugged. Her stomach rumbled again and she sighed. Food would have to wait.

She found the captain sitting at the table going over some maps. He was freshly shaven, and with his neatly combed hair and spotless clothes, he might have been a young lawyer, except for his wind-roughened tanned skin and calloused hands. She had an urge to reach out and touch those hands, though she couldn't think why.

The captain regarded her. "DiCesare, I hear you're bad luck."

Francesca frowned. News did travel fast. "Well, I..."

The captain waved a hand. "At least that's what the men are saying. I don't believe in luck, bad or otherwise." He looked into the distance. "Destiny, now that's another matter."

"I've taken care of it, Sir," Francesca said.

He brushed the maps aside. "Have you now. How, precisely?"

"The doctor has agreed to share his food with me, Sir."

"And when they find some other way to be rid of you?"

Francesca stammered. "I, I don't know."

"I thought as much." He rose, the action quick and light, reminding Francesca what a powerful man he was. He motioned to Francesca's left. "Tuit will see to it."

Francesca looked to her left and froze. A man stood grinning at her. Francesca's breath caught and she took a step away. How had she missed him standing there? He was as silent and unmoving as a statue. She'd seen him around the ship, though she hadn't heard his name. She thought of him as *The Savage*.

He wore nothing but cotton duck trousers and a necklace of shark teeth. He was compact, his smooth-skinned, solidly-muscled body adorned from head to waist with bold black tattoos—circles, swirls, and half-recognizable mythic creatures. Two black bands crossed his face encompassing his eyes and mouth, giving him a menacing grin. He wore his long black hair tied back tight with two protruding white feathers.

"Him?" Her voice trembled.

The captain crossed to Tuit and put a hand on his shoulder. "You see, he's a kind of witch doctor. The men trust him. He's agreed to take the bad luck off you."

Tuit still grinned, his teeth harshly white in their band of black.

"I don't want his help," Francesca said. "Or yours."

The captain shook his head. "Why not?"

"I won't be indebted to anyone."

The captain approached her, his face turning red. "But you'll take food from the doctor."

Francesca's face went blank, her mouth a hard line. That was different, at least it felt different.

"So it's just Tuit and I you object to," the captain said. His voice was angry, but his eyes looked hurt.

Then he scanned her body. "You think we'll want something in return. Something you're unwilling to give."

Francesca's cheeks flamed. That was what she thought, now that he said it. A tingling sensation rippled across her skin. "Won't you?"

The captain sighed as he sat back down at the table. His expression was soft but his voice hard. "If I make it an order you owe us nothing."

Francesca was confused. She had the impression she had hurt him but didn't understand how.

She looked nervously at Tuit. "Surely, Captain, you can't expect me to agree to a heathen ritual."

The captain tilted his head. "Are you devout?"

"Yes, well, no, I mean…" She squirmed under his gaze.

With pupils of so many different faiths at the salle, Papa had banned speaking of religion to maintain peace. Her family went to mass only on high holidays and spoke little of Christianity. There was no need—honor was their religion, and the first rule was to believe in the Church and to defend Her until death.

The captain raised an eyebrow. He stood and moved close to Francesca. She fought the urge to step away. His voice dropped. "So, you'd rather die a horrible death than have Tuit mumble some mumbo jumbo over you?"

"Well, I…" Confusion and a wave of homesickness swept over her. She wished Papa were here. He'd know what to say.

"I'm not asking you to believe it," continued the captain. "But the men will. They will believe the bad luck is gone."

Francesca saw concern in his blue-gray eyes. She felt as though she was being dragged along a fast river as she tried to swim for shore. Was he really trying to help her? Could it be a trick? She twisted her fingers together and dropped her eyes. "What is he going to do to me?"

"I don't know, exactly." The captain took his seat. "You see, his English is not so good." He smirked. "Nothing you'd consider *dishonorable*."

"You're sure, Sir. Nothing…"

He nodded.

Francesca took a deep breath. "Very well."

She headed up on deck both relieved and worried. She tried to imagine what Papa would say, but the question was outside her realm of experience. Still, the idea of Tuit and his "mumbo jumbo" left a bad taste in her mouth. Lost in thought, she sat down next to Carter who handed her a plate of salt pork. She shoveled it into her mouth.

"So," said Carter, "Tuit's gonna change yer luck."

Francesca swallowed and turned on him. "Were you listening?"

"Naw," said Carter. "Lump 'a sugar, cup 'a tea."

Francesca noticed Old Nob and the rest of her messmates staring at her with relief in their weathered faces. It would be better for all of them if she were to go through with it.

She watched Tuit cross the deck and go below. He moved with easy confidence and grace. She leaned toward Carter. "What do you know about Tuit?"

"'Tain't nothin' ta be feared. Tuit's a puffer fish, 'is spikes is all fer show."

She looked at Carter sideways, unbelieving.

"'Is full name's Tuiterai," Carter went on. "He's from some bit a' rock in the South Seas. They says 'e kin predict the weather a week ahead. Some says 'e controls it."

"What does he do aboard ship?"

"He's a striker. Gits us wild food when the larder runs low. Ya know, turtle, sharks, fish, birds, 'e knows 'ow ta catch 'em all, what's good ta eat n' what ain't. But most times, 'e 'elps out Barnacle Face. Ol' Barnacles don't like 'im much. I think it's 'cause Tuit's a better doctor than 'e is."

"A better doctor?"

"Aye," said Carter. He rubbed his chin with a bit of rope. "Barnacle's medicine may be new-fangled, but Tuit's works more of'n." He made a face. "Tastes like mealy worms, but it works. Then 'gain, might just be the way 'e gives it."

"What do you mean?"

"C'mon," Carter said.

Francesca followed Carter back down to the infirmary. Carter opened the door a few inches and they peered inside. The doctor sat at his desk writing notes in a journal. Tuit knelt beside one of the unconscious men. The man gleamed with sweat. The blanket covering him lay flat where the man's left shin and foot should have been. Tuit set a basin of water on the deck, wet a rag, and dabbed gently at the man's neck and face.

"That's Mills," whispered Carter, "Had the fever since we took 'is leg after the last battle."

Mills moaned and came to as Tuit laid the cloth across his forehead. Mills looked around confused and then focused on the savage. "Tuit. I thought ya was me mum."

Tuit helped Mills sit up, then retrieved a bowl from the desk and spooned something into the man's mouth.

"See," said Carter, closing the door. "I'm not sayin' Barnacles don't know what 'e's doin'. If ya need someth'n cut off or sewn up, 'e's your man. But for ol' fashion coddlin' ya go ta Tuit."

Francesca shook her head in confusion.

The night of the ritual, the full moon loomed larger and brighter than Francesca had ever seen. Its azure glow bathed the deck and gleamed on the furled sails. Tuit, dressed only in a loin cloth, his long, black hair falling loose, escorted Francesca to a seat on a barrel set near the mainmast. A nervous shiver ran down her spine as the pirates gathered, whispering and watching with anticipation.

Tuit began by singing a long, slow ballad in his native tongue. He had a rich, melodic voice and the song called up images of endless seas and soft caressing waves. As he sang, he wove scraps of white sailcloth into Francesca's hair creating a wreath around the crown of her head. The moonlight transformed it into a halo of blue.

Once the song ended, Tuit took an unlit torch from Carter. He looked toward the captain on the quarterdeck and gestured toward the lantern hanging above the ship's compass. The captain nodded. Tuit strode to the quarterdeck, kindled the torch in the lantern, then returned to Francesca's side.

He began to dance. At first only his bare feet beat time on the deck. The crew took up the beat, seventy men stomping until the ship resonated like a drum. Then he began to whirl and leap around Francesca. The torch flame arched and flew. He twirled it through the air creating wheels of fire that burnt trails across her eyes. He tossed it into the air and caught it with ease. He danced around Francesca, inscribing symbols in the darkness faster and faster. Just when the flame became one continuous red streak, it stopped.

The stomping ceased. For a moment, the only sound was the creak of the hull and Francesca's pounding heart.

Tuit handed her the blazing torch. She held it in her left hand while he took her right hand in his. He grabbed a knife from a scabbard at his waist, held it over the back of her hand, and looked at Francesca.

She braced herself and nodded. Tuit ran the knife, trailing fire across her hand. Francesca grimaced as blood ran.

Tuit held her hand over the torch, which sputtered and spat as blood dripped into it. Then he let out a war-cry that split the night air and plunged the torch into a waiting bucket of water. With another scream he tossed the water, torch, and bucket over the side.

There was a second of silence, and then a roar went up from the men. Their relief, like a wave of lightness, swept over Francesca. The bad luck was gone.

She hadn't actually believed the superstition, but she felt a giddy sense of release. She wanted to laugh, cry, or shout at the top of her lungs.

The captain approached as the men talked and hooted. Tuit knelt in front of her and gently bandaged her hand. She put her other hand on his bare shoulder. "Thank you."

Tuit nodded.

"Is that it?" the captain asked Tuit.

Tuit shook his head. He patted a tattoo on his shoulder and pointed to Francesca's shoulder. She furrowed her brow. "Must I?" she asked the captain.

The captain grinned. "Consider it a souvenir of your time on the *Destiny.*" He leaned in close to Francesca's ear. His warm breath on her neck made her shiver. He smelled of fresh air and sea spray. "If I understand Tuit's English, his people have no cure for bad luck." He gave a small laugh. "You may be married to him for all I know."

Francesca's fists clenched. *Married!* Was he serious or was he teasing?

The captain straightened with twinkling eyes and turned to the crew. "This calls for a celebration!" He signaled One-eyed Kelsey, who rolled a barrel into the midst of the men.

The crew cheered. Two fiddles, a bagpipe, and drums appeared and a lively sea tune started up. Ale cups passed hand to hand.

A few of the men shook Francesca's bandaged hand and even Old Nob gave her a nod. Her anger at the captain dissipated in the new camaraderie. She gladly took a mug of ale from Kelsey as he passed them around. She asked him how he had lost his eye and that brought an eruption of laughter from the other sailors.

"Burying a moll!" shouted one pirate.

"Dilly dallying with a doxie!" shouted another.

"As a wedd'n gift!" shouted a third.

Francesca wasn't sure what they meant but gathered a woman was responsible for Kelsey's missing eye.

"Bosh!" scoffed Kelsey. "I only said I'd marry 'er *after* she shied the broken bottle at me canister."

"And if ya were naught so boozy, you'd a ducked faster and still have both daylights," added the first.

"I brushed off with the cap'n then and there," Kelsey said to Francesca. "Didn't e'en get me four hundred."

She guessed he was referring to the four hundred pieces of eight every seaman was awarded for losing an eye or a finger aboard ship.

The crew chortled.

After that every man had a story to tell. They showed Francesca their scars and told tales of wounds received in some ridiculous manner. The company roared with delight.

All eyes seemed to be on her—with varying degrees of intensity.

The captain hovered in her peripheral vision. There was something mother-hennish about the way he kept an eye on her. How strange that when Phillip had been solicitous, she thought it endearing, but she found the captain's actions patronizing. She also noticed Agar, the master gunner grumbling to Hal as he glared at her over the top of his cup.

As the night wore on and the second and third barrels emptied, stories and jests gave way to dancing. A drunken crowd gathered around the musicians, clapping and singing, Francesca among them.

The fiddler struck up *Spanish Ladies* and the men turned to sing to Francesca. She blushed and resisted the urge to remind them she was Tuscan, not Spanish.

Farewell and adieu unto you Spanish ladies
Farewell and adieu to you ladies of Spain
For it's we've received orders for to sail for old England
But we hope very soon we shall see you again.

Agar, smelling of alcohol, approached Francesca and growled in her ear. Francesca's eyes went wide, then narrowed to slits. Her cheeks flushed and her hand went to her dagger. As she faced Agar the rowdy chorus of the song started. Miller, Carter's pipe-smoking friend, grabbed Francesca and dragged her into the dancers, singing.

We'll rant and we'll roar like true British sailors
We'll rant and we'll roar across the salt seas
Until we strike soundings in the Channel of Old England
From Ushant to Scilly is thirty-five leagues.

She searched for Agar among the moving forms but couldn't see him. Miller linked arms with her and spun her around.

The pirates grew uncomfortably friendly, taking her hands, putting an arm around her, closing in. Trouble was brewing.

Miller, drunk, pulled Francesca into a bear hug. She smelled rum mixed with spicy pipe smoke on his breath. His whiskers were rough against her cheek. She shoved him away and stepped back, working her way out of the crowd.

Captain Massey, suddenly in front of her, considered at her with piercing eyes. "Everything shipshape?"

"Aye, Sir." She nodded as she moved past him. She didn't want him to see her momentary panic. She sat on a crate in the cool night air. She couldn't see Agar anywhere.

Miller sat next to her on the crate. His hand strayed to her thigh. Without thinking, Francesca made her point.

Miller's shriek pierced the night. Even the bagpipes were no match. The musicians fell silent. *Spanish Ladies* trailed off. All eyes turned to Francesca.

Miller grimaced and groaned with his hand on Francesca's thigh.

Francesca held her dagger, spitted through his hand and into her own leg. Blood spread as she waited for everyone's attention.

Once she was sure all eyes were on her, she yanked the dagger loose suppressing a cry of pain. Miller yelped and hurried off. Francesca rose, seemingly nonchalant, wiping the blade on her injured leg.

"Gentlemen," she said. "Mr. Miller has failed to win my affections." She looked around at them. "Is there anyone else who cares to take a … stab at it?"

Silence hung suspended. Francesca awaited her fate with her chin up. Either they would turn against her, or they would accept her limits.

The captain, surprise on his face, scanned the men. The moment stretched on. Then Kelsey laughed heartily, and soon the rest were roaring, Captain Massey among them.

Agar scowled and turned his back.

As another round of *Spanish Ladies* started up, Francesca walked calmly away making sure not to limp.

When she reached her cabin she locked the door with trembling hands, all pretenses gone. She let out a stifled cry as she dropped to her cot, palms to her thigh, trying to staunch the bleeding. She jumped at a knock on her door. "Who is it?"

"'Tis the doctor, lass."

She unlocked the door. He helped her back to the cot and took a look at her leg. "Don't fret," he told her. "Et's nae as bad as all that."

"It hurts like the dickens."

The doctor smiled as he pulled out a bandage. "Maybe so, lass, but ye ded right. Miller came looking fer bandages. 'A man yer age should know better,' says I, 'than to affront a lady born tae the blade.' They'll mind their manners nou."

"Doctor," Francesca said folding her hands so he couldn't see them shake. "What do you know of that fellow, Mr. Agar?"

"He's a queer fish. Best gunner I've seen, but a bad man to cross. Why?"

Francesca took a breath. "He threatened me. He called me…" she felt her cheeks flame. "The Whore of Babylon. He said a woman who doesn't know her place must be cast out. Then he said a fall from the crow's nest or a tumble overboard, and God's work would be done."

The doctor eyed her over the top of his glasses with concern. "Did he nou?"

She nodded. He examined her face as if looking to see what effect this had had on her. Finally, he sniffed and said, "Well, lass, ye'd best watch yer back."

CHAPTER 14
THE JOURNEY

The next morning, Francesca gritted her teeth at the pain in her bandaged leg as she climbed into the rigging. She smiled at Old Nob's cheerfulness, despite the ache. She and her messmates worked the mainmast companionably, and after their shift, the crew made room for her at their breakfast table.

As she limped back onto deck, Carter, two of the other ship's boys, Rolly and Finn, and Miller, looking sheepish and hung over, scrambled to attention.

"They all wants lessons from Lady Blade," Carter said.

Francesca frowned. "I'm not a lady. My father was a swordsman, not a nobleman."

"Yer as close as we'll e'er get," mumbled Miller around the stem of his pipe. He took the pipe from his mouth with his bandaged hand. "Beggin' yer pardon, Miss, 'bout last night. Me mum, rest 'er soul, long maintained as I was part pig—on me father's side, a course."

Francesca chuckled at the apology. She liked Miller, despite the previous evening. His laughing blue eyes and red-splotched nose gave him a jolly air, and he had watched over Carter. She wondered how he had gotten so thick around the middle on the ship's questionable food. "No hard feelings, Miller." She waved a hand. "Well, men, line up."

Their swords were a sorry bunch of bent blades, but they would do. She got them into proper fencing stances despite Miller's protesting knees. She went to each in turn, rearranging their fingers on the grips, but Miller objected.

"Beggin' yer pardon, but I've been fightin' on an off fer nigh forty years. I always 'eld my blade this way and I ain't been dished yet." He held the pommel like a hammer, blade pointing toward the brilliant blue sky.

Francesca mused. "Then I must stand next to you in battle, since you find uncommonly slow enemies."

Miller scowled.

"Perhaps a demonstration is in order." Francesca faced off against Miller holding her blade as if it were an extension of her arm, pointed directly at his chest. "When you're ready," she said, "swing at me."

As he started his back swing she extended, putting her point to his chest before he even started his downward stroke.

Miller's arm dropped. "I sees yer point, Miss, decidedly so." He let Francesca rearrange his fingers on the hilt. "It'll take some gitt'n use to, but I imagine this ol' sea dog kin still learn a trick 'r two."

Francesca patted his shoulder. She started them on footwork: advancing, retreating, and crossing. And for the first time in months, she felt in her element.

As her recruits drilled, Francesca's mind drifted. For a moment, she was eleven years old again, peeking out of her second-story bedroom window, watching the fencing class below in the flagstone courtyard of Salle DiCesare.

Two dozen young men sweated under the bright sun. The maestro had walked among his pupils calling the drill and correcting a hand here, a lunge there. "Advance. Advance. Lunge. Retreat. Parry. Riposte."

Sebastian, lunging and advancing across the courtyard, had noticed Francesca in her window. He'd stuck his tongue out at her. She returned the gesture.

"Sebastian! Leave your sister be," the Maestro said. He faced the class. "Halt!"

They stopped, wiping sweaty faces and catching their breath.

The maestro shook his head. "Your blade work is dull, your footwork sloppy. Your hearts are not in it. You must learn more than footwork. You must learn the essence of fencing, of manhood, indeed, of life itself."

Antonio rolled his eyes. He'd heard the speech so often he could repeat it verbatim, as could she.

"What sets man apart from the beasts?" asked the maestro. "What is it that earns respect and authority? What makes us fit to sit at the knees of God in the hereafter?"

"Honor," whispered Francesca.

"Honor!" the maestro said. "Courage, strength, honesty, virtue, are but aspects of what?"

"Honor," Francesca murmured.

"Honor!" the maestro said. "And the art of the sword, the art that above all others embodies honor, I pound into your thick heads daily.

All of you," he continued, "are young men of either privilege or means. But privilege can be given, and it can be taken away. Means can be lost as well as won. There is only one treasure a man can hold that cannot be taken from him by fate or by force. There is only one thing that you will always be master of—your own honor. It is a treasure you must guard with vigilance and discipline. Mind your honor and you will always be rich men. Dismissed!"

Francesca shook away the memory. She could teach her pupils to fence, but she had small hope of instilling a sense of honor in pirates. There was only one type of treasure they were interested in.

Still, many of Papa's students might never use their swords. But Miller and the boys would need every ounce of skill she could give them to stay alive once they reached the Spanish Main.

———

After class she went below to the great cabin and knocked hesitantly on the door. One-eyed Kelsey answered it. "What do ya want?"

"I'd like to speak to the captain."

Kelsey frowned and turned toward Captain Massey who sat at the table eating lunch. The captain nodded.

Francesca entered feeling nervous and annoyed with herself for feeling that way. After all, she was the daughter of Maestro DiCesare.

The captain wiped his mouth and leaned back in his chair. "What is it, DiCesare?"

She squared her shoulders. "It's about the tattoo, Sir."

The captain nodded. "I thought as much."

She glanced at Kelsey who stood near the door pretending not to hear what was going on. The whole luck charade had been for him and the rest of the men. Francesca chose her words carefully. "The bad luck is gone, Sir. Is the tattoo necessary?"

"I'm afraid so."

"But, Captain, a tattoo is … unseemly."

He laughed. "And wielding a sword is ladylike?"

Francesca felt color rising in her cheeks. She seemed to always be blushing around him. "A sword can be set aside in polite company. A tattoo cannot."

The captain rose and approached Francesca. His eyes twinkled with amusement. He walked around her, examining her. "You're worried some future suitor from this 'polite company' might be put off by a bit of ink on your shoulder?"

Francesca glared at him. As much as he might belittle her concerns, a tattoo was a social stigma that would brand her forever as an outlaw.

The captain's eyes narrowed, and he twisted one corner of his mouth. "Or has one particular man of this 'polite company' caught your fancy?"

As Phillip's azure eyes and blonde hair leapt to mind, Francesca felt her blush deepen.

Sarcasm filled his voice. "I'm sure he's a paragon of honor."

She grit her teeth. "Compared to some."

The captain shrugged. "Then why isn't he here protecting your virtue?"

"Because he did as honor demanded. He sacrificed…"

"You?" he sneered.

"Everything." She turned away as longing for a life with Phillip swelled in her chest. "You wouldn't understand." She couldn't talk to this man. Even when she knew she was right, he made her feel confused and foolish.

The captain moved in front of her, fire in his eyes. "Aye, I don't understand. Nothing could have kept me from the woman I loved."

Francesca noted the past tense in his words. She imagined she saw tears gathering in his eyes, but instead they hardened to flint.

"Answer me this," he said. "If this suitor's ardor was shaken by such a trivial thing as a tattoo, would you still want him?"

Would Phillip have loved her less if she'd had a tattoo? Of course not. But she didn't want to concede the point. "That's not the issue."

"Of course it is," the captain scoffed. "Who else need ever see the tattoo?"

Francesca scowled. "I'll see it. I'll know it's there. I'll know what it means."

"And what will it mean?"

"That I'm an outlaw, an outcast."

A smirk crept across his face. "A pirate?"

Francesca pressed her lips tightly.

"Well," the captain said. "Aren't you?"

She dug her nails into her palms. She knew her argument was lost. She glanced at Kelsey. The corners of his mouth twitched. "Very well," she said, biting off the words.

———

That afternoon Tuit worked on the tattoo. He had spent hours chanting as he mixed a dark liquid with the ash of a strange nut he had burned, creating ink.

Francesca, shoulders tense, reluctantly rolled up her left sleeve. "Let's get this over with," she growled.

She, Tuit, and Carter sat on deck in the shade of the mainsail between two cannons.

Tuit studied her face. "To my people, tattoo great honor, mark of courage, respect."

She bunched her forehead, regretting her temper. It wasn't Tuit's fault she was being forced into this, and his serene face showed reverence for the process.

She resigned herself. "I'm sorry, Tuit. I meant no disrespect." She scanned the tattoos covering his skin. "At home, are you a great chief?"

Tuit thumped his bare chest. "Great warrior and hunter. Better than chief. More useful."

Francesca laughed. Apparently savages had bureaucracy, too.

Using a piece of charcoal, Tuit sketched a geometric band above her bicep, incorporating a stylized creature of mostly eyes and teeth. Once satisfied, he opened a leather pouch and laid out his tools. One held a short line of razor-sharp needles, bird bones perhaps, set into a long handle. The other tool was a short stick.

Tuit showed Carter how to stretch Francesca's skin taut so he could work on it. A few men gathered to watch. Tattoos were common among them, but they had never seen this method of tattooing.

Tuit dipped the line of needles in the ink and set them against Francesca's skin. She steeled herself. Tuit gave the rake a firm, quick tap with the stick, driving the needles into her flesh.

"Is it bad?" asked Carter as pinpricks of blood welled.

She exhaled. "Not as bad as I expected."

"Cracking!" said Carter, "Do ya think 'e'd gi' me one?"

"Ask him.,"

Carter watched Tuit strike the rake again. More blood oozed.

"Maybe later," mumbled Carter.

The process took hours. Most of the time Tuit hummed to himself, but occasionally they talked. They spoke Spanish since he understood more of that language. Francesca rambled on about Papa and home. Tuit seemed to understand but she wasn't sure.

At one point, he looked at her directly as he dabbed blood from her shoulder. "Tuit best to make women happy." His expression held no bravado. He was merely stating fact. "Excellent mate for Francesca."

It took her a moment to comprehend, then she suppressed a giggle, glad he had spoken in Spanish so Carter didn't understand.

Francesca had to admit, once she had gotten past the black bands across Tuit's face, he was quite handsome. His nose was straight and broad, his generous lips curled in a smile more often than not. His dark eyes held an enticing peacefulness, and she was not immune to his smooth, decorated skin or his gentle hands. She imagined tracing the tattoos swirling across his chest with her fingertips. Her eyes traveled along his strong jaw, broad shoulders, and silken black hair. She felt heat spread down her neck and chest.

Am I insane? He's practically a wild creature. But the thought did nothing to stop her skin from tingling. Finally, she cleared her throat. "Tuit would be an excellent mate indeed," she said. "But not for me."

If he was disappointed, he didn't show it.

"But I hope you will always consider me a friend."

He smiled. "Friend."

"Do you not have a woman at home?" she asked.

Tuit held up three fingers with a gleam in his eye. "All very happy."

Francesca laughed.

The weather warmed as the *Destiny* traveled south along the coast of Africa. By the end of the month the men had set aside their vests or jackets, to work in their shirtsleeves. Francesca sweated in a baggy, gray vest Carter had found for her. It hid some of her curves, minimizing unwanted attention.

Each morning at four bells Francesca awoke with one thought. *I'm closer to Phillip.*

Once she grew accustomed to work in the rigging, she enjoyed it. It was hard on the hands and feet, and she had to always be aware of the danger, but when she finished tying off canvas or loosing a sail, she loved to pause and feel the wind and marvel at the view. According to Old Nob, on a clear day they could see nearly fifteen miles from the top mast trees. Francesca didn't doubt it. And the immensity always filled her with awe.

Somewhere off of Mauritania the *Destiny* caught the trades—strong westward winds that seldom varied in direction or strength. For weeks the trades whisked them across the Atlantic. That was good news for the topmen. They had little work to do trimming the sails.

Early one morning, as Francesca and Carter sat unwinding old rope to be used for caulking the seams of the ship, there was a cry from the crow's nest. "Sail ho!"

A bolt of excitement ran around the ship. It was the first sail they'd seen in weeks.

Captain Massey shouted, "Where is she?"

"Two points off the larboard beam, Sir."

The captain trained a glass out to sea. "What's her nation?" he shouted.

Off duty pirates gathered at the rail staring into the distance.

"I 'ope they ain't Spanish," whispered Carter.

"Why?" Francesca said.

"Makes more work fer me an' ol' Barnacles."

"Why is that?"

The cry came from above. "She's Spanish, Sir!"

The words transformed Captain Massey. His eyes narrowed, his muscles tensed, and seething hatred flowed over his face.

"That's why," said Carter nodding toward the captain. "'E hates 'em somethin' fierce."

"Spaniards!" hissed the captain. "All hands! Clear the deck! After her!"

Francesca and Carter gathered up the pile of rope. "Why does he hate them?" Francesca asked.

Carter shrugged.

"Wear the ship!" shouted Mr. Baldric. "Topmen aloft!"

The bosun's whistle sounded and hands grabbed lines. Francesca and the other topmen hurried aloft to reset the sails.

Captain Massey watched his quarry. "Raise our standard!" he shouted. Then he gritted his teeth and spat, "Come fight me, you bastards!"

The Spanish ship fled, leading them on a three hour-long chase. But there was nowhere to hide on the open ocean. Finally, they approached within cannon range.

Agar's gun crews stood ready. "Ports!" shouted Agar.

The gun ports thumped open. "Starboard! Run 'em up sharp, or your backs'll smart for it." He carried a riding crop to back up his threat. The cannons rumbled forward.

"Across her bow, Mr. Agar!" the captain commanded.

"Forward gun!" shouted Agar. One gun bellowed. Smoke drifted across deck. They watched the shot fall into the water in front of the Spanish ship. She showed no sign of slowing.

The captain faced the crew. "See that, men?" He raised his voice. "Looks to me like she's beggin' for a set to."

The crew cheered.

"Come on then," shouted the captain. "Let's give it to her!"

The crew roared.

"Guns ready!" shouted Agar.

The gun crew hunkered down, ready to touch their burning slow-match to powder. Agar paused, waiting for the ship to come broadside.

Francesca, in the rigging with the topmen, awaited orders. Her heart pounded. From up there she could see the Spanish crew preparing the cannons. They had half the firepower of the *Destiny*, and they looked panicked. She knew exactly how they felt, like a calf being run down by a wolf.

But she also understood why the pirates cheered. Cold fear clutched at her belly, but excitement fluttered around the edges. There was exhilaration in shutting down the mind and giving oneself to the pure animal instinct of battle, and a part of her craved it.

That excitement, she realized in a horrifying flash, was the difference between predator and prey.

Papa's face, awash with disgust, appeared in her mind. Was she becoming the thing Papa hated? The thing that had taken her mother from her and nearly killed her in the womb. Was that what the captain had seen when he had called her a pirate? Had a month among these men turned her into a predator?

No. Her word bound her to the pirates and required her to help capture the ship, but she would do so on her terms. Somehow.

"Fire!" yelled Agar.

Smoke belched from cannons on both ships. Splinters and screams erupted on both sides. Fans of blood painted the decks red. She looked away. So much blood already and the battle had only begun.

A cannonball whistled by two feet below her, creating a perfect round hole in the sail. Her heart pounded harder, and her hands tightened on the rigging. Her eyes met Willy's and she sensed his matching fear.

Courage, said Papa's voice. She gave Willy a determined nod and he returned it.

Below, the gun crews reloaded their cannons. The ships were close now, yards apart. The *Destiny* began to pull ahead.

"Furl the mains'l!" shouted Mr. Baldric.

Francesca went into action. For a while she was too busy hauling and tying off canvas to watch what happened below. Another pair of broadsides thundered. The ship lurched, but she kept her eyes on her job. When she finished, grappling hooks held the Spanish ship.

"Now!" Mr. Baldric cried. Crewmen below pulled the belaying pins and the sails billowed loose. Francesca climbed up to the topsail to help gather it in and tie it off.

"Heave, men!" yelled the captain.

Pirates hauled on the grappling lines. The *Destiny* pitched sideways toward the Spanish ship, the masts swaying wildly. Francesca let out a cry as the world spun. She looked over at Willy again and wondered if her eyes were as frightened as his.

"C'mon, men!" shouted the captain. "Bring our prize home!"

The ship lurched again and again. With a wooden crash and the splintering of the rails, the ships met.

"Boarders away!" shouted the captain.

Pirates swarmed onto the Spanish ship. Francesca and the other topmen wrapped their ankles around backstays and lowered themselves, hand over hand down the tar-covered ropes. Francesca's bare feet landed on the deck. Her body quivered as she grabbed a sword from the weapons rack and headed toward the Spanish ship. She climbed the destroyed rail into chaos.

The fire of battle washed over Francesca, churning with her fear into an intoxicating mix. Instinct told her to rush into the fray beside her crewmates. She fought the urge. The Spanish weren't her enemies. She had to find a way to end the fight quickly.

She watched Captain Massey hacking his way through a group of

Spaniards. He wore his battle clothes, the red coat of a Spanish captain, shorn of sleeves and insignia. He slashed at the Spaniards with ferocious glee.

To her right, Tuit, in only his loincloth, wielding a six-foot spear, had cowed a bunch of Spaniards. A dark stain ran down one Spaniard's breeches.

Francesca spotted the Spanish captain on the raised quarterdeck, fighting with a pirate. *If the Spanish surrender, fewer lives will be lost.*

All else fell away. She rushed toward the quarterdeck, twisting through the writhing bodies, parrying. She mounted the steps in two leaps.

The axe-wielding pirate swung at the Spanish captain. The captain ducked aside, pivoting so his back faced Francesca. With a sword thrust, his opponent fell.

Francesca dropped her blade and pulled her pistol. She grabbed the captain from behind, pressing the pistol into his side. "Your ship or your life," she hissed in Spanish.

The captain struggled. Francesca cocked the hammer on her pistol and he stilled. "*Si, si,*" the captain said.

Francesca pressed him toward the edge of the quarterdeck, overlooking the writhing main deck. "Tell them!" she said.

"Give way men!" he shouted.

The fighting mass paid no heed.

"Louder!" Francesca pressed the pistol harder into his ribs.

"Stop fighting!" bellowed the captain in Spanish. "Surrender!"

Twice more he shouted. Eventually his men heard him. The Spaniards backed off from their opponents, dropping their weapons. The pirates halted, sides heaving.

Captain Massey, sword poised over an unarmed Spaniard, hesitated, tensed to strike, and then snarled in frustration. He dropped his sword arm and turned away. The battle was over.

All told, the Spaniards had lost fifteen of their complement of forty. Six more were wounded, two gravely. The pirates had lost five with seven more injured.

The Spanish ship was stripped bare, and the Spanish captain left with nothing but his breeches before they were allowed to raise sail and limp away. The haul was a good one, not the gold and jewels the pirates hoped for, but tobacco, spices, and dyes that would bring a good price at market. The goods were stowed, the ship repaired, and the decks cleaned all before nightfall.

As the sun faded, the tired *Destiny* crew rested on deck. Captain Massey, carrying a lantern, his face relaxed and jovial, addressed them. "Well done, men! We've a fine day's haul and plenty more fat merchantmen to follow." He addressed Francesca. "That was quick thinking, DiCesare. You may have saved some of these men's lives."

The company murmured in agreement.

The captain's eyes lingered on her as if he had something more to say, but he held his tongue.

Francesca thanked him, contemplating the captain's stormy eyes. She'd never before noticed how they crinkled when he smiled, or the curve of his lips.

Then she derided herself. What good were his compliments? And he wasn't nearly as handsome as Phillip.

Still, she was proud of herself. She had kept her word to help capture a ship while spilling no blood and preventing more bloodshed. Claire's words came to her: "Exactly how do you intend to maintain your honor among these brigands?" Well, she had done the best she could. Hopefully she could keep it up until they reached Jamaica. Then Phillip would help her find a way out of her predicament and she could finally rest.

CHAPTER 15
RÍO DE CAIMÁN

The next morning, as Francesca and her messmates were finishing breakfast, they heard the tweet of the bosun's whistle calling for "All Hands." She and a flood of crewmen climbed onto deck looking expectantly at the captain on the quarterdeck.

The captain raised his voice. "Good news, men! Last night, during first watch, we crossed the thirtieth parallel!"

A roar went up. Francesca turned to Miller with a blank expression.

"'E means we're better 'an halfway there."

Over halfway to Phillip! A tingle radiated all over her body.

The captain waited for them to quiet. "We're getting close men, and you know what that means. Keep your weapons sharp and a weather eye out for our next prize. They'll be coming fast and close from now on. Why, I've heard tell of industrious rogues taking two or three ships a day!"

Francesca gripped Miller's sleeve and whispered. "Do you think we'll stop at Port Royal soon?"

Miller laughed. "If we does, it'll be in chains."

She tilted her head. "In chains?"

"English navy's there," Miller said. "They've a nasty habit a' 'angin' pirates like us. They hoisted Calico Jack and Vane a few years back. Gallows been busy 'er since."

Her stomach dropped. "So, we won't go to Jamaica."

"Not iffen we gots a choice."

Francesca tried to stifle her disappointment, but it welled up as a wave of weakness. To be so close and never see Phillip. She held onto Miller's sleeve, light-headed.

The captain walked forward as a pirate spread a tarp on the deck that contained glittering golden plates and cups taken from the Spanish captain's quarters after the last battle.

Miller leaned toward Francesca saying softly. "Them togs oughta belong ta the cap'n by rights, but 'e likes ta 'and 'em out ta them as done good service."

The quartermaster, Mr. Angstrom, a giant Swede with a long face and a frizzy red mane, cleared his throat. "It's time to pass out a few pips from our last plum. Mr. Adams, step up."

A bald man with a bandaged eye came forward. Mr. Angstrom handed him an elaborately carved gold plate that glinted in the sun. In the center was an etching of a castle and around the rim swirled raised lilies. "This should cover the blinker."

Adams looked it over and ran his fingers along the flowers. "Aye, Sir, an' then some." He gave the captain a wry, toothless grin. "Don't worry Cap'n, a patch can't mar me looks none."

The crew laughed as Adams stepped back into place. The quartermaster picked up a cup. "DiCesare, step up."

Francesca didn't move. She knew what Papa would say. *Better to die with honor than to live with another man's goods.* The captain motioned her forward, but she shook her head. "No thank you, Sir," she said quietly, hoping they would move on.

"What's this?" asked Mr. Angstrom scratching his frizzled chin.

"Pardon?" the captain said.

The pirates gave her a quizzical stare.

"I'm sworn to help you capture these ships, Sir, but the Articles say nothing about accepting the loot."

The captain threw up his hands. "And if I order you to take it?"

Francesca crossed her arms, anger rising. It was none of his concern. Wasn't it enough that she fought his battles and risked her life for him? "I'll toss it over the side, Sir."

The captain's teeth clenched, and the men mumbled.

"She's tenpence to a shillin'," someone said.

She guessed from the way he said it, he was calling her either stupid or crazy. Her anger flashed hotter. "What's it to any of you if I don't want my share? That's more gold for the rest of you."

"Maybe so," said a man who Francesca thought was called Bigalow. He was broad and muscular but with a chubby, baby-like face. "But we don't want no one gettin' uppish or ridin' a 'igh 'orse just 'cause we want our chinkers."

The company mumbled in agreement.

"If you choose to thieve that's your business." Francesca felt the men tense. "At least have the stomach to call it what it is." She glared at their glowering faces. "But I'm not the one you'll answer to, and I've enough to answer for on my own." The fury leeched out of her. She added quietly, "You'll not hear a word from me."

That mollified the men. The quartermaster called the next name. But the captain's eyes bore into her, his mouth a tight line. Francesca couldn't imagine why he cared. According to Miller he'd done the same thing, giving away his "cut."

When Mr. Angstrom finished handing out prizes, the captain went below without a word. The pirates drifted back to their seats or their stations.

Carter turned to Francesca. "What's all 'at about?"

She stared after the captain. "I have no idea why he's upset."

"Not 'im, chucklehead," Carter said.

Francesca laughed. "I'm just doing as Papa taught me."

"Seems ta me, ya earned them beans."

Francesca leaned close. "I expect the Spanish captain those 'beans' belonged to would disagree with you."

Carter's eyebrows drew together, but he said nothing.

Over the next week they chased three more ships. A Dutch ship slipped out of reach as night descended, but they captured two Spanish ships. In both cases Francesca rushed the quarterdeck to force the Spanish captain to surrender. Each time he was dead when she reached him. Trapped on the enemy quarterdeck, unable to end the battle, she was forced to fight. Men died by her hand.

After the first battle she retreated to her cabin. She was not sure she believed in God anymore. How could He let an idiot like Tarrentino kill Papa and leave her in the hands of her enemies? But praying was all she could do for the souls she had killed. So, with tight lips she muttered prayers she had learned in another life.

She dreaded nightfall. The faces of the pirates she had killed in the first battle were bad enough. How much worse would it be when she saw the faces of innocent sailors who were protecting their ship?

This was what Claire had warned her about. But she went over all her decisions and couldn't see where she had gone wrong. She had always made the honorable choice.

The next day she bought a brown leather journal from the doctor. In it she kept track of all the lives and injuries she was accountable for—her *Book of Reckoning*. She had no names, but she remembered each face, their coloring and dress. Entries ran along the lines of:

August 26th, Taking the Santa Theresa
Ginger-haired man with green breaches—slash to the chest—may have lived
Square-jawed Spaniard with eyepatch—run through—RIP

Her journal didn't keep the ghosts at bay, but it helped.

Francesca paused one afternoon as she trained her recruits. Willy and two of Francesca's other messmates had joined, giving her seven pupils to drill.

She pushed damp tendrils of hair off her tanned forehead as she looked out to sea. They had passed inside the Caribbean Islands two weeks ago and now skirted along Costa Rica. The weather had grown hot and moist. Francesca had discarded her vest and sweated in her cotton shirt like the rest of the crew. The heat intensified the smell of tar, livestock, and sweat, but at least at the rail the breeze cut the odors. Three small fishing boats floated off the starboard side, not worth the effort to catch.

Francesca had reached the Spanish Main, but she still had to find Phillip. She could think of no way to convince the captain to visit Port Royal. Doing so would be dangerous. The captain was sure to become suspicious if she argued with him.

Plans to get to Port Royal swirled through her head, each more outlandish than the last. She considered them all, but always came back to the same thing. She had given her word not to abandon ship. Still, if she could just get to Phillip he would come up with a solution.

Well, if an opportunity presented itself, she would be ready. She would learn all she could about the Caribbean. Someone must have a chart that would show where Port Royal was. Miller might be able to teach her something about navigation, and the more she knew about seamanship the better. She was in the perfect place to learn.

Francesca ached for Phillip as she thought of the few intervening miles between them. Her eyes drifted to the soft waves caressing the side of the ship. Along the coast the water was an intense aquamarine. It was a glorious color, and every morning she discovered it all over again. Often in the afternoons she sat at the rail staring into the depths, longing fluttering in her chest. Nothing else was that color except Phillip's eyes.

A disturbance brought Francesca's attention back to her students. Adams, the swarthy bald man who'd lost an eye three weeks ago, climbed up the forward companionway. He held his etched golden plate in one hand. Shouting profanities, he made a beeline for Willy who stood unmoving, eyes huge. Adams grabbed the front of Willy's shirt and shook him and threw him to the deck as a crowd gathered.

Francesca stepped between them, setting a hand against Adams' chest. He shook his fist at Willy around Francesca's side. Willy got to his knees. The captain and Baldric pushed their way through the company.

"What is this?" the captain demanded.

"He stole it! The gutter blood stole it!" Adams's face turned purple as he shook the plate in front of the captain.

A tense murmur ran through the men.

"Calm yourself," ordered the captain.

Francesca knelt before Willy with a tight lump in her chest. Willy's head hung. She put a hand on his arm.

Adams took a deep breath, and his face lightened a shade as he grew calmer.

"Now," the captain demanded. "What happened?"

Adams hugged the plate etched with lilies to his chest. "Me plate. It went missin'. I remembered seein' the li'l sharp millin' 'bout me dunnage, so I op'ed 'is chest and there it were."

Willy's eyes didn't leave the deck. The gathering shifted uncomfortably. Old Nob pushed through the crowd, his face drawn. "'E's a good lad, Cap'n."

Francesca suddenly remembered the ship's Articles. Stealing from another pirate was punishable by death. The blood drained from her face and hands leaving them cold.

"Mr. Brown," the captain said. "Did you take the plate?"

No one stirred. Willy nodded almost imperceptibly.

"I'll be blowed!" swore Old Nob as everyone talked at once. Francesca put both hands on Willy's shoulders. "In God's name, why?"

Willy's eyes darted from face to face. "I never meant ta keep it. I just wanted ta look at it, then Mr. Baldric called fer all hands. I stowed it in me locker 'til I could put it back. 'Til e'ryone was asleep."

"So 'e says," shouted Adams. "'Ow do we know what 'e meant?"

"Me mum," Willy said. "Her name was Lilly."

Francesca's breath whooshed out.

"They was—"

"Sail ho!"

No rush sizzled through the pirates as usual. They stood silent, downcast, and some held their hats in hand, as though Willy was already dead.

Captain Massey turned to Mr. Baldric and said quietly, "Lock him up." Then he pushed through the crew back toward the quarterdeck. "Bearing!" he shouted.

"Hull down, two points off our starboard bow, Sir!"

"General quarters!" barked the captain. The bosun's whistle blew and the men shoved their hats on their heads and rushed to their stations.

Francesca climbed into the rigging with her mind racing. Would the captain condemn Willy to death? He was just a boy. He'd made a mistake. Certainly the captain would be lenient. But in her mind, she saw Willy, neck askew, hanging from a noose.

Another cry came from the crow's nest. "Four ships, captain!" There was a long pause. "Spanish warships!"

Francesca and her crewmates froze. A rush ran through them snapping their necks around—fear.

The captain's body tensed and the familiar mask of hatred descended. "Raise our colors and luff up, Mr. Hart, two points to starboard."

The company stared at the captain, shocked. Baldric stopped in his tracks, his hand on Willy's sagging shoulder. "But Cap'n, that's four ta one!"

He growled. "One man can beat four dogs any day."

The men swore under their breath.

"Cap'n, we're out-gunned and out-manned," Baldric said.

The crew didn't move, but their heads tilted forward, and their shoulders set.

Francesca's eyes snapped between the men and the captain, then out at the huge ships cresting the horizon.

Carter had explained that a pirate captain was elected by the men. He led by virtue of their faith in him and with their cooperation. He couldn't force them into this battle, not if he wanted to remain captain.

Seconds ticked by. Captain Massey's face writhed. "Bollocks!" he shouted at the sky. Then his face relaxed into his usual calm composure. "Very well. Bring us around. And Mr. Hart, get me the chart."

The crew set to work with desperate speed. The ship came about, sending a spray of saltwater over the deck. The sails billowed. Mr. Hart, the sailing master, hurried to the captain's side, charts in hand.

Mr. Hart looked every inch the naval officer he had once been with his set jaw, an air of authority, and careful attention to every detail of dress. Francesca had not heard why he left the navy, but it was not lack of competence. He knew how to get every bit of speed from a sail and exactly how far he could push the *Destiny*. Francesca was grateful they had him as she glanced out at the ships plowing down on them.

"Here." The captain pointed at the chart. "Head South. We'll make for this river, the Río de Caimán. We'll sit this dance out, if we must.

Despite their size, the Spanish warships matched the *Destiny's* speed. She fled with every stitch of sail she could take, but she couldn't lose the ships over the horizon. They dogged her, hour after hour, all day. The more the crew thought about the firepower chasing them, the tenser they became.

Estimates were that the largest Spanish ship carried fifty cannons, which probably threw eighteen-pound balls. The two slightly smaller ships likely carried thirty guns each. Even the smallest probably had double the *Destiny's* firepower.

There was little talk, only nervous fidgeting and eyes inexorably drawn to the warships. Francesca knew the same thing was on all their minds—odds four to one, out-gunned, and out-manned.

In the late afternoon, a cheer went up as the river mouth appeared in the distance, a wide slit in hills of blue green. But they were not safe yet. The river delta, with its maze of sandbars stood between them and the cover of the jungle. If they grounded, they'd be staved in by the cannons.

The captain sent the ship's best lookout up the foremast. Standing on the crow's nest, he leaned out toward the prow yelling directions, guiding the helmsman through the delta by the deepest channel. For those on deck, staring down the warships' guns, it was an excruciatingly slow process.

Francesca, off duty, had nothing to do but watch and will the *Destiny* to move faster. Her shoulders tightened as the warships closed the distance.

Smoke puffed aboard the nearest ship. The report followed a second later and then a cannonball sent up an enormous geyser of water close astern. Spray misted her face. A couple hits by cannonballs that size, and the *Destiny* would be done for.

"Furl the sails! Sweeps out!" yelled the captain.

Francesca saw that the fourth-watch topmen had the sails in hand, so she went to help with the sweeps. As they hauled the long oars from the hold and thrust them out the oar-ports, another pair of geysers blossomed to starboard. Men hauled on their oars as more fountains sprouted around them. A cannonball smashed the starboard stern lantern sending out a shower of glass and splinters.

"Buckle to!" shouted the captain. "Give 'er all you've got! Pull!"

The *Destiny* shot forward with each stroke, finally reaching the river mouth. As palm trees closed around them, they could see the warships dropping anchor.

As the rowers heaved at the oars, the ship moved upriver. The crew's tension melted away.

The river worked its lazy way through dense forest. The hot, green darkness felt claustrophobic after the open glare of the sea. Hundred-foot-tall trees spread lace against the fading sky. The smell of damp earth encompassed them. Francesca closed her eyes, drawing in the scents of flowers and plants and the sounds of animals and birds calling through the foliage. She hadn't realized how much she had missed land.

She opened her eyes. Carter was standing in exactly the same pose with eyes shut, nose raised, mouth slightly open. "Golly," he said.

Francesca chuckled and Carter opened an eye and scowled. "Bugger off."

She smiled. "I know exactly how you feel."

Carter's face darkened. "What'll they do with Willy?"

Francesca looked toward the quarterdeck, a hard knot forming in her stomach. "I don't know." She watched the captain pace, his face flinty and his lips tight. Most likely he was pondering the same question.

After a half hour Francesca spotted small, planted beds of vegetables on shore, squares of greenery identifiable by the slightly more orderly pattern than the riot around them.

The river widened at a sharp bend, spreading into a lake twenty yards wide and twice as long. The *Destiny* could go no farther.

On the starboard bank was a clearing that the plants seemed intent on taking back. Greenery massed at the edges, crowding inward. A group of nine thatched huts hunched in the center as if shying away from the encroaching wilderness.

"Leave off!" yelled the captain to the sweat-drenched oarsmen. They dropped their oars.

Francesca stared shoreward consumed with curiosity and apprehension. When she was young, her brothers had told her tales by flickering candlelight of cannibals in the jungles of the New World. She had only half believed them, until now.

The huts seemed deserted except for a few goats staring at the ship and a handful of chickens scratching in the dirt.

The underbrush to the right of the village moved. Sunlight glinted off the barrel of a musket. As her eyes adjusted, Francesca saw a dozen black men dressed in rags watching them from the forest.

They'd escaped the Spanish into the hands of savages. A couple men held muskets, most wielded makeshift spears. They seemed ready to melt into the foliage at any moment.

Another movement caught her eye. Frightened, dark-faced women and children peeked from behind the huts. Suddenly the savages didn't seem so threatening.

Baldric, Agar, and Captain Massey, at the rail not far from Francesca, watched the village.

"Them heathens would fetch a good price, Sir," Agar said.

A frown ran across the captain's face. "Belay that, Mr. Agar." He turned toward the crew. "Stow the sweeps. Drop anchor! Mr. Baldric, away a boat. Mr. Hart, attend."

Captain Massey and Mr. Hart went below. Francesca followed. This was her chance to convince him to spare Willy if she could. She searched for what to say, but her thoughts were still a jumble when she knocked on the open door to the great cabin.

The captain and Mr. Hart rummaged through a pile of maps.

"Captain, may I have a word?" Francesca said.

The captain glanced at her, then handed an armful of charts to Mr. Hart with a nod. Mr. Hart ignored Francesca as he passed and moved up the companionway. The captain waved Francesca in.

"Sir—"

He held up his hand. "I know what you're going to say. He's just a boy. He made a mistake. I know. But my hands are tied. He's over sixteen and he signed the Articles."

Francesca paused, her mind whirling though defenses. "He didn't mean to keep it."

"But he did."

"Only until…" She saw his hard look and knew that line of argument was useless. She took another tack. "Did you know his mother's name was Lilly? That she died when he was six? Do you know what's on that plate?"

"Then he should have bought it or bartered for it, or asked to see it," the captain said, anger in his voice.

She was out of arguments. She drew near and put a hand on his arm. *Pride be damned.* She pleaded with her eyes. "Please." She saw pain in his face.

"You'd be the first to point out that this is a ship full of cutthroats." He bit off the words. "The only thing keeping the men from each other's throats is discipline—harsh, swift discipline. No exceptions." He pushed past her and headed out.

Francesca emerged on deck, her eyes searching for the captain. He disappeared down the ship's side. She hurried to the rail. Mr. Hart and two rowers were already in a longboat. As the captain settled in, he said to Baldric at the rail. "Muffle the ship while we're away."

"Aye, Sir."

With a sinking feeling, Francesca watched the boat row to shore. She'd failed Willy.

The crew gathered to watch the black men along the tree line. The village men tensed and paced, panther like, muskets aimed at the longboat.

A spike of fear raced through Francesca. She wanted to call out, but the captain raised a hand and shouted a few strange words. The black men nodded and answered.

Francesca frowned. It wasn't Spanish. *Could it be some African tongue?* Here was another puzzle. Whatever the captain said, the villagers lowered their muskets. The captain and Hart leapt ashore. The black men motioned them toward the largest of the huts.

As they disappeared inside, Mr. Baldric faced the crew. "Ya heard the cap'n, muffle the ship!"

All through the humid evening, the crew worked covering anything reflective and muffling or oiling anything noisy aboard ship. They draped the furled sails in canvas painted black with tar, and even painted out the red and gold stripes that graced the ship's sides. The mood was tense as they worked.

Francesca, with Carter and Miller, watched the huts anxiously. They hung over the rail, painting the metal chains and deadeyes at the bottom of the shrouds with tar.

"Ain't we gonna hafta strip this 'ere tar off ag'in?" said Carter, grumbling.

"No doubt," Miller said.

"Then what are we doin' it for?"

"I expects the Cap'n is plannin' on slippin' past 'em warships in the dark," Miller said. "And these are right reflective. They might give us away."

"Slippin' past?" Carter's eyes grew large. "With them big ships lookin' for us? Is 'e daft?"

"Ya gots a better plan?"

"Can't we just wait fer 'em ta bugger off?"

"I doubt they're going anywhere." Francesca rolled her shoulders, trying to release the knots. "Not when they have us so neatly trapped."

"Will they come after us tonight?" asked Carter.

"I doubts it," Miller said. "A man don't go into a hole after a snake. 'E waits fer the snake ta show its snout. Naw, they'll wait, 'specially iffen they 'ave an inkling them ones are 'ere," he said with a nod toward the huts.

"Who are they?" asked Francesca.

"Maroons, I'll warrant. Slaves 'scaped from the Spanish. Word is there are warrens like this 'idden all o'er these lands."

"He's been there for hours. They must have a good deal to talk about."

"Aye," Miller said. "They's probably the only ones who hate the Spanish as much as the Cap'n."

"Why does he hate them so?"

Miller removed his pipe. "The Spanish claim the Main for 'emselves. They ruin any other colony they find."

"Yes," Francesca said. "But the English do the same farther north."

"Aye, but the English didn't murder 'is wife and child and give 'im them ruddy big scars on 'is back."

"Look," Carter said, "there 'e is."

Captain Massey emerged from a hut with a dignified, graying black man. Hart trailed behind with an armful of charts. The captain and the black man shook hands, and the captain turned toward the *Destiny*.

No wonder he hated the Spanish. *A husband and father.* That explained his "no *living* woman" remark. Perhaps she could use that, play on his sympathies. What if Willy were *his* son. She had to admit, she had never imagined him settled. There was so much restless energy about him. The more she learned, the more of a mystery he became.

She noticed Miller grinning crookedly at her and realized she'd been stroking her face with her fingertips as she watched the captain. She probably had black paint trailed across her cheek. She wiped her face with her sleeve.

"A gal could do a heap worse," Miller said, hitching his head toward the captain.

"He's a pirate."

"Aye," laughed Miller. "But better men than he 'ave gone pirate with less cause."

"What are ya yappin' about?" Carter said.

"Nothing," Francesca said, going back to work.

When the captain came aboard, he went straight to his cabin, pausing only long enough to announce, "The hanging is at dawn."

Francesca followed him, but he had left word with Kelsey that he was not to be disturbed.

CHAPTER 16
LOST

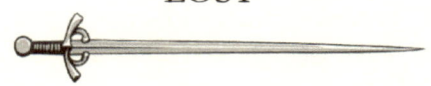

The *Destiny* spent the night under the canopy of trees. Francesca tossed, unsettled by the ship's stillness, plagued by the thought of Willy waiting to die. The captain was right. Discipline had to be maintained, but the punishment was out of proportion to the crime. Or perhaps it was her guilty conscience thinking how she had cheated the noose after killing Tarrentino.

Her body flailed as thoughts spun. Finally, she got up. Willy shouldn't spend his few remaining hours alone. She pulled on her clothes, lit a lantern, then opened her door and peered out. She saw no one but heard the rustling of men in the infirmary tossing and turning. It seemed few were sleeping well tonight.

She made her way down the companionway to the lower deck, then forward, through the hold which was crowded with barrels and crates.

The ship's "brig" was the pitch locker, a closet where barrels of tar, buckets, and brushes were stored. It was seldom used as a brig since the captain generally disposed of prisoners quickly, one way or another. There was no security other than the lock on the door.

The tar smell scratched her throat as Francesca approached the barred window. Willy took his head from his hands and looked up with red rimmed eyes. He stepped to the door. "Francesca."

"I didn't want you to be alone." She put a hand through the bars.

"Thanks," he said, taking it. His jaw muscles tightened in an effort to stop his mouth from trembling. He looked so young with his patchy beard and smooth cheeks that not even work in the rigging had hardened. Francesca opened her mouth but nothing came out. She wanted to offer some hope, but what was there to say?

Willy seemed to sense her thoughts because he dropped his eyes and turned away. "I s'pose it were bound ta end in a noose 'ventually. But I wish it were the law hanging me 'stead of me own kind. It'd be a bit easier ta take."

"I talked to the captain, tried to convince him. He doesn't want to…"

Willy nodded. "Aye, 'e told me so 'imself. I knows 'e's got to. I don't 'old it against 'im."

"How can you defend him? He's condemned you to death!" Francesca's tears welled.

"Don't be startin' that," Willy said, wiping his nose on his sleeve. "I can't hardly stand it ta 'ave someone cryin' fer me. I know I done wrong. It's me own fault. Dis'onorable, that's what *you'd* call it."

"I don't care." Francesca grabbed the iron bars. She just wanted him alive. She pulled at the bars. Of course it was locked. But she knew who had the key and where he kept it.

A week ago, she'd followed Mr. Pitt, the master carpenter, to his cabin, trying to convince him to dull some old swords to serve as practice weapons. Mr. Pitt, who was generally overworked, had refused, but she had seen him hang his keys on a hook just inside his door. He was in charge of the pitch locker so the key would likely be there. No one had seen her come. No one would know if …

Her tears stopped and her face hardened. She looked around carefully, then squeezed Willy's hand. "I'll be back."

She made her way towards the six tiny cabins on the aft hold platform. She heard nothing but the footsteps on watch two decks above and the scurrying of a few rats. When she reached the platform, she set down the lantern and tiptoed onward. She stopped outside Mr. Pitt's cabin and listened to his deep, resonant rumblings. *This must be a sign.* She held her breath as she twisted the handle on his door. It yielded easily. *Another sign.* She reached a hand in and gently searched the wall. Her fingers curled around the cold metal of the keys, lifting them from the hook.

Willy was still at the door when she returned. His eyes flew wide when he saw what she held. "What are ya doin'?" he hissed.

"Getting you out of here."

"Are ya daft? Ya'll be swingin' beside me."

"Hush." Francesca tried the keys. The third one worked, and the lock *snicked* open. She opened the door carefully remembering that it had a tendency to squeak.

"What do I do now?" asked Willy.

"Go over the side, quietly, swim for shore."

"But…"

"You can do it. You'll have to hide until we're gone." She blew out the lantern.

"Then what?" Willy said with a trembling voice.

Francesca searched around in the blackness and put a hand on Willy's shoulder. "Live."

Francesca rose the next morning with dread in her chest. She hadn't slept. She'd been so sure about letting Willy go, but as soon as she lay down, doubts set in.

Papa would say she had undermined the captain's authority, had gone against her oath, and had acted dishonorably. She imagined the disappointment in his eyes, the look that twisted her heart like nothing else could. But would Papa let Willy die? He hadn't wanted her to die for killing Tarrentino. He had insisted she run—a dishonorable act. But it was Tarrentino's dishonorable act that had forced her to kill him. Still, Willy's actions were miniscule in comparison. Her thoughts churned in a loop until she wanted to scream.

She also realized what she had condemned Willy to. In her rush to set him free she had left him alone on a hostile shore, perhaps to die a slow, painful death from starvation or disease. She should have at least given him a weapon or some money, but she'd left him with nothing but the clothes on his back.

When she stepped on deck for her shift, men scurried about, preparing for the hanging she knew wouldn't happen. The captain paced the quarterdeck, a mug of coffee in hand. From his drawn face she guessed he hadn't slept either.

A crewman rushed to the captain and whispered in his ear. She thought she saw a flash of relief before the captain's brows shot down and his face went red. His smoldering eyes met hers. Guilt sent heat rising in her face and she turned away to hide it.

"All hands!" shouted the captain. The bosun's whistle blew and groggy sailors flooded the deck a few seconds later. The captain's voice was harsh. "Men, Mr. Brown has escaped."

The crew mumbled and Francesca tried to catch their mood. She couldn't tell if they were relieved or angry.

The captain went on. "Find him. Third watch, search the larboard bank. Fourth watch take starboard. He can't have gone far in this jungle. Dismissed!"

The captain went ashore. Francesca stood her watch, but there was little to do beyond splicing a few fraying ropes, scrubbing the decks, and waiting to hear the call that meant they had captured Willy.

Three hours into her watch, Mr. Angstrom ordered Old Nob's crew to fill the water casks. Francesca was thrilled. That meant going ashore! She might be able to find Willy. She rushed to her cabin, tied on her sash, and stuffed a pistol, ammunition, and what money she had left into it. If she found Willy, at least she could give him that much.

She joined her messmates hauling empty water barrels up from the hold. They loaded eight barrels into the longboats and headed for the river's edge. They paddled upstream from the village to find cleaner water. They paused at two spots where the bank ran smoothly into the river, but alligators sunned themselves on shore. They kept going. After half an hour they found a small stream gurgling over a pile of rocks into the river. They pulled the boats in.

It was the first time in months Francesca had stood on solid earth. It felt spongy beneath her feet. She was so accustomed to the sway of the ship that now the ground swayed instead.

Old Nob saw her grab at a nearby branch and grinned. "Yer land-legs'll come back in a hour or two."

"I hope so." Stumbling around as though drunk, she'd never be able to find Willy.

She and Nob followed the stream inland a dozen paces and found a pool deep enough to fill the barrels. Water trickled down a two-foot waterfall into the pond. Nob knelt and scooped water into his hand. He sniffed, then drank.

Francesca wondered if Willy could have made it this far without a boat. She doubted it. He knew there were alligators. He would have gotten out of the water as quickly as possible, but he wouldn't want to leave the bank—he might get lost in the jungle, and he would need to drink. If she headed back toward the ship along the bank, she might find him.

"DiCesare!"

She looked at Nob. "I'm sorry, what did you say?"

"I said, this 'll do. Go git the men."

Francesca nodded and headed toward the longboat, then she turned back to Old Nob. He had been fond of Willy. Maybe he would let her go find him.

"What's the hold up?" he said.

"Willy's out there all alone."

"Aye." Nob's face was lined with worry.

Francesca looked around to make sure they were alone. Then she patted the pistol and powder in her sash. "He might have need of these."

Nob froze, his eyes on her face wary. He looked around too, then nodded. "Well, what are ye wait'n fer."

Francesca plunged into the jungle angling back toward the river. After a few paces the foliage made it impossible to tell which direction was which. She paused. It would do no good to get lost. Through the bird calls and rustling she heard the voices of her crewmates. Keeping the voices on her right, she hurried on.

Before long she was at the river's edge. She stayed inside the line of trees and headed back toward the Maroon village. She stopped every few yards and called softly, "Willy! It's me, Francesca!"

She saw no one, though she could occasionally hear the *Destiny* search crews calling through the brush in the distance.

At one point she startled a group of howler monkeys munching fruit in the trees. They were large, about the size of a five-year-old child. Their sudden, booming howls made her jump. Her heart raced as the creatures rushed away through the canopy, branches whipping under their weight.

As she moved on, she became aware of a pair of eyes watching her. She froze. A form materialized out of the jungle. He was one of the Maroons, a tall, broad, black man whose ragged clothing had been disguised against the trunk of a tree. He held a spear, and his face was pulled into a mask of hatred. Francesca stepped back and pulled her pistol. It was unloaded, but he didn't know that. She wished she had her sword.

Then another face materialized to her left. Then another. All of them held that look of rage. They spoke in their strange tongue, but Francesca caught two Spanish words, *Spanish* and *spy*.

Francesca's body went cold as the men advanced toward her. She took a step back and held up her hands. She set the pistol on the ground. There was no time to load it anyway and she needed to convince them she was not a threat. "I'm not Spanish, and I'm not a spy," she said in Spanish.

They continued toward her with their spears pointed at her chest.

Perhaps speaking Spanish was not the best way to convince them she wasn't Spanish. "Please," she said in English. "I'm not a spy. I mean you no harm."

One of them shouted and they rushed toward her.

Francesca fled, her heart thumping. Branches and leaves slapped her face, ripped at her hair and clothes.

Arms wrapped around her midriff and a body thudded into her back. She fell to the damp ground with someone on top of her. She tried to writhe out from under the weight. Her head was yanked backwards by the hair. She cried out. A knife flashed toward her throat.

"Parada!" boomed a deep voice.

The blade stopped inches from her neck. No one moved or said a word. The only sound was her ragged breathing. She tried to turn her head, but her hair was held too tightly.

The man on top of her spoke in his foreign tongue. Again, Francesca caught the word *Spanish*.

"And how do you know this?" the deep voice said. It was musical, mixing Spanish with something more exotic.

"She spoke Spanish," said one of the other men.

"I speak Spanish," the deep voice said. "Does that make me a spy?"

"No, Akinsanya," said the man on top of her, but he didn't move.

"Have the Spanish ever sent a woman spy?" the deep voice said.

"No, Akinsanya," said someone else.

"Let her up."

The hand released her hair and the pressure on her back disappeared. Francesca wobbled to her feet, facing the men. They held their spears ready.

The man who had saved her stood with his arms crossed. He held himself with confidence and authority. His shrewd eyes scanned Francesca. He gave an unfriendly smile, his teeth flashing against wide, dark lips. He wore buckskin trousers and an open vest with no shirt underneath. He was the leader of the Maroons, the man she had seen shaking hands with the captain the previous evening.

"Who are you?" he said in Spanish.

"My name is Francesca DiCesare. I'm a crewman on the *Destiny*."

Skepticism was plain in their narrowed eyes.

"I'm a topman, second watch, Old Nob's mess, honestly."

Their expressions did not change.

"Name the captain and sailing master."

"William Massey is our captain and Mr. Hart is our sailing master."

The leader nodded. "And where have you come from?"

"I joined the crew in England. I don't know where they came from before that," Francesca said.

"What is the name of the escaped man?"

"Willy Brown."

The leader spoke to the others in their native tongue. They lowered their spears and Francesca heaved a sigh.

The leader gave a command and the others disappeared into the jungle. He approached Francesca, extending a hand. She shook it. "Thank you for saving my life."

A genuine smile lit up his dark eyes. "You may call me Juan. I am sorry if they frightened you."

Francesca rubbed the back of her head where it felt as if a handful of hair had been ripped from her scalp. "No harm done."

"We have never heard of a woman pirate. But these are strange times. Why are you alone in the jungle?"

Francesca hesitated. Should she tell him her goal? He might turn her over to the captain. On the other hand, he was an escaped slave, so he must know what it was like to be hunted and to be under a death sentence. He might understand. And the Maroons had a much better chance of finding Willy since they knew the area and were accustomed to the jungle. She had to take the chance.

"I was looking for Willy, the boy who escaped."

Juan frowned. "Alone?"

"Yes, well, he was a friend. I didn't want to capture him, I wanted to give him something."

Juan's frown deepened. "You would disobey your captain?"

Francesca took a breath. "In this case, I must. The penalty far outweighs the crime. It's not fair that he die for what he did."

"Your captain has explained the situation."

"Then you understand."

"I understand this is none of my concern."

"Please," Francesca said. "I need your help."

Juan shook his head. "My people say, if you do not step on the dog's tail, he will not bite you. Your ship is a very large dog."

"Please," Francesca urged. She took out the last of her money. "You need do nothing until we leave. All I wish is to leave some things for Willy. I have a pistol and shot and some money." She held the money out toward Juan.

"And what if we never see this man? What if he has already fed the alligators?"

"Then it's yours. Use it to help your people."

Juan tilted his head. "You would trust me?"

Francesca shrugged. "Your people trust you. And you are Willy's only chance."

He looked hard at Francesca a moment, then took the money. "Very well. I will hold it for this Willy Brown, if he lives."

Francesca took the shot and powder from her sash and handed them over. "I had a pistol, but I set it down."

They retraced her steps and found the gun. Juan tucked it into the waistband of his pants. "What will you do now?"

"Find the men I came with."

"Will they not wonder where you have been?"

She smiled. "I'll tell them I went to relieve myself and got lost."

Juan laughed. "And they will believe that?"

"They have a very low opinion of me."

"Then they are fools," Juan said. He bid her farewell and Francesca headed back the way she had come.

She found her companions filling the second to last barrel. They accepted her excuse, ribbing her about getting lost. Nob noticed the missing pistol in her sash and gave her a tiny nod. She helped them roll the barrels back to the longboat and load them aboard.

All the way back to the ship Francesca stared into the jungle, hoping to get a glimpse of Willy, and hoping she'd done the right thing.

The *Destiny's* search parties eventually returned, streaming with sweat and scratching at mosquito bites, empty handed. Francesca wondered how hard they had searched. She doubted any of them wanted to see Willy hang.

Late that afternoon Juan approached the ship. Two black men, bare to the waist, sun gleaming from their chocolate skin, propelled a canoe toward them.

The crew gathered as Juan climbed up the side. Francesca noticed Agar's hand stray to his pistol. The captain approached the rail and helped Juan aboard. "Welcome."

The man sniffed and rubbed his nose, apparently unaccustomed to the harsh smells aboard a sailing ship. His shrewd eyes scanned the crew and rested momentarily on Francesca.

He faced the captain. "Capitán, we have found no sign of your missing man, but our hunters met a party of Spaniards this afternoon. They came from the sea."

No wonder they thought I was Spanish.

"They will never report back," Juan said.

"Thank you," the captain said.

Juan had a gleam in his eye. "Our pleasure."

The pirates chuckled and Francesca shivered, remembering the knife at her throat.

"What will you do now?" asked Juan. "They will send more soldiers next time." His hand swept wide including the ship and the river bend. "You are up a tree without a monkey's tail."

The captain chuckled. "Indeed we are, but we had little choice. We must sneak past the warships. The moon rises late tonight. At least we will have darkness on our side."

"And your missing man?"

The captain shrugged. "He belongs to the jungle now."

Juan's eyes flicked briefly to Francesca.

Tuit took a step forward. "Capitán, a storm comes. I feel it, here." He thumped his bare torso.

The captain looked at the clear blue sky. "Let's hope your chest is right."

The wind arrived as evening darkened, whipping the trees into frenzied whorls of green and filling the air with the smell of leaf mold and wet earth. The crew worked the *Destiny* downstream, just short of the river mouth, and waited for the light to fade.

According to Miller, the plan was for two longboats full of oarsmen to tow the *Destiny* past the waiting Spanish warships. Sails, he explained, would be too conspicuous, even in the dark, and the ship's sweeps too noisy.

As the last of the light faded, the captain headed for one of the longboats waiting at the side. His eye caught Francesca's and he changed course, approaching. He leaned down and whispered in her ear.

"I won't say I'm not relieved, but if you ever, *ever* disobey my orders again, it'll be you swinging."

Francesca looked up at him, startled. The captain walked away and descended to the first longboat.

"Cast off," he called. The rowers took up oars and bent their backs to them.

Francesca felt the ship move forward. They were on their way. She took her station by the starboard shrouds. Usually, Willy would be to her right; she missed him keenly.

So, the captain knew what she had done, or had guessed. Or had Juan told him of their meeting? In any event, she felt a mixture of relief and guilt. She was glad it was dark so no one could see the look on her face.

The Spanish ships were anchored as near to shore as the ocean depth would allow, their positions marked by four sets of lights twinkling atop the water like earthbound stars. The captain aimed the *Destiny* straight for them— he had no choice. Sounding for depth in the shallows would be noisy and time consuming, and running aground would be fatal. He must head directly for deep water, even though it meant sneaking between the Spanish ships.

Francesca made out the vague forms of crewmates shifting their weight from foot to foot and nervously rubbing their hands together.

As the lights drew closer, all movement stilled aboard the *Destiny*. They barely breathed, but the ship was far from silent. There was an occasional small splash from the rowers in the longboats ahead of the ship. The hull creaked, waves slapped against the *Destiny's* side, and the strengthening wind whistled through the rigging.

As they neared the warships, the sets of lights drew apart, three to larboard, one to starboard. Francesca heard snippets of Spanish voices whipped on the wind. It was difficult to judge distance in the dark, but she guessed the starboard ship was no more than twenty yards away. When the warship's bell rang to mark the hour, she jumped, her heart skipping wildly.

Cool rain spattered across Francesca's shoulder, and she gave mute thanks. It would help hide the ship.

She caught voices coming from the *Destiny*. She tried to locate them and nearly ran into the metal vent pipe that rose from the cooking stove in the forecastle below. The voices grew louder. She glanced anxiously toward the Spanish ship. They might give them away! Francesca felt her way toward the companionway and headed below.

As she descended the stairs, the banked-down coals glowing from the stove vaguely silhouetted a few men. She stopped on the last step when she recognized Agar's rumbling voice. "I tell ya he's gone soft. First 'e brings a bloody woman aboard. Now 'e let that boy go. He ain't willing ta do what needs doing. And now 'ere we are creepin' away with our tail 'tween our legs. Ain't no fit cap'n."

Francesca gulped. They were talking mutiny and it was partly her fault for letting Willy go. She had understood discipline needed to be maintained, but she hadn't realized how fragile the peace was.

"And who would ya stand fer cap'n?" said a voice she didn't recognize.

"Why, Mr. Agar, a' course," said Hal's nasal voice.

Panic speared through Francesca. It was too horrible a thought. Captain Massey might be a pirate, but at least under his command there were no bloody slaughters of weaponless men and no raping of women, and he had not treated Claire and Belle unkindly. Agar's threat leapt to mind. There'd be no one to protect her if he took control.

"You're the cowards," Francesca said, keeping her voice low though she wanted to yell. "Plotting and scheming in the dark." Their silhouettes turned toward her. She drew her sword. "The captain would have taken on all four of those ships if we had let him." A pistol cocked, but she knew they wouldn't risk shooting her with the Spanish warships so close.

"'Tis true," said another voice she couldn't place.

"The captain has brought you riches and kept you safe," she went on.

"Aye," said the first unknown voice.

One of the silhouettes left the stove and approached. She twisted her sword hoping it would catch the light from the stove. Apparently it worked, because the figure stopped.

"Ya gutter bloods gonna listen to a woman?" hissed Agar. "'E's gone soft, I tell ye. 'E let the thief go."

"He did not let Willy go," whispered Francesca. She moved up a step.

"How do you know?" snapped Hal.

"I saw him escape," Francesca said, retreating another step.

The men chuckled. "An' 'eld yer tongue. Proper li'l pirate yer turnin' into," Hal said. "Disobeyin' orders when ya please."

"Now you know my secret and I know yours. I suggest we all keep our mouths shut." Francesca didn't wait to hear more. She hurried up the companionway.

Francesca looked around for the lights of the Spanish ships. They were dimmer through the rain, behind the *Destiny*, but still close. She moved back to her station to watch the lights fading and disappearing into the darkness and the rising seas. She put a hand to her forehead. *It's my fault they were talking mutiny. That's what comes from acting dishonorably.*

Yet she didn't regret letting Willy go.

CHAPTER 17
THE STORM

The next day, as the seas grew heavier, Francesca tried to tell the captain what she had overheard, but he refused to see her. So she turned to Miller. Maybe he could get the captain to listen. She found him sitting on the deck, leaning against the wheel of a cannon, untwisting old rope. She sat down cross-legged next to him and told him what had happened, omitting the part about Willy's escape.

Miller took a few puffs on his clay pipe. "This ain't a navy ship. Iffen Agar wants ta stand fer cap'n 'e's the right ta do so. Tho' it's bad manners ta go fomentin' 'hind the cap'n's back."

"Bad manners!" hissed Francesca. "It's mutiny. He should be hung from the yardarm."

Miller chuckled. "Ya needs to remember what sort a' ship yer on. We choose our cap'ns. Luck's been on our side an' the men credit the cap'n fer that. I expect few would side with Agar now, but iffen the tide changes, well, 'at's a different story."

Francesca shivered. *Captain Agar.* She picked up a piece of rope and untwisted it. "Isn't it my duty to tell the captain?"

Miller shrugged. "Iffen ya like. But the cap'n'd be a fool iffen 'e didn't already suspect as much – an' 'e's no fool."

Francesca realized she was getting in over her head. She hadn't understood pirate politics. Were others trying to undermine the captain, too? Her chest tightened when she thought of him pushed aside for someone else.

He might have forced her aboard, but she felt sure he was protecting her. And he was a good captain: decisive, smart, brave, and, if not honorable, at least not blood thirsty—except toward the Spanish. Surely that could be excused considering …

She added the untwisted rope to the pile and picked up another. Who were those men whose voices she didn't recognize? They had agreed with her. Agar had not yet swayed them. She'd have to identify their voices. *Surely they'll see reason.* Her shoulders relaxed a little now that she had the beginnings of a plan.

Perhaps she'd been foolish to tell them she saw Willy escape. Agar might try to use her admission against her, but she couldn't see how. If she denied it, it would be her word against his, and how he knew—the conversation in the mess—would be sure to come out.

In any case, the captain already knew and hadn't punished her. Agar could try to turn the crew against her, but she was pretty sure most of them would be happy she let Willy go. Even if Agar made the men hate her again, that would be better than his becoming captain.

She tried to figure out the honorable course, but she wasn't sure. At home it had seemed crystal clear, the line between honor and dishonor a chasm too wide to jump. Now it seemed convoluted, twisted like the rope in her hand, and not nearly as easy to unravel.

Over the next few days, the clouds thickened and lowered until the masts seemed to scrape their bellies. The wind came in violent blasts that threatened to rend the sails. Rain hissed on the surface of the riotous waves. Tuit's face became drawn and tense, which made the crew nervous. Though they no longer needed his weather sense. They could all feel the weight and scale of the approaching storm. They whispered the word "hurricane" as they looked at the sky and made the sign of the cross.

The *Destiny* searched for a sheltered port, but the admiral of the Spanish warships seemed to have read Captain Massey's mind. Every protected harbor they approached held at least one of the warships. The captain cursed as he headed due east for deep water. They'd ride out the storm and hope not to be driven upon a reef or shoal.

The crew furled all but the small spritsails, battened down the hatches, added extra straps to keep the cannons in place, faced into the wind, and hunkered down for the show.

Francesca had been at sea for over four months. She had seen some rough weather, but nothing like this. This was a ship-wrecker. For a week the twist and jolt of the deck grew worse until it was impossible to stand or walk without holding on to something.

The men gathered in the forecastle to pass the hours between watches. The roar of the storm made it impossible to talk without yelling. Their tanned skin took on an ashy hue. Their usual camaraderie was gone, beaten out of them by their watches above deck.

Today had been the worst yet. During Francesca's four-hour watch on deck, the rain pelted her horizontally, each drop a bee sting on her face and hands. Waves took on living forms, rearing up like kraken, crashing down on top of her, sucking at her legs, trying to carry her into the sea. They might have succeeded if the crew hadn't rigged lines across deck to hang onto. Fortunately, there had been little work to do in the rigging and she had retreated to the sanctuary of the sweltering mess hall after her shift.

Now she sat dripping wet, her hair and clothes plastered to her, trying to eat breakfast. The cooking fire had been doused three days prior, so breakfast consisted of dry bread, moldy cheese, and water—just like every meal for the last three days. Even if it had been freshly scrambled eggs with piping hot bread, she couldn't have eaten it. Nausea raged through her stomach matching the writhing of the deck. The tables, which hung from straps attached to the deck above, swung wildly with each pitch of the ship. With nearly everyone confined below deck, the room smelled like sweat, moldy cheese, and fear. She pushed her bread away.

One lantern gave a sickly yellow cast to the men's faces. Fear roiled through the room, like a low fog. They were all waiting for the worst, wondering if the ship could take it. She tried not to imagine the ship breaking apart, water spilling down the companionways, her body sliding into the cold depths.

She turned her mind instead to those on deck. The captain had been up there for over twenty-four hours. Five nights ago was the last time Hart had gotten a clear reading of the stars. At the time, they had been two hundred miles due east of the Bahamas. There was no way to know how far they had been blown. The captain must expect them to be cast up on rocks at any moment.

In fair weather, it was easy to forget how delicate a thing a sailing ship was, she thought, like a nutshell floating in a lake and as easily—

Lightning cracked and thunder boomed simultaneously, so close it made Francesca jump and the hair on her arms stand on end. On the bench opposite, Carter's body shook.

Suddenly, the *Destiny* was hit by a landslide. The bow plunged downward. Anything not nailed down hurled forward as water rushed in the air vents.

Francesca tumbled from her seat, sliding in a pile of bodies down the tilted deck. She grabbed the foremast as she passed and dug her nails in. The ship was headed straight down. The ship's timbers groaned. She looked up at the hatch, waiting for it to crash in with a wall of water. Her throat constricted with a stifled sob. *This is it!*

The bow shot skyward, hurling anyone who hadn't found a handhold back toward the stern. Francesca grabbed Carter with one hand as he slid past and then the lantern went out with a crash of shattered glass.

The lower deck became a black meat-grinder as the ship bucked and twisted. Pots and pans that had been jolted loose, casks of food, one squawking chicken still in her coop, plates, silverware, and deck hands all rolled and pitched about the room. Clutching the mast with one hand and Carter's shirt with the other, Francesca saw the faces in her *Book of Reckoning*. She heard Carter crying as he held on to her.

In the darkness the shriek of the storm grew louder. Cannon wheels rumbled overhead amid the roar of the storm. She could smell that someone near her had been sick. She gulped down the bile in her throat. They held on, wondering how much punishment the *Destiny* could take.

The companionway flew open. Murky light flowed over them. Wind and rain poured in, cutting the stink. Baldric stuck his head in shouting, "Aft starboard cannon's broken loose! Fifth watch!"

Old Nob hurried to light another lantern as ten men rushed up the stairs into the storm. The companionway slammed shut. Cannon wheels rumbled and there was a crash amid the roar of the storm.

When the men came back down there were only eight. "Armstrong? Sullivan?" someone asked. They shook their heads.

And then as suddenly as the wave had struck, silence hit, like a vast blanket of stillness laid over them. The wind and rain stopped, and the thunder and lightning faded. The ship settled into a gentle roll. Francesca pried her hand from the mast. She clapped Carter on his shuddering back. "We made it!"

"No, missy," Miller said getting to his feet and brushing off wet bits of bread and cheese. "'Tis but the eye o' the storm."

The companionway thumped open and the bosun shouted, "All hands!"

Francesca made her way up to the strangest sight she had ever seen. Close astern was the storm they had just left. Lighting flashed, wind and rain whipped sideways along the wave tops. The storm arched around them, but overhead was a bright blue, cloudless sky. In the distance ahead she could see the second half of the storm they had yet to pass through.

The deck was in shambles, particularly where the cannon had broken loose and crushed everything in its path. Rigging lines had been ripped and the forward spar was loose. They set to repairs with desperate speed; their lives depended on it.

The captain leaned heavily on the wheel, his clothes and hair drenched and disheveled. He looked as though he could barely stand. He had weathered the full brunt of the storm on deck.

Francesca and the other topmen hurried into the rigging to repair the lines. Some of the furled sails had come loose and were torn and needed mending. But as she worked, Francesca's eyes were drawn again and again to the advancing wall approaching their bow. Perhaps that was why she was the first to spot the other ship.

"Sail ho!" shouted Francesca, not entirely accurately. No sails were in evidence. Two of her three masts were leaning precariously. Her crew worked desperately on repairs. Francesca made out the name in gold letters across the stern, the *Jamaican Queen*. She gasped. The ship was from Jamaica, perhaps even going there. *Jamaica, Port Royal, Phillip!*

Francesca tried to concentrate as she tied off wet hemp lines, but her mind churned. The *Destiny* was unlikely to ever stop in Port Royal. Even if they did, it might be months from now and Phillip could be gone by then. Every day she waited was a day he might receive orders that took him elsewhere. She must reach him soon and here was her answer.

She glanced again at the *Jamaican Queen*. She was closer now and Francesca tried to assess the damage. Other than the masts she looked sound, but was it worth the risk? This might be her only chance.

The captain would never agree to a mercy mission, but what if she offered to take the ship? Once aboard, well, the storm would certainly separate her from the *Destiny*. After that, they might as well head for Jamaica as anywhere else. The chances of finding each other again were slim.

Once in Port Royal she could sell the merchandise and leave the money there in the captain's name. Having done her duty, she could find Phillip.

She thought briefly of Calico Jack's body swinging in the Jamaican breeze. Would the navy hang them if they saved the ship? Well, she would think of that later.

Francesca finished her work and climbed down to deck. She hid her excitement as she joined Captain Massey and Baldric at the rail. They were staring toward the foundering ship. The captain's wet clothes clung to his body. His dark hair, tangled and loose, hung to his shoulders. His hands trembled as he examined the vessel though his glass. Francesca had an urge to reach out and steady his hand. Instead, she clutched her other hand and steadied that.

"Such a waste," the captain said, "she looks like a merchantman."

"All that loot," sighed Baldric.

"Begging your pardon, Sir, but we can take her," Francesca said.

The captain turned to her with eyes sunken and faced lined, his usual intensity gone.

Agar approached in a hurry. "Captain—"

The captain held up a weary hand and Agar paused.

"No one takes a ship in the eye of a storm," Baldric said.

"That wall of water will be here in less than half an hour," the captain said. "And I can't get close without risking the *Destiny*."

Agar looked from the captain and Baldric to Francesca, confusion and interest on his face.

Francesca desperately wanted to save the other ship. Not only could it take her to Phillip, but rescuing it was honorable. It was what Papa would do. Saving the *Jamaican Queen* wouldn't undo the things she had done, but maybe it would help. "I'll take a longboat," Francesca said. "We can take the ship and save some lives."

"We're not in the business of savin' lives," growled Baldric.

"I'll take volunteers," Francesca said.

Agar gave a skeptical laugh.

The captain shook his head. "I'll not risk the boats or the men."

Francesca looked over at the *Jamaican Queen*, even closer now. "You can tie a line to the boat. Haul it back—"

"I said no!" The captain rubbed a hand across his face and turned to Agar. "What is it, Mr. Agar."

"'Ere's a problem with the powder magazine, Cap'n."

The captain gave a weary nod and followed Agar below.

Ten minutes later, as Francesca finished splicing a frayed halyard, she glanced longingly toward the *Jamaican Queen*. The ship was less than a hundred yards away now and the storm wall was nearing. There was one man on the *Jamaican Queen's* deck not working feverishly on repairs. He cupped his hands around his mouth and shouted for help. If only he knew how much Francesca would like to supply it.

A disturbance on the *Destiny's* deck made Francesca turn. Men were hooking a longboat to the windlass, the winch used to lower it over the side. Another group stood nearby with weapons in hand. A spike of elation passed through Francesca as she headed toward them. Rolly, a red-haired, freckled-faced boy stopped her. "Cap'n says yer ta make a go a' it."

Francesca's eyes widened. "He's changed his mind?" She'd never known him to do so before.

Rolly shrugged. "Just deliverin' the message."

Francesca hurried to the gathered men. Miller and Tuit were among them. It was a ragtag group of twelve, not the ones she would have chosen, but she didn't care.

Minutes later they were in the boat and headed for the *Jamaican Queen*.

The storm was moving fast. They were still ten yards away when the second front engulfed them. The longboat was tethered to the *Destiny* as Francesca had suggested. She expected at any moment to be hauled back, and her chance to reach Phillip would be gone.

"Row! Harder! Pull!" Francesca shouted over the roar of the storm. The oarsmen groaned, cursing and straining.

Squinting through the lashing rain, Francesca watched the tilted mainmast of the ship crack and crash into the waves. But the rigging tied it to the ship like an anchor. The ship listed dangerously to one side.

Moments later Francesca's longboat bumped against the hull. She scrambled up the side. The ship's crew worked desperately to free the broken mast before it swamped them. An extravagantly dressed man, finery drooping, arms wrapped through the rail, watched the boarders. He was the man who had been shouting for help. She reached him and yelled over the storm, "Are you the captain?"

"He's dead! And the first mate with him!"

"We're taking your ship!" yelled Francesca.

The man looked Francesca up and down. "Madame, if you can keep her afloat, I'll give her to you!"

Miller shouted, "She's sluggish. We're takin' on water."

The man pointed downward. "There's a crack in the hull."

Francesca's knees went weak, and she grabbed the rail. The ship was much worse off than she had imagined. But at least she could get as many people as possible back to the *Destiny*. She looked over the side and saw their boat being pulled back to the *Destiny* by its tether. She made out Agar at the other end. He'd gotten rid of her at last. Her stomach knotted. *I've done it now. I've killed my friends. We're marooned on a sinking ship.* One of her knees buckled, but the other held. She had to make this work.

Francesca faced her crew. "Tuit, away the mast! Bigalow, take half the men and man the pumps!"

Six *Destiny* crewmen ran below. The others joined the tired group that was hacking loose the rigging holding the broken mast.

Francesca grabbed Miller's arm. "We'd best get her headed into the wind."

"It's no use," shouted Miller. He pointed toward the bow. "No sails. We got no steerage!"

Without the wind pushing them faster than the surrounding water, the rudder was useless. They'd roll at the mercy of the sea until they capsized. Francesca shoved Miller toward the helm. "Man the wheel. I'll set the sails."

She headed forward. The mainmast had fallen, and the mizzen mast leaned precariously; that left only the foremast and the bowsprit. The bowsprit churned through the water every few seconds, so she headed for the foremast shrouds. She grabbed the collars of two of the *Destiny* men who were chopping at the rigging. "I need you on the clew lines!" They nodded and followed.

As Francesca climbed the shrouds, a wall of water headed for the side of the ship.

"Hold on!" she screamed.

She wrapped her arms through the rigging, locking her hands to her opposing wrists. She twisted one leg through the shrouds before the wave hit. The ship wallowed on its side, dragged under by the broken mast.

Francesca plunged underwater. Cold blackness swirled around her, yanking at her hold, tearing at her. She lost all sense of direction.

She fought against rising panic. *Are we capsized? Are we going down? Should I let go?*

149

If the ship had capsized, hanging on would mean death. But she couldn't tell. Was she inches under water or yards? Should she swim for the surface? She couldn't tell which way was up. She wouldn't survive with nothing to buoy her.

She held on to the only thing solid, the shrouds. Her lungs burned. Her blood beat against her temples. Her body screamed to expel breath, to gulp in air. She squeezed her eyes tight and fought the wild pull of the water and the deadly urge to breathe.

Then suddenly, she surfaced with a gasp as a wave broke the mainmast free from the ship. The mast swept past her, dragging along a tangled crewman. In an instant, mast and man were gone. The ship righted itself, flinging her back up into the air.

It took Francesca a few seconds to break her grip on her wrists. Then she climbed as fast as she could.

The mainsail, she knew, was too large. The strength of the wind would shred it, so she climbed higher, to the topsail. She slid out along the yardarm cutting loose the bindings that furled the sail.

"Haul her tight!" she yelled to the men below. They probably couldn't hear her, but they knew what to do. They hauled on the lines pulling the sail taut, then tied them off.

The sail snapped out, bulging with the force of the wind. The ship moved under her. She grabbed a backstay and slid down to the heaving deck.

Tuit met her there. "Mast away!" he shouted, as if she needed to be told.

"Go below! Everyone. Man the pumps!"

Tuit rounded up the crewmen from both ships and shepherded them below.

Francesca made her way to the helm where Miller was fighting the wheel. "Mighty glad ta see ya, missy, I thought ya was a goner," Miller said as Francesca added her weight to steadying the wheel.

The next ten hours passed in a hellish whirl of fatigue and pain. Through the pitch-black night, the crew toiled, manning pumps and buckets and emptying the flooded hold, while the carpenter and his mates worked to patch the crack in the hull.

Francesca and Miller did their best to keep the ship headed into the storm. The whipping rain pelted her face until her skin felt raw. Each breath seemed to contain as much water as air. The wheel bucked like a living creature. Waves washed across deck and sucked at their legs. Francesca's muscles vibrated with fatigue. She cut a length of rope and tied herself to the wheel housing so she could save her strength for controlling the wheel.

The next day, the storm began to spin itself out. As the sea settled down to a dull roar, the crew's pace slacked and one by one they dropped, exhausted.

Francesca untied herself from the wheel housing and sank to the deck. She was surprised to find that not only was she still alive, but she had also saved two dozen lives and was the de facto captain of a Jamaican ship.

CHAPTER 18
THE CAPTAIN'S TABLE

Two days later, the *Jamaican Queen* was still taking on water, though slowly. Francesca had joined the crew on the pumps and buckets. No one had yet gotten any sleep except the ship's owner, Mr. Carlisle, who had collapsed after an hour on the pumps. Francesca suspected it was the first physical labor he had done in his life.

Ankle deep in water, Francesca pushed snarled hair back from her forehead with trembling hands. She stooped in the tight space in the hold, one in a line of men leading up the companionway and onto deck. The man on her left passed her a bucket of water. The weight made her shoulders and back ache and the metal handle had long since rubbed her hands raw, but she didn't complain—they were alive. She handed the bucket to the man on her right and it traveled hand to hand up the stairs, passing an empty bucket coming back down.

Farther aft, four sailors on the two chest-high pumps chanted to keep rhythm, bending and straightening with each stroke of the handle. It would be her turn on the pumps soon and she dreaded it.

Forward, the carpenter and his mates still worked to stop the leak. They too were near exhaustion, their movements slow and awkward. Their hammer blows still echoed through the hold, but they were losing ground. Yesterday the spot where Francesca stood had been dry. At this rate, it was just a matter of time before the ship went under.

Despite it all, excitement buzzed just under Francesca's skin. She trusted

152

the carpenter would stem the leak and the ship, such as it was, was hers. Mr. Carlisle had said so when he had shaken her hand and thanked her for saving his life. His crew took him at his word and now followed her orders. She had expected a fight from the pirates, but none had arisen. Maybe they were too weary to argue. In any case, she was in charge.

The prize, if she could keep it afloat, was a valuable one. According to Mr. Carlisle, the *Jamaican Queen* carried a cargo of silks and satins headed from England to Jamaica. Once Francesca reached Port Royal, she could sell off the goods, leave the money for Captain Massey, and find Phillip.

Word came, along with a descending bucket, that Francesca was wanted on deck. A ship had been spotted. She frowned, worried. They had jettisoned the cannons to lighten the ship. Now, keeping her prize would be harder than taking it. She put a hand to her aching back as she climbed the companionway.

The deck was a wreck. The two broken masts ended in jagged splinters. Frayed ropes twisted like tree roots, among scraps of wood from the longboats that the falling mast had smashed. At least the foremast and bowsprit still functioned, and the billowed sails were pushing the ship slowly toward Jamaica.

Overhead the sky was clear except for a few cottony clouds hurrying after the storm, like kid brothers toddling after their older siblings.

Francesca inhaled air that was still crisp after the storm, with a lingering, electric feeling. One of Carlisle's men, tossing a bucket of water over the side, pointed a finger and she turned to look.

She didn't believe her eyes. The black hull, the tilt of the masts, and the trim of the sails she knew so well—it was the *Destiny*. Somehow, they had calculated how far and in which direction the *Jamaican Queen* had been blown and correlated that with their own position. It was an amazing feat of navigation. Pride flashed through her, immediately followed by a spike of disappointment. They would live, their ordeal was over, but so was her hope of reaching Phillip.

Still, she was happy to see Carter and the doctor at the rail with most of the crew, shouting and waving when the *Destiny* pulled alongside.

"Not bad fer a wee gal," shouted Old Nob from the rigging.

Men joked and hollered as ropes were tossed across and the ships tied together.

The captain's voice rose over the others. "Pipe down! All of you!"

A gap opened at the rail and the captain appeared. Francesca's stomach tied into a knot when she saw his face. It was red-purple, hard as rock. His eyes, locked on her, were chips of stone. He climbed onto the railing and leapt across to the *Jamaican Queen*. Francesca took a step back, gulping. He stared at her then turned to Bigalow and Miller who stood nearby. "Take her back to the *Destiny* and throw her in the brig."

Francesca put a hand to her chest. The men around her did not move. She blinked at the captain. "Wh, what have I done?"

He vibrated with rage. "You disobeyed my orders and left the ship. You risked your life and the lives of my men. If I have to lock you up to keep you alive, I bloody well will!"

"But … but…" she sputtered. "You gave me permission."

The captain's fists pumped. "No, I did *not!*"

She looked around, confused. "Rolly said you'd changed your mind. That I was to make a go of it."

The anger didn't leave the captain's face, but he tilted his head to one side. "Rolly!"

Rolly's red head reluctantly peeked out from behind the doctor. The captain's eyes flicked to him.

"Did you relay that message?"

"Aye, Sir." He inched back behind the doctor. "Just as Mr. Angstrom tol' me to."

"Mr. Angstrom!" barked the captain.

Angstrom stepped forward and ran twitchy fingers through his beard. "I received yer written orders, Sir, an' carried 'em out."

The captain paused at this, and his eyes scanned his men. "Do you still have the orders?"

Angstrom shook his head. "No, Sir."

The captain's eyes scanned the faces of the crewmen, searching. "I intend to get to the bottom of this." He let out breath. "Mr. Angstrom, we'll discuss this in private. Back to work, all of you."

As weary men climbed up the *Jamaican Queen's* companionway on shaky legs, fresh replacements from the *Destiny* thumped them on their backs as they headed down. The captain faced Francesca. His shoulders slumped, and his anger drained away. "I thought you were dead." He ran his hands over his face and went below.

Francesca climbed across to the *Destiny* and stumbled to her cabin.

Someone had sent her on a suicide mission. Agar's dark shape loomed in her mind, but she was asleep as soon as she hit the cot.

A knock on her door woke Francesca what seemed like minutes later. She pulled on her salt-stiff clothes and opened the door. It was One-eyed Kelsey. "Yer invited ta dine at the Cap'n's table."

"Dinner?" Francesca squinted through the dim light below deck. "What's the time?"

"'alf past six," Kelsey said. "Dinner's in 'alf an 'our."

Francesca's stomach growled. She stared at Kelsey trying to sort out the fact that she'd been asleep for over twelve hours. "Very well," she mumbled and closed the door.

Francesca rubbed her face to bring herself fully awake. She'd never been invited to Captain Massey's table before. Why had he invited her now, especially after he'd seemed so angry? Then again, she had succeeded in taking the *Jamaican Queen*. Perhaps he wanted to celebrate her success.

Her eyes popped open wide. Dinners at the captain's table were a formal affair. What was she to wear?

Her options were limited. She had her gray riding habit, the emerald-green dress Claire and Belle had made for her—which she'd never yet worn—her leather vest and buckskin breeches, and her salt-stained trousers and shirt. She scratched her head. Somehow a dress seemed wrong, but her other options were anything but formal.

She thought about it as she washed up in her cabin. She broke three teeth on her comb trying to get the knots out of her hair. Eventually she swirled her hair into a bun at the nape of her neck and got dressed. She would cut the knots out later. She pulled on her buckskin breeches and boots. On top of her shift, she buckled on her ruffled collar and slipped into the long jacket of her dove-gray riding habit. She wished she had a mirror to inspect the effect but shrugged. It was the best she could do.

When the ship's bell chimed seven o'clock, she headed to the great cabin. A few crewmen on the landing congratulated her on her success. The ship's carpenter, Mr. Pitt, patted her on the back with a hand the weight of a cooked ham. Apparently, all she had to do to earn their respect was to take a ship.

In the great cabin, Mr. Carlisle, owner of the *Jamaican Queen*, greeted her graciously. Francesca was not surprised to see him. In general, the *Destiny* did not attack English ships. Not out of patriotism, but because it made good business sense. When the captain sold off loot, he sold it to the Englishmen whose ships plied the seas. Being on good terms with the *Jamaican Queen's* owner might prove useful, so the captain would treat him well.

Mr. Carlisle bowed with a practiced motion. "My lady, what a pleasure to see you without the threat of drowning hanging over our heads." He kissed her hand. "Again, I must convey my deepest gratitude. I am your most humble servant, always."

Francesca pulled her hand away as quickly as was polite and hid it behind her back. Mr. Carlisle's hand was long and elegant—much like him. Francesca's hands were raw from bailing water, calloused from the rigging, and stained black with tar. "Thank you, Mr. Carlisle, but I don't deserve the honor."

He smiled, accentuating prominent cheekbones. "On the contrary," he said as he offered her a glass of wine. "Never have I met such a woman." He turned to Captain Massey. "I wish you could have seen her aboard the *Jamaican Queen* in the heart of the storm, Captain." Mr. Carlisle raised his glass. "She possessed the bravery of Joan of Arc, the wisdom of Elizabeth, and the beauty of Judith."

Francesca's cheeks grew hot as the men clinked glasses. Mr. Carlisle leaned toward her. "The captain tells me it was your idea to save my ship."

"Well, I suppose so," she said. She couldn't admit why she wanted to rescue the *Jamaican Queen*, not in front of the captain.

Captain Massey ushered her to the table, smiling. He wore a tan silk vest and black jacket that set off his dark hair. He looked much recovered, though there were dark circles under his eyes. His intensity was back as he drew out her chair. He leaned close as he slid the chair in, and she smelled rum on his breath. "Indeed, she was most adamant about taking your ship, Mr. Carlisle, despite the fact that she'll have none of the spoils."

"None?" Mr. Carlisle said, sitting.

Francesca took a hasty sip of wine.

The captain seat himself at the head of the table. "Apparently our ill-gotten gains are beneath her," he said with a crooked smile at Francesca. "I had hoped to make a rich woman of her when she first came aboard, but what is a man to do?"

Her fingers tightened around the stem of her glass. Why should she be embarrassed for not accepting stolen goods? She wanted to make a sharp retort but couldn't think of one. She was relieved when Kelsey entered with a tray and they fell silent.

Kelsey deposited a bowl of watery soup in front of each of them and left. Once Francesca's anger abated, her mind whirled. He had hoped to make her rich? Was that true? Before she could form a question, the captain continued. "So, Mr. Carlisle, the question is, why was she so keen to risk her life to save yours?"

"A pirate wouldn't understand," Francesca said.

The captain turned to Mr. Carlisle. "This from the woman who just stole your ship."

Mr. Carlisle chuckled. The captain faced Francesca. "Try me."

Francesca opened her mouth to make a cutting remark, then closed it again. To be honest, her motives were selfish—she did it to reach Phillip. So that she might have a normal, happy life. She had risked her crewmates' lives for her own gain. Perhaps she had done the right thing, but Papa would say it was for the wrong reasons.

"No doubt her concern for her fellow man drove her to it," Mr. Carlisle said.

Francesca looked at him sharply to see if he was mocking her, but his face was sober. She fingered the stem of her glass and glanced sideways at the captain.

With amusement in his eyes, he said, "No doubt."

He *was* mocking her. He was so exasperating. With one word he could make her feel foolish and question the meaning of her existence. She tried to come up with a retort, but everything that came to mind sounded childish. She bit her lip until her anger subsided, then ran her tongue over her lip and tasted a tang of blood. She took a spoonful of soup to hide it.

Mr. Carlisle laid his long fingers on Francesca's wrist. "My dear, the captain tells me you are the daughter of the renowned Maestro DiCesare. Can you tell us what has become of him?"

Sorrow swept through her. She was grateful for the change of subject, but this one was even more painful. The amusement was suddenly gone from the captain's face. His eyes bored into hers. She took a sip of wine to steady herself.

"A dishonorable man killed him, a cheat and a tyrant named Tarrentino." She was surprised by the venom that had risen in her throat. She put both palms flat on the table, fingers stretched. "Papa was unarmed. Tarrentino stabbed him in the back."

Both men gasped as she swallowed the lump in her throat. It was an ignoble way for a fencing maestro to die. Her face hardened. "Tarrentino was craven, and died by my hand."

Something flashed in the captain's eyes. Gratitude? Pride?

"Is that how you came to be aboard a Spanish ship? Were you running?" asked the captain.

Francesca nodded. "I'll hang if they catch me." Her voice dropped to a whisper. "I can never go home."

She saw sympathy in the captain's gaze.

"Exile is a hard road," he said. "There is so much one … regrets."

His hand moved across the table toward hers but stopped.

Mr. Carlisle shook his head. "What did they quarrel about?"

The captain's face went hard again. "Honor, no doubt," he said with disgust. "Why else do respectable men kill each other? I'll wager it was a duel."

Francesca's blood boiled. "What do you know of respectable men?"

"Plenty," he said. "I come from a respectable family. I was respectable myself for most of my life, but I realized that adhering to some idealistic Code of Honor in an imperfect world was foolish and arrogant."

Francesca's fists clenched.

The captain's voice grew soft. "And likely to get you killed."

She saw Catalina's face as her body lay on the dueling grounds. Francesca trembled, barely controlling her anger. "And not adhering gets others killed." She had risen to her feet. "If the world is imperfect, all the more reason to seek perfection in ourselves. To do otherwise is weak and cowardly."

The captain's expression grew serious. "But honor and perfection are two very different things."

Francesca scowled. They were the same. To be perfectly honorable was to be perfect. It was what she strived for, her vow. She had failed, but still she tried. She opened her mouth to speak but Mr. Carlisle cut in.

"Come, my dear, do sit down," he said gently.

She felt ridiculous. Why had she let the captain bait her? Why should she care what he thought? But she did care, and it irritated her.

She sat down feeling self-conscious. "It was a duel," she said. "But the duel had ended. Papa had drawn first blood. We were leaving when…"

The captain prompted her. "When Tarrentino attacked?"

She nodded. "I grabbed Papa's blade … it all happened in a blur. I, I killed him."

The captain looked away. "Seems to me this Tarrentino fellow died much too easily."

"What precipitated the quarrel between your father and this Tarrentino fellow?" Mr. Carlisle asked.

Francesca sighed remembering that day in the market square, the boy, bloody and beaten, at her feet. "A boy. A slave boy. Papa prevented Tarrentino from beating him to death."

Mr. Carlisle gasped. "But how foo…" he stopped himself and dabbed at his mouth with his napkin searching for words. "Why ever did your father get involved? The man had a right to do as he liked with his own property."

The captain bristled, as did Francesca.

"It's not as though they have our sensibilities or feel pain as we do," Mr. Carlisle went on.

Francesca stared in disbelief and the captain exclaimed, "What bosh! How would you know what they feel?"

Mr. Carlisle looked stunned. "Why, it's commonly known."

The captain bristled. "Then I'll tell you what I *uncommonly* know. I lived with a group of escaped slaves for a year after the Spanish left me for dead. They saved my life and nursed me back to health out of the kindness of their hearts. They had little but gave all they could. I had nothing, no way to repay them. They didn't care. They did it because it was right and good." He turned to Francesca. "That is perfection."

Awkward silence descended. Mr. Carlisle cleared his throat. This explained how he had known the Maroons' language. She wanted to ask more, but his expression was distant, untouchable.

Kelsey entered, collected the soup bowls, though Francesca had eaten little of hers. One of the cook's mates brought in a platter sporting a thin, but golden, stuffed chicken. The aroma of cinnamon and spice that rose from it awakened her hunger.

The captain shooed the cook's mate away and carved the meat. Mr. Carlisle opened his mouth to speak, but Francesca jumped in hoping to change the subject. "What about you, Mr. Carlisle? What brings you here?"

Mr. Carlisle picked up a fork. "Call me Henry, my dear. After all, you saved my life.

I can claim no story as dramatic as yours. Rum brought me here. Lots of it. My parents were colonists. They founded a sugar plantation on Jamaica which has grown to over a thousand acres. I've added two rum mills that run night and day, supplying three of my own ships that ply between Jamaica, the American colonies, and England. I was returning from England. I have a seat in Parliament representing the sugar interests, so I spend much of the year there."

As she listened, Francesca shoveled chicken into her mouth in the most ladylike fashion she could manage given how hungry she was. The bird was tough, but she was famished, and the spices and raisins in the stuffing tasted wonderful.

Henry turned to the captain. "My ships have also, when occasion presented, engaged in your line of work, Captain."

The captain gave a slight nod.

"So you can be assured I have no hard feelings. All the best businessmen are opportunists."

"Do you live in Port Royal?" asked Francesca, unable to hide the excitement in her voice. Henry might know Phillip.

"No, my dear." My plantations are to the west of Port Royal near Old Harbor, but I keep an apartment in Port Royal for when I'm conducting business."

"I see," Francesca said, searching for another question that wouldn't give too much away. "And Port Royal, what is the town like?"

Henry shook his head. "As wicked as ever, to be sure, but Port Royal is only a shadow of its former self. Earthquakes, tidal waves, and hurricanes have taken their toll."

"Recently?" she said in alarm, dropping her fork. "Has something happened?"

"Oh no, my dear, not since—"

The captain cut in. "Why the concern?"

"What do you mean?" she said.

The captain scratched his head. "I've seen you less worried about an upcoming battle."

"Well, I have a cousin there." She was a terrible liar, but she couldn't bear to tell him the truth, not after he had mocked her about Phillip leaving her. His eyebrows arched and she looked away.

"A cousin," the captain said with an insolent tone. "And what is this cousin's name?"

"What possible difference could it make to you?"

"Mr. Carlisle may well know your *cousin*," the captain said.

160

Francesca wracked her brain for a name but only Phillip would come to mind. Then she remembered Claire and Belle mentioning Phillip's cousin, Abigail. "Have you by chance made the acquaintance of Miss Abigail Worthington?"

As Henry pondered, Francesca shot a look at the captain. He seemed satisfied.

"I don't believe I've had the pleasure, my dear," Henry said. He turned to the captain. "I've no idea what your plans are, but it's clear you'll need a port to repair my ... I mean your ship. I could make it worth your while to make Port Royal that port."

She stilled herself, trying to hide her excitement.

"I'd be taking a terrible risk," the captain said. "I would need quite a large incentive."

Henry waved a hand. "The risk is minimal. The navy may be intent on hanging pirates, but the townspeople are much more interested in catering to them. Besides, as one of the chief planters on the island, I'm an important assembly member. I can give you a letter of introduction. No one will question you."

Francesca kept her face neutral as her heart beat wildly. The captain tapped a finger on his cheek and Henry continued. "This is a critical time of year for my business. It behooves me to get home quickly. I can promise you twenty barrels of my best dark rum when we arrive."

"Forty," the captain countered.

"Thirty, and the pleasure of showing Miss DiCesare the town."

Francesca laughed and laid a hand on his arm. "Call me Francesca, Henry, after all I saved your—"

"No." the captain slapped the table, making the dinnerware jump.

Startled, Francesca thought she saw a flush under his tanned skin. His expression was suddenly vulnerable. She noticed how rough and weathered his lips were from the storm and wondered what they would feel like against hers. She mentally shook herself. *I love Phillip.* She reached quickly for her glass of wine, knocking it over.

Henry busied himself with his chicken. "I'm so sorry. I should have known."

A strained hush filled the room.

Francesca pushed back a strand of hair. "I am just a crewman like any other."

"Hardly, my dear," Henry said.

One-eyed Kelsey bustled in with a platter of small, round honey cakes which he set in the center of the table. No one moved to take one. Kelsey righted and refilled Francesca's wine glass, took their plates, and left. Silence descended again.

Francesca's mind raced. Was the captain jealous? Why did the thought thrill her? Would he still agree to go?

"Please," the captain said finally, motioning toward the dessert. He reached out and took a cake. Henry and Francesca did the same.

The captain cleared his throat. "This is how it will be. Mr. Carlisle, you will write a letter of introduction naming me the captain of the *Jamaican Queen* and arranging payments for all goods in my name. When we arrive you will be escorted to your apartment by two of my men who will attend you in your *illness*. You will, unfortunately, be indisposed until the *Destiny* and the *Jamaican Queen* leave Port Royal."

At this Henry shrugged. "As long as I'm allowed to meet with my plantation overseer."

The captain nodded, and Henry raised his glass and took a drink.

The captain turned to her. "Miss DiCesare," he said with a glance at Henry, "will pose as the wife of the captain." His voice quavered slightly.

Francesca opened her mouth to protest and then shut it again. He was offering to take her ashore in Port Royal! All she would need to do was slip away.

The captain continued. "No one would suspect a man who brings his pretty young wife aboard ship of pirating."

"Indeed," Henry said, taking another honey cake.

"I will be happy to play my part in your charade. It suits my humor to owe my life to pirates. Though you may appear more bloodthirsty when I eventually tell the tale."

"We can be, I assure you," the captain said with a boyish grin.

"No doubt." Henry lifted his glass to Francesca. "But there is more angel about you than devil, my dear."

"That's kind of you. But my halo may have tarnished of late."

Henry chuckled. "A slight patina only adds to the beauty."

As the honey cakes disappeared, the conversation turned to the latest news from Europe. England was once more at war with Spain and had trounced them at the Battle of Cape Passaro off the southern tip of Naples.

England, France, Austria, and Holland had united to force Philip of Spain to abandon his claims to Italy.

After that, between the wine and the fatigue, Francesca lost the thread of the conversation. The mention of home made her think of Papa. She wondered what he would have thought about her actions. She had saved two dozen lives but stolen a ship. Did the good outweigh the bad? Henry seemed content, but was she? She shook her head. It was all so confusing. She was too tired to puzzle it out, and thinking of Papa made her homesick for the sun-washed hills of Salle DiCesare.

The table had fallen mute. She realized that Henry and the captain had been talking to her and she had missed what they said. She smiled sheepishly. "You must excuse me. I'm still a little worn."

"Of course, my dear," Henry said.

"Perhaps some more rest is in order," said the captain.

Francesca nodded as she stood. "Thank you for dinner."

The men stood and bowed. She realized how much she missed good manners and quiet conversation. She was reluctant to leave.

The captain took her hand and raised his other palm toward her cheek.

She leaned toward it before she could stop herself.

He froze, his hand hovering an inch from her skin. Her breath caught.

"Get some more sleep," he said, dropping his hand. "It will do you good."

Henry bid her goodnight as she headed out. Francesca shook her head to clear it as she walked toward her cabin. She puzzled over dinner as she took off her breeches and riding jacket. As she drifted to sleep, she had one thought on her mind.

Agar may have been trying to sabotage her when he sent her aboard the *Jamaican Queen*, but instead she had gotten just what she wanted.

CHAPTER 19
PORT ROYAL

According to Mr. Hart's sextant, the storm had blown them five hundred miles northwest and deposited them off Florida. They were lucky they had not run aground on any of the islands along the coast.

By the end of the week, the *Destiny* was repaired, but the *Jamaican Queen* still needed work. She carried only one spare mast, so she was one short, and the leak still required men on the pumps around the clock.

The *Jamaican Queen's* crew was grateful to have been rescued. Nearly half asked to stay on under Captain Massey. They treated Francesca with a deference she found embarrassing. Had she saved them for the right reasons, she might have accepted their admiration with good grace. But every time they swept off their caps, asked about her health, or inquired whether there was anything she needed, she was reminded of her selfishness.

Agar seemed to be keeping his head down since the forged orders. When she did see him, his mien held a heightened malevolence, as if he was affronted that she had not had the decency to die.

Francesca still hadn't identified the two voices she had heard plotting with Agar. She had narrowed it down to five men. None of them gave her a second glance or showed any undue interest in Agar, but she kept an eye on them just the same.

At first the crew grumbled as they sailed by ports where they could have made repairs, ending shifts at the *Jamaican Queen's* pumps. But the grumbling stopped when the captain announced that they were headed for Port Royal.

The crew's raucous cheer surprised Francesca. She had thought the crew would rather avoid the town since it had a reputation for hanging pirates. She noticed Henry at the rail sunning himself and went to ask.

Henry gave her his usual bow as she approached. "My lady."

Francesca leaned a hip against the rail and faced into the crisp wind. "The men seem happy to be going to Port Royal."

Henry nodded. "And I'm sure Port Royal will be happy to relieve them of their swag."

"But isn't the English navy there?" She dropped her voice. "Aren't they likely to be hanged?"

"I expect the danger is a part of the thrill, but for the past eighty years Port Royal has been catering to pirates. The town has one tavern for every ten residents. The majority of the population is either pirate or prostitute."

"What is the navy doing about it?"

"Oh, they hang pirates when they catch them. During one month last year, they hanged forty-one. But that's only a drop in the rum barrel, and the townsfolk are not keen on the hangings. A few months back, the locals rushed the gallows and cut down a popular pirate."

"Why would the townspeople want to save pirates?"

Henry rubbed his fingers together. "Gold, my dear. I've heard stories of buccaneers spending two thousand pieces-of-eight on a night of debauchery."

She shook her head in amazement. "Is that even possible?"

Henry grinned. "Believe me, it is."

Francesca looked out over the water. She pushed the hair back behind her ear. "Do you know many of the navy men stationed there?"

Henry shook his head. "Only a few. I've dined with the admiral, of course, and I've met his aides, Briggs and Wilkes, perhaps a few others."

Her voice fell to a whisper. "Have you met anyone by the name of Worthington?"

"I'm sorry, my dear, I don't believe so."

It took three weeks for the *Jamaican Queen*, and therefore the *Destiny*, to limp to Port Royal. They were interminable weeks for Francesca as she paced and fretted. She vacillated between worrying that Phillip had already left Port Royal and imagining what their meeting would be like. She debated what she would say. *Phillip, I'm so sorry for the loss of your wife.* That was an outright lie. She wasn't sorry at all. *Phillip, it's so good to see you again.* That seemed far too weak, so she settled on, *Phillip, at last!* It captured the longing without throwing herself at him.

During those weeks she felt the captain's eyes on her often, especially when she was chatting with Henry. When she and Henry were together, the captain's pace on the quarterdeck quickened and he shouted at the men for no reason. She hated how that thrilled her.

Jamaica finally appeared off their larboard bow late one afternoon, a smoky blue bead on the string of the horizon. The crew cheered and Francesca shared their excitement as it rose like the tide. She was so close!

A few hours later, Henry, wearing his finest frills, joined Francesca at the rail. As they sailed along the south side of the island, he pointed out landmarks and part of his family's plantation. When they neared Port Royal, Henry put a hand over hers on the rail. "Well, my dear, I'll say goodbye now. I'm to be put ashore as soon as we've moored."

Francesca turned to him. "I shall miss our afternoon chats."

"As will I. It has been a pleasure, my dear. Never have I owed such a beautiful woman so much."

She shook her head. "It's I who owe you. I wanted very much to come here, and you made it possible."

"To be honest, I have no pressing business to attend to. I saw your interest in visiting Port Royal and thought it the least I could do to assist you. You mean to visit your cousin I take it, this Worthington fellow?"

"But you promised the captain thirty barrels of rum. Surely not on my account!"

Henry waved away her remark. "You saved my life. I would do much more to repay you, if you would allow me. Surely there must be something I can do for you?"

Francesca thought for a moment, but all she wanted—a home, a life, a love, waited for her in Port Royal. Her excitement must have shown in her face because Henry gave her a rueful look. "I wish you and your *cousin* well. I hope he proves worthy of such an exceptional woman. I admit, I'm jealous, and I'm sure the captain will be too."

Francesca felt her cheeks flush. She looked ahead in the direction of town. On her left, a breeze played over the fields of sugar cane so that ocean waves turned to waves of green as they met land. Ahead and to the right lay a scattering of small islands, not much more than sandbars.

Henry pointed to one of them. "That's Rackhams Cay. That's where they hanged Calico Jack and Vane. Jack's bones hung there for years as a warning to other pirates. Not that it did any good."

They were nearing the mouth of a huge bay, bustling with close to forty ships. Two towns nestled on the mainland on her left, and to her right a town sat so low to the water it appeared to be floating. She had heard that Port Royal was built upon a sand spit, but this town seemed likely to be overwhelmed by the ocean at any moment. "Is that Port Royal?"

"What remains of it," Henry said. "A few years before I was born, over half the town was swallowed up by the sea during an earthquake. Most of the survivors moved there, Kingston." He pointed to the nearest mainland town.

Then he pointed to a red brick wall on the near side of the spit. "Fort Charles. The navy's offices are there. That's where your young man will be."

Francesca examined the fort. She could see its strategically advantageous position with clear lines of fire over the entrance to the harbor as well as out to sea. Orderly red bricks were set atop a base of rough-hewn stones. Black cannon muzzles protruded from the perimeter.

The image popped into her head of her and Phillip running into each other's arms along the parapet with the azure ocean behind them. *Don't get ahead or yourself.*

The next morning, Francesca put on the velvet dress Claire and Belle had made for her. It had cream ruffles around the square, open neckline and Francesca liked to think that the emerald-green set off her eyes. She felt pretty and feminine for the first time in months. That was precisely how she wanted to feel when she saw Phillip.

First, I have to pretend to be the captain's wife. Her chest tightened. She told herself she felt discomfort at the lie, but that wasn't it. Was she nervous about playing so intimate a role? Or was it the betrayal she had planned?

Francesca purposely pulled the laces on her corset overly tight. The whalebone stays pinched her ribs so that she could barely inhale. She liked what it did to her figure, but more importantly, she would have an excuse to feel faint and ask the captain to find her someplace to lie down.

Once alone, she would find her way to Phillip. She would pretend to faint at the captain's feet if necessary, although in that case, she ran the risk he might bring her straight back to the *Destiny*. She would have to see how the situation developed.

Crewmen whistled and shouted playfully when Francesca appeared on deck. She dropped them a curtsy which they greeted with laughter.

Bigalow, scraping the deck with a holystone, called out, "I see Mills was wrong when 'e said ya were a better man than 'e were."

Francesca grinned. "Not at all! Find him a dress and I'll prove I'm a better woman as well."

The men guffawed. Francesca noticed Mr. Hart frowning. As an ex-naval officer, he was firmly against women aboard ship. It seemed he could ignore Francesca in her man's attire, but this, she suspected, was unsupportable.

The town of Port Royal spread before the *Destiny*. The morning was warm, promising oppressive heat later. The line of white wooden shops and taverns was punctuated by an occasional red brick building that had survived the earthquake and tidal wave of 1692. Palm trees added splashes of green against the blue sky. Gulls, flecks of white, darted over the town, their calls crisp. Shouts flew between ships and among buildings ashore as the townsfolk began their day.

Captain Massey appeared from below deck. He stopped short when he saw Francesca and he turned his face away. He tugged at his lapels and cleared his throat.

He wore a navy-blue silk coat that narrowed at his waist and pleated over his hips, accentuating his broad shoulders. Beneath, a gray silk waistcoat laced with blue embroidery and close-fitting gray velvet breeches gave him a distinguished air.

"There's a right fizzin' dandy," called one of the men.

The rest hooted and Bigalow whistled at him as well.

Captain Massey waved them off good naturedly. "You've been at sea far too long."

"Aye, Cap'n," Bigalow said, tilting his head toward town. "When do ya mean ta remedy 'at?"

"In a few days' time," the captain said. "But there will be plenty of entertainment in the meanwhile."

He approached Francesca and offered his arm, leading them toward the manned longboat waiting at the side. Baldric met them with a mocking bow. "M' lord, m' lady," he said. "Yer chariot awaits."

"Aye," grumbled the captain. He paused and stroked the rail of the ship. "Make sure my girl is in good order when I return."

"Aye, Sir."

They descended to the longboat and headed ashore.

"You look lovely, Francesca," the captain said once she'd gotten her skirts situated.

"Thank you, Captain." She put a hand to her coifed hair. "I'd forgotten how much effort it takes."

"It's well worth it, I'd say." He took her hand and slipped a diamond ring on her gloved finger. "Call me Will, Mrs. Massey." The captain held her hand longer than necessary and Francesca felt blood rising to her traitorous cheeks.

She fingered the ring and looked away. "I'll wear the ring, but I won't tell lies for you." She could sense him staring hard at her profile.

He shrugged. "Let me do the talking."

The awkward silence that followed was interrupted by two boats filled with local wenches headed for the *Destiny*. The women hollered and waved while the men whistled and roared from the ship.

"There goes the loot," Francesca said.

"It's theirs to spend as they please." The captain said, preoccupied with scanning the town. "You disapprove."

How else could he possibly imagine she'd feel?

A body hung decaying in a gibbet on a spit of land. Birds had pecked out the eyes and flesh hung loose from the encaged bones. A sign beneath read, "*Pyrate*."

Francesca, eyes locked on the rotting body, and surprised at the acid edge to her voice, replied, "It's just good to see precisely what I'm risking my neck for."

The captain followed her gaze. "Poor sod."

Once ashore, Captain Massey and Francesca wandered past a row of taverns full of raucous music on their way toward the market square.

Drunken men with women on their arms stumbled out of bars reeking of stale beer. They bellowed at passersby.

A boy bumped into the captain and scurried away. The captain swiftly searched for his purse to make sure it hadn't been pinched. Francesca averted her eyes from the gaudy women with painted faces who winked and called to passing men.

Once they reached the market, Francesca was enthralled by the exotic items and foods on display. Captain Massey purchased a slice of watermelon from a local farmer. Francesca looked wary as he handed it to her. He laughed as her eyes widened with the first juicy bite.

"Amazing," Francesca said as the captain wiped a drop of juice from her chin with his handkerchief. "It's like eating a sweet cloud! It just melts away."

"Indeed," the captain said. "And that is only the beginning. There are bananas, pomegranates, seagrapes, prickle pears. A whole rainbow of tastes to experience."

"They'll have to wait until I finish my watermelon," she said with a laugh.

They wandered into a stall lined with reed bird cages. The pens erupted with squawks, twitters, and a flurry of brightly colored feathers. A wizened little man drew them in, a parrot with a scarlet breast perched on his shoulder. The bird screeched, then croaked, "Welcome, come in, come in," to Francesca's delight.

Francesca perused the cages, marveling at the variety and depth of color as the birds fluttered and flashed their wings. Besides hue, there was an amazing variety of sizes, from the large and majestic macaws to tiny lemon-colored warblers.

"Do people buy them as pets?" she asked the captain.

"Some," he said. "Others, for the feathers."

They went on to the next stall laughing and talking, steering clear of the north end of the market where slaves were bought and sold. Neither of them had the stomach to watch.

As they passed a booth full of mammal and reptile skins, a man with a live snake around his shoulders startled Francesca. She cried out and buried her face in the captain's chest. He jokingly pretended to defend her making them both laugh.

As they wandered on, Francesca slipped a hand through the captain's arm. "Captain, I mean … Will. Thank you for showing me the town. How do you know so much about the goods? Have you been here before?"

"No, I've not been to Jamaica, but I lived on Barbados." The captain stiffened. The friendliness and cheer drained from his face, his mood suddenly businesslike.

Francesca was sorry she'd asked. She wished for something to say to bring back his mood of a moment ago, but it seemed irretrievably lost. "Is Barbados much like—"

"No," cut in the captain. He nodded toward an elegant storefront. "That's where we're headed." He hurried their pace.

The sign in red and gold lettering read, "CROWLEY & SONS MERCANTILE," and the shop window displayed women's hats and bolts of silk fabrics. They entered into the scent of exotic spices.

Francesca examined a selection of coin purses embellished with the same colorful feathers she had seen in the market. The captain spoke with an ample, red-cheeked woman who looked to be the proprietress.

The woman beckoned Francesca and led them through a back door into an expansive warehouse full of crates and casks. She hustled them up a set of stairs into a luxuriously furnished office.

"Stanley, we have visitors," she said as they entered.

Mr. Crowley was a tiny, balding man, dwarfed by his enormous rosewood desk. He rose in greeting as Mrs. Crowley introduced them.

"Welcome," he said, shaking the captain's hand and bowing to Francesca. He motioned them to a pair of leather chairs. "What brings you here today?"

The captain handed him a sheet of paper. "Business, I'm afraid," he said with a dashing smile at Mrs. Crowley who hovered behind her husband. Her generous proportions made him look even smaller.

"Business, business," said Mrs. Crowley, clearly disappointed. "Perhaps I could get you some tea." The thought seemed to cheer her.

"That would be lovely," Francesca said.

Mrs. Crowley bustled out as Mr. Crowley examined the sheet of paper. "Working for Carlisle, I see. You could do a lot worse."

He took his time going over the paper, and Francesca could almost see numbers whirring in his head.

Mrs. Crowley bustled in with a tea tray and set it on the corner of the desk. She poured a cup and passed it to Francesca.

"You're lucky to have escaped the pirates prowling these waters," said Mr. Crowley.

"Indeed, we are," the captain replied.

"We hanged Black Sam and his crew last week, yet they still seem to be everywhere." Mr. Crowley watched them closely.

Francesca's fingers trembled and she spilled a few drops of tea. Did the man suspect something?

Captain Massey waved a hand. "Please, you mustn't frighten my wife with talk of pirates."

Mrs. Crowley handed the captain a cup of tea. "Really, Stanley, you'll scare the girl to death." She turned to Francesca. "You must love your husband very much to go to sea with him."

"Well, I…"

The captain took Francesca's hand, squeezing it. "She is the soul of loyalty. She's pledged to follow me wherever I go."

How quickly his moods changed, or was this an act? Considering the Articles she had signed, he was telling the truth—in a way.

Mrs. Crowley sighed as she handed her husband a cup of tea. "Stanley used to gallivant about the ocean. He never took me. Not that I would have gone, mind you. But it would have been nice to have been asked."

Mr. Crowley rolled his eyes as Mrs. Crowley perched on the desk. "Tell me, how did you meet your husband, Mrs. Massey?"

"Ida, I really—" Mr. Crowley started.

Mrs. Crowley waved him quiet. Francesca bit her lip.

After an awkward pause the captain kissed Francesca's hand. "Well, Mrs. Crowley, when first I saw her, she was across the floor amidst a group of men. None of them could take their eyes off her. She was radiant, such spirit, such vigor. I knew then she was like no woman I'd ever met and that she was the one for me. I made my proposal that very night, and we've been together ever since."

Mrs. Crowley beamed, her eyes misty.

Francesca stared at the captain. It was true, though he'd left out the swords and blood. But did he mean the part about her being "the one for him?" Or was he just having fun, twisting the truth to make a point? Mocking her statement that she wouldn't lie by proving he didn't need to.

"That is the most romantic thing I have ever heard," Mrs. Crowley said. "Isn't that wonderful!"

"Yes, dear," Mr. Crowley said with an air of long-suffering patience. "Now, may we please conduct our business?"

Mrs. Crowley sighed. "He has no head for romance." She set down her teacup and rose. "I'll say *adieu*."

The captain rose as she bustled out of the room, then turned to Mr. Crowley. "Now then, where were we?"

Mr. Crowly grinned. "We were discussing how to marry your cargo to my inventory and produce some very lovely numbers," Mr. Crowley said. "And my wife says I have no head for romance."

An hour later the captain shook hands with Mr. Crowley and he kissed Francesca's hand at the door. He said, "Your supplies will be delivered in the morning."

They turned to go as Mrs. Crowley tapped on the window and waved a handkerchief. They waved back and then were off through the market stalls.

Francesca took the captain's arm. "Captain, I mean, Will … I…" She wanted to ask him about what he had said to Mrs. Crowley.

"What is it, Mrs. Massey?" He had a teasing look in his eyes that made Francesca smile despite herself. He could be so charming when he wanted to be, when he wasn't mocking her or ordering her about.

"I wanted to ask you about—"

He stopped dead before a stall, yanking Francesca to a halt. The stall owner, a toothless old woman approached. Captain Massey lifted a bolt of blue and white gingham fabric, his face stricken.

"Five gold pieces," said the woman.

Captain Massey fingered the fabric. Pain etched his face, but he ran a tender hand over the fabric.

"What is it?" asked Francesca tightening her hand on his arm.

His voice cracked. "My wife had a dress made of this. She wore it the day they came."

A chill ran down Francesca's spine.

The woman poked at the fabric. "Four gold pieces. You buy."

The captain's fingers tightened into fists. "They came at night, dragging us from our homes. They cut down the men with machetes. They thought I was dead. I think I was dead." His eyes closed. "I lay there and watched them … Mary …"

He took a deep, shuddering breath. "Caroline got away from them. Mary screamed for her to run. She ran back into the house. Caroline was three. Sometimes she would hide under the bed when she had bad dreams."

Francesca wanted to lay a palm against his cheek, but then his face hardened to stone. An unquenchable rage roared behind his eyes. "The bastards laughed as they lit the house on fire."

With tears in her eyes, she reached up to wrap her arms around his neck. He jerked away, his face twisting with pain. His lips formed the name, *Mary*. He pressed the fabric into Francesca's arms.

He loves her, this other woman who was slain and possibly raped before his eyes. He loves her passionately enough to risk his life every day to avenge her.

A sickening wave of jealousy swept through her chest. No one had ever loved her that way. Not even Phillip.

With a haggard look the captain turned and strode away.

"Where are you going?"

He neither paused nor looked back. "Return to the ship."

The old woman tugged at her sleeve. "Three gold pieces."

Francesca shouted after him. "Captain! Will!"

He disappeared into a tavern with a painted sign of a blue anchor. The woman tugged at her sleeve again. "You buy? Madame buy? Two gold pieces."

Francesca stood shaking, hugging the fabric. Her heart broke, but for him or for herself? She knew that look, she knew the pain of losing loved ones, but would she ever know that kind of love?

"Two gold," said the woman.

Francesca stared vacantly at her. That violent rush of jealousy was more than loneliness. In the past she'd been attracted to him, certainly. There was something compelling in his vitality, his roguish charm, but this was different. She wanted to take away his pain. She wanted to hold him, to soothe and comfort him, she wanted … She wanted to inspire such a passionate love.

"I must be going mad," she said aloud.

The old woman studied her, then rooted around in her pockets. She brought out a ceramic charm on a string and dangled it in front of Francesca. "Cure for madness, two gold pieces."

CHAPTER 20
THE FORT

Francesca stared unseeing at the old woman for a moment then shook her head. She set down the fabric, though her fingers lingered on it. *Get a grip on yourself, Cesca.* She glanced around the crowded market, but people were haggling and laughing as usual. No one but the old woman had seen the exchange between her and the captain.

Shaken and light-headed, she thought perhaps she had tied her corset too tight. She wanted somewhere quiet to think.

Then it struck her. She was alone in Port Royal and she hadn't even needed to faint. This was her chance to find Phillip.

But did she want to? *It's not fair to compare the captain's relationship with his wife to mine with Phillip. We were so young. That sort of passion would have come.* She'd risked her life to reach Phillip. That was passion. How could she know how he felt unless she found him?

But the anguish on the captain's face… There were times when she thought he cared for her. Disobeying orders, leaving, finding Phillip would be a betrayal. But the captain didn't love her. He loved his wife. He'd be angry, but he'd mend.

Her eyes drifted to the alehouse where the captain had gone to grieve or to forget. A fiddle scraped out a sea chantey amid lusty singing. She squared her shoulders. *What am I doing? Why am I even questioning this?*

She couldn't pass up a chance at happiness because of her confused feelings for a pirate. She headed for Fort Charles.

Francesca's head swam when she reached the fort. She had hurried as much as her corset would allow and was short of breath. Her heart thumped as she made her way across the cobblestone courtyard. Between the oppressive heat and the velvet dress, she was bathed in sweat. She barely noticed the towering walls or the guards walking the fortifications. Her eyes were locked firmly on the door to the officers' quarters, where she had been told she could ask after Phillip.

The door opened as she approached. A young man in a gold-trimmed, navy-blue officer's coat appeared. He took off his tri-corner hat when he saw Francesca and escorted her in. "Good morning, Miss. How may I help you?"

Her breath was shallow and her heart beat so hard she had to swallow before she could speak. "I'm looking for Lord Worthington."

The young man tilted his head and thought for a moment. "I don't believe I've had the pleasure of meeting him. But won't you take a seat and I'll check with the captain."

The young man disappeared through a door in the far wall. A few wooden chairs lined the white walls of the waiting room, but she was too nervous to sit. She paced.

What if Phillip had forgotten her? What if he didn't feel the way she did? Her skin blazed all over and she fanned herself with her hands.

The ring on her finger glinted. She yanked it off, dropped it in a pocket, and resumed pacing.

A series of sketched faces tacked to the wall caught her attention. They were crudely drawn "wanted" posters of known pirates. She absently scanned the malignant faces and stopped dead.

There was a sketch of a dark-haired woman. The eyebrows were too thin, the nose a bit long, and the expression too fierce, but it was meant to be her. The sign read: LADY PYRATE and MURDERER.

A blade of ice plunged into her stomach. Her knees buckled and the room spun. Papa's face, full of contempt swam before her. Then the young officer was there, catching her.

"Miss, are you ill?"

Francesca clutched him with one hand and put the other to her tight stays. She couldn't get enough air. She needed to pull herself together; she was making a scene, but she couldn't breathe.

The young man helped her to a chair, and she sat, trying not to be sick. Had Phillip seen the drawing? She had asked Claire to tell him what had happened. She had admitted she was a pirate. Did he despise her now? Was he trying to hunt her down and kill her?

The young man, who had left her side, returned with a glass of amber fluid and an older gentleman also in an officer's uniform. The young officer sat beside her and pressed the glass to her lips. When she took a sip, fire slid down her throat and swirled through her stomach. It steadied her a bit and allowed her to think. If Phillip were trying to capture her, her name would be on the poster. No, it wasn't Phillip. The thought buoyed her spirits a little.

"Feeling better, my dear?" the older gentleman asked. He had a stooped build, thinning hair, and a stern, but concerned face.

"Much, thank you," Francesca said, catching her breath.

"This is Midshipman Davies," said the older man. "And I am Captain Fredricks. What is your name, my dear?"

She took the glass from the young man and took a slow sip to give herself time to think. She couldn't give them her real name. It might cause trouble for Phillip if people knew he was visited by pirates.

"Abigail Worthington," she said, remembering the name she had given the captain. That was twice now she'd lied.

The gentlemen scowled and looked at each other. Did the young man glance at the drawing then back at her? Or was she imagining it?

"I'm sorry, Miss Worthington, it's just that you don't sound English."

Francesca hadn't even thought about her Italian accent. Now she was stuck in the lie. "My mother was from Naples," she said, "I spent much of my childhood there."

"I see," Fredricks said with a disapproving air, as if an Englishman marrying an Italian was distasteful. "And, if I may ask, how have you come here? Are you alone?"

Francesca feigned another dizzy spell to give herself time to think. Why hadn't she anticipated these questions? She'd been so focused on Phillip.

"Thank you for your concern, Captain. I arrived a few days ago. I'm staying with my Great Aunt in Kingston. You see, she has rheumatism. The family thought I might be able to help." She smiled sweetly up at the men. "I'm afraid I'm not accustomed to the heat here in Jamaica."

"My, my," Fredricks said, more comfortable now that he had an explanation for her condition. "It does get hot, doesn't it?"

"I have a cousin stationed here," Francesca continued. "I was hoping to find him. His name is Lord Phillip Worthington."

"Ah," Fredricks said, "A fine young man. He's captain of the Doe. He's cruising for pirates with Admiral Strickland's fleet. I'm afraid he hasn't been here in months and we're not expecting him anytime soon."

Disappointment crashed on Francesca. She'd risked so much to get here, and for nothing. And to make matters worse, Phillip was under orders to hunt down and capture her.

She slumped forward and must have gone pale because the young midshipman was instantly forcing more alcohol down her throat. She sputtered and coughed, fuming at herself.

Of course Phillip wasn't here. Of course he would be at sea, not sitting around port, waiting for her. Of course it would be his duty to apprehend her. How could she have been so foolish? Tears of frustration streamed down her cheeks.

The two men, appalled, fretted and clucked, muttering "please," and "you mustn't."

Captain Fredricks, who she was sure had faced cannon fire and enemy assaults, cowered in front of her womanly display. Mr. Davies looked apologetic as he patted her back and offered her his handkerchief.

Francesca let herself cry. She couldn't help it. And after all, these men would hardly suspect her of being a pirate if she fell apart in their waiting room. Eventually she wiped her eyes and nose on the midshipman's handkerchief and quieted.

"I am sorry to distress you," Fredricks said. "I can see it is a matter of some import."

Francesca nodded. She'd had time to think while she was crying. "It's a family matter, you see. There is bad news from home, I'm afraid. I was hoping Phillip would be able to help deal with a ... delicate situation." These men would never pry into someone else's delicate situation. "Do you have any idea when he will return?"

"It may be months," said Captain Fredricks gently. "Last year the admiral cruised for half the year." He hastily added, "But orders do change. There's no way to know for sure."

Francesca nodded, dabbing her eyes.

Captain Fredricks rubbed his hands together nervously. "I wish there was something I could do for you."

"We could deliver a note to him on the next post ship," suggested Mr. Davies with a look at the captain, who nodded.

"Yes, please," Francesca said. Little good a letter would do, but it was better than nothing.

They led her down a hallway into an office with a writing desk. Mr. Davies supplied paper, pen, and ink and they left her alone to write.

Francesca puzzled over what to say. She wasn't sure if anyone besides Phillip would read the note. Finally, she scribbled:

My dearest cousin,

I've come to Port Royal only to find that you are at sea, out of my reach. I pray news has reached you from the ladies, Henry. Since I left them, my circumstances have worsened. I cannot remain here to wait for you as I desire. I must move on, I know not where.

I've done all in my power to remain in Papa's good graces, but I have been obliged to join my new companions in their activities. Please believe that in my heart I am still as you have known me.

With love,

Abigail F.D. Worthington

She folded the letter and wrote Phillip's name on the outside. She rose, opened the door, and found Mr. Davies waiting in the hall, hat in hand. She handed him the letter. "Thank you. I'm most obliged."

"My pleasure," he said, slipping it into a pocket. "May I arrange a carriage to take you home?"

"No, thank you, I think a walk would do me good."

"Surely you aren't thinking of walking all the way to Kingston in this heat!"

Francesca kicked herself, she had forgotten that her imaginary aunt resided in Kingston. She should have let him call the carriage. She could have had the coachman drop her off wherever she liked, but then, where was she going?

"Indeed not," Francesca said. "I have business to attend to here in town."

"Then at least let me escort you."

"You are too kind," Francesca said, heading for the door. Now she wanted to be away from the fort as much as she had previously wanted to reach it. "I mustn't take up any more of your time. Thank you, Mr. Davies."

As she hurried out the door, she found Mr. Davies at her elbow. "Miss Worthington, you're new to Port Royal. You may not realize how dangerous the town can be for a lady."

Francesca wanted to laugh. The navy men were the danger, not the pirates. She was a pirate, whether she wanted to admit it or not. She stopped and looked at his serious face. His jaw was set. She could see she wouldn't be able to get away from him without making a scene. The last thing she wanted was to draw more attention to herself.

She took his arm, her voice teasing. "You intend to be my protector whether I'm willing or not, don't you, Mr. Davies?"

He gave her a shy grin. "I do, Miss. It's my duty as a gentleman. Where is it that I'm escorting you?"

Francesca had no idea. Other than the market square she was completely unfamiliar with the town.

As they headed toward the gate, she put a finger to her cheek. "I'm to meet a good friend of my aunt. But, how silly of me, the name of the establishment escapes me. I'm sure it will come to me."

"Then how are we to find it?"

"It's this way," she said, nodding in the direction of the docks and smiling. "I'll know it when I see it."

It was past noon, and the heat was oppressive, the kind of heat that saps the will from all but the insects, which fill it with their buzzing. There was no breeze, and sensible folk had all taken refuge inside their shady homes. A few drunkards in shirtsleeves stumbled from one bar to another, occasionally throwing rude comments toward Mr. Davies.

Francesca, sweat dripping along her spine, led the young man randomly through the streets. She searched for someplace that would be appropriate for her to enter where he would be unlikely to follow. She was having no luck. As Henry had indicated, most of the establishments were bars or brothels. There were a few inns, but Mr. Davies might insist on waiting with her for her aunt's friend to arrive.

If Mr. Davies noticed the heat, or her haphazard wandering, he gave no indication. He kept up a friendly chatter that she barely heard. If he stopped to draw breath, she threw out a question about Port Royal and he was off again. She nodded, but her mind was preoccupied with the question of where she was going. Not just here and now, but in the larger sense. She was lost in more ways than one.

She turned right at a corner, her eyes scanning the names of businesses and shops, and stopped. Captain Massey was walking down the street toward her. She ducked back around the corner dragging Mr. Davies with her.

"I think we've gone too far," she said, hiding her panic with a shrug. She didn't want the captain to see her with Mr. Davies. Not only was she disobeying his order to return to the ship, but he might think she was betraying them to the navy, or that Mr. Davies was the cousin she'd mentioned. It would be a disaster if he confronted them.

She hurried the young man back the way they had come. She tried to judge the distance between the captain and the corner behind her, and between her and the next corner. She wouldn't make it without running and Mr. Davies would find that odd. The shops ahead were all taverns. She couldn't duck inside one; Mr. Davies would be aghast.

Finally, she took a couple quick steps ahead and spun to face Mr. Davies. He stumbled to a stop, nearly running into her, but at least he was between her and the corner the captain would pass. As long as the captain didn't turn down this street, he might not see her.

"What is it?" said Mr. Davies, confusion on his face.

"Well," she said, "I guess I must admit that I'm quite lost."

Davies gave her a gentle smile. "I thought as much. If you could tell me the type of establishment, I might be able to help you find it."

Francesca watched for the captain around the young man's shoulder. She prayed he wouldn't see her. Prayed ... yes, that was it. "It's a church."

She saw the captain. His gait was purposeful but not hurried, his eyes on the ground in front of him as if lost in thought. He moved on, past the intersection and Francesca stifled a sigh of relief.

"You mean St. Peter's?"

"Of course!" Francesca focused on the man. "How could I forget?"

"That's only two blocks from here. If you'd told me it was a church, I could have taken you there straight away."

"Well..." She gave Mr. Davies her prettiest smile, the smile she had always reserved for when Papa brought her presents, the smile that made Papa pinch her cheek and call her *my Cesca*. It seemed to do strange things to Mr. Davies' breathing. "I guess I was enjoying our walk."

St. Peter's church was an elegant, red brick building with arched windows and a shake roof. Mr. Davies bowed as he left her at the doorway and asked if he might have the honor of calling on her again. She told him she must speak with her aunt, but not to worry, she knew where to find him.

Francesca entered the relative cool of the building, her shoulders drooping.

The whitewashed walls gave the church an airy feel. Brass chandeliers overhead reflected off the black and white floor tile as glints of gold. The church was laid out in the shape of a cross with ten or twelve rows of pews leading to the altar. Francesca made her way to the left arm of the cross and knelt at the back of the empty church.

Her head dropped onto her clasped hands on the dark wood pew in front of her. She was exhausted. The last few months had been such a struggle, and now there was no end in sight. Phillip wasn't going to ride in and save the day.

She didn't realize she was crying until she felt the tears dripping from her hands. Footsteps approached and Francesca looked up. She wiped at her tears, smearing more than drying them. They felt cool on her cheeks.

A dark-haired woman with a half-grown son and daughter and a little girl moved into the pew three rows ahead of Francesca. Once seated, the woman hugged her older daughter and broke into stifled sobs. The son stared stoically ahead, and the little girl fidgeted and looked around.

A bent old priest shuffled over to them and spoke softly with the woman, his face sorrowful. They must have lost someone, a husband and father maybe. She looked around at the plaques covering the walls—memorials to traders, fishermen, and sailors lost at sea.

Francesca flared with shame at her binge of self-pity. Maybe she was alone, but she was alive. She could find a way out of her situation ... somehow.

The priest gave Francesca a nod before he moved up the aisle toward the altar.

Francesca couldn't shake the wanted poster image. The black eyes stared at her. She had tried so hard to keep her vow and look at what she had become. This morning she told the captain she wouldn't lie for him, but how many lies had she told poor Mr. Davies? What would Papa think now? She sighed and dropped her head into her hands.

Men's voices, arguing near the entrance, echoed through the church. She jerked her head up when she recognized Mr. Davies' voice. She couldn't catch what he said, but heard another man respond.

"Impossible. Abigail Worthington has blonde hair and blue eyes."

Francesca dropped to her hands and knees, crouching between the pews.

Hurried footsteps echoed up the aisle toward the altar. A voice called out, "Priest!"

"Please, gentlemen, this is a church," said the old man's voice.

She strained to make out what they were saying. She peeked over the top of the pew. Five navy men surrounded the priest, who raised an arm in her direction. She ducked down, heart racing. She was trapped. There was no way she could get to the exit without being seen. She had to hide, but where?

Under the pew she saw the wide skirts and legs of the grieving family three rows up.

As boot heels headed in her direction, Francesca stretched flat on the floor, pulled her skirts tight around her, and barrel-rolled toward the legs of the family. She stopped, facing the underside of the pew, as close to the family's heels as she dared.

Her heart thudded in her ears as she lay perfectly still. Suddenly the little girl's face appeared, upside down. Her little brows pulled together in a confused frown. Francesca's body went cold, but she winked, putting a finger to her lips. The little girl smiled and her face disappeared.

Please, God, I've tried so hard, I'm so sorry.

Francesca watched five sets of shining black boots stop in the aisle in front of the grieving woman, just feet from her head. She held her breath.

"We're sorry to bother you, ma'am," a voice said, "but—"

The little girl said, "Mumma, why is—"

"Hush," cut in her brother.

"We were wondering if you saw a young woman in a green dress."

"But—" said the girl.

"You hush," her brother said.

The little heels kicked at the air, but the girl remained silent. The woman made no reply. Perhaps she shook her head, because the boots turned toward each other.

"Adams, search the choir loft. Davies, check the sacristy. The rest of you sweep the church."

"Aye, Sir." The feet headed off in different directions. Francesca said a silent thank you. The little girl's face reappeared. She put her finger to her lips as Francesca had done. Then her face jerked out of sight.

"Stop yer blessed squirmin'," said her brother.

Francesca waited a long time with the tile pressing hard against her back and skull. Once she was positive the boots had disappeared, she rolled back to her spot and rose. She brushed off her dress and hurried toward the exit, stopping just inside the door.

She had to get back to the ship. Luckily, Port Royal was a small town. It couldn't be more than six or seven blocks back to the harbor. The docks were on the northwest edge of town and the afternoon sun supplied the direction, but she would be terribly conspicuous in her green dress.

She peered out searching for blue navy coats but didn't see any. The street was wide and open, too open for her liking, but she'd have to cross it at some point. Hopefully the navy men had moved off.

Beside a brick house across the street grew a row of broad-leaved bushes with red flowers. Among the plants, her dress might not stand out as much. She looked both ways and then hurried across the street. The afternoon heat hit her like a hot, wet blanket, but she made it across with no sign of pursuit. She weaved her way between buildings and down back alleys toward the ship.

Once she reached the harbor, Francesca hovered in the shadows of a covered porch. Unlike the town, the docks were far from deserted. Workers loaded barrels onto carts or off wagons, and boats plied between ships and shore, the men's movements languid in the heat.

She fidgeted, searching for a way back to the ship. She ran her fingernails through the velvet of her skirts. Wet with sweat, she wished she hadn't tied her corset so tight.

The *Destiny* swung at anchor fifty yards out in the bay, but it might as well have been fifty miles. Francesca had no way to get there. She could hire a boat, but the authorities might question the rowers. If they discovered what ship she boarded, not only would she be captured, the rest of the crew would be as well.

The captain might still be ashore so she could ride back with him, but then he would know she had disobeyed orders. And if the navy men saw her with the captain …

Francesca noticed four women approaching from her left. They chatted beneath pastel parasols, waving feathered fans. From their painted faces and low-cut dresses their profession was clear. Their gait was purposeful but unhurried. In their midst was a young man carrying a pair of oars.

One of the brothels must have its own boat. The women might be headed for the *Destiny*. Her green dress would be less conspicuous amid their brightly colored outfits, and it seemed unlikely the authorities would question every brothel.

As they drew near, Francesca stepped out into the hot sun. "Good afternoon, ladies."

The women halted and stared at her, apparently unaccustomed to being spoken to by respectable women. Francesca stood, open mouthed, unable to think of anything to say.

"Good afternoon," said one of the ladies. She was a stunning woman. Golden curls surrounded perfectly arched eyebrows, high cheekbones, and a straight, pert nose. Her skin was creamy, her voice deep and musical.

The women turned to move on and Francesca quickly approached. "Please, may I ask where you are going?"

"To find our destiny," laughed a slender, boyish woman.

"If you're going to the *Destiny*, might I, perhaps, ride with you?" Francesca said, feeling inexplicably shy and bashful.

Now the women bristled and looked her up and down.

"Git yer own way," said a gaudily dressed redhead.

"C'mon, Helen, let's go," said a mousy woman with too much rouge to the stunning woman. "We've enough competition already."

Helen held up a hand and the others quieted.

"No, no," Francesca said. She could feel a blush spread. "I'm not … I don't…" She looked helplessly at Helen. "I'm a crewman."

Two of the women gaped. "Ya expect us ta believe 'at?" the redhead said.

Helen's eyes went over her, reassessing. "Let's see your hands."

Francesca stripped off a glove displaying her tar-stained, calloused hand. "Honestly, I'm a topman." Francesca glanced around feeling exposed. She spotted a blue coat exiting a shop. She looked at Helen, her eyes pleading. "Do you know what flag the *Destiny* flies under?"

"We can guess," Helen said, measuring Francesca.

Francesca glanced back at the blue-coated figure as he headed toward them. Mr. Davies! Panicked, Francesca clutched Helen's arm. "The navy is looking for me."

Helen, following Francesca's eyes, gave a small hiss. She drew Francesca into the midst of the women. "Form up, girls."

The women surrounded her, hiding her among their parasols and skirts.

Gratitude filled Francesca. These women were willing to risk the wrath of the navy to protect a woman they had just met.

"Why didn't you say so at once," Helen said. "You're Lady Blade, aren't you? The woman pirate we've heard the men talking about."

"Well, yes. I suppose I am."

Helen handed Francesca her peacock-feather fan for Francesca to hide her face behind. They moved toward the docks. As Mr. Davies neared, the women catcalled to him, swishing their fans and fluttering their parasols.

"Ooo, look at the handsome young officer."

"I'd like to run up his flag."

"Show us the big gun."

"I promise we won't tell the admiral."

Mr. Davies tried to ignore them, but his eyes were drawn back. From behind her fan Francesca saw the redhead bare a breast to Mr. Davies. The gentleman's coughing fit turned his face crimson. Averting his eyes, he hurried away with the women laughing behind him.

They were still giggling as they approached a small dingy. The young man jumped in, setting the oars into the oarlocks. He helped them into the boat.

Once they were seated and headed into the bay, Helen leaned toward Francesca and put a hand on her arm. "I met Mary Read once. She was one of the woman pirates who sailed with Calico Jack. She was a bold, brash woman, always looking for a fight." Helen scanned Francesca. "You're not like her at all, are you?"

Francesca thought that Helen was not at all what she had expected from a painted lady. She remembered the priest haranguing about wicked women, but these women didn't seem wicked at all.

"I guess I'm not," Francesca said. "Thank you for saving me. It was brave of you."

"Not at all." Helen shrugged, but a proud smile lit her eyes.

"If I may ask, why did you do it?"

Helen looked out over the water, her face pensive. "None of us are who or what we wanted to be."

"Speak fer yerself!" said the redhead.

Helen laughed and nodded toward the woman. "With the exception of Maryrose, our lives and our fates have been decided for us by men." Her expression turned wicked. "I learned long ago that a little rebellion now and again makes it bearable."

As the dingy neared the *Destiny*, Francesca could hear men laughing and singing, intermingled with feminine shrieks and giggles and off-beat music. Francesca grimaced. Noting her reaction, Helen said, "You're the strangest pirate I've ever met."

"I'm not a pirate," Francesca said. "Not by choice anyway."

Maryrose whistled and a few heads appeared at the rail of the *Destiny*. The pirates hollered and waved. Three of the women shouted and fluttered their parasols while Helen waved her fan demurely.

Francesca couldn't imagine how an intelligent, well-bred woman could engage in such work. Helen must have read her mind because she squared her shoulders.

"You must know as well as I do that money is freedom. With enough money even a woman can live as she pleases without being ordered about by men." Her voice went hard. "There's more than one way to plunder."

The dingy bumped along the side of the ship. One-eyed Kelsey, Pitt the carpenter, and Bigalow helped the prostitutes aboard, shouting greetings. When they saw Francesca, they looked disappointed.

"Oh, it's you, DiCesare," Kelsey said. "When's the cap'n comin' back?"

Francesca climbed up the side on her own, a difficult task in her skirts and petticoats. "I don't know."

When she swung over the gunwale, Helen and the other women were already wrapped tightly in the arms of pirates.

Francesca's nose wrinkled. The *Destiny* had been transformed into a floating brothel. Near the mainmast a few men drunkenly played fiddles and drums while couples, in various states of undress, stumbled around, attempting to keep time. Many pairs had retreated to the relative privacy between cannons to complete their tête-à-têtes. Francesca looked away when she spied too much of Tuit's tattooed skin. Carnal noises emerged from the decks below.

The only bastion of order was Mr. Hart, standing stolidly on the quarterdeck, purposefully oblivious to the chaos. Francesca noticed one wench approach him, but his glare sent her skittering away.

Francesca headed for her cabin, but before she reached the companionway, Miller, ale mug in hand, tumbled into her. He was chasing a pudgy, giggling girl with deep dimples in her painted cheeks.

"Pardon, missy," he said, turning red.

Apparently seeing consternation on Francesca's face, he snatched off his hat and gave her a shrug. "E'ry man needs a bit o' muslin now and again." With that he turned and followed the trail of giggles.

Francesca shut and locked her cabin door. She threw herself on her cot, covering her head with her arms to muffle the noise. Her loneliness felt like it had burrowed a hole in her chest and was devouring her from the inside out. She supposed she couldn't begrudge Miller and the men the comfort of soft arms to hold them and hands to caress them. By this time, she had hoped to be firmly wrapped in Phillip's arms, laying her head on his chest and listening to the reassuring sound of his heartbeat. How she ached for that.

Or was it the captain's arms she ached for? It was all so confusing. She wrapped her arms around her body and squeezed.

The captain's words from the marketplace echoed in her head. She pictured a dark-haired little girl in a white shift curled into a ball under her bed as flames crept around her. In her mind, the shrieks of the wenches were transformed into a child's screams.

She loosened her stays, curled into a ball, and waited for the storm to pass.

CHAPTER 21
BACK TO SEA

The next day, as Francesca lay in her cot staring at the ceiling, there was a knock on her door. The captain stood outside, shoulders slumped but jaw hard set. "Francesca, be dressed and ready in an hour. You and I are going back ashore."

A ball of panic writhed in her stomach. "I can't. I mean, I really don't care to, Sir."

His face darkened. "I'm not giving you a choice, DiCesare." He turned to go but Francesca grabbed his arm.

"Please, Captain—Will—don't make me go back there."

"Why not? Yesterday we … you seemed to enjoy it."

"I…" She tried to think of a story, but nothing came.

He tilted his head, suspicion in his face. "What happened after I left you?" She looked away.

"The truth now. You're a terrible liar."

"I didn't come straight back. I went to find my cousin." *Mostly the truth.* She felt him studying her face but didn't look at him.

"You were unsuccessful, I take it."

She nodded.

"Then what happened?"

"There was a wanted poster." She risked a glance at him. He didn't seem angry, just concerned. "It was me."

"Bollocks!" He took a sharp breath and ran a hand through his hair.

"A navy man recognized me," she said, her voice quavering. "I barely made it back to the ship."

He closed his eyes with a pained expression. "That changes everything." He sighed and opened his eyes. "Did anyone see you come back?"

"Just the ladies who brought me."

"Very well." He turned and strode away.

"I'm sorry, Captain," she said to his back.

He paused but didn't turn. "As am I."

Francesca spent most of the next ten days in her cabin. The captain would not allow the crew ashore. Whether that was because of her misadventure, or because one of them might let it slip that the *Destiny* was a pirate ship, she didn't know. It was possible they would be captured and hung. Her messmates said they didn't care about the restrictions, so long as there was a constant stream of *kiddleywinks* from town to keep them occupied. But a few men, including Agar, grumbled.

Francesca was glad she needn't go ashore. Even if she could, she had no desire to; Port Royal had lost its charm. Everything had. Just getting up from her cot was difficult. She did as duty required, but beyond that, she lay in her cabin, staring at the ceiling. The weight on her heart and conscience grew.

Apparently, the captain did not want her to miss Port Royal's good points. When not occupied with ship repairs, he stopped by her cabin with exotic fruits or sugar cane. In another time and place, she might have found it charming. As it was, his visits reminded her why she couldn't return to town.

Francesca answered his knock one afternoon. "What is it?"

The captain stood, irresolute, with half of a fruit about the size of a pear in his hand. The flesh of the fruit was brilliant fuchsia even in the dull light below deck.

"It's a prickle-pear. I thought you might like it." He held out the fruit.

She frowned. "And what if I like it? What if it is the best thing I've ever tasted, what then?"

He looked at her, confused. "Then you have more. Then I bring you all the prickle-pear you can eat."

She'd lost everything she loved. "What is the point in learning to love something new? "No, thank you."

She closed the door, shutting out his worried look, and lay back down staring at the same blank ceiling she'd been staring at for a week.

She tried not to think about him. *I love Phillip, even if I'll never see him again.* Her love for him had been warm and sweet, their relationship built on trust. Her feelings for the captain could not have been more different. How could she be in love with a pirate, after what pirates had done to her family? She couldn't deny the attraction, but there was none of the sweetness she had shared with Phillip.

Perhaps the wound in her soul was calling out for someone who knew her sorrow. No, that didn't seem right. It was something primal reaching out for something equally alive.

Papa had taught her that honor would raise someone above the animal state and free them from base inclinations. But aboard a pirate ship, pledged to obey a pirate, honor seemed ethereal, a pleasant fantasy told to children. What was left? She felt like a cracked china pitcher from which the water had leaked.

Once the *Destiny* and *Jamaican Queen* were repaired and restocked, the captain gave the men a few hours ashore in shifts to see the town. Finally, the crew was recalled, and the ships set sail, the *Destiny* leading the way and the *Jamaican Queen* following behind.

Francesca and Mr. Hart seemed to be the only ones happy to leave Port Royal behind. Mr. Hart had been given command of the *Jamaican Queen* and seemed excited to test his new vessel, and Francesca was happy to have escaped the English Navy.

The *Jamaican Queen* turned out to be a trim, sprightly ship. She was narrow in the waist and carried only ten guns, but she was quick to the helm and fast.

The crew gave her a new name. Gold letters on a deep green background proclaimed her the *Lady Luck*. Francesca liked to think the name was a tribute to her daring adventure in the storm, saving the ship, which cheered her up considerably.

Captain Massey set a third of his crew aboard the *Lady Luck* under Mr. Hart's command, then set sail southeast, robbing his way down the chain of islands to Guadalupe. From there he headed northeast, returning along the windward sides of the islands.

While there was no shortage of merchantmen, few had cargo of real value. Most were filled with everyday supplies being plied between islands: sugar, molasses, fleeces or hides, vegetables, flour, or lumber. Occasionally they found a crate or two of indigo, or barrels of rum or wine, but little of the gold and jewels they hoped for. Few of the merchants put up a fight; their cargo wasn't worth it.

To Spanish captains, Captain Massey was merciless. Other captains discovered that he rewarded those who cooperated. A captain who surrendered immediately might be given a cask of valuable wine. A captain who chose to fight would be beaten, were he lucky enough to survive the battle.

While battles were few, they were hard fought. Francesca did what she could to end the battles quickly, but she was forced to protect herself, and her *Book of Reckoning* grew.

One of those debts was a Spanish captain. They took his ship on a stormy day toward the end of September. The deck tossed and rain blurred her eyes as Francesca put a dagger to the man's throat and demanded his crew surrender.

"Lady Blade," he whispered, as a tremor ran through him. His knees buckled and he slid toward the deck.

Taken aback, Francesca loosened her grip. The man slipped free, turning to her. His swarthy face had a few days' growth of beard, and a scar crossed the bridge of his nose, but it was the look in his dark eyes that made her pause.

"Please," he pleaded, "kill me if you must, but don't take my soul!"

Take his soul? She wanted to tell him she had no designs on his life, much less his soul, but he reached for his pistol. She threw herself on top of him and they grappled for the gun. With a bang and a puff of acrid smoke, the man went limp.

Francesca stood, trembling, shaken by the man's terror of her. How could he believe such nonsense? No one could take a soul but God.

She later learned that more stories about her had traveled from port to port, possibly started by Henry Carlisle. He had said they would sound more bloodthirsty when he told the tale. In one, she had defeated a whole ship full of men. Another told how she could skewer a mosquito with the point of her sword. She rather liked that one, though she refused to admit it. The one she was sure came from Henry gave her the ability to raise a storm on command.

Tales have a life of their own and grow in the telling, but this! She remembered the wanted poster in Port Royal. PYRATE. Despite all her efforts, she had failed, again. Henry Carlisle may have started the rumors, but her actions fed them. And what did this mean for her future? Would she always be hunted? Was there nowhere she would be safe?

Despite her worries, once away from Port Royal Francesca's spirits rose. She loved the ocean; the warm, clear air snapping at the sails spoke to her spirit. She loved watching the crystal bow waves curl from the ship's prow and seeing exquisite green islands rise from the aqua sea. She even loved the brief afternoon showers that slid over the ship, cooling the midday heat. Surrounded by such beauty she could not stay depressed.

Life fell back into its routine. She worked her morning shift, taught fencing classes, and relaxed with Miller, Carter, and sometimes Tuit or Rolly when time permitted, but something had changed. She no longer had hope of rescue, only a determination to change her own fate.

Francesca stayed away from the captain. She didn't want him to see how she felt, and when she was near him, she had the urge to reach out and touch him. But more and more often their eyes met and she detected regret in his face. She wondered what he regretted. Telling her what happened to his family? Bringing her aboard? She had no intention of asking.

Things were not going well for the captain. He commanded two ships and nearly one hundred and twenty-five men who were not getting rich nearly as fast as they had hoped. There were grumblings that the captain's luck had run out, and more and more often the Spanish warships appeared over the horizon, forcing the *Destiny* and *Lady Luck* to skitter away like frightened puppies. Even with two ships he was no match for them.

Toward the end of September, they were cruising off the north coast of Cuba, preying on merchants but finding little of value. During one fruitless battle the *Destiny's* carpenter, Mr. Pitt, was injured along with the carpenter's mate. They were repairing a shot hole near the waterline during battle when a second cannonball peppered them with six-inch oak splinters. Both were expected to recover, but a ship could not do without a carpenter.

Mr. Angstrom convinced the captain to press the prey ship's carpenter, Jose Morales, into service. The captain was loath to have a Spaniard aboard who was not in chains, but Mr. Angstrom's logic was irrefutable, so the captain reluctantly took the man.

Jose, born and raised in Cuba, had rolls of fat that covered a considerable frame of solid muscle. He was amiable enough, but his presence made the captain uneasy, which made the crew edgy.

It was November first and the day had been unsettling, the wind shifting quarters since dawn, as if unable to decide which way to blow. Around noon they had caught sight of a rich looking merchantman and had chased it eastward.

Now they were rounding a headland on their starboard side, chasing the merchant ship into the Bay of Matanzas.

Francesca studied the bay from the maintop. On the left sat emerald fields of sugar plantations, on the right ran a line of blue-green hills. The bay extended far inland. She couldn't see the town because of the curve of the bluffs, only a blue haze of smoke where it was likely to be.

She was glad the merchantman had gotten away. She doubted there would be a fight this time. The captain wouldn't attack a Spanish ship this far into a Spanish bay. There were too many who might come to its aid.

"Sails ho!" came the cry from the crow's nest above her.

The captain on the quarterdeck scanned with his spyglass. "How many?"

"Eight or nine at least, Captain, moored near town."

Captain Massey climbed up into the foremast for a better look. Francesca watched from the mainmast. Rarely had she seen the captain above deck, but he seemed at ease, as sure as any topman. But then, it was difficult to imagine him being out of place anywhere.

The town, five or six miles away, appeared around the headland. A forest of small masts crowded near the town, sails furled. Their prey had drawn within a mile of the moored ships with its Spanish flag flying upside down – a sign of distress.

"Bloody hell!" the captain shouted. "That's the Spanish warships anchored there. Ready about!"

It was not Francesca's watch in the rigging, so she hurried to deck, grabbing lines with the rest of the men. In seconds everyone was in place, turned toward the captain, awaiting orders. They waited. And waited.

"Shall we bring her about, Sir?" shouted Baldric from the foredeck. He squinted up at the captain.

The captain only stared doggedly through his glass.

Mr. Hart must have seen the warships as well because he backed the *Lady Luck's* sails, slowing. He, too, awaited orders.

After nearly twenty minutes the captain wrapped his feet around a backstay and slid down, landing lightly on the deck near Baldric.

"Where is the chase, Baldric?" the captain said, shaking his head.

"Perhaps they've not seen us, Sir."

"If we've seen them, they've bloody well seen us. And the ship we were chasing is within hailing distance of the warships, but I see not a lick of sail nor a man stirring on deck. Either I've failed to impress them or," he rubbed his hands together, "there's something afoot."

He headed toward his cabin. "Mr. Baldric, we'll stand off around the headland 'til dark, then I want you to take a boat and see what they're about."

"Shouldn't we show 'em our heels, Cap'n?"

"Not this time, Baldric, not this time."

Baldric shrugged and turned to the bosun. "Bring 'er about, north by nor'west. Full sail. Signal *Lady Luck* to follow."

That evening, just past dusk, the *Destiny* and *Lady Luck* snuck back toward Matanzas. They stood-to four miles from town and Baldric boarded a longboat with a set of strong-backed rowers to find out what was happening.

Two hours later he climbed back aboard the *Destiny*. The company met him expectantly at the rail. Mr. Hart stood among them, having come over from the *Lady Luck* to discuss plans. The captain put a hand on Baldric's shoulder as the man rubbed the scar on his face.

"The town's aflood with music," Baldric said. "They're deep in their cups already."

"And their watch?" asked the captain.

"Lax, from what I could see, Sir." Baldric handed the captain a crudely drawn map.

Captain Massey motioned to Mr. Angstrom, who lit a lamp and held it up. The captain spread the paper on top of a barrel and Francesca and the men crowded around.

"The bay is shallow 'round the perimeter," Baldric said. "So the larger warships are forced to moor close together, here, where the water is deep." He pointed to a group of dots straight out from town. "Though there's a twenty-gun Corvette here, near shore. She must have a shallow draft." He pointed toward the south edge of the bay.

"And that fifty-cannon behemoth? Where's she?" the captain asked.

"She's 'ere, where the water's deepest." Baldric pointed to the dot farthest out in the bay. He looked up at the captain. "There's only skeleton crews aboard th' ships. Everyone seems ta be in town."

Captain Massey put a hand to his chin, pacing the deck as crewmen backed out of his way. "I can't imagine what's gotten into them."

Mr. Angstrom cleared his throat. "Cap'n, that Spanish bloke hails from this here town."

The captain turned sharply to the Spanish carpenter, Jose, who stood at the rail looking toward Matanzas. Everyone else stared at him as well. Jose must have felt their eyes on his back because he spun toward the crew and sidled away.

The captain took a couple steps toward him, pointing toward the town. "You. What's going on there?" He spoke loudly, as if that would make English more understandable.

Jose coughed politely, fumbling with his hands. *"Perdón, Capitán?"*

The captain glared at him, and Jose bobbed his head apologetically.

Francesca translated the question into Spanish and Jose replied quickly. She turned to the captain. "He says it's All Saints Day, Sir."

"Ask him if they always celebrate All Saints Day falling down drunk."

Francesca relayed the message and Jose answered sheepishly.

"Well?" demanded the captain.

"No, Sir, he says they don't often drink to celebrate All Saints Day, but the warships captured a pirate called El Azote who's been prowling these waters for months. They were to hang him this evening and apparently, they are pleased about it."

At the mention of hanging pirates Francesca felt the crew bristle. Jose must have felt it too since he dipped his head even more apologetically.

"Once we sink those Spanish bastards, we'll have a free hand on the whole Spanish Main," the captain said. "There'll be no one to stop us."

Francesca stifled a gasp as a murmur ran through the company. They shifted uneasily, probably thinking what she was thinking. Sink four warships? Impossible. They knew the Spanish firepower. Francesca added it up: the fifty-gun giant, the two thirty-gun frigates and the twenty-gun Corvette, one hundred and thirty cannons against their combined force of twenty two. Even with the warship crews ashore it would be suicide. They could not sink those ships before their crews got back aboard.

The captain squared his shoulders and set his jaw. She could see he meant to attempt it. *Can he be that blinded by his hatred?* But in her mind she saw a three-year-old girl hiding under a burning bed. *Yes, he could.*

"Master Gunner," he continued. "How many could we put under before they mounted a counterattack?"

Agar scowled, but Francesca, only a few feet away, noticed a glitter of anticipation in his hard eyes. "Not more than one, Captain."

Agar couldn't be looking forward to attacking the warships, could he?

"Leaving us three to fight!" exclaimed a voice among the crowd.

"By the Dikens!" said another.

The captain spun toward them. "I don't care if there's a hundred. I'll have them on the seabed by morning!"

A knot formed in the pit of Francesca's stomach as she realized that Agar wasn't excited about the warships; he was excited about taking the captain's command. If the captain pushed this against the men's will, Agar would seize control.

"Sir," Baldric said, drawing the captain's attention back to his map. "There's a gun tower on the hill here." He pointed to a spot on the headlands about two miles from Matanzas.

The captain turned to Jose, his voice hard. "You. How many guns, what size?"

Francesca and Jose conversed, then she faced the captain. "He says the tower is not yet completed. Eventually it will hold four thirty-six pounders, but at the moment, there's only one."

The muttering was audible now. "A bloody thirty-six," murmured one man. "'At's suicide," another said.

The captain's voice was sharp. "One is better than four." He glared, body tensed for a fight. Venom leeched into his voice. "I'll not run away from Spaniards. Not this time. We're destroying those ships! Tonight!"

The men shouted and cursed. They weren't cowards. Francesca had seen every one of them leap into battle without hesitation, but they were gamblers, and they knew bad odds when they saw them.

A smile crossed Agar's face in the lamplight and he nodded to Hal. Francesca's body went cold. She looked toward Miller and Tuit, but they were too busy yelling, adding their voices to the roar to see what was happening. She had to do something! What would Agar do to the captain if he took over, not to mention her and her friends? If only it wasn't a lost cause.

She remembered her history lessons with Signore Gallo. He was an odd man the students called *La Tartaruga*, the Turtle, because of his bald head and the way he stretched his neck before he spoke. La Tartaruga had two interests: Greek history, and naval history, but naval history was his passion. He made his students work through all the great sea battles since ancient Greece using colored blocks on a blue table. She'd been bored silly, but there was one thing she remembered: when faced with overwhelming odds, all the beleaguered forces used fire ships.

Wooden ships, with their canvas sails, hemp ropes, and timber caulked with tar, lit with ease and were extremely difficult to put out. Laden with gunpowder they were floating bombs. A fireship might give them the advantage they needed. If the crew thought the odds were in their favor …

"Perhaps a fireship, Captain," she said into the din. No one heard her. She shouted it three more times. Still no one listened.

A pistol shout rang out. The silence was immediate. Everyone turned to Agar, who held his pistol in the air. Agar tucked the gun in his belt.

"Captain, the men 'ave spoken. Our luck's gone from bad ta worse an' now ya want us ta take a terrible chance."

The pirates shouted in agreement. Francesca tensed.

He spread his arms wide, turning to take them all in. "Men, now is the time—"

Francesca shouted. "What about a fireship?"

Everyone stared at her. She glanced from man to man. Out of the corner of her eye she saw Agar's face darken.

"A fireship," the captain said, considering.

"Men, don't listen to the hay-bag," roared Agar. He started toward Francesca, but Hal grabbed his arm.

"Sir, we have *Lady Luck*," she said in a rush, "and the wind seems fair. We could sail her into their midst and light her on fire, burn the ships while their crews are ashore. The *Destiny* could stay here. We'd only risk a skeleton crew."

Silence. But Francesca could sense the mood had changed, the tension gone from the men's faces.

Mr. Hart stepped toward the captain. He looked put out. "We do have the weather gauge, Captain," he said, "but t'would be a shame."

Francesca suspected that for Mr. Hart, the idea of burning his crisp little brig seemed sacrilegious.

The captain slapped a hand on Mr. Hart's shoulder. "There's plenty more where she came from. We'll get you another ship."

Agar stared daggers at Francesca, his fists clenching and unclenching. She matched his glare.

He prodded the men, trying to rouse their previous anger, but they had quieted into a thoughtful silence.

Francesca guessed what was going through their minds. Maybe they did have a chance. With luck, they might pull it off. The captain was right; with the warships gone the Main would be theirs and they could plunder where they liked without worry of reprisals from the Spanish.

Agar growled. "Lord save us, she's daft, Sir. A thirty-six pounder would cut *Lady Luck* ta pieces before we could light 'er." He gave her a smug look as the crew tensed again.

"He's right, we can't git past that gun." It was Hal's nasal voice. The men were muttering again as Hal shot Francesca a triumphant look.

Shore batteries, with their height advantage and big guns, were terribly effective at putting holes in the bottoms of ships. A couple well-placed hits from thirty-six-pound cannonballs could easily sink a ship the size of *Lady Luck.*

But Francesca remembered the day she had saved Claire and Belle from the assassins; pretending to be blind had gotten her close enough to be effective. She could use a similar ploy, and she had the advantage of looking and speaking Spanish.

She raised her voice. "I could take that gun, Captain, given gunners, pistols, a picnic basket, and a bottle of wine."

The men looked at her as if she'd gone crazy.

CHAPTER 22
MATANZAS BAY

An hour later, Francesca was crouched in the bushes at the base of a hill. The underbrush, blue in the moonlight, caught at her clothes and prickled her skin. Insects buzzed around her head. Atop the hill sat the pale stone fortification holding the thirty-six-pound cannon. The irregular top of the unfinished tower glowed yellow. There were men up there. The question was, how many?

Her body shook in nervous anticipation—and in horror at what she was about to do.

How could she do otherwise? The captain would have gotten them all killed avenging *her*. Or Agar would have taken over as captain and she and her friends would be dead. The vague outlines of Miller, Carter, and Tuit loomed in the dark. Pirates or not, she didn't want them to die.

Besides the four of them, Agar and his six-man gun crew crouched in the shrubs. Her stomach had sunk when the captain sent Agar with her. It was a logical decision—she needed a gun crew and Agar was the best, but he was the last person she wanted along.

Francesca wore her emerald dress with her hair loose, curling over her shoulders. She planned to play the damsel in distress, but she would need to look the part. Brushing her hair back over her left shoulder, she grabbed the material and ripped it open at the seam. Next, she knelt in the dirt and ground her knees and hands in till they were well stained. She stood and looked toward Miller. "I need your help."

"What da' ya' need, missy?"

"I need you to slap me, hard."

Miller hemmed. "I don't think I could, miss."

"Please. I need to look as if I've been beaten."

"I don't know—"

"Oh, fer Christ's sake," muttered Agar stepping forward and hitting Francesca across her cheek with his meaty palm. She stumbled sideways and Tuit caught her. Blazing white stars filled her vision.

"Blast it!" Miller said, stepping in front of Agar. "She was talkin' ta me."

Francesca took a breath and straightened. "That'll do," she said in the calmest voice she could muster. She'd have a bruise tomorrow. The handprint burned across her face. Perfect.

She turned to Carter. Miller had found him a servant's outfit somewhere in the hold. Carter wore a black jacket that disappeared in the darkness, but his pale silver vest and breeches glinted in the starlight. The outfit was two sizes too large and Carter tugged at the collar.

She hadn't wanted to put him in danger, and had planned to bring Finn, who was older, but Carter had pestered the captain until he gave in. When she objected, the captain said, "Better to take a boy who wants to go."

Carter probably regretted that move about now. She handed him the picnic basket. "Ready?"

"Ready as I'm likely ta be."

Francesca faced the rest of the group, barely visible in the darkness. "Remember, blades only. No guns or Carter and I are done for." She stared hard at Agar's dark bulk. "Wait for the signal, then charge up."

"Aye," replied the company. She thought Agar smirked.

The plan was for Francesca and her team to take over the tower before *Lady Luck* reached the moored ships. Agar's crew would fire the thirty-six-pound cannon on the warships. That would be the sign for the captain to set *Lady Luck* aflame.

Miller opened a spyglass and trained it out to sea. "*Lady Luck's* just outside the bay," he said. "She's movin' at a good clip since we emptied 'er out." He closed the glass. "Ya'd best git a move on."

She nodded. "Keep an eye on Agar for me," she whispered.

"I will, Missy. Two peepers, well peeled. An' remember, iffen it gits topsy-turvy, make tracks back 'ere." He patted her arm. "Good luck, Missy, an' take care a' the boy for me, would ya."

With a nod, she and Carter headed up the hill, angling left of the tower. She searched for the trail that must lead from town to the tower and eventually stumbled onto it. She paused to listen. Insects buzzed. The tower was lost in the darkness.

Francesca laid a hand on Carter's trembling shoulder to reassure him and wished there was someone to do the same for her. Then again, looking scared would be perfect for the part she was about to play.

Jose, the carpenter, had said that with work on the tower and barracks incomplete, the guards were few. But how many were a few? If the numbers were small, she would try to take the tower. If there were too many, she and Carter would return to Miller and lay new plans.

She leaned toward Carter. "You know what you're to do?"

"Aye. Keep close, look scared, an' keep me muzzle shut."

Francesca nodded. "That's it. And whatever you do, don't drop that basket. Ready?"

"Aye."

Her legs trembled, but she squared her shoulders and took a deep breath. Then she let out a strangled cry and ran toward the tower shouting for help in Spanish with Carter following behind.

Francesca ran wildly, looking back over her shoulder as if someone was chasing her. She tripped and fell, losing a shoe, then leapt up and kept running. It was a strange feeling, this headlong rush, pretending to be frightened of something behind her while running toward what she feared. Her feigned fear became an actual panic.

As they neared the tower, men's voices answered her cries. She didn't see them in the dark until she barreled into two men. "Help! Let me go! Please! Let me go!" She struggled against them.

"Easy now, we're not going to hurt you," said one man.

"What's happened?" said the other.

Francesca ceased struggling. Now that she faced her adversaries the thrill of battle rose, like fire in her veins. Every sound, every leaf, became crisp and clear. This was a different kind of battle—a battle of wits—but no less exhilarating. If she were smart, none of her friends would get hurt, but if she failed, they would likely die.

"I … he…" she stammered. "He tried to … oh, please help me! It was so awful! Please, don't let him find me!" She buried her face in a man's chest, squeezing her muscles to make her shoulders tremble.

"Are you injured?" asked the other man.

Francesca nodded and shook her head at the same time. The man wrapped a protective arm around her. "Let's get her inside."

Neither man noticed Carter following, catching his breath.

Francesca trembled as they approached the pale stone wall of the tower. The dark shape of a guard stood to the left of the dark arching doorway.

"Halt! Identify yourselves," the guard called.

Francesca gave a violent shiver and the man with his arm around her mumbled, "Don't be afraid."

"Soto and Vega," announced the other guard. "And guest."

"Guests," Francesca said, her voice uneven.

She held out a hand to Carter who took it. "My servant, he saved my life."

"What's going on?" the door guard asked.

"That's what we're trying to find out," said either Soto or Vega. "We'll take them to the lieutenant."

"It only takes one of you," the door guard said.

The man's arm tightened around her. He felt protective, which could be useful.

"I'll take them," he said, pulling open the door and ushering Francesca and Carter inside. She clung to the man's bicep, thrilled with her victory. She'd gotten inside in minutes, and it had been easy.

The man put a hand over hers. "It will be alright."

He has no idea.

Beyond the entryway a stone staircase curved up along the inside of the round outer wall. Stairs, wide enough for two abreast, glowed from lanterns hanging beneath iron sconces.

The man swept Francesca up the steps. She looked at his weathered face, pronounced crow's feet, and soft brown eyes. Something in his manner reminded her of Papa. Guilt washed over her. This man wasn't her enemy. He was kind, and she was deceiving him. She wanted to run away.

If he knew who I was he'd be trying to run me through, she told herself sternly. *Besides, Lady Luck must be close now. It's too late to turn back.*

They came to a landing with three wooden doors swathed in iron. According to Jose, the third would be the powder magazine where the gunpowder and shot were stored. She would need that later.

They started up the next flight. Ahead she saw the night sky and a lantern's glow and heard voices squabbling. Francesca's steps faltered. The story she had made up suddenly seemed unbelievable. She'd be found out and then she and Carter would be dead.

The man sensed her hesitation. He stopped and took her gloved hands. "You needn't fret." He smiled. "I don't know your name."

"Francesca," she whispered.

"I'm Manuel. I promise, no one will hurt you, Francesca."

Her eyes closed. Very soon he might be trying to kill her. She let him lead her up the last few steps.

The round room, open to the night sky, was perhaps twenty paces across. A low stone wall went all the way around. Arches were completed on the far side, but wooden scaffolding on the near side indicated work was continuing. On her right, aimed over the bay, gleamed a massive, brass thirty-six-pound cannon.

A lantern sat in the middle of the floor surrounded by six kneeling men— the gun crew, most likely. Though a handful of money and dice lay between them, their eyes were on her. They were unkempt, with dirty faces and stained clothes.

Opposite Francesca, a guard raised a musket and pointed it at her. Carter leaned against her. He trembled as he clutched the basket in both hands.

Nine men. Carter and I against nine men. Is it even possible? Will Carter muster the courage? Will I? She shuddered.

"Sir," Manuel said.

A Spanish officer in a red and gold uniform turned to look at them. He'd been leaning on the parapet next to the cannon, staring toward town.

"At ease," he said to the guard with the musket, who lowered his gun. Those on the floor went back to their game.

The officer's gaze traveled over Francesca, like a cat sizing up potential prey and finding it not worth the effort.

She despised him immediately. She longed to wipe the dismissive look from his face, and with that desire her courage returned. But she had a part to play so she huddled into Manuel's arm and kept her eyes wide with fear.

"I take it this is the source of the screams I heard."

"Yes, Sir. Miss Francesca…" Manuel said.

"Lady Montenegro, daughter of Don Carlos of Seville," she said in a trembling voice. "We've only recently arrived."

The officer's expression changed from annoyance to calculated hope. He straightened and licked his lips. She could almost hear his thoughts, *a Don from Seville must be an important man, and he has a daughter.* Manuel's arm around her tightened.

The officer approached, took Francesca's gloved hand and bowed, kissing it. "Lieutenant Diego Delgado at your service, my lady." He straightened and put a hand to her chin, tilting her face to look at Agar's handprint across it. "You've been treated poorly since your arrival. I apologize for my fellow islanders. Tell me what happened."

Francesca shivered, partly at the lieutenant's touch, partly at the bold-faced lie she was about to tell. "I, I met a gentleman at the party in town. At least, I thought he was a gentleman. We went for a picnic—"

"At this time of night?" the Lieutenant said.

Francesca buried her face in Manuel's chest. "I shouldn't have, I know. But all those months confined to my cabin aboard ship. I ... He..." Her voice dropped to a whisper. "I was so frightened."

"How did you get away?" the Lieutenant said.

"My servant," Francesca said, laying a hand on Carter's shoulder. "He hit him with the basket and we fled."

The lieutenant ruffled Carter's hair. Carter's body went rigid. He could have no idea what they were saying.

"Sir," Manuel said. "I'll take a few men and hunt the cad down."

"No!" Francesca said, panicked. The last thing she wanted was for a search party to run across the *Destiny's* men. She hadn't planned on the Spaniards being quite so gallant. "You mustn't."

"But, my lady, he assaulted you," Manuel said.

"I don't want to cause any more trouble."

"It is no trouble to avenge such a lovely young lady," the lieutenant said, probably thinking about how grateful it would make her rich father.

"But..." Francesca racked her mind for a reason they shouldn't rush out to defend her honor, "I'm afraid it would put you in an awkward position."

Manuel looked confused.

"Ah," the lieutenant said with a scowl. "Our cad is an official, a high ranking official."

Francesca nodded. The lieutenant sighed as he strolled back to the parapet. "Other than a fright and a bit of a bruise, no real harm has been done." He gave her a condescending smile. "Perhaps it would be best to keep this among ourselves." He gazed out toward town, Francesca forgotten now that she might be a liability to his career.

Her anger flared that he would cover up another man's misconduct, then she caught herself. *You're starting to believe your own fairy tales and time is running out!*

Manuel, too, seemed outraged by the lieutenant's about-face. His arm around her tightened. She needed him to calm down and let her go if she was to move on with the plan.

She smiled at him. "I've learned my lesson. I shan't go anywhere without my chaperone." She put a hand to her throat. "Please, may I have a drink of water?"

"Of course, my lady. How thoughtless of me." Manuel ran down the steps and returned with a goblet.

Francesca sipped slowly, spilling a few drops as her hands shook. They were out of time. She and Carter needed to either return to Miller or make their move. Nine men were far too many, but she did have surprise on her side. She might get them down on the ground without a fight. If she went back to Miller, they would make an armed assault and people would certainly die.

She raised her eyebrows at Carter. He straightened, set his shoulders, and gave her a quick nod. She drained the water and handed the cup to Manuel. He disappeared down the stairs. She only had moments. Francesca took the basket from Carter. "Lieutenant, I have a bottle of my father's best Madeira I'd like to give to you and your men for saving me." She set down the basket and she and Carter bent over it.

Francesca opened the cover. Beneath the bottle of wine, and some slices of ham, were four primed and loaded pistols. Nine men, four shots. Her heart raced. It was lunacy, but the pistols were the best chance for everyone to come out of this alive.

She pushed the ham aside and she and Carter each grabbed two pistols. Just as Manuel reappeared, Francesca and Carter spun back to the Spaniards. The lieutenant had closed half the distance. He came to an abrupt stop with an expression of shock and anger. Manuel stared in confusion.

"Hold!" ordered Francesca, trying not to look Manuel in the eyes. "Now, face down, all of you!"

The unarmed gun crew was quick to comply, but the guard with the musket hesitated.

"Shoot the guard," Francesca said to Carter in Spanish cocking her pistols.

Carter cocked his pistols as well. He couldn't understand Francesca, but the guard did. It was enough to get the man down on his stomach.

Manuel stood stunned.

"Please, Manuel," Francesca said softly. "I don't wish to shoot you, but I will."

"Who are you?" he said as he knelt.

"It's Lady Blade," hissed one of the gun crew.

"It can't be," whispered another.

"My name *is* Francesca. On your stomach, please."

Manuel laid flat on the stone floor.

"Their weapons," Francesca said to Carter.

Carter kicked the guard's musket away, then, releasing the hammer on one pistol he stuck it in his belt. He pulled the man's rapier from its sheath and tossed it by the musket. He hurried to Manuel and did the same, though Carter tucked the sword under his arm.

The lieutenant remained standing, hands raised in a placating gesture. A pistol hung from his belt, but Francesca doubted it was loaded. He also wore a rapier at his side. Her eyes narrowed, "I said, *down!*"

The officer looked her over dismissively. "A bird like you won't kill me. You haven't got it in you."

Francesca lowered her gun to aim at his groin and raised an eyebrow. "You may survive."

"You have only four shots and there are nine of us."

She shrugged. "So, which of you want to die?"

None of the gun crew moved, but one whispered, "It *is* Lady Blade!"

The officer went down on one knee. "What is it that you want?"

"We need to borrow your cannon." She tipped her head toward the lantern and said to Carter. "Give the signal."

"If it's big guns you're interested in, I'm the one you want," the lieutenant said with a leer.

The corner of Francesca's lip curled in disgust. Carter grabbed the lantern. As he moved toward the parapet a shot sounded from down the hill where Miller and the crewmen waited. Francesca instinctively turned toward the sound.

The weight of the lieutenant's body plowed into her. He grabbed her wrists, driving her backwards.

She fell with the small of her back against the wooden scaffolding and his bulk against her. The impact knocked the wind from her lungs and the pistols from her hands.

He sneered as he held her pinned. "This is no Lady Blade."

The guard started to rise, but Carter moved toward him, aiming for his head. The man went flat again.

Shouts and gunshots filtered up from below. Everything was going terribly wrong.

Francesca brought her thigh up hard, kneeing the Lieutenant between the legs. He gasped and she shoved him away enough to wriggle free.

She lunged for one of her pistols, but he grabbed the back of her skirts. She strained for the gun. Her stockinged foot slid on the stone floor.

He yanked hard on her skirts and fabric ripped as he flung her stumbling backwards. She tripped over a prostrate man and fell to the floor.

Manuel and the guard started to rise. Carter's pistol spat. The bullet sparked off the stone floor and the men dropped back onto their stomachs.

Francesca leapt to her feet, drawing a knife and kicking off her remaining shoe. She faced the lieutenant, who had drawn his sword.

He rushed at Francesca, swinging.

She dodged, lunging in with her knife and slicing the back of his wrist.

He retreated, cursing.

She stepped sideways toward Carter and held out her hand, her eyes on the lieutenant. The hilt of a sword slapped into her palm and she grabbed it.

She faced the officer with a wicked grin that set him back on his heels. He circled, thrusting carefully, judging her skill.

The gun crew watched from the floor.

"Com' on, Francesca," urged Carter, "tuck it in his breadbasket."

Footsteps pounded up the stairs. Was it her men or more Spaniards? She had to finish off the lieutenant quickly if they were to have any hope.

Carter sidled over to one of the pistols she had dropped. He set down his spent pistol and picked up the loaded one. He raised both, aiming for the top of the stairs. *Smart boy*, she thought, *it will be my fault when he dies.*

The lieutenant rushed Francesca. She sidestepped, turning as he passed, and shoving him toward the parapet. The wall caught him mid-thigh and his momentum tipped him over the edge. He caught hold of the stone lip with one hand.

Carter yelped behind her, and Francesca spun back toward the sound. Carter's eyes were wide, and his eyebrows pinched in fear. Manuel held Carter by the collar, his pistol jammed into Carter's side. He growled, "Drop the weapons."

Francesca's breath caught. She looked into Manuel's stone hard eyes.

"Please," she pleaded. "Shoot me if you must, but he's just a boy. Don't hurt him."

Carter's breath hissed, rapid and shallow.

Manuel's hand holding the pistol trembled. "I said, drop the weapons."

Seven sets of Spanish eyes stared at Francesca. If she dropped her weapons they'd be on their feet in seconds. There was sure to be a fight. If it was Miller and the others rushing up the stairs people would die. If more Spaniards were on the way, she and Carter were dead already.

She shook her head. "I'm sorry Manuel. We only want the cannon, please."

The footsteps were nearing. Francesca's nerves stretched, muscles vibrating with tension. All eyes flicked to the stairway.

Miller and Agar appeared with the others bunched behind them, swords ready.

"Stop!" yelled Francesca.

The *Destiny* men hesitated in the doorway, taking in the situation. Manuel cocked the trigger on the pistol pressed to Carter's side.

Francesca set down her weapons and took a few steps toward Manuel. "You're a good man, Manuel. The boy's name is Carter. I know you don't want to kill him. You're trapped. Give me the gun and no one will be hurt, I promise."

No one moved for a second, then Manuel released the hammer on the pistol. Francesca's breath released. Carter yanked free and ran to her.

A pistol spat. Everyone jumped.

"No!" cried Francesca as Manuel toppled backwards. She jerked her head toward her shipmates. Agar lowered a smoking pistol.

"You bastard!" She went to Manuel as her crewmates flowed into the room.

"If you can't keep the situation under control, I will," spat Agar.

Francesca knelt beside Manuel. His eyes were staring, dead. "I'm sorry, Manuel," she said as she closed his eyes. This time she had a name for her *Book of Reckoning*.

Francesca rose. There was still one life she could save. She stepped over to the parapet and looked down at the lieutenant.

He breathed heavily, feet scrabbling at the sheer stone wall. "Help me!"

"Will you behave yourself?" she asked as Miller came to her side.

"Si, si, anything," he gasped.

She and Miller pulled the lieutenant up. He lay on the floor, body spasming. Tuit stood over the Spaniards brandishing his spear.

Francesca put a hand on Carter's shoulder. "Well done, Carter."

He gave her a strained smile. "'At was a bit too 'airy fer my taste."

"You and I both."

Then she scanned her men—everyone was there. They hadn't lost anyone, but Hal's arm was bloody just above the elbow. "What happened?" she asked Miller.

He hitched a thumb toward Agar. "I'll tell ya later. Let's git this done."

Agar's crew had already taken over the cannon. Agar pushed Hal toward the stairs. "Powder an' grapeshot, now! An' keep it comin'."

Gunfire erupted from the town and Francesca looked out into the darkness. She vaguely made out the shape of *Lady Luck's* sails headed toward the moored warships. Miller handed her the spyglass and she put it to her eye.

In the light of the largest warship's stern lanterns, skeleton crews opened gun ports and loosed cannons, but they had enough hands to man only two or three guns. She swept the glass across the waterfront and saw men with torches piling into boats. *They're too late.*

Francesca focused on the *Lady Luck*. One lantern burned on deck illuminating scattered tinder. The sails looked well-trimmed to collide with the largest warship, the fifty-gun behemoth with the name *Intrépido* scrawled across the back.

A dozen pirates waited in a longboat at the *Lady Luck's* stern. Captain Massey, the only one left aboard ship, tied off the helm, then paused, running a hand over the wheel housing.

A cannon spat aboard the *Intrépido,* and a bit of the ship's rail disintegrated. That spurred the captain. He opened the lantern, illuminating the deck, bent over it for a moment, then stood. Light flared at his feet. The captain hesitated a second and then ran headlong for the stern of the ship.

They must have poured gunpowder or kerosene over the tinder because before he reached the stern, flames leapt like lightning across the deck. Captain Massey paused as flames spread.

The thought flashed in her mind that if the captain died, she would be free of her oath to him. *Not that way.* This had all been for him. Manuel had died so he might have his revenge. It would be too cruel if he died too.

The captain swung down into the longboat filled with crewmen. They bent their backs and headed out to sea.

Already the *Lady Luck* lit the night sky. Flames licked up the lines like rats scurrying from a sinking ship, outlining the rigging in glowing yellow. The Spanish fired their cannons, hoping to sink *Lady Luck* before she came alongside, but the holes they put in her only fanned the fire.

As *Lady Luck* brushed against the *Intrépido*, crewmen poled her away, but she was close enough. Half of one flaming sail twisted loose in the wind and fluttered into the *Intrépido's* rigging, setting it ablaze. Burning embers wafted into the *Intrépido's* sails and the warship blossomed red.

The boats from shore reached the *Intrépido* just as the *Lady Luck* did. They might have put out the fire, but Agar's gun crew had not been idle.

"Fire!" shouted Agar. The cannon thundered and the percussion hit Francesca like a fist in the ribs. The parapet shook and smoke covered the scene. As the smoke cleared, she saw the effects of grape-sized shot raining down on the *Intrépido*. Some men lay dead on deck, others ran for cover. One of the burning sails shredded, peppered with holes. In the mayhem, the fire gained the upper hand.

Francesca scanned the glass over town. The two flaming ships painted it crimson. Panicked people ran in every direction.

She refocused on the *Intrépido*. The crew abandoned ship, some jumping and swimming for shore, most crowding into the boats. It would only be a matter of minutes before the fire reached the gunpowder magazine.

Turning lazily, pushed on by wind, *Lady Luck* floated toward the next warship, a thirty-gun brig. Along the way she lit up two small fishing boats. Once burnt free of their anchor lines, they too became floating firebombs.

Agar's crew cranked the cannon around and focused on the ship that *Lady Luck* was approaching. With shot raining from above and death floating toward them, some of the brig's crew took to longboats. Some fought on, wetting down the deck and chopping mooring lines. Francesca admired their courage but doubted it would save the ship.

Suddenly the *Intrépido* exploded in a white-hot flash that seared her eyes and sent flaming debris hundreds of feet in every direction. A half second later the sound and shock wave hit, knocking Francesca back. Then the *Lady Luck* exploded too, enveloping the brig in her flaming death throes.

Francesca stared in amazement as burning debris landed on the town, the countryside, and on nearly every ship in the harbor. She shook her head in horrified awe. The Turtle's stories had completely failed to describe the holocaust one burning ship could unleash.

Francesca scanned the fourth and smallest warship, a sleek twenty-gun corvette. She rode upwind, near the far shore, safe from the *Lady Luck* and from Agar's cannon, but not from the *Intrépido's* flying debris. Her crews had rowed over from town and frantically smothered the flames kindling aboard her. It looked as though they might succeed.

Another thirty-gunner, moored a dozen yards from the *Intrépido*, was now seriously aflame. Agar must have seen his opportunity to put her under as well. He shouted at his men as he grabbed a handspike, "Haul 'er round two points and load the thirty-six-pound shot."

Francesca had had enough, but she still had one more order to carry out. She was to blow the tower's powder magazine as they retreated.

She wanted their Spanish prisoners outside, quickly. More guards would be arriving soon. She pulled two of the Spaniards to their feet, pointing at Manuel. "Carry him."

They lifted the body and she and the other crew members hurried them down the stairs.

As soon as they were outside, the Spaniards started yelling for help. There was no point trying to stop them. Already she could see the torches and hear the shouts of approaching soldiers. They would be there in minutes.

She darted back inside, racing up the steps. "Avast firing!" she shouted.

Agar paid no attention. "Prime the gun!" he shouted to his men.

Francesca put a hand on his shoulder. Agar gripped her hand, turning to face her and squeezing so hard she thought the bones would break. His face held undisguised hatred. "I give the orders to the gun crew."

Francesca yanked her hand away. "Very well," she seethed. "I'm blowing this tower whether you are here or not." She turned on her heels and raced down the stairs.

"Avast firing!" Agar yelled to the gun crew. "Back to the boat!"

Moments later, in the powder magazine, Francesca stuffed slow-match into a cask of gunpowder and set it alight. Then she and the *Destiny* crewmen careened down the hill through the brush toward their longboat as twigs and thorns slashed at their faces and arms. They heard angry Spanish shouts and saw at least fifty men heading for the tower along the trail from town.

Then the tower exploded in a white-hot flash behind them, searing the view of the hillside into her retinas. Stone and mortar rained down. Francesca covered her head with an arm as she scrambled downward.

She cried aloud, "I'm sorry, Papa, I'm sorry!"

CHAPTER 23
MASTER AT ARMS

Francesca clambered up the side of the *Destiny*. Early dawn lit the eastern clouds with a soft golden glow, but to the south a harsher orange light marked the location of Matanzas. Another explosion flashed in the distant sky, the sound blast following seconds later.

The men cheered as they grabbed Francesca's arms and helped her aboard. She managed a weak smile. But it wasn't physical exhaustion alone that bent her shoulders. She still felt Manuel's protective arm around her. She hadn't meant for him to die. Or to cause such widespread destruction. Sink the warships, yes, but the last thing she'd seen as they rowed away was two of the town buildings bursting into flame.

"What news?" asked the captain. "How many have you lost?"

"None, Sir," she said, though Manuel's imaginary arm tightened around her. Hal climbed over the side. "One injured, Sir. The two largest ships and the tower blown."

"And the other ships?"

"One on fire an' well-holed," Agar said, "They may keep 'er afloat, but it'll be some time 'fore she sails."

"Well done!" Captain Massey exclaimed. He turned toward the crew. "Men, the Spanish Main is ours!"

The crew's roar echoed through Francesca's hollow interior.

Captain Massey continued. "Three warships blown to Hades and scarcely a man injured, thanks to DiCesare!"

214

A thrill ran through her at the pride in the captain's voice, but she hated that she felt that way.

"Huzzah!" shouted the men.

"In recognition," the captain continued, "I propose we make her our master at arms."

Francesca froze. *An officer?* They didn't have a master at arms aboard the *Destiny*, but it sounded important. Her emotions clotted her throat. *I should be punished, not promoted.*

"Belay that, Captain!" shouted Agar. "I've done served as master gunner fer two years! That title is mine by rights!"

Her stomach knotted as Agar pushed through the men. He stood before the captain, fists clenched. "'Tis bad 'nough havin' a woman aboard, yet you propose ta not only carry 'er, but set 'er over us. No, by God, it's unnatural. We'll not stand fer it!"

Francesca's breath caught. Agar hated her already and a promotion would only make matters worse. She wished the captain hadn't brought it up.

Captain Massey frowned and shook his head. "You're the best gunner in the West Indies, Mr. Agar, no doubt about that. But her strategy has just destroyed our biggest threat on the Main. She's a good sailor and a first-rate topman. She's done good service to this ship and proved her worth more than once."

She felt a flush creep from her cheeks down her neck.

Agar raised a fist. "She don't belong here. This is no place for a woman. She'll be the ruin of us all."

Miller, scowling, started toward Agar. Francesca grabbed his arm and held him back.

"Yer talkin' bilge water, Agar," Miller shouted. "Ya've no cause to badmouth DiCesare!"

Captain Massey looked around at the crew. "We'll put it to a vote. What say you, men?"

There was a long, uncomfortable silence. The only sound was the creak of the hull and the wind in the rigging.

Francesca's throat eased. Now they could all forget the ridiculous notion. Agar had a fierce reputation. Many had felt his whip when they'd been too slow swabbing or priming their cannon. They wouldn't want to anger him by siding with the captain and that was fine with her.

Then a resonant chant swelled among the men. "Lady Blade, Lady Blade,

Lady Blade, Lady Blade," until the entire crew, short of Hal and Agar were shouting. The night sky thundered with her name.

The hair on Francesca's arms stood on end. A rush of pride washed over her like hot water. For an instant she wanted to scream *YES!* into the blackness overhead, but the impulse passed quickly. She had once told Phillip how much she wanted to be seen for who she was and what she could do. Well, these men saw her, and while they liked what they saw, she couldn't.

The men were clapping her on the back and shaking her hand. She nodded mechanically.

Captain Massey laughed. "Master at Arms it is." He grew serious. "And, Mr. Agar, if the situation won't suit you, I'm prepared to set you ashore at your earliest convenience."

He replied through tight jaws. "I'll not abandon ship."

"Very well," the captain said. "Master at Arms, join me in the great cabin, once you've changed your togs."

"Yes, Sir." She wanted to be alone to wrestle with her conscience and add to her Book, but it would have to wait.

Francesca took Miller's arm and pulled him with her toward her cabin. As she headed below, she could swear she felt Agar's eyes on her back. Once out of view, she asked Miller, "What happened. How did Hal get injured?"

They stopped outside of her cabin and Miller dropped his voice. "'Bout what you'd expect. Agar pulled a pistol after ya said not ta. I tried ta take it from 'im and the damned thing went off. Hal 'appened ta be in the way."

Francesca frowned. Agar was a master gunner. Guns didn't "just go off" in his hands. He had meant to get her and Carter killed up in the tower. He'd probably hoped to take out either Miller or Tuit in the bargain. Luckily, Miller had caught him. "Thank you for keeping an eye on him."

Miller straightened and brought the knuckles of his right hand to his temple in a pirate salute. "At yer service, Master at Arms."

Francesca's eyes pricked and she shook her head. She didn't want her new rank to get in the way of her friendships, especially since she didn't want the rank. Or maybe she was just overtired.

Miller saw her expression. "Sorry, missy, I was just funnin' ya."

She smiled weakly and looked down at her tattered dress, "I'd best get changed."

Her thoughts were in turmoil as she shed the gown for her trousers and shirt. *There must be a way out of this promotion. Surely there are better candidates.*

When she joined the captain, he was at his table, pensive, as though he had something painful to do. He studied her as she closed the door.

She spun to face him. "Captain, I don't believe I'm qualified—"

"Bollocks," he interrupted.

"Pardon?"

"I said, bollocks. How do you think I became qualified to captain this ship?"

"Well—"

"By captaining her. You'll learn by doing."

"And if I choose not to?"

"Odd, I don't remember offering you a choice." He sighed. "This means no more dangerous work in the rigging. You'll be down here, safe on deck with … us."

She had the impression he meant to say *with me* and her breath wavered. Still, leading a band of pirates went against everything she believed in. "I'm sure Mr. Agar would be much better suited."

"Mr. Agar is an excellent gunner, but he is not subtle. His solution to every problem is a lead ball. I appreciate your more," he searched for a word, "circumspect approach."

Francesca's anger flared. "You think I'm deceitful?"

"The dress and the picnic basket were your idea. Left to my own devices I'd have lobbed shot at the whole place. Maybe we would have succeeded, maybe not, but the butcher's bill would have been much higher."

He had a point. She had learned to think her way around problems instead of plowing through them. Perhaps her plan had cost lives, but how many more would have died if the captain had followed his plan?

The captain waved a hand. "That's not why I brought you here." He took a small wooden box from his lap and laid it on the table. He touched it gently, rose, went to the sideboard and poured himself a drink. He returned, perching on the edge of the table close to her, bottle and cup in hand.

"You've done well, Francesca."

Her first name seemed so intimate coming from his lips. Her legs wobbled.

"I know this is not the life of your choosing," he said. "And that you scorn our winnings."

"You mean your loot." She hadn't meant it to sound so harsh.

Captain Massey took a drink, then shrugged and set down the cup and bottle. "The Spanish loot the New World, I loot them. But, as you will. The point is, you should have recompense."

"Then let me go, Captain. That's all I want."

"I see no chains. Your word holds you, not me." He picked up the wooden box and held it on his outstretched palms. "I want you to have this."

"No thank you, Sir," she said with a superior air.

"It's not stolen, Francesca," he said with a hard edge. "It's mine, and I would like you to have it."

Francesca paused; she could see this meant a lot to him. He was so close now. The urge to lay a hand along his cheek was almost overpowering. She wanted to turn away, but curiosity got the better of her. She opened the lid.

Inside an intricate piece of equipment glowed gold in the lamplight. A sextant. There was an eyepiece on one side and an elegantly etched arc on the other. An inscription read: *To my loving husband, with all my love, Mary. May you always find your way home.*

Francesca gasped and her eyes went to his. How could he part with a gift from his wife? How could she take it? "I couldn't."

"Please," he said with a plea in his voice.

She looked at him confused and touched. She shook her head. "Why?"

"I want you to have something of value. I can think of nothing I value more." He shrugged, seemingly lost for words.

She saw the pain in his storm-blue eyes, and the plea. She wanted … she wasn't sure what she wanted. "You're sure?"

He nodded once.

"Thank you, Captain." She gently closed the lid. Her hands lingered as she took the box from him, her fingers touching his palms. He wrapped his hands around hers for one brief moment before letting go.

"I'm so sorry…" She couldn't finish.

The captain picked up his drink. He seemed to search for words as he rolled the liquid around the cup. He swallowed the drink and poured another. "I've made them pay dearly for that day."

"Does it work, Captain?"

He looked at her. "The sextant?"

"No, I mean." she swallowed hard. "I killed the man who stabbed Papa. I took my vengeance." She shook her head. "But it only made matters worse. Does blood wash away your pain?"

"Yes," he said decisively, his face hardening. Then the lines of his face wavered. "For a time." He shook his head and his shoulders sagged. "Some days there is not enough Spanish blood in all the world."

Francesca reached out, but he turned his back and said, "Dismissed."

The flame of jealousy had returned, and there was more she wanted to say. She wanted to tell him about Manuel and what a good man he was. She wanted to ask him about his daughter, Caroline, but she could tell from his tensed shoulders she would get no more out of him. She turned quietly and left.

Francesca stood at the rail considering the captain's gift as dawn turned the sea to liquid gold. She held the sextant in the crook of her arm, solid in form but elusive in meaning.

But she didn't have long to ponder. Mr. Hart hailed her from the quarterdeck, "Mr. DiCesare."

Francesca came to attention, confused by the form of address.

"Come here, if you please."

Francesca hesitated. Only officers and helmsmen were allowed on the quarterdeck, and in all the months she had been aboard, Mr. Hart had never once spoken directly to her. He had refused to admit her existence.

She walked toward him solemnly, conscious of her new position aboard ship. She liked Mr. Hart, even if he didn't like her. His straight back, dark, greying hair, and steel-grey eyes brought Papa to mind.

Mr. Hart spoke in low tones. "Mr. DiCesare, I am thoroughly against women aboard ship, but as we are to work together as officers, and as you have proved yourself to be of use, I have decided to ignore your unfortunate gender."

He seemed to be waiting for a response, but Francesca was not sure how to take this pronouncement. She settled on, "Most kind, Sir."

From there he launched into a history lesson of the station of Master at Arms, eventually getting down to what was required of her.

Traditionally, the master at arms had three roles: to oversee the procurement and maintenance of all arms aboard ship, to train the men in small-arms proficiency, and to act as sheriff when crimes were reported aboard ship.

She would report to Mr. Baldric, the first mate, and was allowed two masters' mates to help her in her duties. On a military ship the master gunner would report to the master at arms, but, Hart explained, the chain of command was more malleable on such a ship as the *Destiny*. She and Mr. Agar would have equal rank.

Francesca left the quarterdeck overwhelmed. She had so much to do and learn. She headed quickly toward her cabin before anyone else could call for her attention.

As she lay down on her cot, she had to admit, she was a good fit for the job. She already had about a dozen fencing pupils; now she would be able to teach everyone. As for the cleaning and procurement, that was no more difficult than her housekeeping chores at Salle DiCesare—easier, since now she could order the crew to do the work. Only the sheriff aspect of the job daunted her. Well, she thought as she drifted to sleep, she could only try her best.

Francesca threw herself into her new duties. It helped her forget Manuel and the town she may have burnt to the ground.

Her first act was to appoint Miller her master's mate. Both Carter and Tuit were spoken for by the doctor, or she would have chosen one of them as well. Instead, she chose Rolly. He was a pleasant boy, if a bit lazy, and he was crazy about swords, pistols, any sort of weapon. He was also the most gifted of her fencing pupils.

Next, she inventoried all the ship's small arms. It was a big task, and difficult given that many of the men had their own weapons stashed about the ship. She was as thorough as circumstances allowed. Together with Miller and Rolly she went through all the crates and racks of swords, pistols, muskets, daggers, pikes, hatchets, spears, pole arms—the list went on and on. She inventoried all the shot and powder for the small guns. She set crews to work, testing and cleaning the armaments. Swords that were badly damaged she sent to Mr. Pitt to dull the edge and blunt the point to make practice weapons.

One afternoon, as she was setting up a fencing lesson, One-eyed Kelsey appeared at her elbow. "Cap'n's askin' after ya, DiCesare. 'E wants ya in the great cabin."

So, a week after the burning of Matanzas, Francesca found herself again knocking on the great cabin door. She hadn't seen much of the captain since his gift and was unsure what to expect.

"DiCesare, come in," the captain said briskly. Mr. Hart and Mr. Baldric already bent over the table scattered with charts.

The captain filtered through the charts as Francesca approached. He spread one over the top of the other. "Here," he said, pointing to a spot on the Panama coast. "Portobello. This is where all the Incan gold and Peruvian silver that the Spanish mine, scavenge, and steal awaits shipment to Spain. According to the Maroons we encountered, a week from now their armory will be stuffed to the rafters with more riches than you can imagine."

"I don't know 'bout that, Sir," Baldric said, grinning. "I have a good imagination."

The captain looked at them conspiratorially. "We, my friends, are going to take the town."

Mr. Baldric eyes widened as Mr. Hart gave an excited laugh and rubbed his hands together. Francesca shook her head, thinking she must have misheard him.

Baldric straightened. "How many souls, Captain?"

"Do Spaniards have souls?" he murmured under his breath. "We'll be outnumbered five to one, and there are guns on both sides of the harbor."

Hart seemed to be enjoying the prospect immensely, but Baldric was incredulous. "You jest, Captain."

"This is our best chance. I believe those warships we sunk were on their way to Portobello to protect the shipment. That means there will be few Spanish troops to deal with. We're more than a match for any Spanish rabble in town. Besides, if Henry Morgan took Portobello, so can we."

"That was nearly fifty years ago, capt'n," Baldric said.

"Aye, so the bastards won't be expecting any trouble." The captain clapped Baldric on the shoulder.

Francesca could not believe he was contemplating such a brazen act. "Captain, you mustn't."

"It can, and will, be done," he said. "How is the question."

"But Captain," A knot formed in her stomach. "Attacking ships full of armed men is one thing, but the town will be full of innocent women and children."

The captain's face slipped into its mask of hatred. "Innocent? Believe me, the Spanish have no such compunction."

Francesca saw the little girl under her bed.

The captain must have seen something in her face. His temper flared. He grabbed her by the arm and pulled her toward the chart. "Look, DiCesare, there are tons of treasure in that town, and I'll have it. No matter the cost."

She yanked free. "Take the treasure yourself! I want no part of this."

The captain's eyes were chips of ice. "You will do as I say. You swore loyalty to me and this crew, or have you forgotten?"

Francesca leaned in, voice dropping low. "You needn't remind me of what I owe to whom, nor is it disloyal to point out when someone is in error."

"Master at Arms," he seethed. "Give me your opinion before I have you strung up for mutiny!"

She paused, taking a deep breath, trying to calm her fury. How could this be the same man who had given her the sextant? She turned to Mr. Hart and Mr. Baldric for help but met only curious stares.

Her eyes settled on the map of the unsuspecting town. "Don't do this, Captain," she pleaded softly.

He made no reply.

Well, if she couldn't dissuade him, maybe there was a way to contain the damage. She focused on the map.

Portobello was a small town nestled in a deep bay on the north coast of Panama. The chart marked gun sites on both sides of the bay. If those guns were to concentrate fire on one ship, she wouldn't last long.

"We'll need a second ship to draw some of the fire," Mr. Hart said.

"Aye," agreed Mr. Baldric. "And a sturdy one at that."

The quicker they were in and out, the fewer people would be injured. "Could we pretend to be the Spanish ships they're expecting?" she asked, "The ones from Matanzas?"

"They'd figure it out soon enough, but that might get us close before they opened fire," mused the captain.

Francesca pointed to a spot on the coast south of the bay. "I would land two parties here, one to take this fort, and the other to enter the town from behind. With the ships bombarding, and their city overrun, the inhabitants would likely leg it into the jungle."

"It's a goodly-sized fort," Mr. Hart said. "She'd be a bugger to take. And the guns to the north still daunt us, Sir. There will be no shelter from them once inside the bay."

"And we risk grounding the ships," Mr. Baldric said.

"Then leave the town be!" Francesca said. "There's riches enough afloat and ready to hand."

"Enough!" snarled the captain. "We're taking that town! Mr. Baldric, set a course for Panama. I'll inform you all of my decisions. Dismissed."

The captain sat down on the lockers under the aft windows and looked out to sea. Baldric and Hart exited, but Francesca paused in the doorway.

"Captain."

He refused to acknowledge her.

"How many little girls will be in that town, Captain?"

His hands curled into fists, but he remained silent. She turned away.

Francesca swore under her breath as she emerged into the bright afternoon sun. A dozen pupils practiced fencing drills on deck. Miller approached, hooking a thumb toward the men. "The natives got restless, so I started 'em drillin'."

Francesca grimaced. The last thing she wanted was to deal with a bunch of idiots pretending to be fencers. "I'm in no humor—"

Just then she spotted Carter, shirtless, sparring with Rolly and dropping his guard. It was a small thing, really. She'd been working all week to break him of the habit and any other time she would have simply corrected him and moved on.

"Carter, what have I told you!" she snapped.

She grabbed a blade, motioned Rolly away and sparred with Carter. She backed him across deck becoming more and more aggressive. Carter, nervous, parried clumsily. Francesca lunged and slid her blade across his upper arm. The blades had been dulled, but not enough. Blood welled.

"Owwww!" Carter dropped his sword.

Francesca gasped, dropping her blade as well, "Bloody hell, Carter, I'm sorry."

Tuit approached, taking a look at the wound.

Miller drew Francesca away to the far railing tilting his head and giving her a fatherly look. "Ya'd best tell ol' Miller what's gnawin' ya 'fore ya run someone through."

Francesca squinted at the sparkling ocean. She didn't know what to say. How was she to explain that all her life she had tried to live up to Papa's expectations, but the harder she tried the more she fell short? That she missed Phillip. That she was attracted to a man who would soon force her to go against everything she believed, and that everything was wrong, and she felt angry. She wanted to throw something, break something. Instead, she leaned on the rail and looked out over the ocean. She felt trapped aboard the *Destiny*. "All that goddamned water."

"Well, aye, there's a bloody lot a' it. But ya must 'ave partic'larly refined tastes fer it ta offend," Miller said, squinting into the sun.

Francesca gave a short laugh, despite her foul mood. "Have you ever made a promise you couldn't keep?"

"Sure, missy, reg'larly." He set his pipe between his teeth. "But it don't worry me none."

"I mean a blood oath, and the harder you try to keep it, the more it slips away." As she spoke, she was once again on the dueling grounds, Tarrentino dead and Papa reaching up to her. Her shoulders gave an involuntary shake.

Miller turned her to look at him. "Now, miss, ye're too young ta be makin' promises a' that sort."

"But what do you do?" She gripped the rail.

He lit his pipe, puffing spicy smoke around his face. "Well, there 're two types a people ya kin make promises ta. Those ya care 'bout an' those ya don't." He blew a smoke ring that hovered in the air between them. "If ya don't cotton to 'em, the promise don't matter."

"And if you do?"

Miller put a fatherly arm around her shoulder and headed her back toward Carter and the others. "Well, then ya hope they care 'nough about you ta understand if ya fail." He cocked his head toward Carter who sat on the deck nursing his bandaged arm. She nodded and walked toward the boy.

Perhaps Miller is right. Papa would understand. I'm doing the best I can. She was so tired of fighting her fate. Maybe piracy was the path intended for her. But she hadn't heard Papa's voice in so long. Had he abandoned her completely?

Carter flashed Francesca a hurt look as she sat down next to him.

"I'm sorry, Carter."

Carter stuck out his chin. "Will it scar, do ya think?"

"Perhaps," she said, guilt welling.

Carter brightened. "That would be first rate! Then I can strip me sleeve an' say 'I copped 'is in a set-to with Lady Blade, the famous woman pirate.'"

Francesca reached for him. He tried to evade her, but she was too quick. "I'll tell you what you copped." They struggled and Carter giggled. Francesca got a hold of him and gave him a raspberry on the back of his neck.

Carter shrugged her away, trying to look tough. "I'm gettin' better, ya know. I've some fizzin' sword work, an' I'm a fair shot. I just wonder, what's it like ta kill a bloke? After all, you've killed scores."

Francesca's winced as though slapped. Her *Book of Reckoning* had grown thick. She looked at him sharply. "Don't be in haste, Carter. The deed is simple enough. Living with it, that's the rub."

She put her face in her hands. "You're a good lad. You should go home. We both should."

Carter shrugged, "Ain't no 'ome ta go to. 'Sides, I'd be bored, as'd you. I've seen yer mug when ya board a ship. You love it, admit it."

She hung her head. Denying it would be a lie. Not that she loved the killing, but the fighting—the rush of fire that filled her being, that ate up her sorrow and her confusion and left her completely and thrillingly alive. Only in battle could she stop her brain and live in the present, with no thought for the past or future. Could she live without it? Would she want to?

Carter chatted on while Francesca sat dreading the upcoming battle. She knew firsthand what sort of hell this one small ship could unleash. She'd seen grown men reduced to quaking shells. In her mind she envisioned an infant being cut from the lifeless body of her mother, as she had been. She saw children gripped in panic, fleeing for their lives. Some of it wasn't hard to imagine since she'd seen it from a distance that night in Matanzas. A peaceful town engulfed in flame, and herself the cause of it. She shuddered.

CHAPTER 24
PORTOBELLO

To distract herself from their course toward Portobello, which she could neither change nor stop, Francesca threw herself into her work.

She set Mr. Pitt to making wooden practice blades and organized fencing lessons for all the men. There was not enough room for everyone on deck, so she taught them two messes at a time. With the quartermaster's permission, she gave small cash prizes for those who did the best—which stopped the complaining, mostly.

She also set up pistol and musket practice. Targets were towed alongside the ship and prizes handed out for the best shot.

She didn't think about the fact that she was making them more effective at killing. She was teaching her friends to defend themselves. And every day the wind took them closer to the coast of Panama and to Portobello. Now, when her eyes met those of the captain, all she saw was a hard-edged resolve.

On the afternoon of November thirteenth, as men gathered on deck for pistol practice, the lookout shouted, "Land ho! Off the starboard bow!"

Francesca didn't want to see the coast. She knew it was Costa Rica. In a few days' time they would reach Panama.

She concentrated on handing out pistols, powder horns, and shot to the men. She was alarmed when Agar appeared with his hand extended. Agar had

226

his own pistols and was good with them. He needed no training. He had flatly refused her sword training, and she remembered the captain's words, "His solution to every problem is a lead ball." But she could think of no excuse to deny him a gun, so she handed one over.

Francesca tried to keep an eye on Agar as the company loaded their weapons, but Tuit took most of her attention. Tuit had never fired a gun and hated the noisy, smelly things. But she had insisted he at least know how to handle one in case the need arose.

Francesca showed him how to check that the weapon wasn't primed before he started. She had him sit down, prop the gun up vertically, and pour the proper amount of powder down the muzzle. He had no problem dropping in the lead ball and wadding and tamping it all down, but as he filled the primer pan, he accidentally cocked and pulled the trigger. With a flash of light and smoke and a terrific *pop* the gun went off. Tuit leaped to his feet, throwing the pistol across the deck.

"Bloody hell!" shouted One-eyed Kelsey who stood near the line of fire. Francesca had to take a few deep breaths before she could pacify Kelsey and calm Tuit.

After that Tuit wanted nothing to do with the gun. It took the combined efforts of Francesca and Rolly to cajole him into trying again.

Meanwhile, Miller organized the rest of the men. They loaded their weapons and took turns shooting at a target towed off their starboard side. Bigalow, the best shot on board, demonstrated how to take a breath and hold it before pulling the trigger.

While the others were shooting, Tuit got his pistol loaded and stepped to the rail. Francesca helped him aim down the sights, and he pulled the trigger. The pistol bucked, and he leapt backwards into Francesca throwing the gun away. As she reeled back, flailing, a searing pain ripped along her right hip and there was a scream behind her.

Mills, who had lost a leg a month ago, fell to the deck bleeding from his truncated thigh.

"Doctor! Get the doctor!" yelled Francesca. She moved toward Mills, putting her hand to her hip and wondering what had happened. Crewmen surrounded Mills staunching the blood that ran scarlet across deck. Francesca took her hand from her hip. Blood. She spun and caught Agar staring at her, smoke rising from his pistol.

"Damned thing misfired," he growled, throwing the pistol on the deck.

"You should have Mr. Pitt look at the thing." He headed below without a word to Mills who writhed in pain.

Francesca's heart skipped a beat. That bullet had been meant for her. If Tuit hadn't bumped into her...

The doctor was hustled up onto deck and into the crowd surrounding Mills.

Francesca picked up Agar's pistol and looked it over. It looked fine. *I had better tell the captain before someone else gets hurt.*

Hal and a greasy, unkempt man named Able approached her.

"We seen the 'ole thing. The damn gun aughta be destroyed 'fore someone else gits popped in the shanks."

Hal leaned toward her and dropped his voice. "We'll swear as much. Anyone who says otherwise kin go whistle."

A tide of hatred welled up and settled in the back of her throat. So they would back Agar and it would be her word against theirs with no proof either way.

She pointed the unloaded gun at Hal. "Tell Agar, what's good for the gander is good for the goose." She cocked it and pulled the trigger. Hal flinched at the click. Francesca tucked the gun in her sash turning to Mills.

Over the next few days, the *Destiny* traveled south along the coast of Costa Rica toward Panama. Distant mountains rose blue from a sea of palm trees. Carter and Rolly stared at the golden sand beaches, but Francesca ignored them. She flew into a flurry of activity trying to forget not only Agar's attempt on her life, but what lay ahead.

Her hip rarely bothered her once bandaged, but Mills was not so lucky. The lead ball had lodged against his femur and fever had set in. The doctor had removed the ball. Mills would make it, or he wouldn't.

A few days later, off the coast of Panama, the *Destiny* captured a ten-gun Spanish brigantine in a hard-fought battle. Once she was repaired, they had all they needed for their raid on Portobello.

When the day came, dread settled over Francesca as she watched the men paint a new name on the captured ship, *Tempting Fate*.

Francesca could feel a storm brewing. The evening air was hot and heavy. Angry clouds gathered and crouched, as if preparing to spring.

The captain's plan was four-pronged. Francesca would head inland leading twenty-five men and attack the town from behind. Mr. Baldric would take four gun crews with swivel guns and attack the south fort from inland. The ships would bombard from the bay. *Tempting Fate*, flying a Spanish flag, would get close to the northern gun platform, then rake it with grapeshot. If they couldn't destroy the guns, they could kill the gun crews. The *Destiny* would focus on the town itself.

Francesca's team was ready. She could feel excitement growing among them. They rubbed their weapons for luck and licked their lips at the prospect of gold and blood.

Francesca's mind played images of what would happen. She saw the bodies of children and smelled blood and gunpowder. Screams filled her mind as she lurched to the rail and threw up over the side. She couldn't attack a town full of innocent people. *He can't do this,* she thought as she wiped her mouth on her sleeve. Her hands balled into fists as she headed for the great cabin.

Francesca burst through the open door feeling wild and desperate.

"Why are you here?" demanded the captain. He was ready for battle in his blood-red jacket and his face hardened to stone.

Her voice cracked. "Captain, please don't do this. Don't force me to do this."

"Bloody hell!" the captain said. "You're leading the landing party!"

Her voice dropped. "Will, I swore to my father—"

Whump! His fist hit the table. "Don't you dare lecture me about your bloody honor. Your father was a master swordsman. How many people do you think he killed? That's what the bloody swords are for! Don't be so goddamned naïve."

Anger ripped through Francesca. "You can't begin to know a man like my father."

"Can't I?"

"You're a … a…" She could think of no word worse than 'pirate' and that would only make him laugh. She trembled with unspent rage.

They stood silent, anger matching anger.

She ground out the words. "Why is Portobello so important?"

"What would you have me tell the men?" he countered.

"It's not about the gold," she said.

"That their master-at-arms doesn't want to play because someone might get hurt?" he spat.

"It's about making them suffer the way you suffer, isn't it? You want women and children to die."

The captain's face contorted. "What I want is my business. Your job is to do as I tell you."

Francesca's eyes bored into his. "Is that what they would want?"

His face went red-purple as he grabbed Francesca and shoved her toward the door. "Get on that boat before I have you keel-hauled!"

She paused in the doorway, not looking back. Claire was right—she'd been doomed since the day she returned to the *Destiny*. If only she'd kept her word and gone to find Billy.

Her words were choked. "I've been a fool to think I could maintain some shred of honor here, with you. If my fate is to become a ruthless killer…" Her shoulders slumped.

The swollen clouds rumbled with menace. Francesca, Carter, and twenty-four *Destiny* crewmen slogged through swampy ground that looked solid but gave way beneath them. The underbrush grew close, and the still air was stifling. Carter sunk up to his knees in mire and Francesca hauled him back to solid footing.

"Keep moving," she scolded. "We have an hour to reach town, and the storm could strike any time."

"I'm trying!" said Carter shaking muck off his legs.

Francesca hadn't wanted to bring Carter, but the captain had insisted. Insurance, she guessed. The captain knew she would do whatever she must to protect Carter. Now she supposed it was just as well; there would be no safe place in this battle. Carter had been thrilled when the captain charged him with setting off the rocket that would begin the concerted attack. She was sure Carter hadn't thought about anything beyond that task.

Francesca's stomach sank with each sucking, muddy step. A black pit grew inside her. She would be lost tonight, either in body or soul. She tried to resign herself to it, but the harder she tried, the angrier she became.

The undergrowth thickened to a green wall, so they pulled out their blades and hacked through.

Francesca emerged on the bank of a wide, frothing river that had not appeared on the map. "By all the saints!"

It began to rain.

It took them forty-five minutes to get everyone across. Tuit swam the river like an otter with a rope and fastened it to a tree on the far side. With their pistols, shot, and powder held over their heads, they waded through the chest-deep water, clinging to the rope.

Francesca stuffed her pistols back in her soggy sash as the last men across dumped water out of their boots. They'd lost too much time. Evening had deepened and soon they wouldn't be able to see where they were going. The rain came down in fat, warm drops that blurred her eyes, and thunder rumbled overhead. Then she heard it: cannon fire.

They turned to the north. Orange flashes painted the undersides of the clouds.

"By Satan's beard!" Miller said. "It's too soon!"

The attack was not supposed to begin until her group was in position. This could not be good.

"C'mon men!" yelled Francesca. She ran into the brush with her crew at her back. She sped through the darkening night, the mud sucking at her feet and her heart hammering.

The town was eerily quiet when they arrived. The cannons had ceased firing. Some of the adobe buildings had been reduced to rubble and random fires lit the night, glittering off wet pavement. Was the battle over? Had they won or lost? She hesitated as the men looked to her for direction. Then she heard gunfire nearby.

"Carter, the rocket!"

Carter fished it out of his bag, careful to keep the fuse dry, and stuffed the back end into the ground. After a couple tries, the fuse finally lit, and they stepped back to watch it shoot skyward with a hiss and a erupt into a shower of sparks.

"Crikey!" exclaimed Carter as it burst into blue flame fifty feet above.

Suddenly, townsfolk flooded from every direction carrying not only the usual weapons, but hoes, scythes, fire irons, anything they could lay their hands on.

Francesca stood on a precipice. The rain-slicked cobblestones flowed out from her mud-covered boots, yet a gaping abyss yawned in front of her. To move forward was unthinkable. But to disobey orders, to break her word, to leave her shipmates to die on an enemy shore was equally impossible.

Anguish filled her. Part of her had known all along that this day would come. *Fight!* a dark corner of her mind screamed. *At least for a while you'll feel nothing.*

The number of townsmen swelled, fifty or sixty at least, advancing warily. So many. She spotted a boy about Carter's age carrying a fire iron, eyes huge with fear.

Francesca's company waited for her word, tightly wound, and ready to pounce. Still, she froze. *Papa! What do I do?*

Carter touched her arm as he hid behind her. "Francesca?" he said in a tremulous voice.

She looked back at him and saw Miller and Tuit staring at her with concern. Their eyes galvanized her will. She couldn't leave them trapped on a Spanish coast. They'd be hunted down and killed. She must get them back to the ship and the only way was through the town.

"Stay here!" she ordered Carter. Then, with a scream that gave voice to her fury, she fired into the knot of innocent townsmen. Pistols erupted all around her and bodies fell. As one, Francesca and her men streamed into the town with swords drawn.

———⸙———

In the pouring rain, Francesca had no idea she was crying until she tasted the salt. Once she'd started the attack, reckless abandon came over her. She had nothing left to lose, and she took it out on the Spanish faces that arose and fell in front of her.

She had no idea how long they fought or against how many. She only knew they had to keep moving together in one murderous mass, this way and that, to avoid being surrounded. And that no one stood long before her well-trained men. White-haired old men and red-cheeked boys fell—each a lump of dirt tossed on her grave, a page for her book.

At some point they encountered Baldric and his crew. She was happy to let him take control. She was beyond exhaustion, beyond caring. Soon the captain and his company and the remaining crew of the *Tempting Fate* joined them. As their numbers swelled, the last of the townsmen dropped their weapons and ran.

Steady rain fell, though a slight lessening of the darkness signaled the dawn. The smell of damp earth and wood smoke felt heavy in Francesca's lungs. In the dim light she saw bodies littering the town. She turned to her bloodied company who wobbled on their feet.

"Good work, men," the captain said, clapping one pirate on the shoulder and almost knocking him over. The captain looked exhausted but elated. "To the armory."

They followed him mechanically, dragging themselves along.

As they passed a small, gray stone church they heard a woman shriek inside. With what strength she had left, Francesca rushed for the door and inside.

The church was cold and damp, the nave lit by a forest of votive candles. The shiver that ran down Francesca's spine came only partly from the chill. Women and children, some injured, many crying, cowered on the steps of the unyielding stone altar. Before them, Agar, wet and bloody, struggled with a beautiful young Spanish woman, her dress torn from her shoulder.

Francesca flew into a rage and attacked. She plowed into Agar, knocking him flat. She was immediately on top of him, a knee on his chest. She raised her dagger, ready to strike.

"Christ!" hissed Agar, fear in his eyes.

"Francesca!" yelled Carter.

She stopped, quivering. Her whole being wanted to plunge that dagger down, but she couldn't, not with Carter watching. She shook with barely controlled rage. Her voice hissed, echoing in the silent nave. "Give me cause and by God, I'll bathe these stones in your blood."

Agar made no move. He barely breathed. She waited, willing him to struggle, to hit her, to do something to give her a reason. He didn't.

She lowered her dagger to his neck and drew a tiny line of red across his throat. "If anyone, anyone, touches these women, I swear I will post your balls on the yardarm."

Still he made no move.

"Is that clear?"

Agar gave the tiniest of nods. Francesca rose and he scuttled away.

The tearful woman held her torn dress. "I had not thought to find a friend among these curs," she said in Spanish.

"I am not your friend," Francesca said, thinking of the bodies lying lifeless outside. How many loved ones had this woman lost?

She turned toward Agar. Switching to English she spat, "But I'll not let cowards wage war on women."

Agar dropped low, as if he might rush her. She fell into a fighting stance willing him to charge. They stared at each other, tense, considering.

Perhaps Agar saw the raging chaos in her eyes, beyond caring if she won or lost, only desiring an outcome. He backed down, his face red with rage.

Disappointed, Francesca headed toward the *Destiny* crew gathered in the doorway. The captain stood in their midst, his face drawn and lips tight.

Hal whispered something, then Agar's sneer echoed, "What, challenge a woman? I'd sooner duel with a dog. But mark me, Hal, no one calls Faulke Agar a coward and lives."

When Francesca emerged, the rain had eased to a drizzle. The crew followed the captain through the gray dawn to a windowless stone building with iron-wrapped double doors. Shooting away the lock, Captain Massey swung the doors open. They gasped.

Miller lit a torch, illuminating row upon row of chest high stacks of gold and silver ingots disappearing into the darkness. The captain threw open a chest revealing gleaming pieces of eight and gems glittering deep red and green. Barrels stacked to the rafters called to be opened and explored, and racks of weapons glinted.

The men stared, rapt, but Francesca turned away, cold and empty. She walked, not sure where she meant to go.

Passing the corner of the armory, she caught a line of advancing Spanish soldiers out of the corner of her eye. She turned, shocked.

A shot echoed through the stone street and pain exploded in her left shoulder, knocking her backwards. She slammed onto the muddy cobblestones.

The world spun in slow motion. The captain's face appeared, full of horror and disbelief.

Carter and Miller threw themselves toward her.

The Spanish advanced.

The crew drew weapons. She tried to shout for them to run, but no sound came.

The captain yelled, "To the ship! Fall back!"

He was close now, lifting her in his arms. Pain seared through her shoulder. She tried to scream, but darkness crept in from the edges of her vision and overtook her.

PART III

A NEW PATH

Tho much is taken, much abides; and tho
We are not now that strength which in old days
Moved earth and heaven, that which we are, we are,
One equal temper of heroic hearts,
Made weak by time and fate, but strong in will
To strive, to seek, to find, and not to yield.

Alfred Lord Tennyson

CHAPTER 25
AFTERMATH

Francesca rose slowly to consciousness, level upon level, out of darkness and into pain. As she broke the surface, her head felt stuffed with cotton. She couldn't sort out what had happened, nor could she move. She managed to turn her head toward her left shoulder, which screamed with pain. She expected to see a hot poker spit through it, but it was simply bandaged.

She groaned and Captain Massey leaned over her, his face full of concern. She was on a cot in the *Destiny's* infirmary. The captain sat on a stool next to her. The other cots held bodies, some quietly moaning.

The captain looked terrible. There were dark bags under his eyes and a week's worth of growth on his chin. His hair was unkempt and dirty. Still, she was happy to see him and would have smiled if it didn't require so much effort.

And then she remembered.

Portobello flooded back—the innocent faces, the sword in her hand, the blood. Her stomach convulsed as the memory crystallized.

"Doctor!" called the captain.

The doctor appeared above her looking worse than the captain. He put a cool hand to her forehead and looked over the top of his spectacles with bloodshot eyes. "Es it bad, lass?"

She nodded, as tears pooled in her eyes.

The doctor disappeared and reappeared with a cup. He sat on the cot, lifted her head, and she sipped. "There ye go, lass. A wee bit o' laudanum will ease the pain."

Francesca turned her face away. "Not this pain. Why couldn't you let me die?"

She felt the captain shudder, but she didn't look at him. She couldn't. It would have been fitting and proper if she'd died—justice would have been served. But here she was.

Already the draught was working. A numbing mist moved outward from her stomach. It did ease the pain, but what was the use? When the drug wore off, the agony would be waiting.

The next few days were a laudanum-induced haze.

She remembered snatches of conversations. She recalled the doctor asking her about Billy England, and realized she'd been calling Billy's name in a half-remembered dream. She tried to explain about her promise to Papa as he died to find Billy, and how, as a child, she had been afraid of being sent to him when she misbehaved. But with her befuddled thoughts, she doubted her explanation made much sense. And the captain had worn the oddest expression.

She also recalled seeing Carter, his chin trembling while he gulped back tears, but she didn't know why. And once she heard the captain and the doctor discuss her. She listened, not caring, and watched from under half-closed eyelids.

"Doc," the captain said, cradling his head in his hands, "what would you call a man who would trade the life of one woman he..." his voice cracked. He swallowed hard. "Who would trade the life of one woman to avenge another long dead?"

The doctor, placing inky black leeches on the bare chest of a patient, peered at the captain wearily over his spectacles. "Fool comes tae mind."

The captain blew out some air. "She'll never forgive me."

The doctor approached, put a hand on the captain's shoulder and tilted his head toward her. "Why nae let her leave, lad?" He motioned around. "She's nae suited to thes."

The captain shook his head. "But she is. With a sword in her hand, she's a Fury come to Earth."

"Her arm, her head, aye, but..." He patted his chest and shook his head.

The captain's shoulders slumped. "How can someone be so suited to a

life and so completely unsuited at the same time?" He sighed deeply. "We …
I suppose it's no use."

After that she had drifted to sleep.

The next time Francesca woke she refused the doctor's offer of laudanum.
The pain was a part of her now. She'd have to learn to bear it.

For the first time, the captain was not beside her.

"Doctor, when was Portobello?" she asked, though really, it made no
difference.

The doctor said, "Why, et must be ten days nou. Ye were fev'rish fer a
week, lass. Eh did nae think ye'd pull through."

"And my arm?" She could wiggle her fingers, but she couldn't lift her arm
without pain shooting in all directions from her shoulder.

"Ye were damned lucky. The arm'll be fine, in time. Considerable blood
loss, but the ball passed through wi' but wee nicks on the clavicle an' shoulder
blade. It was the fever that vexed us, but ye'll be right 'nough nou."

The captain appeared in the doorway, hesitating when he saw her awake.

"I should ask what happened," she said, avoiding the captain's eyes as he
sat down beside her.

"We were routed."

She had guessed as much. "Carter? Miller? Rolly?"

"The boys are fine." He hesitated.

"Miller?" asked Francesca, looking toward the doctor.

The doctor's shoulders slumped. "We brought back the yellowin' fever
from the damned swamp."

She closed her eyes. "Dear God."

"Ten stricken, four dead," the captain said. "Miller's alive. He's a tough
old bla'guard. Claims he's been yellow before." The captain shrugged.

"May I see him?"

"Nae, lass. Give it a wee while. Gain a bit o' strength first."

The doctor went to another patient. The captain gazed hesitantly at her
and she turned away. His chair scraped the floor as he rose.

"Why did the battle start so early?" she asked.

He sat again and ran both hands up his face and over his head. "Baldric's
men at the south fort were discovered. Both of the gun batteries opened fire

on us." He closed his eyes. "*Tempting Fate* went down and Mr. Hart and half his men with her."

Francesca was engulfed in a wave of sorrow.

"I was on the *Tempting Fate*," said a voice from the far cot.

"Mr. Jenkins," the captain said. "How are you faring?"

He held up the stump of an arm and his voice wavered. "I'll live. But I'll naught play me bagpipe again." He paused. "Still, it's due to Mr. Hart I'm alive. He was a first-rate commander, Sir. He got as many of us off as 'e could."

"Tell us what happened," the captain said.

"Well, Sir, the first bloody thirty-pound ball from th' north gun took out our foremast, topplin' it into th' mainmast. One lucky bloody shot, an' we was dead in th' water."

Jenkins ran his remaining hand across his face. "She was a doomed ship, Sir. No luck in 'er. The next shot broke 'er back, smashin' the keel amidships. We could tell she was goin' down, Sir, but me an' the men, we kept our stations.

I was at the forward starboard gun. We was firin' back at a mad pace, but it weren't no use. We was at th' far end of our range, and couldn't move closer. Our shot had no bite. But those thirty-pounders kept comin' and comin' and comin'…" his voice trailed off.

Jenkins was quiet for a moment. His voice cracked when he continued. "They was knocking th' ship apart around us, Sir. One shot knocked o'er me cannon and took me arm with it." He took a breath. "I can't cotton ta 'ow the fire started, but Mr. Hart gave the command ta abandon ship. He went below ta save th' men trapped down there." He wiped at his face. "He ne'er came up, but 'e got 'em out."

Francesca wiped away a tear trickling toward the pillow.

"He will be missed," the captain said.

"Cap'n," Jenkins said. "Why didn't the *Destiny* come ta our aid? How could ya leave us ta go under like 'at?"

The captain shook his head. "We couldn't help you, Mr. Jenkins. I would have been there if I could have."

"Why not?" asked Francesca.

The mask of hatred fell across his face. "I expected the guns to attack, but not the bloody townsfolk. We'd disturbed a hornet's nest. They boarded boats and swarmed the *Destiny*, twenty, maybe thirty boats full. We blasted many of them out of the water, but they kept coming. They poured over the rails. We abandoned the cannons for hand-to-hand fighting. I, we…" He stopped. "There was nothing we could do to help you, Mr. Jenkins, Jesus, we could not have saved ourselves."

Francesca stared up at the ceiling. She could imagine the scene, bodies writhing across the *Destiny's* deck, the *Tempting Fate* breaking apart.

"It was your rocket that saved us," the captain said to her. "That blue flash was a gift from heaven. The Spanish abandoned the *Destiny* to defend the town, so I took the men who were left and followed. You know what happened next."

Francesca nodded. She remembered the next part—Agar in the church, the treasure, and the Spanish infantry. "Where did the soldiers come from?"

The captain shrugged. "I'd guess they were from the warships we burned at Matanzas.

I suspected they were on their way to Portobello to protect the gold. Burning their ships slowed them but didn't stop them. When we fought our way back to the bay, we found it full of fishing boats crammed with soldiers." He rubbed his face as if erasing the memory. "They'd taken the *Destiny*."

"That was a bloody bad spot down there on the beach, Sir," Jenkins said. "Seein' enemies on our ship an' all 'round. And them fresh an' us fought out. We was all shakin' in our boots. And me 'alf dead from loss a blood. Me an' the men, we was ready to lay down our arms an' beg fer mercy."

"Believe me," the captain said through tight jaws. "You would not have received any."

"How did we get the ship back?" she asked.

The captain got a far-off look in his eyes. "I didn't think we could do it. I didn't think we had the strength left to retake her. But you should have seen Tuit, he was magnificent."

"He was a gorgeous bloody spitfire," Jenkins said.

Cold realization spread through Francesca's chest. She hadn't seen Tuit once since she'd woken.

"He roared like a lion and rallied the crew," the captain said, his voice catching. "When a Spanish lieutenant shot him dead, the men went wild."

"No," breathed Francesca. She put her good arm across her eyes.

The captain paused. "I've never seen the men fight so hard. We tossed the last of the Spanish bastards overboard and limped out of the bay."

"It were a miracle, Cap'n. A goddamned bloody miracle," Jenkins said.

Francesca pictured Tuit's deep, calm eyes in their band of black. She remembered the feel of his hands and his brilliant smile. Gone. Grief poured through her. She touched the tattoo on her left arm, glad now that she had it. It was a tribute to a brave warrior with healing hands and a gentle heart.

At length, she wiped her eyes and nose, and took her arm from her face. The seat next to her was vacant. She looked around for the captain, not wanting to miss him, but unable to stop the longing. *It's his fault that Tuit and Hart are dead.*

"He'll be back," said the doctor as he sat next to Francesca and removed the bandage from her shoulder. "He cannae stay away."

"How many altogether, Doctor? How many did we lose?"

The doctor gave a weary sigh. Francesca noticed how his hands trembled with fatigue.

"Nigh everyone's been injured one way or t'other." He paused. "From two ships and a hundred an' fifty men, we're down tae one ship an' forty-eight men."

Her body went cold. More than a hundred souls lost. She wondered about One-eyed Kelsey, Mr. Baldric, Mr. Angstrom, Bottom the Cook, Mr. Pitt the carpenter, and Old Nob and the rest of her messmates. How many of them were dead?

No wonder the captain looked miserable. She almost felt sorry for him.

It was another three days before Francesca left the infirmary, and then only because the doctor made her. She might have lain there forever staring at the ceiling, but the doctor needed the bed.

"Get yer arse up on deck an' get some fresh air," he ordered. "Et'll knock the cobwebs out o' yer noggin."

Cobwebs, is that what the people of Portobello are now?

Carter helped get her arm in a sling then took her good arm, acting as her crutch. Even so, she almost passed out when she stood up.

As she hobbled out of the infirmary, she saw that the floor of the landing and the great cabin held wounded lying on pallets. *So many.*

"Who's running the ship?" she asked Carter as he helped her up the companionway.

"We're spread mighty thin," Carter said. "We gots twenty men split 'tween three watches, and us boys 'ave been put ta work. I'm a topman," he said, puffing his chest.

Francesca gasped. "But you're what, twelve?"

Carter laughed. "A twelve-year-ol' boy is better 'n a one-armed girl any day."

Francesca gave him a weak smile. "No doubt."

As they reached the deck, Francesca took a lungful of air. The freshness was a relief after two weeks of the stench of sickness and death in the depths of the ship.

Lowering clouds sent a rumble of thunder across the ocean. Banks of mist drifted off their starboard bow.

Francesca and Carter had arrived for a burial-at-sea. Three men had died of yellow fever during the night. Their bodies lay on deck wrapped in canvas. Hats in hand, the crewmen waited for the captain.

She looked around. Nearly everyone was bandaged. Mr. Pitt had a bound leg and a crutch under one arm, Mr. Baldric a wrapped bicep. Bottom the Cook's wooden leg was missing and even Agar had a dressing around his head. *Tuit is dead and Agar lives,* she thought bitterly.

The thing that struck her most was not their injuries, but their attitudes. They were beaten men. Their shoulders slumped and their faces hung slack. There was no hope left in their eyes, except for Agar. His eyes smoldered with hatred as he stared at her.

She remembered his words in the church, "No one calls Faulke Agar a coward and lives." He would be even more dangerous now.

She spotted Miller near the rail. He looked bent and gaunt, his hair straggly, and a yellow tinge to his skin, but he was up and on the mend. She and Carter hobbled toward him, but he held up a hand as they approached.

"It's right good ta see ya, missy, but I wouldn't want ta be turnin' ya yella."

She stopped. She didn't care what happened to her, but she didn't want Carter to get sick. "It's good to see you too, Miller." They turned as the captain drew near the three wrapped bodies.

"None of us," the captain said, scanning the men, "are fit to sit at the knees of the Almighty in the hereafter."

A bolt of recognition hit Francesca. Those were Papa's words—*honor made us fit to sit at the knees of God.* Papa was speaking through the captain. She closed her eyes as misery washed over her.

"We all have grave sins set against our souls," he continued. "But neither are we without our credits." He stood at the head of the first body. "Five years I sailed with Bigalow. He was a good hand before the mast, and never once did I hear him utter an ill word 'gainst man nor beast."

The men nodded. Francesca thought of Bigalow's baby-face, such a contrast to his muscular hulk of a body.

The captain stepped to the second body. "Kelly was a top-notch sailmaker, and a bang-up son-of-a-bitch. Once I saw him lay into five Spanish bastards to save his messmate's skin." Again the crew nodded their assent.

She had rarely spoken with Kelly, but he'd always treated her with respect. He'd come from the *Jamaican Queen* and had never forgotten that it was Francesca who had saved them.

The captain stepped to the third body with a sigh. "Smitts was a first-rate topman and played a rippin' fiddle. His gift will be sorely missed."

"Smitts," whispered Francesca. He had been one of her messmates. How many meals had they shared? He was about her age and had a sweetheart in England named Emma. How long would Emma wait, hoping?

The captain walked among the men. "If I were to stand before the Almighty today, I would tell him this: Judge these men if you must, but against their sins set the good they've done to the likes of us and have mercy on their souls."

"Amen," muttered the crew. Two pirates came forward and heaved each body in turn overboard as the crew stood transfixed.

Agar growled something to Hal.

The doctor, nearby, turned to them with a glare. "What was that Mr. Agar?"

Agar drew himself up until he towered over the doctor. "I says, This is what comes a' carrying a woman 'board ship."

The doctor's fuzzy brows lowered. He scowled at Agar over his spectacles. "Nou ye'll be blamin' yellow fever on the lass?"

"We all know what bad luck it is to carry a woman, and burning *Lady Luck* was her idea. All our luck's burnt with her."

There was a murmur among the men, but whether in agreement or not, Francesca couldn't tell. *Maybe he's right, maybe I am bad luck.*

Agar looked around at them. "Least I've the guts to say what the rest of ya gutter bloods are thinkin'."

The muttering grew louder.

"Speak fer yerself," one man said. "She's done good service by me."

Men nodded and a few agreed. Warmth spread through Francesca that they thought better of her than she did of herself.

Agar's face twisted into a sneer, but before he spoke the captain stepped toward him, red-faced. "Agar, don't think for a moment I've forgotten your actions in that church in Portobello. It is only because we are so short-handed that you're not in the brig."

"I told ya, Captain, I never meant ta harm the wench."

"And I told you I don't believe you." The captain scowled. "But as rape is a capital offense, I'm forced to give you the benefit of the doubt."

Agar smiled and the captain's eyes narrowed.

"But be packed, Mr. Agar," the captain said. "I intend to set you ashore at the nearest English settlement once more of the injured are back on their feet."

Francesca sighed with relief. Agar gone. No more threat hanging over her, no more watching her back. It couldn't come soon enough for her.

Agar opened his mouth, but a call from the maintop interrupted him. "Three ships to starboard! Comin' out a th' mist!"

All eyes turned seaward. Dread spread among the company. No one moved. They expected more bad news, and why not? Their luck had run out.

The call came. "English warships hard by!"

Agar glared at Francesca. "She's killed us all."

Francesca dropped her eyes.

"Stow it, Agar," the captain growled.

Francesca scanned the crew. They had already done the math and given themselves up for dead. The warships had the weather gauge and were close at hand. In half an hour they'd be in firing range. The *Destiny* had no hope of outrunning them and no means of defending herself since there were not enough able-bodied crew to man both the cannons and the sails. They were as good as in the noose. She supposed they all belonged there.

Her eyes met the captain's. At first, she saw only sorrow, but his features hardened as he gazed at her. He turned purposefully toward Mr. Baldric. Suddenly he was himself again, barking orders and rubbing his hands.

"Mr. Baldric," he said, striding to the quarterdeck, "the Union Jack at the mainmast, if you please, and the quarantine flag on the fore."

"Aye, Sir," Baldric said, relaying orders to the men.

"Mr. Miller, if you'd come here, please. Doctor, I'd like any yellow fever patient who can walk on deck. Have the rest carried up."

"Captain, I protest," the doctor said, "fresh air es contraindicated—"

"As is hanging," snapped the captain.

The doctor nodded brusquely and gave orders to a group of men who disappeared below.

The captain turned to Miller. "Today is your lucky day, Miller. You're to be captain."

Miller looked less than pleased. "Captain? Sir?"

"Those ships will have us in their glasses in a minute, and they'll be in boarding range in three quarters of an hour. They must believe we're a merchant vessel rife with plague, and I must say, you're looking the part."

Francesca nodded. That was certainly true. The captain hustled Miller toward the quarterdeck.

"Tell them we're traders out of Port Royal on our way to St. Thomas. Whatever you do, don't let them board the ship."

The yellow fever victims were being brought up and deposited about the deck.

"Anyone not ill, below decks and keep quiet," the captain ordered. He turned to Carter. "Get her below and see that she stays there."

Francesca and Carter headed toward the companionway. Below deck, she moved toward her cabin, but Carter pulled her to a halt.

"Don't ya wanna see what 'appens?" Carter said.

"Aye, Carter, but I need something from my cabin." There was a little time left before the warships arrived. If they were captured, if she was hung for her crimes, Francesca wanted all those she injured represented in her *Book of Reckoning*. She owed them that much.

With Carter's help she gathered the book, pen, and ink. Then they headed toward the fo'c'sle where the men messed. The room had vents in the low ceiling that let in light and air. There they could hear what happened on deck, though they wouldn't see much.

When they reached the mess, there were over a dozen crew members gathered near the air vents listening.

Francesca sat at a table, opened her Book, and wrote:

November 26th, Portobello.
Young man with metal casque – slash to the side – may have lived.
Square jawed Spaniard with eye-patch – run through – RIP

Her hand shook.

Boy with a machete — slash to the arm — will most likely lose it.
Old man with a long beard — RIP.

She made it through half a dozen entries then stopped. She remembered a figure arising in front of her, remembered him falling, but no more. No face, no clothes, no age, nothing. Her throat constricted. *What kind of monster can't remember? Are there others I've forgotten?* But then his face crystalized—the dark eyes, shaved head, and dark goatee—and she went on writing.

"Crikey," Carter said. "'Ow can ya sit an' write at a time like this? They're git'n' close!" He stood atop the table that Francesca wrote on, pressing his face against the wood grating of an air vent trying to see what was happening on deck.

"I have to, Carter."

A voice commanded them to heave-to. Minutes later the *Destiny's* forward motion stopped. The ship rolled on the waves.

Francesca finished and closed the book. It was complete. The only thing left to do was to pay for her crimes.

She looked up at Carter. "Can you hear anything?"

"I think a boat's comin' o'er. I can 'ear the oars."

Francesca wanted to climb up on the table, but she was too unsteady. She could only imagine the pain if she fell on her bad shoulder. She stood and tucked her Book in her sash.

She thought about hobbling up on deck and giving herself up to the British, but it would put all her friends' necks in the noose as well, and she couldn't do that.

Miller called, "Hold! Ya mustn't come up! We've yellowjack aboard."

There was a muffled voice from the boat.

Miller sounded hesitant. "Why no, Sir."

"We're boarding your ship," shouted the British voice loud enough for everyone in the forecastle to hear.

The men all stared upward, listening with grim faces.

Francesca's muscles tightened and fear clotted in her stomach. *Carter and Rolly, they're so young.*

There was a long pause then the clipped British voice yelled, "Blast it! Up the side, men, or you'll answer to the cat-o-nine-tails."

"They're comin' aboard," whispered Carter. "Marines, from th' red coats." He paused. "They don't look keen on it. They're bunched at the rail."

She understood their reluctance to board a quarantine ship. And if they doubted the quarantine flag, the yellow fever victims should convince them. *Perhaps that will be enough.* But she didn't hold out much hope.

"Miller's goin' up ta th' bloke in th' blue coat," said Carter. "The marines are backin' away."

"Twill be their deaths, Sir, if yer men was ta go below," Miller said.

"I'll go myself," the man said.

"I'll not let ya do that, Sir," Miller replied.

"Out of my way!"

"Now, now, no need for 'at."

"The bloke pulled a pistol," hissed Carter.

Francesca's fingernails dug into the fabric of her breeches, and she listened for the shot that would mean Miller was dead.

"Beggin' yer pardon, Sir, I'd like ta oblige, but it's fer yer own good," Miller said, his voice wavering.

He's a brave man, thought Francesca.

The tension was thick in the forecastle.

"If you don't move, I will signal that ship," the navy man said, "and she will hole you from stem to stern and put you on the bottom."

No one in the mess moved or breathed.

Finally, Carter said, "Bloody hell, Miller's stepped aside. The bloke's head'n fer the companionway!"

Calm washed over Francesca. It was over. All that was left was the gallows.

But suddenly everyone was moving. Where they thought they would go, she couldn't imagine. The only exits were past the companionway, and there wasn't time to reach them.

Carter jumped down from the table and grabbed Francesca's good arm, dragging her behind Bottom's cook stove. The bolt of pain from her shoulder blinded her, and she swallowed a cry.

Footsteps thudded on the companionway and a voice commanded, "On deck! Now!"

Someone yelled and metal scraped—the metallic ring of a sword pulled from a scabbard. A pistol shot rang out, ear-splitting in the enclosed space. There was a cry of pain and a thump, like a body hitting the deck. Who had fallen? She leaned toward the edge of the cook stove to peek, but Carter pulled her back.

"'E bloody shot me," said one of the men.

The voice commanded again, "I said, on deck!"

There was silence for a moment, then she heard someone being lifted and steps shuffling toward the stairs.

She closed her eyes with a sense of relief. She moved to join the men trudging up the companionway, but Carter held her back.

"Are ya daft?" he hissed.

"It's no use, Carter." His fingers dug into her bicep. When she turned to him, his eyes were dilated and his mouth trembled.

She sighed, her voice soft. "In a few minutes they'll search the ship. There's nowhere to go." She tried to reassure him. "You're under sixteen and you didn't sign the Articles. They won't hang you." *I hope.*

Carter's grip tightened. "But they'll 'ang you!"

She wrapped him in her good arm. "It's all right, Carter."

He held her tight. "First ma and pa and all me brothers and sisters. Then Tuit died an' you was shot an' Miller all Yella. I can't … I don't want ta be alone."

They heard footsteps on the companionway and the doctor's voice. "Lass? where are ye?"

"Here, behind the stove, Doctor." Carter's arms around her tightened even more.

"I'm sorry, Carter," she said, resting her cheek on the top of his head. "I wish things were different."

The doctor joined them. He put a hand on Carter's shoulder. "It's time tae go, lad. They're waitin' fer us on deck."

Slowly Carter released her, but he took the last of her strength with him. She slumped against the stove, drained. Her legs shook.

"Help her," the doctor said.

Carter took his place as her crutch and helped Francesca toward the companionway and the doctor followed.

The sun had burnt away the mist and felt hot on her skin as she stepped onto deck. Close at hand was a British ship, perhaps twenty feet longer than the *Destiny*. In the distance were two much larger ships-of-the-line.

A handful of red-coated marines pointed their muskets at the crew who formed forlorn groups, unmoving. Captain Massey stood in front of

Francesca, his back to her, each arm held by a marine. He argued with someone in front of him who was blocked from her view, presumably whoever was in charge.

"You must see that she's cared for. She's injured," the captain said.

An angry voice responded. "You're in no position to make demands."

"Captain," she said. "I want to speak to them."

The captain turned, giving Francesca one glimpse of his anguished face before her eyes focused on the British officer behind him.

Blood hissed in her ears and her knees gave way. She leaned heavily on Carter as the doctor stepped toward her extending a hand.

It was Phillip.

CHAPTER 26
CLAIRE'S LETTER

Francesca and Phillip stared at one another across fifteen feet of deck. Red-coated marines awaited orders with muskets ready. The defeated *Destiny* crew grouped together, waiting. And Captain Massey, his face twisted, stood watching. The ocean itself seemed hushed.

Memories flashed through Francesca's mind in an instant. She and Phillip racing through silver olive groves on horseback, her golden maestro teaching her to fence in the stone barn, their decision to run away together, and then, Catalina.

"Francesca! At last!" breathed Phillip, joy shining from his face.

She didn't notice either of them moving, but suddenly his arms were around her. She looked up at his aqua-blue eyes and his perfect face.

"What have they done to you? Bastards!" Phillip said, glaring at the captain. "I'll see them drawn and quartered for this."

His voice was deeper, harsher, but it was him.

"Phillip," she said, trying to reassure herself this was not some after effect of the laudanum.

"It's me," he said with the voice she remembered. "You're safe."

The words were comforting, and Francesca expected relief, but the feeling didn't come. Somehow it was all wrong. *Why hadn't he come sooner? Before...*

Phillip turned to a nearby marine. His voice grew commanding again. He motioned toward the *Destiny* crew. "Take their weapons and secure them in the hold. Search the ship for others."

"Aye, Sir," said the marine who barked orders to his men.

"Ready the boat," Phillip said. "I'm taking Miss DiCesare to the admiral's ship. Mr. Adams, you're in charge while I'm away."

"Aye, Sir."

Phillip motioned to the men who held the captain's arms, "Bring Massey."

Francesca gave a muffled cry when someone jostled her bad arm as they were handing her down into the red and white longboat at the *Destiny's* side. She was soon seated in the front with Phillip next to her, his arm around her.

The marines hustled Captain Massey into the back and the rowers took up their oars.

"What happened to your shoulder?" Phillip said as the boat moved forward. They headed for the largest of the three English ships which rode the waves a quarter mile off.

"A musket ball," she said, cradling her arm.

"My God, Francesca." He turned to glare at the captain.

"It wasn't him; it was a Spanish soldier. And the ball passed through, I'll be fine."

Phillip rubbed his face. "I'm sorry I didn't find you sooner. I've been searching for months."

"Searching for me?"

"Of course, for you. I received a letter from Lady Claire Henry. She told me what happened. I've been searching ever since."

"Oh, dear Claire," she whispered.

He brushed a stray hair back behind her ear, "The admiral keeps me on a short leash, but I've boarded every ship we encountered for months hoping to find you."

"Did you get my letter from Port Royal?" she asked hesitantly. Did he know she'd been pirating? She'd admitted as much in her letter.

He shook his head. "We've not had mail in quite a long time."

Francesca chewed her lip. "What exactly did Claire tell you?"

He took her good hand, his palm hard and calloused, like hers. "She told me you saved her and her sister. How you went up against three men carrying knives and swords, and how you beat them armed with nothing but a wooden cane." She heard pride in his voice.

"My brave little Francesca," he said, tightening his arm around her. "But it was a terrible risk. You shouldn't have done it. Your father would have been quite cross with you."

"Papa." Francesca's chest tightened and she closed her eyes. She disagreed. Papa would have wanted her to. She wished she could tell him she had heard Papa's voice urging her on, but she feared she would sound crazy.

"Claire told me about the Maestro's death and that you had avenged it. She told me you were running for your life when she met you. I'm so sorry, Francesca. You've been through so much."

She nodded and swallowed hard. "I was so frightened, Phillip. I missed you."

Phillip laid his cheek against her head, regret heavy in his voice. "I should never have left you. This is all my fault."

"No. It was my decision."

His face twisted in anguish. He glanced back at the rowers, then dropped his voice. "If I hadn't left you, you would never have been on that ship when the pirates attacked, you wouldn't have been forced to stand against them, and you wouldn't have had to sacrifice yourself for Claire and her sister's freedom."

She stared at her hands. Claire had made her sound nobler than she deserved. She heard Claire's words on the day they said goodbye.

"You've chosen this path, not out of honor, but out of a need for ... that you couldn't abide a quiet life in the country with us."

Why had she gone back to the *Destiny* that day? She could not now truly say. It was clear Phillip still thought her spotless. *Do I have the strength to tell him the truth?*

Her *Book of Reckoning* dug into her ribs. "Phillip, well. You see…"

She fell silent and looked out to sea. *He will hate me.*

"What is it?" Phillip said, turning her face to his with a gentle hand.

She avoided his eyes. "Nothing."

He frowned, but let it go.

They were approaching the largest ship. It had four masts and she guessed it was over two-hundred feet long. Most of her sails were furled, displaying her spider's web of rigging. The ship's sides were navy blue with yellow and white stripes just below the rail. At least twenty guns bristled from its side.

"The *Horatio*." Phillip's face grew hard. "Don't worry, Francesca, Massey and the rest of them will get what they deserve. Hanging pirates is the admiral's one joy in life."

Francesca felt sick to her stomach.

As the boat bumped against the *Horatio's* side she said, "Please, Phillip, you mustn't say anything. Please."

Phillip gave her a puzzled look then turned his eyes up to the deck fifteen feet above. "Permission to come aboard?"

"Aye, Sir."

He stood and helped Francesca to her feet. "You needn't worry about them."

"But Phillip—" Then she was being handed up the side. Someone grabbed her bad arm, and she cried out again. A moment later she was on deck.

In the commotion of getting aboard Captain Massey moved close to her.

"Say *nothing* to the admiral. That's an order," he hissed.

"Shut your mouth, Massey," Phillip said.

Francesca couldn't tell the truth. If she admitted what she had done, her friends would all hang. She couldn't condemn them. But to lie? To bear false witness? Also impossible. The captain was steering her down the only possible course. Say nothing and let the chips fall as they may, but that seemed no more honorable than her other choices.

Her thoughts whirled as Phillip guided her aft. She barely noticed the gleaming white decks or the precision and snap of the navy men they passed. Her ears were tuned to the captain's footsteps with his attendant marines close behind her.

They were whisked into the great cabin before she could decide what to do.

The aft of the ship faced the late morning sun. Light flooded the twenty-foot arc of stern windows, glittering off the waves, gleaming off the whitewashed floor, and reflecting up to the snowy ceiling. The dark-wood furniture and Oriental rugs floated in lightness, like a naval officer's idea of what heaven would look like. The cabin was at least four times the size of the one on the *Destiny*.

At an ornate desk against the blinding windows sat Admiral Strickland. The silhouette of his bald head, thick neck, and rounded shoulders seemed owlish, but his heavy jaw, and grey assessing eyes dispelled the impression. His nose was flattened and crooked, as if it had been in the way of too many fists.

Leaning on Phillip, Francesca approached the admiral. On Phillip's other side were the two marines holding the captain. The captain yanked his arms, but the marines' grips held.

Phillip saluted the admiral.

"Well, Captain Worthington, who have you brought me today?" The admiral leaned back in his chair.

"Sir, I'd like you to meet a very old friend of mine. May I present Miss Francesca DiCesare, daughter of the illustrious Maestro DiCesare."

The admiral stood, tugging at the bottom of his blue jacket making the golden epaulets on his shoulders dance. He came around the desk and took Francesca's hand in both of his. His hands were large and soft, as if he wore oversized gloves. "It is an honor to meet you, my dear. Your father's reputation is well known in England."

"Thank you." Francesca thought of the "wanted" poster in Port Royal, doubting the admiral would be so cordial if he knew the truth.

The admiral addressed Phillip. "To what do I owe this pleasure?"

"I ... we rescued her, Sir. She was a prisoner of this man, Massey, and his band of pirates."

The admiral's face stiffened, and he turned toward the captain.

The captain gasped in outrage. "Pirates? We're traders out of Charlotte Amalie bound for Port Royal, Admiral."

"Then why were you trying to scare us away with a quarantine flag?" demanded Phillip.

The captain's eyes narrowed. "That was for your own good. I've lost ten of my men to yellow fever."

"And they caught yellow fever in Charlotte Amalie, did they?" the admiral said, clearly disbelieving.

There was a quick knock at the door.

"Enter," the admiral called.

A navy man popped in, then snatched off his hat.

"What is it?" the admiral said.

"We've sighted the mail packet from Port Royal, Sir."

Too late, thought Francesca.

"Very well," said the admiral.

The man disappeared, shutting the door.

"Yellow fever aside, Sir," Phillip said. "They've kept Francesca captive aboard their ship for months."

"My men had nothing to do with it, Admiral. They're simple sailors. I'm the one to blame," Captain Massey said.

Francesca's throat constricted. The captain was protecting his crew. It was noble of him, but while he had committed many crimes, holding her captive was not one of them. "I'm sorry, Admiral," she said. "Phillip is very gallant, but he has been misinformed. I was not a prisoner. I went aboard of my own volition."

"You were forced," Phillip said, looking indignant.

"I was only forced to make a decision," she said.

"You were a passenger aboard this man's ship?" asked the admiral.

She opened her mouth, but the captain cut in. "Aye, aye, a passenger. She was in no way involved in any of the ship's activities."

She looked at the captain. His eyes pleaded with her to keep her mouth shut, to let him save her life. Francesca wanted to tell the admiral that she had been a crewmember—that she had bled and sweated and worked with them. But as an innocent bystander and Maestro DiCesare's daughter, she could plead for the men and argue for their lives. As one of them, she could not. She held her tongue.

The admiral scratched his chin as he examined her. He took her aside out of earshot of the captain.

"My dear," whispered the admiral. "I can see you've been ill-treated. If you're afraid of reprisals by that man, you needn't be. I can promise you every protection. Is there anything you wish to tell me?"

I wish to tell you I was master at arms, that I've boarded a dozen Spanish ships, that I plotted the burning of Matanzas Bay and led the attack on Portobello. "No, Sir."

The admiral turned to the others. "As to the question of pirating, that is easily answered. Captain Worthington, search their hold. If they are honest traders, there will be records of purchases and sales. Unless there is a manifest entry and a bill of lading for every item in the hold, I'll see them hang. In the meantime, take Massey to the brig. Dismissed!"

Cold fear swept through Francesca's stomach. Their loot was sure to damn them.

As the marines hustled Captain Massey out the door, he looked back over his shoulder at her. "Francesca, please, there is something I need to tell you." The marines yanked him out of sight.

Francesca reeled as the captain exited. It might be the last time she would see him alive. Phillip steadied her and she gave him a weak smile.

"My dear, I fear all this has been rather trying for you," the admiral said. "Captain Worthington, find somewhere for our guest to rest."

"Aye, Sir."

As Phillip helped her from the cabin, she realized how tired she was. This was her first time out of bed since she had been shot. It was only noon, and she was already exhausted, her shoulder throbbing.

"Let's let you lie down," Phillip said.

Francesca nodded. She had no intention of sleeping, but she needed somewhere quiet to think of a plan.

Phillip escorted her to a small, but lavish guest cabin with a four-poster feather bed and she sank down wearily. "Phillip, the men on the *Destiny* are my friends. Most of them, anyway."

He brushed the hair back from her upturned face. "I'm here now. You don't need them." He kissed her lovingly on the forehead. Then he left, closing the door behind him.

Francesca sagged onto the bed. What was she to do? How could she save them? There was no way to get back to the *Destiny*. Even if she had a longboat, she couldn't row it with her injured shoulder. And how could she get the captain out of the brig? And if she did, what would happen to Phillip? Would they court martial him? But if she didn't do something they would all die. Thoughts whirled through her head, but none offered any hope.

Francesca awoke with a start. *Asleep! Dear God Almighty, I fell asleep with all their lives on the line!*

She jumped up, making her head spin with vertigo. Once the room steadied, she hurried for the door. In the hall, she approached the first navy man she saw. "Excuse me, please. Can you tell me what time it is?"

"It's six bells in the noon watch, ma'am."

That made it three in the afternoon. *I slept for three hours!*

"Can you tell me where Captain Worthington is?"

The man touched a knuckle to his forehead. "He's with the admiral in the great cabin, ma'am."

Her mind raced. Was he back already from the *Destiny*? Was he telling the admiral what he found? She couldn't remember which way she had come. "Please, could you take me there, quickly?"

The man led her this way and that, but she noticed little of it. She was running through defenses in her mind. All of them seemed just as inadequate as they had before she fell asleep. The man stopped so abruptly Francesca ran into him.

"Here you are, ma'am."

She looked up at the door to the great cabin. "Thank you."

As the man nodded and hurried off, she heard raised voices inside.

Her hand shook as she knocked.

"Come," called the admiral.

Francesca opened the door and peered inside. The admiral sat at his desk. Phillip leaned over his left shoulder looking at a sheet of paper in the admiral's hand. To her right stood Captain Massey, Mr. Baldric, Mr. Angstrom, and Agar—the *Destiny's* officers. Their hands were manacled and a pair of marines with muskets stood behind them. Captain Massey and Agar looked angry; the others looked terrified. The scene had a feeling of finality to it, like a trial.

"I tell you, those were a gift for saving his life," the captain said, frowning. He saw Francesca. "Is that not true, Miss DiCesare?"

She hurried to the admiral's desk. "If I may be of service, Admiral. What is the issue, Sir?" she asked.

"My dear," the admiral said. "We're discussing the lack of documentation for anything in the *Destiny's* hold. I can only assume it has all been stolen." His face darkened. "Pirates are the scourge of the seas. I've taken an oath to hunt down and destroy them, and I take that oath seriously."

Francesca felt the blood drain from her face. She was too late. "But what in particular were you discussing?"

"We were discussing the twenty-five barrels of fine dark rum I found," Phillip said.

"Those were a gift, Sir. I can vouch for that. They belonged to Mr. Henry Carlisle, a plantation owner from Port Royal. We came upon his ship in a storm and I ... well, you see, the *Destiny* crew saved Mr. Carlisle's life, and he was most generous in his thanks."

"That's as may be, my dear," the admiral said. "But it doesn't account for the rest of this long list, like the chest full of gold doubloons, the cask of emeralds, the two tons of cocoa, the silver plateware, the three crates of indigo dye, or the personal effects and correspondence of one Señor Ramírez de Arroyo."

Francesca pleaded with Phillip with her eyes. "I'm sure explanations can be found for everything."

"But not for this," Phillip said, pulling a folded paper from his pocket. "Admiral, this is a letter from a young English woman of high standing, named Claire Henry, whose ship, the *Santa Ana*, was boarded and taken. In it she identifies the ship as being renamed the *Destiny* and identifies Massey as the captain."

Francesca gasped. Claire's letter!

Phillip looked at the captain, gloating. Francesca closed her eyes. A void opened between her ribs. It was her fault. She had asked Claire to write that letter. Agar had been right when he said she would be the ruin of them all.

The admiral took his time reading. Francesca's eyes met the captain's and she hoped he saw how sorry she was. He seemed strangely at peace, and that made it all the worse.

There was a knock on the door.

"Come," the admiral said without taking his eyes from the letter.

A navy man entered and set a stack of papers on the desk. "Mail from Port Royal, Sir."

The admiral nodded and the man left. Finally, the admiral folded the letter and handed it back to Phillip.

He turned to Francesca. "You've had quite an adventure, my dear. You are your father's daughter. I can give you no higher praise than that."

Francesca's eyes stung. She wanted to say something, some defense for her friends, but no words came.

The admiral brushed the stack of mail aside as he rose and straightened his coat. "As for the rest of you scoundrels and thieves, I find the officers and crew of the *Destiny* guilty of piracy on the high seas. The punishment, whereof—"

A piece of mail peeking from the stack caught his eye. He pulled a paper from the pile and stared at it. His jaw tensed and he faced Francesca. "I suppose there is an explanation for this as well."

He turned the paper toward her. Her own eyes stared at her from the wanted poster.

Calm spread over her. The truth was out. No more lying. "There *is* a perfectly good explanation, Admiral. I was not a passenger. I served as the *Destiny's* master at arms."

It was a relief. But then she saw Phillip's face blanch and heard the captain's indrawn breath.

"I am extremely sorry to hear it," the admiral said. "The punishment, whereof, is to hang by the neck until dead, dead, dead. May the Lord have mercy upon your souls."

The captain and Phillip both spoke at once and the admiral raised a hand to silence them. "The verdict has been rendered. Captain Worthington, you know the procedures. Take them out and hang them at once."

Francesca's legs went weak, and she leaned heavily on the admiral's desk. She put a hand to her *Book*. She had an overwhelming urge to bolt for the door, but where would she go?

"Admiral," the captain said in a voice equally panicked. "May a condemned man have a last wish?"

The admiral waved to the marines, and they prodded the captain and the others toward the door. "Pirates do not merit last wishes."

"Please, Admiral," the captain said. "I need a word—" but the marines shoved him out the door.

She turned to Phillip whose face was ashen.

"Pull yourself together, Worthington," the admiral said. "I expect you to do your duty. Take her out with the others."

Phillip seemed frozen in place. Francesca couldn't be angry with him for showing the admiral Claire's letter. He had meant to avenge her, to protect her, and punish the captain. He couldn't have known what she had become since then. Pity surged through her. His inability to move freed her limbs and she took his arm. "Come, Phillip."

Together they moved out the door and up the companionway onto deck. Phillip's actions were stiff, mechanical. "Why didn't you tell me?" he whispered.

Francesca leaned her head against his shoulder. "I didn't want you to hate me."

"I could as soon hate the air I breathe."

"Had I told you, you would have been forced to lie to the admiral."

There were tears in his voice. "My God, Francesca. What is a lie compared to your life?"

"And let my dishonor become yours?" She shook her head. "It's better this way."

"No!" he said. "I'll get you out of here. If we can get to my ship, we can make a run for it. I know the admiral's tactics and my ship has the advantage of speed. We'll—"

"Stop! I won't let you do it! I won't let you throw away your career, your life, for me."

"A sensible sentiment, for a pirate," said the admiral just behind her.

Francesca jumped, then turned. She hoped he hadn't heard what Phillip had said.

He glowered at Phillip. "We'll discuss this indiscretion at a later date." He stopped a sailor who was hurrying past. "Have the rest of the *Destiny* crew brought over and prepare to string them up from the yardarm."

An hour later, the *Horatio's* whitewashed planking blazed under a burning sun. With the sails furled there was little shade for the crowd on the expansive sweep of deck.

Francesca stood at the rail with Phillip's arms around her. Carter, Miller, and the rest of the *Destiny* crew were rowed over in longboats and bunched together, thirty pirates in all. They stared toward the mainmast in silence as five nooses were tossed over the yardarm and twirled in the breeze.

Two rows of red-coated marines with muskets shouldered stood at attention on the raised foredeck looking down on the condemned. Compared to the spotless navy men, the *Destiny's* crew looked like mangy strays.

Francesca and Phillip had spoken little during the preparations. Only his arms, slowly tightening around her, spoke of his rising tension. He crushed her to him in an iron grip that she had no wish to lighten.

She watched with a strange detachment, her brain refusing to accept what was about to happen. Something or someone would save her, save them all. *This can't be the end, it can't.*

The captain, Angstrom, Agar, and Baldric, with their hands manacled behind their backs, were prodded up the companionway and marched under four of the five nooses. A marine with shackles advanced toward Francesca and Phillip. As the man neared, Phillip's arms tightened still more, forcing the air from her lungs.

"Admiral's orders, Sir," the marine said.

Phillip didn't move. Francesca closed her eyes. If she couldn't change things, at least she could end it with dignity. She pulled Phillip's arms from her waist and turned her back to the marine. The man wrenched her bad arm behind her, and she cried out as agonizing pain shot through her neck and spine.

She looked up at Phillip as the manacles snapped around her wrists. His jaw trembled.

The marine escorted her to the fifth noose that bobbed in the breeze and turned her to face the rest of the crew. She stood shoulder to shoulder with the captain.

As the admiral approached, Phillip hurried to his side.

"Sir," Phillip said, "you can't hang her."

"Bah," the admiral waved the objection away. "They are all vermin, Captain. I understand you have an attachment to the woman, but our duty is clear." He nodded to a marine holding a drum and a slow beat began.

Captain Massey leaned toward Francesca, his eyes more intense than she had ever seen them, his face tight with emotion. "I'm sorry, Francesca. I never meant for this to happen."

Francesca tried to concentrate, but the pain in her shoulder throbbed in time with the drumbeat. Her mind wouldn't focus. She wanted her last moments to be clear. She wanted to say something important, but pain blurred her thoughts.

Slowly the captain's words to her registered. She could hear his sincerity, but it didn't matter anymore.

"Everyone's sorry," she said.

Francesca caught sight of Carter among his crewmates, tears running down his face. *At least I won't have to watch him die.*

"I must tell you something," the captain said.

Phillip and the admiral stopped a few paces in front of them.

"As I was saying, Sir," Phillip said to the admiral. "There is no proof they have waylaid any English ships. Judging from their cargo they've only harassed the Spanish, who are currently our enemies. They could be considered heroes."

"Nonsense," snorted the admiral. "Any aid they have rendered the English cause was completely unintended. You know that as well as I." The two men moved down the row past a wild-eyed Mr. Angstrom.

Beyond Angstrom, Agar railed at the admiral, at the crew, and the heavens, spewing bits of Bible verses. Francesca caught something about "breastplates" and "judgment".

The marine slowly beat his drum. Another marine stepped in front of Francesca. He had freckled skin and avoided looking her in the eyes. He reached up for the noose and lowered it over her head. It settled loosely against her collarbone and burned her skin where it lay.

Her heart raced wildly. So, the admiral planned to do this the painful way reserved for pirates. Instead of a quick drop that would break their necks they'd be hauled up off the deck. It would be a slow and agonizing suffocation.

A blue-coated navy man read loudly from the Bible, trying to drown out Agar, whose ranting only grew louder. The drumbeat swelled. Francesca wanted to clap her manacled hands to her ears.

Agar's voice rose over the sailor's. "Then shall the thunderbolts and hailstones full of wrath be cast, and the water of the sea shall rage against them, and the floods shall drown them..." Agar raged on.

Francesca tried to pray, but no words would come. She figured it was just as well.

"Francesca," the captain said. "Francesca!"

She turned toward him.

"Do you remember a boy your father adopted in England?"

"Papa. He hated pirates," she said, thinking of the many ways she had failed him. She hadn't heard his voice in so long.

"A lad named Billy?" the captain continued.

The name caught her attention. "Pardon?"

Agar railed on: "Thus iniquity shall lay waste the whole earth and overthrow the thrones of the mighty..."

The captain looked at her with those penetrating eyes. "He raised the boy for three years before he returned home." He spoke each word slowly. "That boy was named Massey."

Francesca barely noticed as the noose tightened around her neck. "What are you saying? You're Billy England?"

"When first I saw you fighting on deck, I knew who you had to be," the captain said. "You're so like him."

Francesca felt as though the world had turned upside down. Her ears began to ring.

The captain rushed on. "He was like a father to me. At first, I wanted you near me because of him. Now I—" His words strangled off.

The pressure on Francesca's throat grew and she gasped. "Christ Almight—" Then her feet swung free, and her neck was on fire. She writhed and struggled to get her hands loose. She thought she heard Phillip arguing with the admiral over the pounding in her ears.

This is it. Her body fought for breath. Her whole being demanded air, demanded life, demanded she get free. The burning in her throat and chest made the pain in her shoulder insignificant. She kicked. Twisted. Writhed. Her body turned on its rope. She faced the captain. Billy England. *How ironic,* she thought, as darkness narrowed her vision. *Some might say it was destiny.*

As her vision went black, she heard Phillip shout, "The Isthmus Project, Sir! The pirates can help us!"

CHAPTER 27
LAMB WITH ROSEMARY

Francesca awoke with her head, neck, and shoulder throbbing. She took a deep, rasping breath, for only a sliver of air, as if the inside of her throat was swollen nearly shut. She put her hand to her neck and swallowed, grimacing at the pain that tore down her esophagus. *Either I'm alive or I'm in hell.* The skin under her fingers felt raw. *Maybe both.*

She was in an infirmary; there were cots, one holding a sleeping man she didn't recognize, and the usual jar of writhing leeches on a desk in the corner. The smell of medicine was undeniable, but it wasn't the *Destiny's* infirmary.

The yellow fever patients had been taken aboard the *Horatio*, so she probably wasn't there. Maye one of the smaller navy ships.

She tried to sit up, but the pain in her head and shoulder exploded in blinding proportions. When her vision cleared, she stared at the ceiling, wondering why she was still alive. She'd given Justice every opportunity to kill her, yet she lived.

Were the others alive? The captain's face arose in her mind, his blue-gray eyes boring into hers. Her heart twisted at the thought that he might be dead.

Then she remembered him saying, "The boy was named Massey." Her heart twisted again, this time with anger. *Billy England! How could he not tell me!* It had to be true; no one would lie while they were being hung. *How could he!* She remembered her first days aboard the *Destiny*, the numbing fear, the isolation, how she mourned Papa. He could have comforted her, shared her grief, eased her fears. Could have.

Betrayal added bitterness to her anger. How, if he loved Papa, could Billy turn pirate? How could he go against everything the DiCesare name stood for? It was the ultimate betrayal of everything Papa had been and everything she strived to be. She hated him for it. She wanted to beat her fists against him and scream.

Then she realized he might already be dead, and a gulf opened in her chest leaving her confused. *I want him dead!* Or she wanted to want him dead, but couldn't.

Had Papa known Billy was a pirate?

Impossible. He would never send her to a pirate, and Papa had thought Billy was still in England. Did he know about his wife and child?

"Papa," she said aloud. It came out as a whisper. "What do I do now?"

There was no answer. She tried to imagine her brothers or Phillip turning pirate. It was unthinkable. Then again, they hadn't lost wives and children to murderous hands.

How much the captain must have loved his family to give up everything to avenge them. No one had ever loved her that much.

Not true, she told herself. Her brothers had risked their lives to protect her at the duel. She didn't for a moment doubt Papa's love—and Phillip, her Phillip, had been willing to give up everything to be with her, until she convinced him otherwise.

Yes, whispered a corner of her mind, *but he was convinced.*

Oh, hold yer clapper, she said to herself, thinking of Carter and hoping he was alright.

I'm not going to find answers lying here. Francesca gritted her teeth, swung her legs over the side of the cot, and sat up. She waited until her head stopped exploding and spinning before she rose to her feet. She wobbled out of the infirmary with nausea swirling through her stomach and climbed up on a whitewashed deck.

The ship she was on was slightly larger than the *Destiny*, and the two ships were lashed together amidships, the wood of their hulls thudding and creaking with each gentle wave.

Francesca twisted to look around, since her head refused to turn on her shoulders. Shadows were lengthening toward evening. Was it the same day as the hanging? How long had she been asleep?

The two large English ships rode a half league off their stern.

None of the sailors paid her any attention. *I guess I'm not a prisoner.* She scanned the *Destiny* deck. It was manned by navy men. Were the crew locked up, or dead?

She wanted to talk to Phillip and find out what had happened, but she felt as though she were strangling. She needed the doctor.

With only one functioning arm, Francesca clambered awkwardly over the rail. The *Destiny's* deck was a couple feet lower than the navy ship's, but she eased down without jolting herself too badly and headed down the *Destiny's* companionway. Injured men no longer covered the floor of the landing. She entered the infirmary: no doctor.

She searched through the doctor's medicines, found a tin, opened it, and sniffed. The contents looked like lard and smelled minty, like the ointment her governess, Senora Bianchi used to slather on her scrapes as a child. Salle DiCesare, home, rushed to mind so sharply that a hand seemed to squeeze her heart and she had to steady herself.

She scooped ointment with her fingers and rubbed it on her neck, feeling the fire quench, on the outside at least. Too bad she couldn't rub the goo on the inside of her throat as well.

As she sighed with relief, raised voices drifted across the landing from the great cabin. It was the captain's voice, harsh and raspy—he was alive. Relief and anger rushed through her simultaneously, making her head pound harder and her eyes smart.

She couldn't make out the reply, but she thought it was Phillip's voice.

"It's been two days! Where is Francesca?" the captain demanded.

"Safe from you!" It was Phillip.

Francesca moved toward the door. She'd been out for two days?

"I was trying to help her," the captain said.

Whump. It sounded like a fist on a table. "When?" shouted Phillip. "When you forced her to become a criminal, or when you got her shot and hung?"

Francesca crossed the landing. The door to the great cabin was ajar and she stepped up to it. She wanted to see Phillip—wanted his comforting arms, wanted him to tell her everything would be alright. But the captain was there.

Phillip sat at the edge of the table glaring at the captain who stood with his back to Francesca. The captain's hands were chained behind him and his knuckles were white where he gripped the chain.

Phillip's voice was menacing. "I could kill you myself for what you've done to her, but the only way to save her life was to save your miserable life as well."

So, Phillip, her handsome hero, had saved her. She opened the door softly. "Phillip?" The word burned her throat and came out squeaky. She took a step into the room.

The captain spun to her. The raw, red band around his throat stood out.

"Francesca!" Phillip rose and hurried to her, concern in his eyes. "You shouldn't be out of bed, not after all you've been through." He put an arm around her and turned her back toward the door.

She put a hand to her fiery throat. "I've slept long enough. What happened? Why am I still alive? Are the others—"

"Everyone's alive," the captain said.

Francesca ignored him, despite the relief his words gave her. She focused on Phillip, who coaxed her back out the door.

"The admiral reconsidered," Phillip said. "He has a plan and could use the pirates' help. It's nothing you need to concern yourself with."

"What plan?" she asked.

"I need to deal with Massey. Get some more rest, my dear. I'll see you in the morning." He closed the door.

"But…" Francesca frowned, staring at the door. She leaned against the frame, frustration growling in her chest. A chair scraped against the floor and her ears perked up.

Phillip cleared his throat. "Now, Massey, I suggest you shut your mouth and listen, or I'll shoot you and deal with that cretin, Baldric. What the admiral is offering is your ship, amnesty, and free rein of English ports in exchange for your aid."

So the admiral wants to make a deal. What could he possibly need our help with? He hates us.

Captain Massey gave a rough laugh. "You'll have to excuse me if I'm skeptical of a naval officer offering a pirate free rein."

She heard paper rustling, then, after a pause, the captain said, "Ah, the overland route." Francesca thought she heard a touch of admiration in his raspy voice and her curiosity piqued.

The men's voices fell too low for her to make out. Just as she was leaving, the captain raised his voice.

"No! No! No! It will never work."

"You will address me as 'Sir'," commanded Phillip.

"It will never work … *Sir,*" Massey said, his voice thick with sarcasm. "You're talking about weeks of slogging through the jungle on short rations and questionable water. Most of the men will starve before the end and those still alive will have little fight left."

"It must work," Phillip said. "Or you are all dead."

"We're dead either way," the captain said. "You might as well stretch our necks now. Unless…"

"Unless what?"

There was a pause, then Francesca barely made out the words. "I may know someone who can help."

Their voices dropped low again. Francesca listened for a minute more, but only caught a word or two so she gave it up.

She headed up on deck to find out where the *Destiny* crew was being held. She wanted to see Carter and Miller. Then she wanted to sleep—for a year.

On deck, she stopped a passing sailor. The man had an emotionless face and steady brown eyes. "Excuse me. Can you tell me where the pirates are?"

"In the hold," he said.

Of course. There were few other places aboard ship you could keep thirty men where they wouldn't be in the way.

"Thank you." She headed for the companionway.

"No one is allowed down there," the sailor called after her. "Not without Captain Worthington's permission."

She paused. She should have suspected as much. Was Phillip trying to keep her from helping the pirates, or was he trying to protect her from them? She would need to talk to him about it.

Francesca went to the rail. The setting sun painted the sky and sea with wide swaths of pink and lavender. Blue-gray clouds, like downy cotton ropes, floated across the sky. The glow of the sunset softened the edges of the ships and turned the rigging into a whimsical web. Francesca inhaled the warm evening air. She hadn't expected to see another sunset and she was suddenly thrilled to be alive.

As the sun faded, so did her energy. Instead of returning to the infirmary, she headed for her cabin. *Funny how it's become home.*

The next morning Francesca discovered she could breathe easier and turn her head a few inches in either direction as she went up on deck.

Crewmen were disengaging the two ships and making ready to sail. Phillip paced the *Destiny's* quarterdeck, oblivious to the light mist that dampened his hair and jacket.

Francesca hesitated. The quarterdeck was sovereign territory for a captain, and she was not exactly sure of her position aboard ship.

Phillip waved her over.

Francesca admired how handsome he was: his flashing blue eyes and perfect cheekbones, the dimple in his chin beneath full, sensuous lips. Though his hair, which was a riot of gold when they were at the salle, was now clipped short and neat. She caught her breath when he smiled at her.

"You're looking better," Phillip said. "How are you faring?"

"Much improved," Francesca said, swiveling her whole body to look around from the quarterdeck since turning her head still hurt. The *Destiny* seemed the same, except for all the unfamiliar faces, yet she felt out of place.

"Phillip," she said, putting a hand to her throat. "I mean, Captain Worthington, what is to be … what am I aboard your ship?"

He took her hand. "You are my particular friend and honored guest," he said, kissing her hand and giving her a ravishing smile.

She glanced at the helmsman and moved closer to Phillip. "You mustn't. How will it look for a navy captain to have a pirate as a … friend?"

"You are not a pirate," he said.

"Unless you can magically remove my name from the *Destiny's* articles, no court martial in the world would believe you."

His mouth stretched taut at "court martial."

She dropped her voice lower. "I love you too much to let our relationship ruin your career."

Phillip hesitated, emotions warring across his face. "An ally, then," he said, "for the moment."

Francesca nodded. Ally she could live with. She looked around the deck. "Are the rest of your allies still in the hold?"

Phillip shot an angry look but didn't answer.

"How long do you intend to keep them there?"

"As long as necessary. Half my crew is on the *Doe*. I'll not have the pirates outnumber us."

Us? Which side was she on? She didn't want her crewmates locked up. Did that make her one of them?

"May I see them?" she asked.

"I would rather you didn't," Phillip said, frowning.

"Why?"

"Because they've done enough harm already."

They grew quiet.

"Where are we headed?" Francesca asked as the sails unfurled above them, and sailors hauled them taut. The ship began to move forward.

"You needn't worry about that," he said.

Needn't worry? She opened her mouth, but Phillip took a couple paces forward.

"Mr. Robins, bring us a point closer to the wind, if you please," he shouted.

"Phillip, I—" Francesca said.

He turned back to her giving her his most gorgeous smile. "Listen, Francesca, I've duties to see to now, but would you do me the honor of joining me for dinner this evening?"

Her cheeks flushed. "Of course."

He headed for the bow, leaving Francesca wondering what she would do for the rest of the day.

As evening approached Francesca had a sailor bring her a basin of water and cleaned up the best she could. Getting into her repaired emerald dress with one hand was nearly impossible, and the lacing turned out crooked. She wanted to swirl her hair up, but couldn't raise her arm, so she left it long and loose. She looked at herself in a borrowed mirror and gasped at the raw stripe around her throat. She cut a strip out of her petticoat and wrapped it around her neck. It looked a little odd, but it hid most of her wound.

She stared at herself in the mirror. She almost looked like the girl who had fallen in love with Phillip. Almost. There was something dark in her eyes, layered over with grief. She tried smiling, laughing, even grinning, but nothing hid it. Her hand shook as she set down the mirror.

She sighed, remembering her dream that Phillip would swoop in and rescue her. Now here he was, and here was the captain, and nothing made sense anymore.

As Francesca raised her hand to knock on the door of the great cabin, a man bustled out, nearly running into her.

"Excuse me, Miss." He turned to Phillip. "She's here, Sir."

Phillip ushered her in and kissed her hand. "You look beautiful, Francesca."

She smoothed her skirts. "Thank you."

He scanned her face and body. His eyes met hers.

"Different. You look different." His head tilted to one side. "More beautiful than ever." His fingers tightened, almost to the point of hurting, then he released her hand and turned to the sideboard.

She noticed Phillip's hands shook as he poured a glass of wine and handed it to her.

As she accepted the wine, she tried to also accept the unreal situation. The goblet was the same one the captain had held when he proposed the wager that set her on this journey. Phillip ushered her to the same seat she had occupied when she and the captain dined with Henry Carlisle. In her mind this cabin was synonymous with Captain Massey, yet here she sat with her Phillip. Everything seemed backwards and inside out.

She studied him. This was her first chance to really see what the last three years had done to him. His voice had changed; it was harder and deeper. He was broader in the shoulders and thicker through the chest. He was as handsome as ever; even more so, now that the sun had tanned his fair skin, making his blonde hair more golden and his aquamarine eyes more dazzling. His jaw was set with an air of authority. A scar ran from his right eyebrow to his ear. He too had seen battle.

"How are you faring?" he asked once the steward had laid the first course of braised quail.

"Well enough," she said putting a hand to her throat.

"I'm sorry," he said, raising his hand to his own neck.

Francesca shook her head. "We're all sorry for something, but this was not your fault. I deserved no less."

"I doubt that," Phillip said, taking her hand. "I doubt it very much."

She looked away, still unable to admit what she had done. "So, where are we going? What's the plan? How did you convince the admiral to spare us?"

His eyes dropped and he picked at his quail. "You needn't worry about that."

"I'm not worried, Phillip," she said, unable to keep the annoyance out of her voice. "I'm curious. I want to know what's happening. I think I'm entitled to know why my sentence has been commuted."

He sighed. "Do you remember Signore Gallo's naval history lessons?"

She rolled her eyes. "Of course, the way he pounded them into our heads. But what has that got to do with anything?"

"Then you remember learning about Sir Francis Drake."

"He was a naval hero over a century ago."

"A hero to the English. To the Spanish he was just another pirate."

Francesca nodded and Phillip continued. "The Spanish called him *'El Draque'*—the Dragon. With the English queen's permission, he hounded the Spanish for decades."

"What does that have to do with us?"

"Well, in 1573, Drake took forty-five men—English, French, and escaped slaves—hiked inland and waylaid a Spanish mule train carrying treasure across the Isthmus of Panama. They made off with more than 100,000 gold pesos—as much gold as forty-five men could carry—and buried the rest in hopes of retrieving it later."

"That's the overland route," Francesca said. "You mean to take another gold caravan."

Phillip nodded. "The admiral has been talking about little else since I met him. That adventure made Drake the most powerful man in England, and that is exactly what the admiral wants."

"But what has that to do with us?"

He looked at her sharply on the word 'us.' "You're not one of them."

"You know what I mean. Why not hang us? How does the *Destiny* fit in?"

Reluctantly, he went on. "Times have changed since Drake. According to international law, military ships are only allowed to take the goods of nations they are legally at war with. And while Spain is an enemy today, she could be an ally tomorrow and we might not get word for a month or two."

She still didn't see how that tied in with them.

He gave a crooked smile. "But there is a loophole. It's always legal to take treasure from pirates."

She gasped. "You want us to take the treasure so you can take it from us."

"Them, Francesca, them," he said hotly. "I don't want you involved. It's too dangerous."

She scoffed. "Too dangerous? I was a topman, Phillip. I've already been shot and hung. I've boarded a sinking ship in the eye of a hurricane. I've taken a Spanish tower with just a twelve-year-old boy. I've attacked..." She realized she was boasting about her criminal exploits. Her voice dropped to a whisper. "I've killed men, Phillip, too many."

He put a hand under her chin and tilted her face to him. "Were any of them unarmed?"

The question caught her off guard but was easy to answer since she knew each face and event by heart. "No."

"Were any of them not intent on killing you?"

"Only one," she answered, thinking of Tarrentino. "And he meant to kill Papa."

Phillip squeezed her hand and gave her a moment to compose herself, then he went on. "Did you gain by their deaths?"

"Only by staying alive," she said, shaking her head. "But I did help others gain."

"Because you were under oath to do so," he pointed out. He kissed her hand. "By any Code of Honor I have heard of, including your father's, you are entirely blameless. Massey carries the burden of your sins for forcing them upon you."

His logic seemed too simple and convenient, yet she could find no fault with it.

"It is as much my fault as Massey's," he said quietly. "I taught you to fence. I started you down this path. I see now why the maestro forbade it."

Francesca was silent. Did he mean that Papa saw what she would become? That he knew what evil lurked in her soul?

He squeezed her hand. "Francesca, every man aboard this ship has killed. I have. But none of us have sleepless nights or wish to get ourselves hung. Those dead men were simply in the way, in the wrong place at the wrong time."

"You were doing your duty."

"As were you," he said. "Do you remember what you said to me that night in the stable?"

Francesca shook her head.

"You said our duty doesn't change with the worth of the recipient. You convinced me to obey my father, a horrible man, because obeying was the right thing to do. That's what you've done as well. That doesn't make you a pirate."

Francesca wiped at a tear running down her cheek. Would Papa have thought so? She wanted to believe him, but couldn't.

The steward ushered in the second course—Phillip's favorite from his days at the salle, roast lamb with rosemary. Just the smell brought dinners at home with her family so fully to mind that Francesca had to close her eyes for a moment.

Phillip inhaled. "The smell is perfect, isn't it? The seasoning is not exact, but it's as near as I could come without the recipe. I always carry the spices with me."

The talk turned to friends at the salle, family, and happier days, carefully avoiding the horrible events that brought those days to an end.

By the time the third course of roast beef with sauerkraut arrived Francesca was feeling the effects of the wine, her full stomach, and her injuries. Sleep threatened to overwhelm her.

Seeing her exhaustion, Phillip rose and came to her side. "Perhaps we'd best get you back to your cabin."

She nodded as he helped her to her feet.

Talk of her brothers had brought Carter and Rolly to mind. "How long do you intend to keep my friends in the hold?" she asked as they left the great cabin.

"Until we arrive at the Río de Caimán in Costa Rica."

"That's where I let..." She had almost said that was where she let Willy go, but she wasn't ready to admit that yet. "That's where we met the Maroons."

"Aye. Massey seems to think they can help us head inland."

She unlocked her door. "I see. And how long will it take to get there?"

"A week, if the weather holds."

"Phillip, you can't leave them locked in the hold all that time. They'll be little use to you in the jungle if you do."

"We'll let them out in shifts for exercise. Don't worry about them. You need to rest." He kissed her on the forehead and turned to go.

Francesca struggled against weariness. She grabbed his arm. "Let them out, please."

He turned back to her. "They can't be trusted. Massey can't be trusted."

"Massey, no," she said, bitterness rushing through her momentarily. "But perhaps you can trust Billy England."

"Who?" asked Phillip, taking her hand.

"Do you remember my brothers and me threatening each other, 'I'll tell Papa and he'll send you to Billy England'?"

He smiled. "I do. I even used it on Sebastian once or twice, but I had no idea what it meant."

"Billy was Papa's other son."

Phillip's jaw dropped and he stared, aghast. "You mean, he's related to you?"

She shook her head. "No. Papa said Billy was family in feeling if not in blood. He never told us more."

Disbelief and anger played across Phillip's face. "How do you know it's him? The chances of the two of you meeting on the high seas are nigh impossible."

She put her hand to Phillip's cheek. "And it's impossible that I'm here now, with you. But I am." She leaned into him. He wrapped his arms around her, the arms she had longed for, strong and comforting. She had come home. She stood on her tiptoes and closed her eyes as their lips met. Soft, sweet, warm, exactly how she remembered. She wanted to stay like this forever, but she heard footsteps on the companionway.

She pulled away from him. "I'm learning to accept the impossible." She entered her cabin and softly closed the door.

CHAPTER 28
THE MAROONS

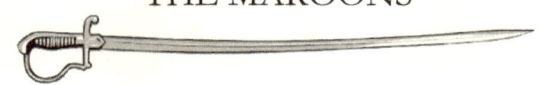

The next morning Francesca awoke thinking of Phillip's kiss. It was the first time in ages she had not opened her eyes thinking of the debts in her *Book*. Those thoughts came rushing back soon enough, but for a moment she had been free.

She remembered his words about honor and could see no holes in his argument. She had only attacked armed men intent on killing her and had taken none of the spoils. Perhaps Phillip was right, but if so, why did she still feel guilty?

She dressed and headed for the hold. She missed Carter and Miller. When she reached the companionway, a burly sailor stopped her.

"Sorry, Miss, you are not allowed to see the prisoners, Captain's orders."

The man was a foot taller than her and bulging with muscles, so she headed up on deck.

Phillip, on the quarterdeck, held out a hand as she approached. She didn't take it.

"Why may I not see the prisoners?" she asked.

"Because they've bewitched you into thinking you are one of them. It's for your own good."

"My own good?" she said heatedly. "I am not a child. I can determine what is for my own good."

"And you've done a first-rate job so far."

She ignored the sarcasm. "Some of them are my friends."

"They are not your friends, they're pirates. They'd as soon slit your throat as look at you."

"How do you know that? You don't even know them."

"I know that because," he said, articulating every word, "it is in their nature."

"I suppose you think it is in my nature as well."

"Of course not!"

Francesca spun toward the stairs, but Phillip grabbed her injured arm. She cried out in pain, and he released her. "Sorry Francesca, but where are you going?"

"To the hold," she said. "One way or another."

"You're not one of them."

Francesca held her ground. Finally, Phillip raised his voice to a nearby crewman. "Adams, take her to the hold."

"Aye, Sir."

The hold was the *Destiny's* storage room, located at the bottom of the ship, along the keel. Any water that seeped into the ship—no ship was absolutely watertight—gathered there. It was damp, rank, and uncomfortable. In bad weather, when the hatches were shut, it was pitch dark. This morning some light filtered down the companionway. There was no level deck; the wooden plank floor curved out and upward from the keel until it became the vertical sides of the ship.

The admiral had confiscated most of the *Destiny's* loot, but the space still held fifty barrels of drinking water along with crates of supplies.

As she entered, the pirates cheered, and everyone spoke at once asking how she fared and what was happening above deck.

She held up her hand to quiet them and told them she was on the mend and that they would be released when they reached the Río de Caimán.

There were iron rings pounded into the timbers for tying crates and barrels into place. Through each ring ran a length of chain, and each chain had a manacle at either end fastened around the wrist of a pirate. Her eyes met those of the captain, chained toward the prow. She flicked her eyes away.

"About bloody time they let us out!" shouted One-eyed Kelsey.

"Aye!" added Mr. Angstrom. "Some bloody manners! They ask fer our aid an' then lock us down 'ere!"

"Aye!" echoed the men.

She shrugged. "I think Phil ... Captain Worthington is looking for some assurance you won't mutiny."

The crew grumbled.

"You seem very friendly with this Phil … Captain Worthington," Captain Massey accused.

Anger and hurt seethed through her. She turned to Miller and Carter. "He studied under my father. We were close."

A few men gave each other nudges and winks.

"He taught me to fence when my father forbade it," she explained, the temperature rising in her cheeks.

"And just what sort of assurance might we give him that he would trust?" the captain asked.

Francesca shook her head. "I don't know."

"An' why should we trust 'im," Agar said. "How do we know he won't hang us all after 'e gets what 'e wants."

"He is an honorable man," Francesca said.

"'Onorable men don't make others do their theivin' for 'em," Miller said.

Her voice softened. "He's obeying orders. He has no choice, but he'll keep his bargain. I'm sure of it."

Captain Massey waved her over. She meant to ignore him but found herself moving his way.

Agar, at the other end of the captain's chain, growled as she approached. "I said she'd be the death of us all."

"Not dead yet, Agar? More's the pity," she hissed.

The captain twisted around to Agar. "I'd thank you to remember that it was her friend who saved our necks from the noose."

As Francesca sat, she arranged her face in a neutral mask.

The captain hesitated. Finally, he said, "There is only one vow I can make to your friend he might believe. Tell him I swear upon the soul of the man I called Father, Thurio DiCesare, to keep faith with him."

Rage swept through Francesca at the captain's oath. She gritted her teeth to keep from swinging at him. She rose trembling.

"I hated you when you first came aboard," he said quietly.

"The feeling was mutual," she said through clenched teeth.

"I hated your brothers, too."

"I suppose you hated Papa as well."

"No," the captain said sharply. "I hated you for taking him away from me. It was because of the three of you he left me in England."

Francesca remembered how jealous she had been whenever Papa had spent time in England with Billy. How must he have felt when Papa went home?

She shook her head. She wasn't going to feel sorry for him.

"If you hated me, why did you force me to stay aboard?"

"Because I owed it to Father not to set you ashore penniless. You know what happens to pretty young women who are penniless."

"Claire and Belle would have taken care of me."

"Their father was dead. How do you know he wasn't mortgaged up to the eyebrows? Even if they were rich, how long do you think their mother would want a girl with a sword around once her daughters were safe?"

"That was none of your affair!" Everyone was staring, but she didn't care.

"Two or three months aboard ship and I figured I could set you ashore wherever you liked with enough money to live royally for a lifetime. But no, you wouldn't take any of the bloody money." The captain was yelling too. "What the hell was I supposed to do then?"

"You could have put me ashore and let me find my own way."

"I tried. In Port Royal I arranged for Carlisle to send you back to England. But you disobeyed orders and set the whole English navy after you!"

"Well, I…" Surprise dulled her anger for a moment.

"Besides," he said quietly. "You were all I had left of the maestro, a—"

Anger hit her in the ribs. She remembered all the sorrow and fear she had suffered alone. Sorrow he could have shared, fear he could have eased. "You could have told who you were! Why didn't you tell me?"

The captain fell silent for a moment. When he spoke, his voice was tinged with regret. "I wanted to tell you. I tried, but you were so goddamned self-righteous."

She stood. He was a coward to blame her.

"And," he whispered, "I was ashamed."

"You should be." Francesca growled as she stormed away.

A week later the *Destiny* and the *Doe* lay anchored in the Río de Caimán, near the Maroon village. Francesca stood next to Phillip examining the settlement. Little had changed. The warm air smelled of lush vegetation and damp earth. Massive trees still vaulted over the river. The jungle still threatened to overtake the small clearing with its meager huts. But this time the Maroons waved and called, while children capered along the riverbank.

Francesca was thinking of Willy when Captain Massey came up on deck. He was clean-shaven, unchained, and rubbing his wrist. Two marines, one with pistols, the other carrying charts, followed him.

The captain headed for Phillip, giving him a nod, but his eyes were on her.

"We should take Francesca with us to speak with the Maroons," the captain said.

Phillip's face darkened. "Address me as Sir, Massey. And it's too dangerous."

"There's no danger, *Sir*," the captain said, making "Sir" sound like an insult.

"I hardly think you are an adequate judge."

The captain winced. "She knows Spanish," he said. "We may need a translator. Unless you speak Spanish ... *Sir.*"

Francesca held her breath. She remembered Juan, the leader of the Maroons, speaking English well. There was no need for a translator, but she wanted to ask about Willy, so she kept quiet. Why did the captain really want her along?

"Very well," Phillip said, frowning. He put a protective arm around her as they and the two marines moved toward the waiting longboat.

Once on land, Francesca followed Captain Massey and Phillip into the largest of the huts. The two marines followed.

Juan waited at a rough-hewn table. His high forehead, broad face, and straight back lent him a dignified air despite his ragged clothes. His heavily lidded eyes seemed to possess some ancient wisdom, like a benevolent African king.

The impression was heightened by the two well-muscled black men in loin cloths who stood guard behind him. Francesca recognized one of them from her meeting in the jungle, but she was not sure which. Their faces were identical: same high cheekbones, wide lips, and dark chocolate coloration, even the same build. *Not just brothers, twins.*

Juan rose and shook Captain Massey's hand. "Welcome, Capitán. It is a pleasure to see you again."

At the man's acceptable English Phillip shot the captain a venomous look. One side of Captain Massey's mouth ticked up.

"*Kiswahili,* Juan," the captain said. "It's good to see you. May I present Francesca DiCesare and Captain Worthington."

As Juan shook their hands his eyes lingered on her. She tensed, wondering if he would say something about their meeting in the jungle, but then he turned to Captain Massey. "Where is Mr. Hart?"

The captain sighed. "He did not survive our attack on Portobello."

"A pity," Juan said. "He was a fine man."

Juan looked out the door of the hut and called out. As he sat back down his eyes lingered on the captain and Francesca's throats. "I see death has paid you a visit."

The captain placed a hand to his neck. "Aye, but the devil hasn't got us yet."

Juan laughed. "The devil is patient. He will wait. My people say: When a man is coming toward you, you need not say, 'Come here.'"

The captain chuckled and Phillip frowned.

Juan grew serious. "Why have you returned?"

Two young Maroons carried in three wooden chairs, placing them around the table. They sat.

"The overland route you spoke of," Captain Massey said, "we mean to attempt it."

Juan leaned back in his chair with a deep breath. "So," he said, nodding. "It is well. Any enemy of the Spanish is a friend of ours. Many years ago, another English did also."

"Aye," Phillip said. "Drake waylaid one of the gold caravans over a century ago. He got away with more Spanish gold than they could carry."

Francesca frowned, thinking of Miller and Carter. It seemed like a dangerous journey for an old man and a boy. She turned to Phillip. "Do you mean to take all the pirates across the Panama isthmus?"

"Aye, I do," answered the captain. "If Juan's men will help us."

"They are not my men, Capitán. I am no commander. They are free men, so the choice is theirs. But our hatred of the Spanish slavers has not changed since those days. Our people say that Spanish blood runs gold because gold is all they love." His eyes sharpened and a hard edge crept into Juan's voice. "Many of these Maroons will join you if you mean to make it flow."

A chill ran down her spine.

"Surely the shipments must be heavily guarded these days," she said.

"Not as strongly as you might think," Phillip said. "None have attempted it since Drake, and a century is a long time to be vigilant. Still, the road has improved. We shall have to move more quickly than he did."

"For two hundred years slaves have died building and improving that road so that Spanish Kings can grow fat off the riches of these lands. Many of us will help you. We Maroons have hidden camps in the jungle that can provide rest and food."

"Excellent!" Captain Massey said, rubbing his hands together. He motioned to the marine standing behind them. "You, charts."

"I give the orders," Phillip said, but he nodded to the man, who spread the charts on the table. The group bent over them.

"According to the admiral's spies," Phillip said, "there should be a gold caravan leaving Panama City for Portobello on the sixteenth of December. We know the time, and we know the route, but we know little of the Camino Real, the road through the jungle. Do any of your people know it?" Phillip asked Juan.

"I traveled that road once, under the overseer's whip. But that was many years ago. There are others who have done so more recently."

Juan turned to the doorway and called out. A few minutes later a black man with a limp entered. He had wild hair, angry, distrustful eyes, and was missing three fingers.

According to Miller, the Spanish punishment for slaves who tried to escape was taking a finger, an eye, or a hamstringing. It was clear this man had made many attempts before he succeeded.

A boy brought in another chair and the man sat with them. He had traveled the Camino Real only a year prior.

Phillip explained to Francesca that the Camino Real, the "King's Road," connected Panama City on the Pacific Ocean with Portobello and Nombre de Diós on the Atlantic Coast. It wandered through hills, swamps, over rivers and through valleys for fifty miles, wide enough for two mule carts to pass in opposite directions. "It is an amazing feat of engineering," he said.

"Almost as amazing as their ability to enslave the entire native population and half of Africa to build it," the captain said with venom.

Juan nodded. "Four thousand men were used up and discarded building this road. Many thousands more have walked it in chains with bent backs, as I did."

"Here," Phillip said, obviously trying to change the subject and pointing to a spot on the map.

Francesca followed his finger. Half-way between Panama City and Portobello a bridge spanned the Chagres River. Captain Massey and Juan nodded.

They hashed out their plans. Under Juan's guidance, a three-part force—Maroon, pirate, and navy—would hack though dense jungle to reach a remote spot on the Camino Real. There were easier, well-traveled paths, but the Spanish had spies everywhere. Once they reached the road, they would lie in wait just beyond the bridge over the Chagres River. When the mule train crossed the bridge, they would hem the Spanish in, and the battle would begin.

Meanwhile, the *Destiny* and the *Doe* would harass the Caribbean coast to make sure the Spanish did not suspect their real objective.

It was a dangerous plan. Phillip would, no doubt, feel it was too dangerous for her, but how could she let her friends take the risk without being there to help them?

"How many soldiers travel with the mule train?" Phillip asked Juan and the wild-haired man.

They spoke in Spanish, then Juan turned to Phillip. "He tells me that most times, sixty or seventy soldiers travel with the treasure, but sometimes as many as one hundred."

"We'll have surprise on our side," Captain Massey said with a wicked smile. "I like our odds."

When at last they shook hands and rose to leave, Francesca lingered behind the others, taking Juan aside.

"Juan, did you ever find Willy Brown, the boy who escaped from the *Destiny*?"

Juan smiled, "You mean the boy you let go."

"Is he here? Is he well?"

"Willy was here. He was a fine young man, and he was happy for a time," Juan said, sadness in his voice.

Her chest tightened.

"He died a fortnight ago of yellow fever."

Her shoulders drooped.

"Ah, be at peace," Juan said. "He lived brightly while he was here and died well-loved. A man can hope for little more."

Francesca nodded. At least she had given Willy that much. "Thank you."

Francesca joined the others waiting at the boat. As they rowed back to the *Destiny*, the captain whispered in her ear. "Did you find out what happened to him?"

She glared at him. He was the one who had condemned Willy to death. "Justice has been served."

His shoulders slumped. Then the boat bumped against the hull of the ship, and they climbed up the side.

With the plan in place, they made ready for the journey down the coast to Panama. There were water casks to fill and food to prepare for all the extra mouths. Phillip's ship, the *Doe*, was given a new name, the *Adventure*. If the admiral's plan was to work, no one must suspect the English navy was involved in the attack on the gold train.

Since only a handful of the Maroons spoke English, Francesca's translating skills were needed everywhere. She enjoyed the task, her strength was returning, and her shoulder was recovering well.

She tried to ignore the captain, but her eyes had a mind of their own. They sought him out and followed him as he worked.

I love Phillip. I do.

The day before their departure, the twin brothers, Abuu and Baakir, appeared carrying an injured man. He had been beaten and left for dead by his owner. Deep gashes covered his body, and one leg was broken, yet he had crawled far enough from his master's plantation for the brothers to find him.

Francesca was no stranger to violence, but this was different. To beat an unarmed man nearly to death was incomprehensible. She realized the anger she felt toward the plantation owner must be nothing compared to what the Maroons felt.

That man, Addae, fought for life despite his agony showed the Maroons' strength. The doctor bandaged the wounds and gave him laudanum for the pain, but the prognosis was not good.

That afternoon Francesca came across Miller and Carter sitting on a log, rubbing their boots with tallow and beeswax.

"What are you doing?" she asked.

"Waterproofin'," Miller said, around the stem of his pipe and puffing a cloud of smoke over his face. "Hikin' through the jungle'll be mis'rable enough withouten we gots wet feet."

"And this will keep your feet dry?"

"Naw," Miller said.

"Dry-ish," said Carter.

Francesca sat down next to them and pulled off one of her boots. They had been a gift from Old Nob's mess when she was promoted to master-at-arms. She hadn't needed them much aboard ship, but she was glad she had them now.

Phillip frowned as he approached. "What are you doing?"

"Keeping my feet dry-ish when we head into the jungle."

"We?" he said. "I couldn't possibly take you along."

She looked up at him sharply. "I am not one of your men to be ordered about. Stop treating me like, like…"

"Like a lady?" He took her arm and helped her up. They moved a few feet away from Carter and Miller. "Like my lady?"

Francesca's little thrill at being called *his lady* didn't change anything. "I won't be left behind like a spare handkerchief."

He put a hand to her cheek. "I'm trying to protect you, Francesca. It almost killed me when I received Claire's letter, and then on the *Horatio…*" He shuddered. "There will be snakes, alligators, natives, yellow fever, not to mention the Spanish. I can't let anything happen to you. Not when I've finally found you again."

Her anger melted. She wanted to lean against his chest and feel his arms around her, but there were too many people around, so she took his hand. "You won't lose me. But I can't watch everyone I care about venture into the jungle and not know what becomes of them. Besides, how will you protect me if I'm alone on a ship full of men? If you go, I go as well."

He sighed, "We'll see."

———†———

The following morning Francesca was on deck, helping with the last of the loading when Phillip came up from below. She suppressed a laugh. He had changed into "pirate" gear: cotton duck trousers, tall boots, and a grungy linen shirt under a loose, dilapidated coat. His bearing was so naval that the clothes looked completely ridiculous. Like a costume. He would never look like anything but what he was.

Francesca joined him at the rail. His shoulders tensed as he watched Juan, the captain, Baldric, and some of Juan's men board one longboat, and a dozen Maroons crowd into another. More awaited their turn.

"I don't like this," he said. "I don't like any of it."

"You've made a good bargain," she said. "It's in their best interest to cooperate. They've no cause to mutiny."

"Since when have pirates needed a cause?" He shook his head.

Agar's dark face flashed through Francesca's mind.

She knew Phillip had been stewing over the best way to manage this voyage. With the admiral off harassing the coast, Phillip had sixty men, two ships to handle, thirty pirates to watch, and now he would have to keep an eye on twenty-five Maroons as well.

Originally, he had mentioned putting half of the pirates and Maroons on his ship, the *Adventure*, but he'd abandoned that idea. If the pirates seized both ships, his problems would be doubled.

He had decided to keep the pirates and the Maroons on the *Destiny* but move the shot and powder to the *Adventure*. He had arranged elaborate signals between ships. If a signal was missed or given improperly the *Adventure* would open fire on the *Destiny*.

Francesca also knew he had debated about where she should be. He would rather she be on the *Adventure*, away from the pirates, but he needed to be on the *Destiny*, and he wanted her close. That suited her. She would have demanded to stay on the *Destiny* anyway. She wanted to be with her friends, she was curious about the Maroons, and, well, the *Destiny* was home.

The longboats bumped against the hull. Navy men gathered as Maroons, carrying spears, machetes, and a few belongings, climbed over the side.

The Maroons fidgeted, ill at ease. Those born in the New World had probably never been on a ship before. But many had likely been chained in the hold of a ship when they were torn from their homes and pressed into slavery.

"We can't ask them to go in the hold," Mr. Baldric said as he climbed over the side.

The *Destiny* crew still slept in the hold at night, under guard, though no longer in chains.

"Aye," the captain agreed. "Make space on deck."

"For now," Phillip said, frowning. "We'll discuss it later."

Agar approached Captain Massey nodding toward the Maroons. "Cargo, Sir?"

"Allies, Agar, and I expect you to treat them as such."

"But, Sir," Agar said, indignant, "you can't be serious."

"Dead serious," the captain said.

"Massey, I'll see you in the great cabin," Phillip said.

"Aye," the captain said, adding a belated, "Sir."

As the Maroons gathered, Francesca, Juan, and Miller made space forward on the main deck, sliding crates, barrels, and ropes out of the way. Baakir, one of the twin Maroons, beckoned Juan urgently to the rail. Francesca followed.

Below, in the longboat, two men tried to help Addae, the beaten and near-dead Maroon, up the side of the ship. He shrugged away their help. He grasped the rope ladder and shook as he pulled himself up a rung. Blood stained his bandages and he groaned, raising his weight to the next rung. Agonizingly, he worked his way up the side. Francesca and Juan grabbed him as he passed out climbing over the rail.

She looked at Juan as they lowered him to the deck. "You can't bring this man!" She knelt beside Addae whose breathing was labored.

"Leave him be!" Juan said sternly.

"He's dying. We must get him ashore." She called to Miller. Together they started to lift him.

"Put him down!" ordered Juan, pulling a knife on Francesca and Miller. Baakir and Abuu materialized at Juan's sides, spears in hand.

All eyes turned toward them. The Maroons, pirates, and sailors tensed. The marines leveled their muskets at Juan and the brothers. The Maroons readied their machetes and spears.

"I said leave him be! He can die here as well as anywhere," Juan said.

"Why won't you help him?" pleaded Francesca.

Juan glanced around the crowd, then put away his knife. The others relaxed.

Juan looked weary. "I am," he said softly. "I can free their bodies, but only they can free their souls. These men need to spill Spanish blood to believe they are free, and I cannot convince them otherwise." He knelt beside her. "He would die fighting, if he could."

Juan felt for a pulse, then closed the dead man's eyes.

"I'm sorry, Juan," she said.

He heaved a sigh. "As am I."

———————┼————————

That night, the two captains and Francesca, in the great cabin, debated about lodging for the Maroons. Captain Massey shouted at Phillip. "You can't do that to them!"

"They will do as they're told!" Phillip insisted. "They're making it nigh impossible to work the jib and the fore gallant."

"I don't care if they're using the jib as a hammock. You'll not force them into the hold," the captain said. "Not on my ship."

"May I remind you," Phillip said, "it is not your ship until I get my gold!"

"They stay on deck!"

"They go below!"

The captains turned to Francesca.

"DiCesare?" Captain Massey said.

She looked off to one side. She hated to side against Phillip, but—

Drums thundered overhead. An unearthly wail and a strangled horn joined the beat. They looked at each other and rushed out.

They emerged amid mayhem. The Maroons on the main deck were wailing, stomping their feet, tearing their hair. Some beat drums or blew ram horns.

On the foredeck nervous marines readied their muskets, unsure whether to open fire.

Phillip bristled. "I'll put a stop to this!"

As he took a step, Captain Massey set an arm across his chest to stop him. "Leave them be!" he growled.

The marines, seeing the captain's movement, turned their muskets on Captain Massey and the crew.

The Maroons grew wilder, screaming and howling.

The pirates grabbed whatever was handy—marling spikes, hammers, ends of rope—and faced the marines.

Agar appeared at the captain's elbow. "They're working up to an attack, Captain."

"No, Agar. This is a funeral," the captain said.

The Maroons hoisted the body of Addae above their heads. They carried the body around deck, wailing. The pirates and the navy men worked their hands on the handles of their weapons.

"How do you know, Captain?" Francesca asked.

"I lived with Maroons after the Spanish left me for dead."

Juan, at the head of the Maroon procession, raised an earthen goblet calling out in his African tongue. The other Maroons fell silent.

In the silence the captain said bitterly, "The Spanish hunt them like animals. I saw plenty of funerals."

Juan poured a dark liquid on the deck and the Maroons lowered the body quietly. Juan took a crude stone amulet from around Addae's neck and made a sign of the cross on Addae's forehead.

Phillip straightened and pressed Massey's arm away. "Very well, but I'll have that deck spotless by morning."

He motioned the marines to lower their weapons and turned to go below.

Francesca stopped him, saying softly, "It's only a few days. They should stay on deck."

Phillip gave a slight nod as he continued on his way.

Francesca let out a breath as she moved to the ship's rail.

The moon had plunged below the sea's rim. Stars glittered and reflected off the ocean so vividly it appeared as though they sailed through the heavens.

The Maroons wrapped Addae in a cloth and lowered him to the water's edge. They held him there for a moment, between air and water, stretching a wake of stars behind him before he slipped beneath the waves.

Captain Massey followed Phillip below and the rest of the crew returned to their duties and conversations.

The Maroons, twenty-four in all, took seats forward on the deck. A borrowed lantern painted their faces in an orange glow.

Carter appeared at Francesca's side. "What was 'at all 'bout?"

"I imagine that's their way of saying goodbye," she said.

Baakir took a position at the rail staring into the night. Like his twin brother, Baakir was tall with broad shoulders, a smooth, wide chest, and narrow hips. Their hair fell in corkscrews down their backs.

The twins were so similar that Francesca told them apart by their attitudes. They were two emotional sides of the same man. Abuu harbored all the fierceness of a man subject to a lifetime of wrongs, and with it the furrowed brow and flashing eyes. Baakir's face was serene, full of Abuu's missing peace and steadiness.

Baakir sang in Spanish with a clear voice that matched the rising and falling of the sea.

"I know this tune," Francesca told Carter. "We sang it back home with different words." She translated:

"From Mother torn,
from Mother's arms,
Mother land, Mother love.
To toil and tempest and death.
But in the dark of night,
and deep of dream,
my soul flies home."

Juan motioned Francesca over. She sat on a coil of rope next to him, and Juan held out the amulet he had taken from the dead man's neck. "Addae died in your arms. It is for you to fight his enemies."

She paused, then curled Juan's fingers around the amulet. "I have my own battles to fight; I cannot fight his as well."

Abuu called sharply, "Akinsanya."

Juan turned and Abuu neared, speaking angrily in his language. Juan handed him the amulet and Abuu put it around his neck. A dozen other amulets hung there.

Abuu gestured toward Francesca and spoke again.

Juan turned to her. "Your dark hair, he asks if you are Spanish."

She shook her head. "Italiano."

The Maroons questioned Juan and he raised a hand saying, "Lady Blade." They nodded approval.

"They have heard of you, Lady Blade," Juan said. "They have heard that you strike fear into the hearts of the Spanish."

She hugged her arms around herself. "I have no wish to be feared," she said. "Please, call me Francesca. What is it the men call you, Juan?"

"Akinsanya, the name my madre gave me. I was born aboard a slave ship after my padre was killed, and she had great hopes. It means, 'The hero avenges.'"

"Ah-KEEN-sahn-yah," Francesca sounded it out. "Is that why you've come? Vengeance?"

Juan tilted his head toward the Maroons. "Them, yes, but I take no comfort in it." He laughed. "One of your countrymen said, 'The best revenge is to be unlike he who performed the injury'."

"Marcus Aurelius, wasn't it?"

Juan nodded.

"You know your letters?" she asked.

"Spanish, Greek, and Latin."

Francesca gaped in amazement. Half those aboard the *Destiny* could not write their names. "How…"

"My mother and I were purchased by a lawyer to tend his house. When I was still young his eyesight began to fail. He taught me to read and write so I could help him with his work. He was a kind man. He let me read any books I pleased from his library."

"And you ran away?"

"No!" Juan said. "I stayed with him until the end and mourned his passing. He had given me much. My people say that knowledge is better than riches. I have found it to be so."

Juan gazed beyond the lamplight. "But he had been sick for a long time. He died leaving many bills unpaid. Although he had signed the papers giving me my freedom, his creditors did not care. I was sold and put to work in the cane fields, so I ran away. I was a free man, no matter what they said."

Francesca nodded. "If you haven't come for vengeance, what have you come for?"

"I come because a soul has no color, and dreams cannot be bound. I come because all men and women should be free." Resolve crept into his voice. "There will be many slaves forced to carry the Spanish gold. I will free them."

Francesca scanned the Maroons who looked curiously back at her. *Freedom. Does such a thing exist?* Papa had said choice was an illusion, that one was bound by duty and necessity, but that was different than being bound by another man.

She admired the strength of these people. They deserved what freedom they could wrest from the world. She thought about the upcoming battle, of the slaves who would be marched fifty miles in chains with loads on their backs. She could help them. Certainty blossomed. Here was a cause she could believe in. She could give those people freedom. Here was something she could work for, fight for, a wrong she could set right.

She nodded. "I will do all I can to help you. It's an honorable goal."

Juan gave a dry laugh, his teeth flashing white. "Thank you, Lady Blade, we will gladly take your help, but honor is a white man's curse. We know only what is right."

She glanced at him. "You don't believe in honor?"

"I have read these *Rules of Honor*. To administer justice and protect the innocent, to respect life and freedom are good ideals. And I admire the man who never abandons a noble cause."

She nodded and Juan went on.

"But some are impossible. What man can live his life never going back on his word, especially when foolishly given? Why must one obey authority when it is misguided?"

Juan shook his head. "Such rules are as likely to lead to ruin as not. It is the heart that decides what is right, not rules."

CHAPTER 29
JUNGLE BEASTS

Clouds dotted the brilliant sky as the *Destiny* and *Adventure* ran smoothly with a steady breeze abaft their larboard beams. They were headed south, parallel to the coast of Panama. The turquoise water near the shore and strip of pale sand created a double ribbon topped by the dense green of the jungle.

Francesca taught fencing class on deck. A handful of pirates and a few Maroons drilled as Francesca walked among them, correcting a hand here, a lunge there.

She noticed Phillip and Captain Massey watching her from the quarterdeck and turned away. She was not getting along with either of them. Phillip and the captain, however, were getting on better, maybe because they had a common problem: her.

They had hammered out a working relationship. Phillip let Captain Massey handle day-to-day decisions, since most of the crew were Massey's men. Phillip stepped in when he felt the need, and the captain did not question him in public. What happened behind closed doors was anyone's guess. The marines took orders only from Phillip.

Francesca's feelings toward Captain Massey were so confused that she did her best to avoid him. She had so many questions, like, why had Papa adopted him but not brought him home? Where and how had they met? But she was afraid to hear the answers. What would the answers say about Papa, about her and her brothers, about the captain? She was angry, hurt, sad, and so many other things she couldn't name. Easier to avoid it all.

He had tried to speak with her once when he found her alone outside her cabin. She had pushed past him, but he grabbed her arm.

"Please, Francesca, I need to speak with you."

"You need! What about what I needed when I first came aboard?" She tried to keep the tears out of her voice. "I was frightened and lonely and grieving. You could h—" The tears gripped her throat. "You, you could have told me." She swallowed hard and turned away.

Since then, he hadn't pressed the matter.

Phillip, on the other hand, had become so overprotective she felt smothered. She supposed he was treating her as he would any lady—the way most ladies enjoyed being treated. But she wasn't like most ladies. She wished Phillip could treat her like the captain did. He never patronized or coddled her. It irked her that she preferred the captain's treatment to Phillip's.

Francesca called a rest for her fencing pupils, and they wiped their foreheads. Phillip had forbidden real weapons, so they lowered their wooden practice blades.

"Captain! Sandy Point off the bow!" came the call from the main top.

They had arrived. From here they would head inland toward the Camino Real. According to Juan, it would be a two-week trek through dense jungle. There were more traveled routes, but avoiding any settlement or native village was the only way to be sure they would surprise the Spanish caravan.

On the quarterdeck Phillip scanned the horizon and Captain Massey turned to Baldric. "Assemble *our* crew."

"Aye, Sir," Baldric said. "All *Destiny* hands on deck!"

The pirates turned out, staring expectantly at Captain Massey. Phillip nodded to the marines on the foredeck, and they came to attention, muskets shouldered. Phillip watched with folded arms as Captain Massey addressed his men.

"Men, as you know, we've made a deal with the devil … or in this case, the English Navy." The pirates booed, and Captain Massey saluted Phillip.

Phillip's jaw muscles worked.

"Out of this exchange we get, first, to keep our necks and our ship. Second, free rein of English ports and a free hand on the Main. And, perhaps, a little gold into the bargain."

Phillip raised an eyebrow but said nothing.

The captain continued with gusto. "And what do they ask in return? That we attack Spanish dogs and take their treasure!"

The crew cheered.

The captain gave a harsh laugh. "Perhaps we should pay them for the privilege."

The crew hooted and roared.

The captain's face grew serious. "But this is no project for the timid. Nightmarish beasts prowl the jungle, and Spanish soldiers guard their hoard. I'll not take men who question their mettle. I want only the bravest. Men with wills of iron and arms of steel. Men whose spirits will encompass all for the taste of blood and the glint of gold. Who will go with me?"

With a shout the crew volunteered en masse. Francesca grimly scanned the eager faces thirsting for blood.

Phillip stared at the captain with a degree of admiration, mixed with scorn. Francesca guessed the admiration was for the captain's knack of firing up his men, and the scorn was for needing to. Navy men required no encouragement.

She knew the captain's speech was mere show. All the pirates who were healthy enough were going. Their choice was to go or be hanged. By letting them volunteer, the captain would have an easier time leading them. Taking unwilling men into dangerous situations almost inevitably led to conflict, and with three different leaders—Phillip, Juan, and Captain Massey—this journey promised more than enough conflict already.

The ships anchored off a wide sand beach. The longboats were swung out on the winch, lowered to the water, and loaded with supplies.

An odd mixture of anticipation and dread settled on Francesca as she climbed into one of the boats with Carter and Miller. Ever since she was a child, she'd longed to see the jungles of the new world. She'd read stories about snakes large enough to swallow men whole, jungle cats, strange creatures with the bodies of pigs but snouts like an elephant, and mysterious natives. Now it seemed a lot less romantic than in her books, but no less fascinating.

The oarsmen bent their backs and pulled for shore. The boat cut through the turquoise water breasting the frothy breakers. The rowers jumped out, running the boat up the beach, sand hissing under the prow.

Twenty-four Maroons, twenty-three *Destiny* crewmen, and thirty English sailors prepared packs.

Francesca eyed the jungle. At first the brush appeared to be a solid wall of green, but as her eyes adjusted, she looked into dark, primeval hollows and started at the sudden movement of branches and leaves. This dark wilderness called to her. She was eager to be immersed, away from the harsh light of day.

She drew her attention back to her companions on the beach. Marines handed out muskets to the pirates and to any Maroon who would take one. From now on, everyone would need to be armed.

Four horses from the *Adventure* stood loaded with gear. Agar and Hal loaded a fifth with two swivel guns, miniature cannons about three feet long.

Phillip appeared at her side and lifted her pack. "I'll take that," he said.

Francesca took the other strap. "Thank you Phillip, but there's no need. Juan has most of my gear. It's not heavy."

He gently tugged at it. "I insist."

She tugged back. "Thank you, but I can manage."

Phillip pulled harder. "I couldn't possibly let you."

She yanked it away. "I'm not an invalid! Stop treating me like one."

"Very well," he said, holding up his hands in surrender.

When Miller helped her on with the pack her injured shoulder throbbed, and for a moment and she wished she'd let Phillip take it, but when she got it situated her shoulder settled down to a dull ache.

Captain Massey approached as she, Miller, and Carter prepared to set out. He rubbed his hands together excitedly. "Ready to take some treasure?"

"I'm ready to free the slaves. As far as the treasure goes," Francesca turned inland, "you can choke on it."

Juan and Captain Massey led the way. Francesca, with Miller, Carter, and the rest of the *Destiny's* men, followed. Phillip's men brought up the rear and the Maroons spread out along the sides of the column, watching for danger.

Shafts of sunlight penetrated the jungle canopy. Painted birds flashed by in every color, calling and twittering. Monkeys chattered at their approach and skittered away. Insects buzzed in Francesca's ears and brushed her skin.

She walked alongside Miller who looked pale and lacked his usual zest since his bout with yellow fever. "Well enough for this, Miller?" she asked as he missed his footing and slipped on a root.

"Aye," Miller said. "Though no doubt I'll be wishin' meself back aboard ship and out on the wide sea in no time." He looked her over. "I could ask ya the same."

She rotated her shoulder and glanced around the jungle. "Suits my humors."

"Aye!" said Carter, scrambling over a fallen log. "This is grand!"

Carter's enthusiasm soon waned as the jungle closed in, growing thicker and thicker, until they were forced to hack their way through with machetes and swords. The humidity was unbearable; they seemed to be breathing water. It was slow going, made even slower by the pack horses that balked at every rustled bush.

Francesca sensed the rising unease among the seamen. They were unaccustomed to the closeness and unnerved by the leaves and vines clinging to their skin. Like her, they probably imagined insects, and worse, crawling everywhere.

Captain Massey and Juan, at the head of the line, were joined by the twins, Baakir and Abuu. They hewed, pushed, and pulled at the living wall in front of them. The captain stripped to the waist to keep the twigs and thorns from catching his shirt, and Francesca saw pale scars crisscrossing his back. He paused to catch his breath and wipe the sweat from his face. He said to Juan, "If it's like this all the way to the ambush we'll be a year getting there."

Juan shook his head. "Only to the top of the first line of hills."

"Hills?" asked the captain. "You mean we'll need to go up?"

The twins broke through a line of vegetation revealing a nearly vertical rise. A groan went up from the men.

"Bollocks!" the captain said. "The horses will love this."

Abuu and Baakir scrambled up the slope, which was less heavily wooded than the land below. At the top they fastened lines for the men to cling to as they climbed.

Pulling, pushing, and cursing were required to get the horses up. By the time the party topped the hill, they were exhausted, and darkness crept across the jungle floor. They worked their way down to a flat area and set up camp.

As they ate, mist oozed out of dark hollows, swirling around tree boles, held at bay by the flicker of two cooking fires.

Francesca noticed the Maroons building themselves small lean-tos of branches covered with banana leaves, but she was too tired to follow their lead.

As she wrapped herself in her blanket, Phillip sat down next to her.

"I'm sorry, Francesca. I know you are displeased with me, but to be honest, I don't know what it is I've done wrong."

She sighed. "I'm the one who should apologize. You've been a perfect gentleman. I'm just not accustomed to it."

He grimaced. "Are you saying you want me to bully you and treat you as a pirate would?"

"No, of course not. I just wish you could treat me like one of the men."

He looked confused. "But I love you as, well, as a woman."

She put her hand on his arm and smiled into his deep blue eyes. "That makes me very happy, but now is not the time." She looked away. "Perhaps it's asking too much."

"That's really what you want? To be one of the men?"

She nodded.

"Well, I will try," he said, shaking his head. "But promise me one thing."

"What?" she asked as one of the marines called for Phillip's attention.

"Promise me that when this is over, when we're back in Port Royal and the admiral has granted your pardon, you'll give up playing at fencing and fighting." He rose. "Promise you'll be who you really are."

He didn't wait for an answer but headed toward the man who had called him. Confused, she watched him go. *Who does he think I am?*

———

Francesca woke disoriented. She hadn't slept on solid ground in so long that the earth seemed to sway beneath her. Once she cleared her head, she realized the heavy dew had soaked her blanket and clothes. She was damp and clammy, and when she moved, every joint ached.

A moment later she recognized what had awakened her. One of Phillip's men was calling for him sharply and bodies were rousing and moving toward the yelling. With a groan, she got to her feet, still wrapped in her blanket, and followed the sound. Mist clung about camp, hiding roots that tripped her sluggish steps. The men gathered in a ring staring at something on the ground.

"Unlucky bastard," someone said as she elbowed her way through to get a look.

A marine lay on his stomach with his face turned to the side and surprise in his staring gray eyes. The man had been mauled by a jungle beast; his throat torn out and a gaping hole in his side. A chill swept through her and she scanned her companions' faces, stunned by the fact that it had happened silently, while others were on watch two dozen feet away. Death aboard a pirate ship was a noisy affair, not this stealthy death in the dark.

"Jungle cat from the looks of et," the doctor said kneeling beside the body. "Probably dead b'fare he knew what hit 'em, poor sod."

Captain Massey knelt and turned the body over.

"'Ow can ya tell it were a cat?" asked Agar pushing through the crowd and kneeling as well.

The doctor indicated claw marks torn across the man's stomach, and a bite taken out of his neck. "See here. The cat wrapped him en his claws from behind, sunk his teeth en his neck, and bore him tae the ground in one go."

"It's Daniels," Phillip said, identifying the victim. He turned to the men. "How did this happen? Who was on watch?"

"He was," said one of Phillip's men.

Captain Massey shook his head. "The watch is nigh useless in the mist. Fetch spades."

"Is 'at what killed 'im, Doc? The bite ta the neck?" Agar leaned over examining the body.

"Goodness, nae," the doctor said. "The bite crushed hes windpipe, sure, but didnae kill him. The beast broke the man's neck after he fell."

The men paled.

"'Tis an ill omen, Sir," Miller said.

"Never mind omens, Miller," Captain Massey said. "Back to breakfast, all of ya. We've a long way to go yet."

Most of them moved off, but Agar grabbed Hal's arm and held him in place. Francesca moved back but lingered behind a bush. If Agar was interested, she wanted to know why.

"Ya can read all 'at from this 'ere body?" Agar said to the doctor.

"'Tis the bleedin' ye see," explained the doctor. "A body'll nae bleed much once et's dead." He looked at Agar over the top of his spectacles. "I'd nae idea this interested ye, Mr. Agar."

Agar shrugged. "All God's creatures, Doc."

The doctor took off his spectacles and wiped them on his sleeve. "The yarns I could tell ye. I was en Africa a few years back—"

"What about his flank there?" interrupted Agar.

"Oh, aye." The doctor settled the glasses back on his nose. "Beast ate hes liver. Left the rest. Either we startled et, or et had nae taste for long pig."

Hal, looking ill, hurried into the woods. Phillip, carrying a, worn Bible, approached followed by a few of his men. Phillip put a hand on the doctor's shoulder. "I'd like to say a few words over him, doctor, if you're done."

"Oh, aye," the doctor said, rising. "An interesting case, but I'll nae keep ye."

Agar rose, humming to himself as he rejoined the crew. Francesca watched him go, puzzling over why he was in such a good mood.

Except for Agar, it was a somber party that broke camp and set out on a gentle downhill slope. The underbrush thinned and they made good time for three or four hours, but eventually the jungle closed in again until they were forced to push their way through foot by foot. Francesca wondered if it were possible to drown in a sea of vegetation.

When they broke through to a clearer part of the forest, they stopped to rest and eat. Phillip leaned against the knobby trunk of an ancient tree as monkeys scolded above. Juan squatted next to him to discuss the trail ahead. As Francesca walked toward them, Phillip shrugged off his pack and dropped it to the ground.

The pack erupted in a hiss.

A silver and black five-foot-long snake darted toward Phillip. He flung himself backwards, tripping.

As the snake shot forward, Francesca froze in panic.

"Phillip!" she screamed.

The snake lunged, mouth gaping, but was brought up short by the pack on its tail.

Juan's machete struck the snake's head from its body. Francesca swallowed hard, heart pounding.

"Is it poisonous?" asked Phillip, breathing heavily.

"Indeed," Juan said. "The most poisonous in these lands, a Fer-de-Lance." He lifted the body, admiring the snake's silver and black diamond-patterned back and pale-yellow belly. He grinned. "It will be delicious."

After that, the landscape changed, as did the weather. A heavy mist fell from the hot humid air until Francesca gasped for breath.

They left the hills for swampy country where they couldn't tell water from earth. What looked solid would give way to muck underneath. The olive-colored slime sucked at their legs, sapping their strength. At least the trees grew less close and they glimpsed gray sky overhead, but the branches dripped with tattered rags of ghostly yellow moss.

They slogged, searching for solid footing and hauling each other out of the mire when necessary. The captain came alongside Francesca as she trudged, his face full of concern. "How are you faring?" he asked, reaching out to steady her as she slipped in the muck.

"Fine, Sir." She straightened and hurried her pace. He kept beside her.

"I just meant, with your shoulder."

"I'm fine, really." When he didn't respond she said, "As well as can be expected."

They were silent and awkward, and eventually, the captain moved off.

When the group found a patch of solid ground, they set up camp early. That evening, she followed the Maroons' example and built herself a lean-to of umbrella-sized leaves to keep off the mist and dew. As the light dimmed, the mosquitoes came out, putting an end to any camaraderie. The only relief was to roll themselves in blankets, cover their faces, and try to sleep.

The next few days were no better. The veiled sun and rising mist leeched away color until they moved through shades of gray. The trees were ominous shadows. Even the jungle creatures were hushed by the fog.

Juan led them single file along narrow hummocks of earth between mires, testing each step first with the shaft of his spear.

One of the men, misjudging his footing, made a splash, blaringly loud in the unnatural quiet.

"Careful, lads," Miller said, his voice strained.

Phillip, following Juan, vented his frustration. "How much longer can this blasted fog last? It's been three days! Three bloody days, damn it!"

"My people say: Tomorrow is pregnant, and no one knows what she will give birth to," replied Juan.

"Indeed," Phillip said. "I only hope the baby is dry."

The head of the line moved onto solid ground amid thick brush. The men passed, covered in goo and unnerved.

One of the horses in the swamp spooked, lunging and kicking. It hauled the man leading it off his feet as it reared back. Men dove for the reins as the other horses bucked and plunged as well.

"Grab them!" shouted Captain Massey as two horses plowed into the swamp. In seconds they were stuck and sinking fast.

"Get their packs off, quickly!" shouted the captain, wading in with many of the men, the olive-green water up to their chests. "We need rope! It's in my pack."

"I'll fetch it." Francesca stood on the bridge of land and had seen where the captain dropped his pack among the bushes. She sprinted for it.

She found the pack and tore the coil of rope loose. As she rose and spun toward the others, she started in alarm. Agar stood in front of her. The butt of his musket smashed into her face.

Francesca came to with a jolt of fear.

She was gagged, lying in a tiny clearing, her hands tied and over her head. Hal knelt on her arms and held her shoulders down. Agar straddled her thighs, knife in hand.

She struggled, her heart racing. She wasn't far from the others; she heard them splashing and cursing. Then she heard Phillip's outraged demand. "What is this?"

He found me! But then she heard a muffled reply and Phillip shouted, "Alligators? Blessed Mother of God!"

He wasn't coming to help her. Francesca struggled harder.

Agar seemed oblivious to what was going on with the others, or perhaps he just didn't care.

He dragged the tip of his knife across Francesca's stomach. Blood welled and she gave a muffled cry, writhing helplessly.

Suddenly she realized why Agar had been so interested in the man killed by the jungle cat. She knew what he was up to. Her eyes widened and her breath came in gasps around the gag. Claw marks were just the beginning. She remembered the gaping hole in the man's side, his torn-out throat. She fought harder.

"Out of the water! Now!" shouted Captain Massey in the distance.

Francesca tried to call out, but Agar pressed a hand to her throat.

Hal grimaced. "Can't we break 'er neck first?"

"No!" spat Agar. "Ya 'eard the doc. She won't bleed proper. Claws first."

"'Sides," he said haughtily, "it is just. The Bible says, 'And I will judge thee, as women that shed blood are judged; and I will give thee blood in return.'" He dragged three more lines across her belly as she writhed.

Francesca panted for breath. *Please, God, I can't die this way.*

"Now for the throat," Agar said. "Hold her still." His fingers tightened on her windpipe. The bloody knife came toward her neck.

The bushes behind Agar rustled and Francesca battled to wrench herself free. Wrestling to hold her still, Agar didn't notice the bushes move until Juan stepped out two paces away, musket in hand.

"Leave her be!" Juan said, sighting down the barrel of the gun.

Agar glanced at Juan then pressed his knife to Francesca's throat. The scene swam before her eyes.

Juan cocked the hammer. "I said, leave her!"

Agar eased his pressure on her neck, and she sucked in air. Agar looked at Hal, tilting his head toward Juan. "What do you know, Hal, a cur defending his bitch." Agar turned to Juan and rose. "You cannot hurt me. God protects the righteous."

Juan tightened his grip. "Hold or I will shoot."

There was a shout, "Kill the beasts!" and a barrage of gunfire erupted from afar. Juan flinched and Agar lunged at him, bloody knife flashing red.

Her legs now free, Francesca twisted and wrapped them around Agar's knees. Off balance, Agar missed his target. He reeled but didn't go down.

Agar grabbed the barrel of the gun.

Juan fought to pull it away from him.

Francesca drew her legs in, pain spearing through her belly. She kicked at Agar with what strength she had left. She caught the side of his knee and heard something snap.

Agar screamed.

With an earsplitting *bang,* Juan's musket went off.

Agar's knife flew as he crashed to the ground, half his stomach blown away. He put a hand to his belly with a look of bewilderment.

Hal crawled to Agar's side. "No!"

"God protects..." Agar's breath sighed out and he went still.

Francesca sat up, crying out in pain. She yanked the gag from her mouth and tasted blood. Captain Massey and Phillip, with a few men behind them, appeared from the brush.

"Bloody hell!" the captain roared, surging forward.

Phillip grabbed his arm and yanked him back. The captain spun on Phillip, and looked as if he would take a swing at him, but Phillip pushed past the captain.

"God Almighty, Francesca," Phillip hissed as he helped her up. She rose unsteadily, holding her tied hands to her bloody stomach. Agar lay with Hal bent over him.

Captain Massey growled at Hal. "He treated you like rubbish. Why do you care?"

Hal cringed, his eyes on Agar's staring face. "My name's not Hal. Hal was his brother's name. I never had no family b'fore."

The others were silent as two of Phillip's marines grabbed Hal and dragged him from the clearing.

Miller and Carter appeared. Carter rushed to Francesca, flinging his arms around her, making her gasp in pain. "Crickey, what's 'e done ta ya?"

"I'm all right," she said, grimacing.

Carter kicked at Agar's body. "I'd kill ol' cribbage face meself if'n 'e warn't already dead."

"As would I," the captain said through tight jaws.

Francesca slumped against Phillip, weak, shivering, and sick to her stomach.

Phillip turned to his men. "Fetch the doctor. Make camp, away from the swamp. We'll stay here tonight."

CHAPTER 30
A MATTER OF HONOR

"I think my tooth is loose," Francesca mumbled. The doctor gently kneaded her swollen face, bloody from the butt of Agar's musket. She lay ice cold and trembling uncontrollably in a lean-to the Maroons had built for her.

"Well, leave the tooth be," the doctor said. "With luck et well tighten up again. Nae bones broken, that's good news. Nou let's see that belly."

Francesca drew up her sliced shirt. The doctor peered at her stomach wiping away blood. "Hmm, superficial," he said.

"It doesn't feel superficial."

"Nae, I dinna imagine so." He indicated the final cut Agar had scraped across her skin. "I'd like tae put a stitch or three in here. If ye can handle et."

She nodded and the doctor grabbed his pack, drawing out a bottle. "A wee nip o' medicinal whiskey will help wi' the pain."

Francesca took a couple gulps. Heat trailed down her throat and pooled in her stomach, making her exterior feel colder. She lay back, waiting for the whiskey to work, feeling giddy and frightened by turns. Giddy that Agar was dead and frightened at how close he had come to succeeding. A few more minutes and they might have found her face down like Daniels and never have known what Agar had done.

The captains' muffled voices filtered to her from beyond the quiet camp, arguing.

"How is it my fault?" yelled the captain. "I was chest deep in muck trying not to be eaten by alligators."

"You brought the man along," yelled Phillip.

"I told you I didn't want him, but you gave me no choice," the captain shouted back.

Before she could hear more, Carter, Miller, and Juan appeared around the side of the lean-to.

"Can we see 'er now?" Carter asked the doctor.

"Aye," the doctor said. "For a wee while. I'll stitch her up once the whiskey mellows her a bet."

They sat next to her.

"'Ow are ya, missy?" Miller said.

"I'll be all right." She tried to smile, but it hurt her face.

"When I seen what 'e did ta ya, I coulda..." Miller shook his head in frustration.

"Why would 'e do that?" Carter asked.

Juan put a hand on Carter's shoulder. "He was a *bwana nunda*, a half-man, who feels powerful only by making others powerless. I have seen many like him. Had he been one of my people, we would have driven him into the jungle to die like the beast he was."

Miller shrugged. "Aye, 'e'll lie there now. But I wager no beast will 'ave the stomach ta touch 'im."

She shivered. "I hate to think there are more like him out there."

Phillip and Captain Massey appeared. Captain Massey's jaw was taut, and he licked at a split lip. Phillip, frowning, held a hand to his stomach.

"How is she?" the captain asked the doctor.

"The wounds'll heal," the doctor said.

"Th' good Doc gave 'er some medicinal whiskey to calm 'er nerves," Miller said. He took a swig and handed the bottle to Francesca, who took another nip as well.

"Cap'n," said the doctor to Phillip. "We'd best move away from thes bog as soon as can be."

"Yellow fever?" asked Phillip.

"Aye. We've two feverish nou and et'll only get worse."

"The men are exhausted," Phillip said. "And Francesca needs rest. I'll not move them tonight." He ran a hand through his hair. "Daniels and Agar dead and two horses lost already."

"And a good deal of ammunition spent on alligators," Captain Massey said. They fell silent.

307

The captain looked across camp to where Hal sat, chained to a tree. "What do we do with him?"

"We clap him in irons and hang him when we get back to the ship," Phillip said. "There must be a trial and an execution."

"An' 'aul 'is worthless carcass through th' jungle in chains?" Miller said incredulously. "Sir, I says shoot th' bastard now and be done wi' it." He crossed his arms. "I'll gladly do it meself."

"It would be as good to let him go," Juan said. "If he runs, the jungle will punish him. If he stays, your laws will."

Phillip considered, then nodded. "Very well. We'll release him, but I'll set a couple marines to watch him."

"And," Captain Massey added, "if he comes within a cables length of Francesca, I say we put a ball between his eyes."

"Aye," they all agreed.

"Nou if ye'll excuse us, gentleman," the doctor said. "The lass has an appointment with a needle and some catgut."

Everyone left, except Phillip, who knelt beside Francesca.

"Please, promise me, from now on you'll let me protect you." He took her hand. "I swear, I won't let anything happen to you, ever."

Francesca gave him a weak smile. "I'll try."

Phillip tenderly brushed the hair back from her face, then rose and left. "I think that's what I'm afraid of," she said quietly.

"What are ye afraid o', lass?" the doctor asked over the top of his spectacles.

"That nothing would happen to me, ever."

"Wouldnae that be a good thing?" He threaded the catgut through the needle.

She shook her head. "Don't listen to me. It's just the whiskey talking."

———— ⊢ ————

That night the wind came up, pulling the mist away in streamers and giving them a break from the mosquitoes.

By morning a steady rain had set in, denying them a hot breakfast. After soggy biscuits were handed around to grumbling men, Phillip called, "Ready the march."

Francesca got to her feet unsteadily, one hand holding her bandaged stomach. Miller hoisted her pack onto his shoulder. She gave him a grateful, wincing smile and he winked.

They finally left the swamp behind. The underbrush opened up, allowing them to walk two abreast so that despite the rain, their spirits improved. Francesca chatted with Miller and Carter, until she noticed the captain walking near her, then she fell silent. The captain sighed and moved on ahead.

The next morning four more men had fallen ill with yellow fever. The two who had been sick before seemed miraculously well, but Miller warned Francesca that it might not last. If the fever returned in a few days, there was little hope they would survive.

Francesca wondered who would be next. "Is there nothing we can do to protect ourselves?"

Miller shrugged. "Just pray that yer luck holds out."

The next morning four more men had fallen ill with yellow fever. The two who had been sick before seemed miraculously well, but Miller warned

After three more days, another fifteen members of the company had fallen ill. Those who succumbed earlier were being carried by sets of Maroons. One was vomiting blood.

As they set up camp, the doctor approached Phillip.

"Ye cannae drive the men like this. They're sick and tired."

"What would you have me do, Doctor?" Phillip snapped. "Time is not on our side."

The doctor made no reply.

"According to Juan, we'll reach a Maroon camp tomorrow. We'll leave the sick there," Phillip said in a conciliatory voice. "How many?"

"Twelve o' yer men, nine from the *Destiny*."

"From seventy-seven down to fifty-four. God help us."

The next morning, three men did not wake. Graves were dug, breakfast eaten, and the line trudged on.

Tall, straight trees soared one hundred feet overhead. Occasional beams of slanted morning sun sifted down. The underbrush clumped here and there, often opening and giving glimpses into the distance, then closing again.

Captain Massey stood next to the line of men watching them pass.

Francesca, near the back, ignored him as she approached, but he held up a hand. "DiCesare, a moment."

She frowned but stepped out of line. "Sir."

The captain waited for the others to pass and fell in behind them, Francesca at his side.

The captain ran his eyes over her, as if measuring how she was doing. They walked silently for a while.

"I won't have you treating me like this," he said.

"I've reported as ordered, Sir."

He studied her face, but she had arranged it into an emotionless mask. "You know my meaning. Yell at me, curse me, but don't ignore me."

He waited for her to respond. Finally he said, "About your father…"

Francesca straightened. "I'll thank you not to speak of him," she said, jaws tight.

"He was my guardian."

"I'll not hear it." She hurried her pace, but he grabbed her arm, stopping her.

"Hold, Francesca. He meant a great deal to me."

"After the things you've done, you're not fit to clean his boots!" She tried to stem the rising tide of anger but it rippled through her chest until she thought she would burst.

The captain gripped her arm harder. "Everything I've done was to avenge the woman I loved."

She yanked her arm free.

The captain went on. "Thurio DiCesare was not the saint you think him. He did terrible things."

Somehow Francesca's sword was in her hand. "Don't ever say his name!"

"I'm sorry, Francesca. I'm sorry I forced you into this. I'm sorry I got you shot, and hung." He paused. "Your father did many things he was not proud of. I know. I was there."

Red swam before her eyes. She attacked, her training taking over her body.

He dodged and drew his sword.

"Liar!" she shouted. "My father was an honorable man, he lived and breathed honor, and I've failed him because of you. Because of you I broke my oath!"

She attacked again. The captain backed away parrying furiously. She lunged and pressed as the captain retreated. Finally, she paused, her free hand to her tortured stomach. "Do you think I care about a ball in the shoulder? Do you think I'm afraid to die?" She attacked again. The captain kept out of reach until his back came up against the trunk of a tree.

Francesca paused, panting, not sure where her words were coming from, but meaning every one. "I despise you for what you've made me do! I despise myself for doing it! I hate what I've become because of you! And I hate how you make me feel!"

She began to lunge.

The captain tensed.

"Francesca!"

She froze. It was Phillip.

She dropped her sword tip and turned. Phillip stood ten paces away, mouth agape, with a handful of men behind him. Francesca spotted Miller, his face twisted with concern and Carter looking expectant.

Phillip stepped forward, red in the face. "Enemies all around and you two at each other's throats? Outrageous! I will not have it!"

Francesca faced him, all anger gone.

"Jesus," Phillip said. "You're bleeding again."

She looked down and saw new red lines across her shirt.

"Massey," Phillip said, jerking his head in the direction of the men.

The captain, silent, passed by him.

Phillip stopped Francesca. "The rules say I should clap you in irons."

She shrugged. "Do as you please." She pressed by, but he stopped her again.

"Would you have killed him?"

She heard a hint of hopefulness in his voice. Or maybe she imagined it.

"We'll never know, will we?"

In camp that evening, Francesca's anger buzzed beneath her skin making her irritable. She couldn't shake the captain's words. *Thurio DiCesare was not the saint you think him. He did terrible things.* Obviously, the captain was lying, but she couldn't stop the thought, *What things?*

Her uneasiness spread among the men. They fidgeted and argued, keeping a watchful eye on her and the captain.

Francesca sharpened her sword, the metallic scrape of her whet stone setting her teeth on edge. She tried to ignore the situation and especially the captain. Phillip's question, *Would you have killed him?* echoed in her head. She honestly did not know the answer. She had been furious, more enraged than she could ever remember feeling, yet … *I couldn't have. Could I? What kind of a person am I? And, is it really him I'm angry at?*

She glanced around the clearing. Men gathered in bunches around the cooking fires or stood talking in small groups. Some lay sick and coughing. Her outburst had done nothing to improve morale. Well, it was none of their affair. What was she supposed to do, let the captain sully Papa's good name?

An argument started among several Maroons around a fire. Two of them, Abuu and a large man she thought was named Kintu, jumped to their feet, machetes in hand. They slashed at each other, knocking over a cooking pot as men scrambled out of their way.

Francesca moved to intervene, but Juan arrived first. He stepped in, livid, knocking their blades aside with his spear.

"What is this foolishness? Why do you raise your hands against each other? Have you not enemies enough?"

Abuu raised his chin. "He insulted my family honor! He said my mother is a witch."

Juan pushed his face within inches of Abuu's. "Do you believe your mother is a witch?"

"No, Akinsanya."

"Then what do you care what he thinks?"

Abuu had no answer and Juan slapped him, hard. Juan turned on Kintu. "Would you cause strife among us at the enemy's gate?" Juan slapped him as well.

Juan spit on the ground. "Honor. Show me this thing. Bring it here and lay it at my feet. What use is it? You cannot eat it nor drink it, nor hold it in your hand." He rested his spear against Kintu's breast. "It will not keep your wife warm at night when you are lying dead for it." Juan turned and strode away. "Fie!"

The men dropped their heads.

Francesca watched Juan, confused and teary-eyed, as though he had slapped her. Juan took his seat in front of another fire, picked up a whet stone and angrily sharpened his spear point. Francesca drew near, her eyes stinging. "How can you say that honor doesn't matter? It's … it's everything. I've tried so hard to—"

"Tell me, what has this gained you?"

She dropped her eyes and her voice cracked. "Well…"

He stopped sharpening. She sat down next to him.

"You white people are so confused up here." He tapped her on the forehead with his whetstone, then went back to sharpening. "I have seen this 'honor' used over and over to cover a multitude of sins. Look at Abuu and Kintu, ready to cause each other grave harm."

Francesca stared into the fire.

"Your head may follow these rules, but your heart knows what is right and what is wrong. You cannot follow both." He went back to sharpening. "Now you confuse my men as well."

Francesca rubbed her face. Papa had always said that what was honorable was right, yet she felt the truth of Juan's words. She had made honorable decisions that had made her heart sick.

She raised her eyes and looked around the camp, searching for the captain. He wrapped himself in a blanket and lay down. Guilt lodged in her chest. She had justified her attack by telling herself she was defending Papa's honor.

She slept little that night. She stared at the green canopy overhead with one question on her mind. *What terrible things did Papa do?*

Just after noon the next day, the tattered company dragged into a Maroon fort surrounded by a palisade of hewn logs. There were no children playing, no women singing while at their chores, just grim, battle-hardened men. From this fort they launched attacks on Spanish plantations, ranches, and homesteads to free their brethren. Even with their Maroon escort, the inhabitants stared suspiciously as the white men passed inside.

One man in particular stared at Francesca. He had one obsidian eye and a gash where his other had been. It was probably her dark hair and olive skin he stared at, thinking her Spanish, and it made her shiver. Baakir whispered to the man, probably telling him who she was. His eye never left her, but a grin spread across his face—one that made her skin crawl.

Phillip clapped one of his marines on the shoulder. "Buck up men, another day and a half we'll be at the ambush point. The gold and the glory are nearly ours. Rest. Replenish the supplies. We march at dawn." The exhausted men dropped their packs.

As a late afternoon breeze picked up, stirring the leaves around the fort, Francesca stood in front of a hut, the doctor re-bandaging her stomach where she'd torn the stitches. Carter rushed up grinning, a brilliant green snake wrapped around his arm and hand. Its body was about an inch thick, and its tongue flicked in and out.

"Francesca, look what I caught!"

"Get that away from me," she said.

"Look!" said Carter, as Juan and Phillip approached.

"Mmmm, looks delicious," Juan said.

"Belay that! I mean to keep him. What do they eat?"

"Insects, rodents, I should think."

Carter beamed. "He'll feast aboard ship then."

"Maybe you should go find it something to eat," Francesca said, eyeing it warily.

"Aye, aye," Carter said. He hurried toward the gate.

Phillip leaned against the doorframe next to Francesca, "Juan thinks we should leave the horses here."

"They have been slowing us for over a week," Juan said.

"Well," Francesca said, "this is one party where it won't do to arrive late."

Phillip sighed, "I hate to lose the swivel guns. They are our only real fire power."

"They can be mounted here to cover our retreat," Juan said.

"Very well," Phillip said. "The horses and guns will remain, along with the sick. What is the count, Doctor?"

"Twenty-six," the doctor said, tying off the bandage.

"See to it," Phillip said.

Juan and the doctor set to their duties. Phillip ran a hand over his face. "Fifty men, no swivel guns, and a hundred Spanish to face. Heaven help us."

Francesca rested a hand on her bandaged stomach. They were hardly in condition to fight, but it was too late to turn back now. "Maybe some of the Maroons here will join us."

"Aye," Phillip said. "They'd make good fighters."

She nodded and suppressed a shudder, thinking of the way the maroon had stared at her. Then she noticed the captain across camp. Since their fight yesterday his words had been gnawing at her. *He did terrible things.* The captain had to be wrong. She needed to talk to him.

She started toward the captain, but Phillip put a hand on her arm. "Francesca."

She turned back to him. For a moment she had forgotten he was there.

Phillip took her hand. "Francesca, if we survive this jungle, I want ... well, I hadn't planned it like this, but..." He got down on one knee. "Will you marry me? No running away together this time. A proper wedding. I have some land outside Bristol. An estate with a garden."

Francesca caught her breath. This was what they had both wanted, dreamed of, when they'd fenced together at the salle in secret. Back when Catalina was still alive. But a feeling had been growing, the same feeling as when she first saw Phillip on the *Destiny* deck. It was wrong, she was wrong, it was too late.

She wanted to go home, she wanted the Phillip of her youth, the boy that had raced her through the olive grove and met her at night in the cellar to fence, not this flesh-and-blood man standing before her. Not this naval captain.

He gazed at her with hopeful eyes.

"Please, Phillip, get up." She pulled him back to his feet, glancing around to see if anyone had noticed.

"Well, will you marry me?"

She dropped her eyes. "No, Phillip."

His hand tightened around hers. "But I love you, Francesca."

She laid a hand on his cheek. "I love you too, and I always will. You're one of my best friends. But we've both been in love with dreams."

"What do you mean?"

"You want someone to take care of and protect. You want a lady to pamper, someone who paints, or embroiders, and throws society functions."

"Well, you told me in your letters how you were managing the salle. You could manage the estate. And we'd have children, together."

"While you're at sea," she said, looking away. More than anything, it sounded lonely.

"I'd be home as often as I could. I thought that's what we wanted, a quiet home and children to raise? We could even fence now and then, as long as no one sees. Surely you want those things too?"

"No, I don't think I ever did. I want a life full of adventure. I want to see the world. And I no longer need anyone to take care of me. I'll never be a proper lady, Phillip."

"You could be, I know it."

She put a hand to her scarred throat. "And when our society friends learn that I was hung as a pirate?"

He blanched and looked away. "You said you loved me."

"I do. I love the handsome hero who would charge in and save me from a harsh world, but…" She gave him a tiny smile. "I've learned to save myself. Now I need something else."

"What is it you need?"

"I don't know exactly." She thought of the captain's passion for his dead wife. Passion was certainly part of it, but there was more to it than that. She wanted a partner, not a protector. She wanted … she couldn't seem to put the rest into words.

"It's him, isn't it? Massey."

"No, this is about us."

"He's changed you, ruined you, wrecked your life, and our life together." His hands squeezed hers and his face twisted with frustration. "I'd like to kill him myself."

She shook her head. "I have changed, but I've done it to myself. It started the day Papa died." She grew thoughtful. "Maybe my life is ruined, as you say. I don't know where it's taking me, but I know it's not an estate with a garden."

"This is what you want?"

She shook her head. "No. It's not what I want, but this is the way it is. I know I would make you most unhappy as your wife, and it would break my heart."

Phillip was quiet, then he kissed her hand. "If you change your mind, I'm willing to take that risk."

She smiled and wiped her eyes as he moved off. She heaved a sigh, feeling as if she'd lost a part of herself, something precious that she could never get back. But she couldn't live in the past, she had to move on. She leaned against the frame of the hut. If the past was gone, why was it so difficult to let it go?

———⚓———

"Francesca," called Carter, later that day. "I fed me snake a big ol' moth an' now, watch this." His new pet slithered from one hand to the other and up around his shoulders.

"Keep that thing away from me," she said as the snake stretched toward her, tongue flicking.

"Are ya scared?" said Carter, thrusting it toward her and then dancing away.

"If you want it alive, keep it away."

She noticed Captain Massey headed out of the fort. "I'll be back, Carter. I need to talk to the captain."

"Are ya gonna kill 'im this time?" Carter said. "Can I watch?"

"I'm not going to kill him. I'm going to apologize." She'd been feeling worse and worse about her attack. Juan had been right; she'd been wrong. And she needed to know what Papa had done.

Francesca found the captain in a small clearing just off the trail. A stream, two feet wide, burbled along the jungle floor. The captain knelt on the far side with his shirt off, splashing water on his face and neck. The filtered, late afternoon light threw the lattice of scars on his back into sharp relief.

He looked up. "Come to finish me off?"

She thought she detected a hint of hopefulness as he wiped his face and pulled on his shirt.

"I came to apologize. I shouldn't have…"

He sat back on a mossy hummock next to the stream. "No, you were right." He shook his head. "All the wretched things I've done, and I've made you do."

Francesca stepped closer and leaned against a tree. "I understand why. I haven't…" she looked away. "Since Port Royal I haven't been able to get the image of a little girl under her bed out of my mind."

He wrapped his arms around his knees, looking away. "My actions weren't honorable."

She shrugged. "No. Human, perhaps." The captain looked at her, surprised. "But they haven't changed anything or made things right, have they?"

She stepped forward and sat down across the stream from him. She plucked at some leaves. "My mother was killed by pirates," she said.

She heard him suck in a breath. "I didn't know," he said softly. "No wonder—"

"—I hated you," she finished for him. "I know you hate me too, but—"

"I don't hate you, Francesca," he said, laughing. "Maybe I did at first, but not for long. I couldn't hate you. You were so proud and stubborn and determined, and so capable. You were just like your father," he chuckled, "except female, and beautiful." His face grew serious. "And in battle, my God, Francesca, lovely and deadly, wild and controlled at the same time. No, I don't hate you."

A fire smoldered behind his eyes that made her skin tingle. Had he looked at his wife that way? The thought brought with it a spike of jealousy.

She cleared her throat. "You said Papa did terrible things. What did he do?"

He looked away.

"Please," she said, "I need to know."

He sighed. "He murdered my real father, for one."

"What!"

"It was before you were born," he explained. "Your father was establishing Salle DiCesare at the time. He came to England to make his reputation as Europe's finest sword master. He had a lot of competition back then: Thibault, Carranza, Pacheco de Narváez. In France there was Le Perche and Besnard. He issued challenges to them all, but none would face him, so he challenged their students, the English and French nobility. He would meet people at parties and events, offense would be given, and a challenge accepted. Two or three duels a week, I think he said."

"So many!"

"It worked. His reputation as a sword master grew quickly and the noblemen sent their sons to study under him."

"And your father?"

"My real father was a nobleman, though he had inherited nothing but blue-blood and debt. He scratched out a living on worn-out land. The maestro didn't realize he had no sword training until too late. He might as well have murdered him."

Francesca drew in a sharp breath. "He never told us."

"It was just another duel to him. I doubt he gave it any thought until our vicar dropped me on his doorstep. He told him, 'You made an orphan of him. He's yours now.'"

Francesca stepped across the stream and sat next to him, putting a hand on his arm.

"Until that day, I don't believe he ever thought about the implications of his duels, of the families of those he wounded or killed. Once he did, it haunted him. I suspect that's why he took me in, to atone."

"Oh Will, you must have hated him."

"I didn't understand what was happening at the time. I was four years old. He was a good father, kind and loving. My real father had never had much time for me. In some ways, I thought myself lucky."

"What did they duel over?"

He shrugged. "He never could remember. 'A matter of honor' he would say." A bitter edge crept into the captain's voice. "I decided early on that if honor meant killing over slights that weren't worth remembering, I wanted none of it."

Francesca remembered being so jealous of the time Papa spent with Billy. Now it made sense. Now she knew why Billy had meant so much to him, and why he had never told them the truth.

She thought about Juan's words. According to the rules, Papa's actions had been perfectly honorable, but that didn't make them right. Even Papa had used honor to justify his wrongdoing.

"He made everything seem simple, but it's so complicated now. I miss him so," Francesca said.

"I know."

"Some days, I…"

"I know."

Tears welled. She couldn't stop them. She covered her face with her hands.

The captain moved closer and put an arm around her. "I do have a knack for bringing out your strongest humors. All bad ones it seems."

She dropped her hands and looked at him. "Not all bad."

She lingered for a moment, his arm around her, his side warm against hers. She felt the damp moss beneath her hand, the moist smell of loam and life all around. His eyes, in the gathering dark, seemed full of wildness and anguish that mirrored her own. He drew a breath as she leaned in.

His lips were softer than she expected, tentative. He kissed her cautiously at first, unsure, but then with abandon.

A wave of fire swept over Francesca, tingling every nerve in her body. She clutched him tight and gulped him in as though she were drowning and he was the air. Her skin ignited wherever he touched her. *Oh, God!* She pressed against him. This was the passion she had yearned for. She tore at his shirt wanting to feel his skin. His hand slid down to her hip. He pulled her on top of him as they fell back on the soft moss, entangled. He clutched the nape of her neck as his lips trailed fire down her throat. Her fingers curled into his skin. He...

"Cap'n! Francesca!" Miller's voice, not far off, stopped them cold. Others called their names in the distance. They lay still, their hearts pounding together. Miller crackled through the underbrush, moving closer. Trading alarmed looks, they jumped to their feet, straightening their clothes and hair as Miller appeared.

"Cap'n, I'm glad the missy hasn't run ya thro—" He stopped short when he saw Francesca brushing leaves from her hair and the captain tucking in his shirt. A smile cracked across Miller's face and he rocked on his heels. "Beggin' yer pardon, Sir. Cap'n Worthington wants ta shut th' gate."

The captain cleared his throat. "Of course."

Miller stuck his pipe between his teeth. "Ya know, Sir, as I was once a young man..." He paused and lit the pipe. "But am now old an' slow. It might, Sir, iffen ya like, take me, ohhh, 'alf an 'our at least ta find ya."

Francesca's cheeks flamed. For half a second, the captain looked as though he were considering Miller's offer, then he frowned. "Lead on, Miller. We're right behind you."

They entered the fort under Phillip's watchful eye. The men were recalled, the gate shut. Francesca lay down near the fire burning brightly in the center of the fort. As she pulled her blanket around her, Miller gave her a knowing look and laid a finger beside his nose to let her know her secret was safe.

She furrowed her brow and turned over. While she appreciated his confidence, she was conflicted about what had happened. He was still a pirate, but now she ached for his arms, for the smell and taste of his skin.

She squeezed her eyes shut. Somehow, in the space of two days, the world had turned on end. Forward was back, up was down, honor was wrong, and loving a pirate felt right. She pulled her blanket over her face and thought about Papa—Papa who had murdered Will's father over a point of honor.

CHAPTER 31
BATTLE'S EVE

Before dawn, Francesca awoke to Will and Phillip shouting, rousing the men.

"Up! On your feet! Move!" yelled the captain.

Francesca opened her eyes and groaned. It wasn't yet light out. Miller hurried past and she called to him. "What's going on?"

"Bad news," Miller said. "One a' them Maroons arrived last night from Panama City. Th' damned mule train left early."

"Oh, no!"

"They's likely ta be at the bridge tomorrow mornin'. We gots ta make quick sticks or we'll miss 'em."

She got to her feet and rolled her blanket. "Can we make it?"

"Aye, we can," Miller said. "Question is, will we be too rung out ta fight."

The men broke camp and shouldered their packs in record time. With only cold rations on the run, and a day's fast march ahead, they were grim.

The only ones not grumbling were the captain and Carter. From the way Will looked at her, Francesca knew their kiss was the cause of his good mood. Carter's mood she attributed to his new pet, who had gone to sleep under his blanket instead of trying to escape overnight.

By midday, the heat was unbearable. She tried to wipe the sweat from her eyes with her sleeve, but it was soaked through with perspiration.

Baakir and Abbu led the way, followed by Juan and Phillip. Francesca hiked with Miller and Carter as they hurried through the underbrush. Captain Massey and the rest of the men followed. Carter's snake, wrapped around his upper arm, stared at Francesca, tongue flicking. "Carter, must you carry that horrid thing?" she asked.

Carter shot her a look. "I'll not have you speak of Mr. Baldric that way."

Miller chuckled. "Mr. Baldric?"

"Aye, this way I tell *him* what to do," said Carter. "Not that he minds me, but I can tell him all the same."

"Just don't let t'other Mr. Baldric hear ya, lad," warned Miller.

Francesca, hypnotized by the snake's iridescent emerald scales and topaz eyes, reached toward it. "I'll admit it's rather beautiful, in a repulsive way."

The snake gathered to strike.

Someone snatched her waist from behind. "Sssst!"

Francesca nearly jumped out of her skin. She turned to see the captain laughing. "Will!" She flushed. "Don't do that, Captain."

His laughter trailed off as they emerged onto a ridge and paused to catch their breath. Below, the jungle canopy stretched away, a carpet of green. In the distance, the sun glimmered on sapphire water.

"Is that…" Carter said.

"Aye," the captain said, "the Pacific Ocean."

Miller took a draw on his pipe. "And she's the biggest, wildest stretch a sea there is."

"You've been there, Miller?" asked Francesca.

"Aye. The sea itself is pretty tame, mind ya. 'Tis gettin' there round the Horn at'll kill ya."

Juan pointed out a break in the canopy, a slash across the green rug below. "There is the Camino Real. That is where the mule train will be."

The captain's high spirits evaporated. "We'd best be more careful."

At dusk, the straggling line of men entered a clearing. Phillip, at the head, raised a hand. "We'll camp here."

The company shrugged off their packs and sank to the jungle floor. "No fires and no noise tonight," Phillip said as thunder rumbled nearby. "Check your weapons, men. You'll want them sharp." He turned to Juan. "Send out the scouts."

Juan gave directions in Swahili. Abuu, Baakir, and Kintu nodded and disappeared into the undergrowth as silent as jungle cats.

Phillip's face hardened as he turned toward the Camino Real. "Massey, Juan, Francesca, with me."

Francesca's nerves tightened as she followed Phillip into the brush. They moved cautiously forward another hundred yards, then the ground broke away and a dozen yards below lay the King's Road.

It was an impressive piece of work, slightly raised from the jungle floor and about eight feet wide. Francesca remembered what the captain had said. The Spanish had built it over two hundred years ago, forcing the native population to do the labor. Loaf-sized rocks were hauled to the site, carefully placed, then hard-packed with clay to create a smooth surface.

Francesca, bathed in sweat from simply walking through the jungle, couldn't imagine what that labor had been like. Even two hundred years of mule carts had barely rutted it, and it was well-maintained with the encroaching jungle cut well back.

"I'd give my eyeteeth for those swivel guns now," Will said, his voice weary.

Juan sounded worried. "This point is most remote, giving us escape time should the alarm be raised."

"Let's see that it isn't," Phillip said.

To their right the bridge spanned the Rio de Chagre. Huge boulders had been rolled into the river and halved tree trunks laid on top and clayed over. The result was a wide, sturdy bridge that looked as if it would last forever.

"We'll wait for them to cross," Phillip said. "Once they are on this side, some of my marines will take the bridge to cut off their retreat."

"Aye," the captain said. "We'll need men farther up the road to keep them from bolting forward as well. And if we station a group on the far side of the road, we'll catch them in crossfire. They'll have nowhere to go."

"The mules are trained to follow the lead of the head mule," Juan said. "If the first mule lies down, the others will follow suit."

"I'll order my marines to see to it," Phillip said.

"Where will the slaves be?" asked Francesca.

"Near the rear of the column," Juan said. "That is where the Maroons will attack."

Francesca nodded. That was where she'd be as well.

Back in camp, the men cleaned and sharpened weapons. A few raindrops fell noncommittally around them. Francesca overhauled her own weapons, cleaning and oiling her pistols and checking that she had enough dry powder and ammunition. She noticed Abuu and Kintu return and talk excitedly with Juan. She headed toward them as Phillip and the captain drew near.

"Well?" Phillip asked.

"We are in time," Juan said. "The Spanish camp four miles south. They will be here in the morning."

The captains' shoulders relaxed, and Phillip took a deep breath.

Juan's face clouded. "Capitán, they are three score and one hundred strong."

Both captains' faces blanched, and fear gripped Francesca.

"One hundred and sixty soldiers," breathed Phillip.

"And us with sixty-five tired men," Captain Massey said.

Phillip shook his head. "That's more than two-to-one. Pure folly. Impossible."

"Bloody hell!" the captain said.

They were all silent for a moment, then the captain threw up his hands. "So be it!"

His face hardened. "If I die at the hands of the Spanish, so be it, goddamn it! They killed me once, and I've killed them for five years. It's time to end it once and for all! I've not come this far through this blasted jungle for nothing."

Phillip gave a determined nod. "We take our positions at first light."

Through the misty evening, men sat in cheerless groups eating cold rations. Word had gone out about the odds, and as the weight of that knowledge settled on them, they spoke little, and their faces were grim.

Francesca, Miller, and Carter joined Juan and a few of the Maroons who quietly contemplated the coming battle.

Carter tried to lighten the mood. "What'll ya do with yer share a the gold, Miller?"

Miller knocked the ashes from his pipe and refilled it. "Supposing I'm still this side a' the turf, I'll make it inta a collection a' solid gold pipes," he said with a wink.

"What 'bout you, Juan?" Carter shot a skeptical glance at Miller.

"I have no use for gold, Chico."

"Francesca?" said Carter.

324

She didn't respond. She watched Will walk among his crew offering words of encouragement. The men's faces lighten for a moment, buoyed by his presence. Juan and Miller noticed her gaze.

"Ah, missy," Miller said laying a finger beside his nose, "ya'd make a handsome couple."

She furrowed her brow.

Carter screwed up his face in disgust, but Juan nodded. "A woman without a man is like a meadow without rain."

She shook her head. "He is everything I hate in myself."

Juan put a hand over hers. "Hearts do not meet like roads, neat and smooth."

"No," laughed Francesca. "More like bulls charging. But it matters little. If I live, I know what I must do." An idea had been growing in the back of her mind, but she didn't dare mention it to anyone.

She looked at Juan. "You were right. I have followed my head, not my heart. But I've chosen my master at last. I'll do what's right, not what's honorable."

"Do what?" Carter asked.

"Never mind," she said.

"Well," Carter said. "I'm going to buy lots of chocolates."

As dawn approached, Francesca stared at the inside of her banana leaf lean-to drumming her fingers on her chest. She listened to insects chirping and men breathing, punctuated here and there by a snore or a mumble. She envied the men's ability to sleep anytime and anywhere. She was too anxious to sleep; tomorrow her fate would be decided. Hugging her blanket around her, she got up and headed out of camp, nodding to Baakir and Abuu who stood watch.

She'd gone only a few paces into the jungle when she heard Will's voice behind her. "Francesca." She turned.

"Where are you going?"

"Nowhere." She shrugged. "I couldn't sleep."

"Me neither."

He approached quickly—a black silhouette barely visible against the underbrush.

He pulled her close and she melted into his arms, returning his insistent kisses. It felt so right, but she hesitated. "Will, I've been thinking."

He buried his face in her neck breathing in the scent of her skin. "Me too, my Cesca, thinking and thinking, of nothing else."

His lips caressed her neck and her knees went weak. She leaned into him. *Papa was right. Choice is an illusion. Even who we love is not up to us.*

"Will, if tomorrow, if I don't..." Her breath shuddered as his lips caressed her earlobe. "If I don't survive..."

His body went rigid. He pressed her away, his hands tight on her arms. She could feel his breath on her face but could barely see his eyes.

"You must live. I couldn't bear it otherwise. Promise me you will stay away from the battle, far away."

She shook her head. "I need to free the slaves."

His fingers tightened on her arms, digging in. "No! You mustn't, you can't. Not now." He drew her close again, his arms encircling her waist, his lips trailing along her jawline, finding her lips. "Not with so much ahead of us," he whispered. He kissed her as if to draw her soul from her body.

Tears of bliss and despair moistened her eyes and she eased herself away from him. She wished she could promise him anything, everything, but she couldn't. "What can you possibly see ahead of us?"

He cupped her face. "You and me. The open ocean. Freedom. Adventure."

She looked away. "Piracy."

He said nothing.

Francesca bit her lip. *Papa was wrong. I do have a choice. If not in who I love, then in what I do about it.* "I'm sorry, Will." She shrugged away his hands.

As Francesca stepped back into camp, faint light in the east silhouetted the jungle canopy. Birds, roused by the predawn, chirped, darting across the clearing. The men tossed and stretched, waking.

How many of us will survive the day? She took a breath, trying to still the stirred-up energy inside her. She must be focused today to survive.

She still felt the echo of his arms around her and his lips on her throat. *Focus, Francesca.*

She noticed the captain had not followed her back to camp. Where was he? *Stop thinking about him.*

A fist of fear squeezed her insides. *What if Will dies today?* She shook her head violently. *Stop! Concentrate on your goal.*

She thought about the slaves, the back-breaking labor, the beatings, the humiliation. She could change that misery for these people. She could take charge of her own life and give them the chance to do the same.

Miller was the first to rise. The captain appeared out of the undergrowth a few paces away and Miller headed toward him.

Her eyes met Will's, but she couldn't read the emotions battling across his face.

"Please, be careful," she said softly. She wasn't sure if he heard her or read her lips, but he nodded.

"I love you, Cesca," he mouthed as Miller reached him.

She swallowed the lump in her throat. *What if...* then she stomped the thought down. There were far too many *ifs* to consider this morning.

"Day is fast approaching, Sir," Miller said to the captain, wiping the sleep from his eyes. He looked up at the clear sky. "She'll be a fair one, I expect, but a right Jezebel."

"Aye, Miller," the captain said, clapping him on the shoulder. "Ready the men."

———⊢———

They were a somber bunch that rose, swallowing rations, grabbing weapons, and preparing for battle. Only the Maroons seemed eager to be off to the Camino Real.

Francesca noticed the captain and Phillip exchange worried looks. Will stepped forward, drawing himself up to address the men, but Phillip brushed past him. Phillip cleared his throat and kept his voice low, though he spoke with energy.

"Men, now is the time for glory! Today is the day of victory! We fight for our country, for King George, for England and all we hold dear. If we stand together, if we fight with honor and with courage we cannot lose! You all know your duties. Stand. Fight with us and victory will be ours!"

The marines raised their muskets. Some of the navy men nodded. The pirates and the Maroons looked skeptical.

"It's nearly bloody three ta one," mumbled a pirate. They grumbled as they went back to packing their gear.

Captain Massey raised his voice. "I know you're tired. I know you've been over-marched and underfed. I know you're sick of this damned jungle and bloody tired of the mosquitoes. I know the last thing any of you want are three-to-one odds."

A murmur ran through the men. Captain Massey put a hand on one man's shoulder.

"The Spanish are tired too. They've been marching almost as long as we have. They're little better off." He shook his head. "Aye, they have numbers on their side, but that's all they have. Sure, in a fair fight they have a clear advantage. But we're pirates." A wicked grin spread across his face. "We don't fight fair."

A laugh ran through the crowd.

He jumped up onto a log. "Remember what we're fighting for. We're fighting for our *Destiny*. And she's a fine, saucy gal. We're fighting for our freedom. We're fighting to be our own masters, to go where we please and do as we want, to take our lives in our own hands."

His voice dropped lower but gained in intensity.

"Sure, you could leg it out of here. The navy has a comfortable noose waiting for you, but I'd rather go out fighting." He jumped down into the midst of the men.

"If I'm marked to die, then I'll do it with a sword in my hand spitted through the stomach of a Spaniard! To hell with the hangman's noose! I'll die with a shout in my throat and freedom in my lungs! It's a fight for me lads. It's a good way to die, and the best company I could ask for to die with!" He turned and headed toward the battle site. "What do you say, men? Are you with me?"

A wave of energy swept the men, their weariness and the odds forgotten. Weapons raised, the company gave a throaty growl as they plowed past the captain toward the Camino Real.

CHAPTER 32
A NEW BEGINNING

As the crews stormed toward the Camino Real, Francesca grabbed her weapons and her *Book of Reckoning* and followed.

Nearing the ambush site, they crept forward, muskets in hand. They reached the top of the hill as pale morning sun lit the empty road below. Juan signaled Abbu and Baakir, who slid onto the brush in either direction. At a signal, twenty men hurried down the slope, across the road, into the brush on the far side. Ten of the marines went north and ten south to the bridge to stop anyone from escaping their trap. That left only twenty on the rise above the road.

So few, thought Francesca, watching them crouch in small groups amid the brush at the lip of the hill. To the north, where the head of the mule train would be, she saw Miller and Carter kneeling behind a fallen log, checking their weapons. She joined them, crouching next to Miller.

"'Bout time," he whispered.

She shook her head. "I can't stay. I'll be fighting with the Maroons."

"What!" Carter cried.

"Hush." Francesca glanced up the road.

Carter wrapped his arms around her. "Ya gots ta fight with us."

A lump formed in her throat. "I'll be there, Carter. I promise. I'll find you as soon as we free the slaves."

Miller's face clouded. "It's a terrible risk, Missy. The Spanish fear the Maroons a damn site more 'an they fear us. That's where they'll be aimin' their muskets."

329

"It's what I have to do." Her hand strayed to her Book. "Be careful, both of you. I'll see you soon." She put her hands on Carter's shoulders. "Keep low. Stay out of the battle. Worst comes to worst, remember what I taught you."

"Take care, missy," Miller said. "I ain't prayed much, but God bless ya."

She moved out of view from the road. The captain and Phillip approached, the captain arguing with Kintu, the large, muscular Maroon.

"Is everything ready?" Francesca asked.

"Aye," Phillip said. "Kintu just returned. The Spanish are a mile off."

She put a hand on Phillip's shoulder. "Be careful."

"Please, Francesca," Phillip said. "Can't I persuade you to stay out of this battle?"

She shook her head.

"I can," Captain Massey said, nodding to Kintu who scowled but gripped Francesca's arm.

"Come," Kintu said, pulling her back toward camp.

"What are you doing?" She tried to wrench free.

"Keeping you safe," Will said.

"You can't do this!" hissed Francesca.

"I can. You're a member of my crew."

"Let go! I want to fight! Phillip, help me!"

Phillip shook his head. "For once I agree with Massey."

"You bloody hypocrites!" Francesca growled. "All your pretty speeches about freedom and being our own masters, about honor and duty for everyone except me. Was it all complete bollocks? Or am I not a person to you?"

Kintu stopped as uncertainty crossed the men's faces.

Francesca looked up at Kintu and spoke in Spanish. "Please, I need to help you free your people. I've done terrible things and I need to make amends. Please, do me the honor of letting me fight at your side."

Kintu released her. "The honor is mine, Lady Blade."

Captain Massey spoke angrily in Swahili and Kintu argued back.

Will's shoulders slumped. "For God's sake, Kintu, keep an eye on her." He stepped toward Francesca, but she spun away and headed toward the south end of the ambush, where the Maroons crouched, waiting.

Francesca still fumed as she found Juan, Abbu, and Baakir hunkered down amid the colossal, ribbon-like roots of a massive tree. Each held a musket and one more lay on the ground. Juan handed her the gun and she checked that it was primed and ready.

Juan wrinkled his forehead. "Is this where you wish to be?" He nodded toward the other end of the ambush.

She followed his gaze to where Phillip and Will joined Miller and Carter. As her anger subsided, she regretted her words; Will was only trying to keep her safe. She wanted to go to him, but the Spanish would arrive any moment.

"This is where I belong," she said.

A man on a bay horse trotted into view wearing the blue coat of the Spanish infantry. With him came a sound, soft at first, but swelling until the ground shook with it: boots thudding against hard-packed clay. The scout rode by Francesca, then passed the spot where the captains hid, and rounded a corner out of view. She shot Juan a concerned look. They couldn't let the scout escape and raise the alarm, but they also couldn't shoot and give themselves away. Juan nodded reassurance.

The rumble of feet and cartwheels swelled. The sun glinted off muskets amid a sea of blue uniforms. Francesca sank down behind the twisted roots. The sound hollowed as the Spanish marched onto the wooden bridge.

She did a rough count. Eighty soldiers walked four abreast in loose order. Behind them rolled six mule-drawn carts, piled high with chests and barrels. The officers rode on the carts with a few passengers.

The slaves came into view next. There were about fifty, over half men, the rest made up equally of women and children. Most wore rags and bent under heavy loads, the sun gleaming from their sweat-layered skin. A few of the women wore what looked like cast-off dresses from a brothel.

The slaves shuffled forward in three separate lines. Each slave's ankle held a manacle through which a long chain passed. The slaves could move forward or backward along the chain, like a bead on a string. Two of the lines walked next to each other. The third trailed behind.

A man on a huge white Percheron horse rode alongside the slaves, his armor glinting. He carried a whip that lashed out and cracked across the back of a woman who stumbled. She cried out and the man following steadied her.

Francesca glanced at Juan, Abbu, and Baakir. Their knuckles were white where they clenched their weapons and rage filled their eyes.

"We shall have to be quick," whispered Juan. "The Spanish would rather see their slaves dead than free."

Another group of eighty infantrymen followed the slaves. They slouched more than marched, their muskets slung carelessly across their shoulders. They looked inattentive, expecting no trouble. Why should they? It had been a hundred years since anyone had ambushed a mule train.

As the last infantry crossed the bridge, Francesca glanced at her companions. Juan's eyes narrowed and the twins exchanged looks and grabbed their guns tighter.

She looked along the lip of the hill to where her friends were. *Please, God, if you're there. Protect them.*

Phillip rose to his feet, sword raised. "Fire!"

Muskets bellowed. Bullets flew from both sides of the road. Infantrymen crumpled like dolls. A dozen at the back turned, fleeing across the bridge, but Phillip's men on the far side cut them down.

Francesca took aim at a knot of soldiers, but hesitated. Then a slave fell to the ground. The Spanish were already executing the slaves.

She took aim and squeezed the trigger. The soldier grabbed his leg. Francesca reloaded and fired again, dropping the man. She reloaded and scanned for threats to the slaves.

The infantrymen, regrouping, fired back. Iron balls thumped into the root Francesca hid behind, and smoke hung in the hollow. After coughing and wiping sweat from her eyes, she reloaded, peered over the roots, took aim, and fired. She reached for more ammunition, but it was spent. She dropped the musket.

Bark, twigs, and leaves rained down. The firing from the ridge grew sporadic as ammunition ran out.

Abbu and Baakir now held machetes, their faces shining with anticipation. Juan's face held resigned dignity as he turned to her.

"Fortune guide you, Lady Blade."

She drew her sword. "And you, Akinsanya."

The captain shouted, "Boarders away!"

As Francesca rose, an ear-splitting scream from the Maroons stunned her and paralyzed their enemies with fear. Even the pirates, accustomed to brutality, were checked for a moment by the ferocity of the Maroons.

Francesca leapt down the hill into chaos as the second company of infantry rushed to meet them.

Out of the corner of her eye, she saw the captain and Phillip plunging into the melee to the north.

Now all Francesca knew was the slash, parry, and twist of battle. Smoke filled her lungs. Bodies pressed in and instinct took over. She stabbed and cut as bodies fell.

She was still at least twenty yards from the slaves with thirty infantrymen in between, when a woman's scream split the air. *They're killing the women and children!* Infantrymen tried to encircle the Maroons, hemming them in. They would all be cut down.

"We must get to the slaves!" she shouted to Juan.

"Go! We will follow."

Francesca, her blade singing, backed up the hill breaking free of the writhing crowd.

She scanned the north end of the battle where the captain would be and saw Carter running down the hill shouting and pointing behind him.

Thirty infantrymen appeared on the rise. They must have swung around behind the attackers. They fired into the writhing mass below.

As Francesca dodged around knots of combatants, toward the huddled slaves, she saw Phillip reach the wagons where the Spanish officers cowered with the passengers.

Then she was ducking and weaving between groups of fighting men. A woman passenger shrieked, and Francesca cast a glance that direction.

An officer used the woman as a shield against Phillip. Phillip took careful aim and shot the officer over the woman's shoulder.

When Francesca reached the slaves, they cowered together in a frightened mass of bodies and limbs, the loads they had been forced to carry held in front of them. A few lay dead; one wailing woman was injured. They scuffled away from Francesca, their faces taut with fear.

"I'm here to free you," she said in Spanish.

Her words had no effect. They flinched away as she examined the chain to find the lock that would free them from each other. But they were so bunched up she had to search among their dust-caked legs to find it.

She had just found the first lock when Juan, Baakir, and Abuu reached her.

Hooves pounded and a slave screamed.

Francesca rose and spun around. The enormous white Percheron approached carrying the overseer, a burly man in a shining silver breastplate. His face appeared lumped together out of the same clay as the Camino Real. He held a pistol and shouted with rage as it spat.

Abuu twisted and fell to his knees.

Baakir screamed and flew to his brother.

Francesca pulled her pistols, handing one to Juan. "Shoot the lock."

Then she faced the overseer.

He dropped his spent pistol and pulled out his whip. Francesca had one shot. Her rapier would be ineffective against an opponent on horseback.

She took aim.

His whip flicked out, licking a line of skin off her wrist. She hissed in pain, nearly dropping her pistol.

The next flick wrenched the gun from her grip and opened the skin across her knuckles.

She leapt backward. The overseer's eyes shone as he swung again.

Francesca stepped into it, the whip smarting across her upper arm and whipping around her body. One arm pinned to her side, she grabbed with her free hand, twisting the whip around her wrist, digging her heels in, and pulling.

The overseer lurched forward, off balance, but quickly recovered.

He hauled on the whip, but she held firm. He backed his horse, yanking Francesca off her feet and dragging her ten paces along the road. Then he spurred his horse straight at her.

She ripped at the whip around her chest and screamed as the horse reached her.

The horse balked, rearing up, its white mane flashing above her. Hooves the size of dinner plates slashed the air.

"Kill her, damn you!" yelled the overseer to his horse.

She twisted as the hooves thundered down. One skimmed the back of her skull, yanking out a handful of hair, pinning her to the road. She cried out.

The horse reared again, hooves flailing.

Francesca tore off the whip. She lunged up, grabbing the cinch strap that held the saddle in place.

The horse bucked, nearly pulling her arm from the socket.

She held on, tugging at the buckle with her other hand.

The overseer swung his whip at her, spooking the horse. It shot forward, dragging her along beneath it.

Then the buckle came loose.

Francesca fell to earth curling in a ball as one hoof scraped the skin off the back of her thigh.

She looked up in time to see the horse rear and the overseer and saddle slide backwards, crashing to the road. The horse bucked and took off. A mob of freed slaves rushed past her, surrounding the overseer.

As his screams faded to gargled rasps, Francesca wobbled to her feet and looked toward Juan. He had reloaded her pistol and shot away the second lock.

Francesca scanned the battle. To the north, Phillip leapt atop one of the carts and raised his bloody sword. "To me! C'mon men! Up the hill!" Then he twisted and lurched as if hit by a musket ball. He half jumped, half fell from the cart.

"Phillip!" she cried.

Will took up the call. With a shout, swords in both hands, he raced up the hill where at least thirty Spanish soldiers stood.

Her breath stopped.

A dozen pirates and marines fell in behind the captain, Miller and Carter among them. Fear squeezed at her stomach. She wanted to rush to their aid, but there were more slaves to free.

Juan, out of ammunition, pounded on the last lock with a rock, but it held. Francesca found the pistol the overseer had struck from her hand and shot away the lock. The last chain rattled free.

Seeing the Maroons being hewed down by the Spanish, the slaves grabbed what weapons they could and ran to their aid.

She took a deep breath. She'd done what she had set out to do. The slaves were free, and the Spanish now had fifty more enemies to face.

She raced up the hill toward her friends, Juan close behind.

At the top, knots of men fought, whipping the underbrush into frenzies. Bodies littered the ground, but she couldn't tell who had the upper hand.

She spotted Phillip and one marine fighting four Spaniards. Phillip looked half dead; blood painted his side and he panted for breath, using two hands to lift his sword. The marine next to him went down. Phillip backed away, parrying furiously against four men. She ran.

Phillip went down on one knee. "No!" she yelled.

Will, shoulder down, barreled into the Spaniards, knocking them away from Phillip. A sword in each hand, he faced the soldiers.

But another Spaniard had followed the captain, running toward his back, blade extended.

"Will!" Francesca charged. She dove for the man's knees, knocking them out from under him. He went down hard.

The captain turned, surprised. Their eyes met, then he yelled in pain as a Spaniard slit open his shoulder.

Francesca grappled with the man she had knocked down. He rolled on top of her, raising his sword. She grabbed his arm, but he forced the blade toward her.

With a white flash, a sword pierced the man's side. His body collapsed onto Francesca.

She shoved him away and saw Phillip on his knees, one hand to his bloody side, the other holding the blade that had saved her. He sagged to the ground but tilted his head toward the captain. "Help him."

Francesca jumped to her feet.

One Spaniard had fallen, three remained. The captain's right arm was blood-red, but he fought hard.

She flew to his side, kicking a Spaniard in the stomach. A slash to his neck and he crumpled.

Now the odds were even. Francesca caught a grin on the captain's face. She and Will both lunged and the Spaniards dropped.

The captain leaned over, hands on knees, catching his breath. "Thank you, Cesca." He nodded toward Phillip, who lay on the ground panting. "Find the doctor. I'll see if we have any men left to rally." He ran off.

She scanned the underbrush for the doctor.

Two dozen paces away she saw Carter and Miller fighting a monster of a Spanish soldier. The man was big, but fast. Too fast for Miller.

She stood transfixed, only able to yell out as the man felled Miller with a slash to the head. Miller raised his arms to protect himself as the soldier swung again.

Carter stepped in and parried the blow.

Her knees went weak as the giant turned on Carter. She was too far away to help. *Remember what I taught you.*

Carter parried two hefty blows, but the second nearly tore the blade from his hand.

The huge man raised his arm to swing again.

Carter threw up his free hand and his snake slithered up his arm, startling the soldier and giving Carter an opening. He buried his blade in the man's chest.

The man toppled backwards, yanking the hilt from Carter's grip. Carter stood over him, staring.

"Oh, Carter," Francesca murmured.

A moan from Miller brought Carter back. He dragged Miller into the brush and Francesca scanned the battle.

She couldn't see the doctor anywhere. But the pirates had gained the upper hand and now outnumbered the Spanish. She spotted Will, rallying his men, fighting a knot of eight infantrymen.

Juan sprinted toward them and jumped into the fray, dropping two opponents in quick succession with his spear. The Spaniards gave ground.

"Surrender," shouted the captain, panting. "And I promise you mercy."

She ran toward them, repeating it in Spanish.

Another Spaniard fell and that was enough. The few left atop the hill surrendered, dropping their weapons.

Pirates and navy men lowered their swords.

She took in the carnage. Bodies of the injured and dead covered the ground, and she closed her eyes.

Francesca, Juan, and Will hurried to the rim of the hill. Below, the battle was ending as well. The few Spanish still standing begged for mercy, but received none from their former slaves. Juan sighed. "There is no cure that does not cost."

"I saw the faces of your men down there," the captain said. "Kintu would have killed me if I hadn't called out in Swahili." He shook his head.

"They are not my men—"

"I know, they are free men," interrupted the captain. "But they didn't look it. I've not been free either, not for a long time."

Marines on one of the carts broke open chests and casks revealing mounds of gold, silver, and gems. Francesca squinted at the dazzling glare from the treasure.

She turned quickly away. "Miller!"

She ran to where she had last seen Carter and followed the trail of blood.

She found them under a tree. Carter knelt at Miller's head, his red hands pressed to Miller's bloody forehead. Blood trickled from Miller's nose.

"Oh, God!" she exhaled.

Carter looked up with a tear-streaked face. "Help me, Francesca! I can't hold it in."

She knelt, pressing her hands over Carter's. Miller's hair and the ground around him were soaked with blood. His eyes stared into space. She thought for a moment that he was dead, but his chest moved slightly.

"Oh, God," she muttered, then yelled, "Doctor! Doctor!"

Miller twitched his hand, but his eyes didn't move. "Missy, that you?"

She put a hand to his cheek. "It's me, Miller." She turned her head. "Doctor!"

"Can't see nuthin'."

"I'm here," she said, wiping her tears on her sleeve. "Don't worry, the doctor will fix you up."

"Got any rum? Head hurts like a son-of-a-bitch."

"No," she said, her eyes swimming. "But the doctor will bring some."

"Think I'll sleep now."

"No! Miller, stay with us."

"I's proud a ya, missy."

She couldn't answer.

Miller's hand twitched again. "Carter?"

"Aye," he said.

"Yer a good lad. Mind Fran…" He trailed off. "Do as she…" With a rasp, his breathing stopped.

"Miller? Miller?" She shook him. "No!"

The doctor and Will appeared through the brush and hurried to them. The doctor put a hand on Carter's shoulder as the boy wailed. Will knelt beside Francesca. She buried her face in his chest and let harsh sobs take her. He wrapped his arms around her and rocked her. "I'm sorry. He was a good man."

She nodded against his chest. "A pirate and a good man."

———————

Francesca and Carter buried Miller on the hill facing west, with his pipe and tobacco so he could have a smoke while he watched the sun set. When they finished, they stood looking down the hill to where men tended to the wounded. Juan headed toward a group of newly freed slaves. Navy men scooped glittering treasure into packs and bags.

"Miller's gone," Carter said. "And I killed a man."

"I know," Francesca said putting an arm around his trembling shoulders. There was no way to soften it. She knew the terrible finality, the gaping void that killing a man opened.

"You had no choice," she said, knowing it was true, but also knowing it

Lady Blade

wouldn't change how he felt. They stood for a while, staring down the hill, seeing nothing.

———✝———

Over the next few hours Francesca and Carter helped the doctor tend to the injured. Once the gash along Phillip's ribs was sewn and bandaged, he was back on his feet. Food and water were passed around.

The bodies of the Spanish were too many to bury so they left them as they lay. Their own dead, they sank in the river, hoping to spare them from the desecrating hands of the Spanish.

Twenty Spanish soldiers and a handful of passengers had survived. They were guarded by marines, for their own protection, from the Maroons.

Both captains had lost nearly half their men and Juan, most of his Maroons. The wounded would need help on the return trip. Luckily, the rescued slaves offered aid in exchange for sanctuary in Juan's village.

Still, there was the treasure to transport. The bulk of it was gold pesos, but there were also bars of silver, chests of turquoise and other precious stones, and casks of jewelry.

In the hot sun, men packed treasure into anything they could carry. The cart mules and eight horses were tied in the shade, awaiting loads. The captain and Phillip discussed what to do with the prisoners while Carter made crutches for the injured.

Juan waved Francesca over to the freed slaves. They crowded around her, touching her arms and hands, thanking her. One woman, holding a young girl, took Francesca's hand and placed it on the girl's head. "You gave us our lives and our chil'ren's lives. How do we thank you?"

She shook her head as she stroked the girl's cheek, then leaned in and kissed her on the forehead. Francesca was happy with what she had helped accomplish, for their freedom, but she had seen the Maroon villages. She knew they had a hard life ahead of them. They'd be hunted their whole lives. Keeping their freedom would be as hard as gaining it. She wished there was more she could do.

Francesca left them and wandered up the Chagre River. She found a quiet spot, took off her boots, set down her *Book of Reckoning*, and waded in up to her knees. The water felt clean and soothing. She wanted to lay on its surface and float away, like her fallen friends, but she couldn't. She had been steeling herself for what was to come since the end of the battle. She had made a choice and now was the time to put it into action.

Stooping, she cupped the clear water in her hands and washed the blood and sweat from her arms, face, and neck. She stood, feeling drips of water trickle down her chest and back, the flow of the stream against her shins, listening to the voices of her comrades. She knew she was stalling.

She waded to the bank and sat, pulling on her boots, then picked up her *Book*. It had felt good to free the slaves, to do something right, to pay back a little of her debt. She rubbed the *Book* thinking of something Papa had said. She'd done something wrong; she couldn't remember what, but she remembered telling Papa how sorry she was. He shook his head. "It's all well and good to be sorry, but that doesn't change anything. You must do better."

She thumbed through her *Book*. Guilt was useless. It wouldn't undo what she had done, but she could make up for it, if not to the people she had injured, then to others. She could balance her *Book* and then lay it to rest. Freeing the slaves counted for something, as did saving Henry Carlisle's crew. She couldn't atone as a pirate, but then, she already planned to change that. She tucked her *Book* back in her sash. *Papa, am I doing the right thing?*

She didn't expect an answer. After all, she was planning to do something dishonorable. She planned to break her vow to the captain and crew. But an answer came out of the rustle of the trees and the quiet shushing of the river. *Follow your own path.*

She thought about the rules that had defined her life, Senora Bianchi's rules, Papa's rules, The *Destiny's* rules, God's rules. None of them were right, at least, not always. She had one rule now. Do what your heart and your mind tell you. Do what is right, because it's right, not because it follows someone else's rules.

She rose then, climbed the hill, and made her way back to last night's camp. She scrambled down the hill with her pack, headed for the horses. Will and Phillip were packing up treasure and arguing. Will held a goblet of gold.

"Francesca!" he called.

She didn't respond. Three horses were bridled and saddled. She picked a black one that reminded her of Achilles and untied it.

Will's voice grew closer. "What are you doing?"

She didn't want to see his face when she told him, but she had to. She faced him, and Phillip beside him.

"I'm leaving," she said.

Confusion filled their faces. The captain took a half step back, reeling. From the corner of her eye, she saw Carter and Juan hurrying over.

"You can't," Phillip said, "I forbid it."

"You've got the admiral's treasure," she said softly but firmly. "I shall, unless you take me back in chains."

Phillip's mouth opened and closed.

"No! You can't!" cried Carter, crumpling at her feet. "Don't leave me! Not you, too."

He looked up at her. "Take me with you."

Francesca's heart twisted. "Carter, it will be dangerous, I don't know what—"

"I don't care! Please, I can't do this alone."

"Carter," she began, then stopped. Would her journey be any more dangerous than life as a pirate? There was no way to know. "Grab your things, and be quick."

"Crikey! Ya mean it?" he said, jumping up.

"You've got one minute."

Carter grinned and darted off. She watched him go, wondering if she'd given him a second chance or a death sentence.

"You can't leave," Phillip persisted. "Think about your future. Where will you go, what will you do?"

"No one knows their future. I'll follow the road. I'll do what I must and what I can, but I'll no longer do what I'm told."

She swung up into the saddle. "Take care, Akinsanya."

Juan raised his hand. "Farewell, Lady Blade."

The captain put his free hand over hers, gripping so tightly she winced. His chin trembled. His blue-grey eyes were stricken. "Please," he said softly.

A battle raged inside her. She wanted to tell him she loved him but that she couldn't live his life. Not without killing what was left of herself. She needed to do as Papa had done; find a way to atone. She wanted to tell him so many things. But her words wouldn't change anything.

She stroked Will's cheek. The wind-roughened skin, the prickly stubble of beard, the stormy eyes, and soft lips—she committed them to memory. He turned his face into her hand.

"Goodbye, Will."

Carter returned with his pack and his snake. Francesca frowned when she saw "Mr. Baldric" but gave Carter a hand up onto the horse behind her.

"Francesca," Phillip said. "Don't do this, I beg you."

"Goodbye, Phillip."

She turned the horse and headed over the bridge, toward Panama City and the Pacific coast. She felt Carter twist around and wave his arm.

"Bye Cap'n!" Carter called. "Tell ol' barnacle face g'bye fer me! Bye Juan!"

She didn't look back. If she did, she wouldn't be able to go on. She let the horse walk unguided since her eyes were too full of tears to see the road.

"What are they doing?" she asked Carter, half expecting Phillip to send men after her. She wouldn't put it past him to clap her in irons.

"Cap'n Worthington's gone back ta the treasure."

She nodded, unable to speak.

"The cap'n and Juan are staring at us. Juan's sayin' somethin' in the cap'n's ear."

Francesca wiped her tears and straightened her back. She was a DiCesare—the maestro's daughter. She couldn't give in, not even if it ripped her to pieces.

"The cap'n's stuffin' the gold cup inta Juan's hand," Carter said, a trace of confusion in his voice. "'E's headin' fer the horses."

She tightened her grip on the reins.

"Crikey! Now 'e's gallopin' this way."

Racing hooves approached and she wiped at her tears. The captain pounded past her, then turned and reined in his bay, blocking her path.

She pulled up her horse.

Will was smiling, almost laughing, his eyes intent on her face. "I can't let you go."

She stifled a sob. She didn't want it to end this way. "Please. Let me pass."

He shook his head, the laughter leaving his eyes. He took a ragged breath. "I can't."

Agony swelled through Francesca's chest. She longed to be with him forever aboard the *Destiny*. Passion, adventure, freedom, and the ocean called to her. The wild side of her thrilled, hoping he would force her back. But at what cost? She would lose her soul. She would cease to be Francesca DiCesare. She didn't know who Lady Blade was, only that she despised her.

Her hand strayed to the pommel of her sword. "I'm sorry, Will. I love you, but I'd rather die here than go back to pirating."

The captain tilted his head, then let loose a thundering belly-laugh. "That's my Cesca. Always ready for a fight."

She shook her head in confusion. Her heart was breaking, and he was laughing at her.

He saw her expression and sobered. He urged his horse forward until he and Francesca were side by side.

"I'm afraid I misspoke," he said softly. "I should have said, 'I can't let you go *without me*.'"

Her breath caught. Could it be true? Would he give up his command, his ship, his gold, everything?

He put a hand on her arm. "I've been a slave to revenge for five years. I've let it rule me, control me. But you freed me, Francesca." His hand moved to her cheek, his thumb stroking her trembling lower lip. "I love you, Cesca. Where you go, I go."

Joy tingled along every limb and bloomed in her heart. She leaned forward, pulling him toward her for one deep, lingering kiss.

"Ewwwww," Carter said.

Francesca drew away, laughing. She kicked her horse and shot away shouting over her shoulder, "You can come, if you think you can keep up!"

Will laughed as his horse reared, spinning, and he bolted after her.

ABOUT THE AUTHOR

Catherine Thrush is a creative powerhouse. She has worked as a glass artist, an illustrator, a web designer, a screenwriter, and a novelist. She wrote her first book, Quest of the Faes at the age of eighteen. It was published while she was in college working toward her studio art degree. Her screenplay and historical fiction manuscript, Lady Blade, have won several contests and led to her continuing work writing the Lady Blade series of novels.

Catherine took up fencing with Salle DeCesare in her twenties and has been studying it ever since.

She and her husband Thomas Thrush founded the company Urban Realms to sell books and products they've created related to RPG gaming—one of their favorite hobbies.

Originally from Wisconsin, Catherine and her husband Tom lived in California for many years, and now call Portugal home.